The Magus of Hay

Also by Phil Rickman

THE MERRILY WATKINS SERIES

The Wine of Angels
Midwinter of the Spirit
A Crown of Lights
The Cure of Souls
The Lamp of the Wicked
The Prayer of the Night Shepherd
The Smile of a Ghost
The Remains of an Altar
The Fabric of Sin
To Dream of the Dead
The Secrets of Pain
The Magus of Hay

THE JOHN DEE PAPERS

The Bones of Avalon
The Heresy of Dr Dee

OTHER TITLES

Candlenight
Curfew
The Man in the Moss
December
The Chalice

Phil Rickman

The Magus of Hay

CORVUS

First published in hardback in Great Britain in 2013 by Corvus,
an imprint of Atlantic Books Ltd.

This paperback edition published in Great Britain in 2014 by Corvus,
an imprint of Atlantic Books Ltd.

This novel is entirely a work of fiction.

10 9 8 7 6 5 4 3 2 1

A CIP catalogue record for this book is available from the British Library.

Paperback ISBN: 978 0 85789 868 5
E-book ISBN: 978 0 85789 867 8

Printed in Great Britain.

Corvus
An imprint of Atlantic Books Ltd
Ormond House
26–27 Boswell Street
London
WC1N 3JZ

www.corvus-books.co.uk

My father had a seven-year-old boy killed.

It had to be done. I understand this fully.

Earlier, he'd murdered the boy's father.

On Christmas Day.

Perfect timing.

The slaughter reveals important qualities in my father: he did what was <u>necessary</u>, untroubled by accusations of cruelty and bleatings about mercy, and he clearly had little regard for the Christian religion which has held back the progress of mankind for so long (although all the signs are that it won't survive much longer).

My father understands the role of violence in mankind's striving for perfection. Who amongst us would not respect a man of pure descent from a northern race bred to kill and prosper?

I speak of my father in the present tense because he lives on in me. My aim is to restore to him what was his. When the time is right I shall make a blood sacrifice in his name, and this will be my ascendance to the Fourth Degree.

What I am saying to you in this article is that you should search for your own true father. Search through old records or, if you have the money, employ a genealogist to find the ancestor with whom you should connect in order to fulfil your earthly destiny.

Somewhere in your ancestry your father is waiting, sword drawn, for your summons.

from an article by Frater J.
in the newsletter 'Dark Orb',
Autumn, 1985

PART ONE

MAY

'Hay-on-Wye remains as it was in
the fifteenth century – a tightly-
walled medieval city.'

RICHARD BOOTH
My Kingdom of Books
(Y Lolfa 1999)

… by 1460, the castle was described
as 'ruinous, destroyed by rebels and
of no value'. In 1498, a survey reported
that the town, as well as the castle,
was ruinous. The whole area within
the town walls was described by John
Leland in 1538 as 'wonderfully decaied'.

WELSH CHRONICLES ONLINE

1

A rebuilding… maybe

IT WAS THE kind of place they just never would have considered living in. At one time. When he'd loved the empty hush of a cold night and the whingeing of old timbers in a gale. Oh… and when he could walk across the yard without a goddamn stick.

He said, kind of tentatively, 'Don't you love it… just a little?'

Facing Betty in the curve of the alley, where there was a café and sandwich bar with outside tables, people having morning tea and fooling themselves this was summer.

'"Love"'s not quite the right word,' Betty said. 'Though *little* certainly fits.'

It was a stone building, maybe a former outhouse, somewhere between a stable block and a pigsty. Most of its ground floor seemed to be a bookstore.

Robin was silent, looking up over the roofs of the shops to the castle's ivy-stubbled stone, his fingers curling with the need to paint it. She must've seen him catch his breath when they drove over the long bridge across the Wye that was like a causeway between worlds.

There weren't many towns left in this overloaded country that you could see the whole of from a distance, nesting in wooded hills, the streets curling up to the castle, warm grey walls under lustrous clouds. He'd been here a dozen times but never before with that sense of electric anticipation, that sense of intent, Jesus, that sense of *mission*.

'So, could you maybe like… grow to love it?' he said.

Betty gave him the long-suffering look.

'I know what *you* love about it. You love how close it is to the castle. If it wasn't for the castle you wouldn't even consider living up an alley in the middle of a town.'

Ah, damn, she knew him too well. Robin took a step back. Here, in this alley, the castle was so close that one of its walls seemed to be growing out of the roofs of shops. Including *this* shop, virtually in its foundations. If he could hop, he'd be hopping. Come *on*. How often did you get a chance like this, to be *almost part of a castle*?

And make money. How could they not?

'And let's be honest.' Betty looked up. 'As castles go, it's not the most scenic. Some medieval walls, most of a tower. A knackered Jacobean mansion somebody built inside, only it keeps burning down. But then – I keep forgetting – you're American.'

Two young guys walking down from the main road gave Betty long glances, the way guys did faced with a lovely fresh-faced blonde. She had on the shocking-pink fleece with the naive flower motif that made her look sixteen, unzipped to below her breasts, swelling the tight T-shirt underneath. Robin couldn't see her expression because the sun was suddenly dazzling him through a split in the rainclouds, and she was spinning around, canvas bag springing from her shoulder on its strap.

'Bugger! We're overdue.'

'What?'

'Car park. Ten forty-six on the ticket. They're complete bastards now, apparently.'

Shouldering her bag and stomping off up the alley, away from the café, towards the main road. Robin didn't move, not ready to lose the ambience of a different era. An old lady was ambling past wearing a tweed cap. She was whistling. He didn't recognize the tune, but how many places did you actually encounter an old lady whistling? He hissed and tightened his fists until his nails dug into his palms, then limped off after Betty. A tug on his hip as he drew level.

'I suppose they're not actually bastards in themselves,' Betty said, 'they're just – according to that woman in the ice cream parlour, you probably weren't listening, you were gazing around – they're under orders from the council that anybody gets a ticket, even if they're only a minute over. Councils are so desperate for cash they're mugging tourists.'

'Betty!' Robin was wringing his hands. 'Fuck the goddamn parking wardens! Fuck the council! Whatta we *do* here?'

She didn't answer. He followed her out to the main road which was called Oxford Road, although it in no way could be said to lead to Oxford on account of Oxford had to be something like a hundred miles away and comparable to Hay only in its book-count.

Across this road, over the chain of vehicles and beyond the wide, sloping parking lot prowled by bastards, hills of pool-table green were snuggled into the Black Mountains. The hills between the mountains and the river. The flesh between the bones and the blood. And in the middle of this right now, the centre of everything, was the grey-brown town, the only actual *urban space* where Robin had ever totally wanted to be since leaving the States. They could make it here. Get something back. Maybe not all of it, but some of it. A start. A rebuilding. Maybe.

Betty said, 'I think it was bullshit.'

'Because?'

'You only had to look at his face when he smiled. He wanted to cause trouble. Not for us, for the guy in the shop. That's my feeling.'

Betty's feelings. You did not lightly ignore Betty's feelings.

'We could at least ask,' Robin said. 'Not like we got anything to lose.'

Betty stood with her back to the sign that said Back Fold and another bookstore on the corner. Three bookstores in this one short, twisting alley with a pole at its centre, phone or power cables spraying from it like ropes from a maypole. Robin looked back down towards the third bookstore, its window unlit. The shelves inside had seemed far from full. It had looked like a bookstore waiting to die.

Or get reborn…

'OK.' Betty threw up her arms. 'We'll get another parking tick— no, *I'll* get it. You go back. There might even be nobody in there.'

'Said Open on the door.'

Over the door it said *Oliver's Literary Fiction.* Robin walked back down there, peered into the window, saw a short rack of hardback novels by Martin Amis and Ian McEwan, A. S. Byatt, Margaret Atwood and like that. He tried the door. It didn't open.

Why was that woman *always* right? He shouted after her.

'Bets!'

But she'd gone. He hated that his wife could now move so much faster. Hated how old ladies would cut him up in a supermarket aisle.

But then the door of Oliver's Literary Fiction opened, and…

Oh my God.

The man in the doorway, in his collarless, striped shirt with the brass stud, his severe half-glasses, looked like nobody so much, Robin thought, as the guy with the pitchfork in Grant Wood's *American Gothic.* It was the kind of face that only promised more humiliation.

Humiliation. How all this had begun, on a cold, rainy day when spring was an ailing baby squirming feebly out of winter's womb. Just under a week ago.

They weren't broke, but they weren't far off.

Robin's income had been smashed around the same time as his bones. They'd sold a house in the sticks, into a falling market, for less than they paid for it. They'd taken out a mortgage on a humbler dwelling. Now they were having difficulty paying the premiums and Betty had to work checkout at the Co-op.

One day Robin had been sitting, feeling hopeless, staring at the wall.

The wall was all books. Like all the other walls in the living room. And the hallway and the bedroom. And he was thinking, *We're never gonna read all these books again.*

Collecting a rueful smile from Betty who, it turned out, had been thinking pretty much the same for several months, wary of approaching the issue because some of those books had great personal significance. They'd each brought a few hundred into the relationship and they'd bought one another more books, over the years, as inspirational presents.

But, hell, there it was. Circumstance.

So they'd driven over to Hay, the second-hand book capital of the entire universe and gone into the first shop they found with a sign that said BOOKS BOUGHT.

The name over the shop was G. Nunne. Robin had walked in with a holdall full of books, dumped it on the counter, told the guy there was another fifteen hundred back where they came from. All on the same subject. A collection.

The guy took a cursory look. He was built like an old-fashioned beer keg and had one of those red wine-stain birthmarks down one side of his face.

'All more or less like this?'

Robin, who'd brought along what he judged to be the most valuable, beautifully produced, hard-to-find volumes on their shelves, had nodded.

The guy had rolled his head around on cushions of fat.

'Market en't good.'

He had, surprisingly, a local accent. Robin had figured that all the booksellers here were, like, London intellectuals.

'See, you can get most of these as e-books for a few quid,' G. Nunne said. 'Nothing's out of print these days. So… I'd need to take a look, but I'm guessing…' blowing his lips out, considering '… three, four hundred, the lot?'

'You mean these… these here…?'

'No, the lot. Fifteen hundred, you said?'

'*What?*' Close to dropping the stick and dragging the guy across the counter by the lapels. 'You'd make ten times that much. Hell, what am I saying? Twenty times... thirty times... maybe more...'

'But even if that were true, I'd have to sell them *all*, wouldn't I? How long you think it takes to even get your money back? What percentage of customers are looking for weird books? You think that's so bloody easy in a double-dip recession, *you* try it.'

Big silence. Betty drawing a long, hissy breath. Robin leaning forward on his stick with the ram's head handle.

'You know what?' Robin had said. 'We might just fucking do that.'

Betty going, 'Robin...'

G. Nunne looking unperturbed.

'Fifteen hundred books en't a bad start. It's how most of us got going, flogging our own. Then you wind up like me.' A toothy wheeze. 'Life sentence.'

G. Nunne was like walled in by books, all the shelves loaded up, hundreds more stacked up either side of his chair. He scratched his nose.

'Nice little shop gonner be up for rent soon, I reckon. Back Fold. Have a look. Small but perfectly formed. Like its owner.'

And then he'd done the smile.

They hadn't checked it out. Not that day. Too annoyed. Too deflated.

No smile from Mr-American-Gothic-but-actually-painfully-English pitchfork guy.

'And who told you that?'

Who tewld you? Now, *here* was a London intellectual.

'Just a... guy in town.' Robin followed him inside. 'He said the store might be up for rent. Soon.'

'Bookseller, was it?'

The cold stare over the glasses.

The guy switched on lights, an antique gas mantle, electrified, a magnesium glow over mainly empty shelves. It certainly looked like an outlet for old books. You could spend a week cleaning and dusting and it would still smell musty. You could replace the gas mantle with halogen spots and it would still look Dickensian-drab.

Which was kind of good. Wasn't it?

'And you're looking for an outlet, are you?'

'Could be,' Robin said.

'A *book*shop?'

'You even get a choice in this town?'

Though evidently you did have a choice now. Driving slowly down the main street with its painted hanging signs which were probably newer than they looked, he'd noticed two new womenswear stores and an outward-bound emporium. Most likely by-products of the new wealth the book trade had brought.

'So it *is* gonna be available for rent, Mr, um…'

'Oliver. Let me say from the outset that we have *never* offered this shop for rent and anyone who told you otherwise is being deceitful and possibly malicious.'

'Malicious?'

Jeez.

'There's a small but pernicious element here that seeks to cause unrest.'

Mr Oliver's short, sandy hair was parted in a Victorian way over a thin, scholarly face on which disapproval was always just a blink away.

'I apologize,' Robin said, 'if we were in any way used by these bas— elements.'

'You've had previous experience of the book trade?'

'Books. I have experience of books.'

Robin turned. Betty was back.

'My wife,' Robin said. 'Betty Thorogood. I'm Robin Thorogood.'

Small exchange of nods.

'Well,' Mr Oliver said. 'If you leave your contact details, I may possibly be in touch.'

When they left, the lights went out.

'Holy shit,' Robin said.

2

Without light

THE BEDROOM HAD fitted wardrobes, floor to ceiling, and lemon walls on which the shadows of trees trembled. It overlooked a garden, well screened with silver birches and larches and woody extras: unnecessary gates, two beehive composters, a Gothic arbour, like a boat stood on end, with a seat for two.

The bedroom had twin beds with quilted bedheads and matching duvets, one blue, one light green. Also, a typist's chair. Merrily had been shown directly up here. No living room chat, no offer of tea.

Ms Merchant, Sylvia, sat on the side of the blue bed facing the green bed.

'This is mine. When I awoke in the morning, I'd see the sun over the trees at the end of the garden, and then Ms Nott's face on her pillow. She tended to awake before me but would not get up in case that disturbed me. When I awoke, her eyes would often be open and looking at me.'

Ms Merchant was what used to be known as a spinster. An early retired secondary school headmistress with a *live-in companion*, who used to be her secretary. Used to be alive.

Rather than go to her parish priest, as was usual, Ms Merchant had made a direct approach to Sophie at the Cathedral gate-house office.

Merrily hovered by the typist's chair, metal-framed, in the bay window.

Sylvia Merchant nodded.

'Please...'

'This was...?'

'Ms Nott's office chair. I bought it for her when we retired. From the education authority.'

Sylvia Merchant had moved from Wiltshire to Hereford, the town of her birth, with Ms Nott, on retirement. She had a long, solemn oval face, short bleached hair solid as an icon's halo.

Merrily lowered herself on to the typist's chair, the light-green bed between her and Sylvia Merchant.

'And... she worked for you for...?'

'Twelve years. For ten of them, we had separate homes.' Ms Merchant's soft voice trailed the faintest of Hereford accents which somehow made her sound even more refined. 'But, as times – and attitudes – were changing, it seemed silly, as well as uneconomical, to pay two lots of council tax, insurance, water rates, all that.'

Merrily nodded. There was a murmur of traffic from the Ledbury road. This was Tupsley, the main southern suburb of Hereford, uphill from the town. Away from the main road it had these secure, leafy corners.

'Ms Nott managed the garden,' Sylvia Merchant said. 'I've hired a girl. It's not the same. Not yet, anyway.'

'Looks wonderful. I don't talk about mine.'

The movable backrest of the typist's chair was fixed at the wrong angle, thrusting her forward. To keep herself steady, she had to push her feet into the carpet and her hands into her knees. Sylvia Merchant didn't seem to notice.

'Tell me about yourself,' she said. 'I'm sure I must have seen you around the Cathedral. Which we've always thought of as... our church, I suppose.'

'Well, we're based – Deliverance, that is – in the Bishop's Palace gatehouse office, as you know. Although I tend not come in more than once or twice a week. I have a parish to...'

'Ledwardine, yes. Not *quite* as charming as it was when I was a child, though it's resisted most of the excesses. We park there

18

regularly, on the square, to walk the lanes on summer evenings. And occasionally have dinner at the Black Swan. Sad to hear about the manager losing an eye. He was quite a pleasant man.'

'Still is. And handling the situation brilliantly. Sometimes, I suspect he rather likes wearing a black eye patch, although it—'

'Deliverance,' Ms Merchant said suddenly. 'I'm not sure I like that word. In this context.'

She was sitting up, straight-backed. She wore a white blouse and jeans with creases. You could imagine her sitting just like that in her office when some kid was pulled in for smoking in the toilets. Last of a breed, perhaps.

Merrily shrugged.

'Oh. Well. Nor me, really. I even prefer the term it replaced...'

'Exorcist.'

'... in a way.'

'Although I gather,' Ms Merchant said, 'that you don't perform that function very often these days.'

Sounding as if she'd gone into it. The Internet?

'Well, that's true,' Merrily said. 'Some of us go through an entire career without once facing a major exorcism. It needs special permission from the Bishop, anyway. And usually the involvement of a psychiatrist.'

'And may only be applied against evil. A word seldom used these days.'

'Shouldn't be allowed to slip out of use, though,' Merrily said.

Beginning to think she should have worn the full kit. The blue sweater and small pectoral cross... this looked like one of those situations where friendly and casual were inappropriate.

'So,' Ms Merchant said, 'how would you describe your main function?'

'Well... essentially...' Never an easy answer to this one. 'We try to help people deal with problems often dismissed as irrational. Which covers... quite a lot.'

'You take such matters seriously.'

'Always.'

Ms Merchant nodded. She was expecting jokes?

'I have to say you seem quite young for this.'

'I'll be forty soon.'

'Have you *known* bereavement?'

'I'm a widow.'

Don't ask, Ms Merchant. Really, don't ask.

'Bereavement is a challenge,' Ms Merchant said.

Ms Nott, Alys, had died a month ago following a stroke. She'd been cremated at Hereford, her ashes sprinkled on the garden, below the arbour. Telling Merrily about this, Sylvia Merchant had displayed no emotion, as if the ashes had been seeds. This was unusual. Normally, helping someone with this particular problem, you'd be faced with an uneasy mix of gratitude and the most gentle form of fear.

'Erm, when did you first...?'

Ms Merchant extended her long legs, in surprisingly tight jeans, to the base of Ms Nott's light-green bed.

'Three days after the funeral, I awoke, as usual, at seven prompt. The sun was shining, much like today, but it was a cold morning. The winter wasn't letting go. I'd look down, as I forced myself to, every morning, at Ms Nott's pillow.'

Each of the beds had a pillow in a fresh white pillowcase.

Pushed unnaturally forward by the typist's chair's tilting back-support, it was hard not to look towards the pillow on the light-green bed. There was a shallow dent in it, as though a head had recently lain there.

'She was smiling at me,' Ms Merchant said. 'As usual.'

Merrily nodded carefully.

'Although her eyes were without light.' Ms Merchant took a considered breath. 'And I wasn't sure she could see me.'

3

The crown

BETTY SAID, 'No, hold it.'

Watching Robin trying not to lean on his stick at the top entrance to Back Fold. His wild black hair was not so wild any more and not so black.

He was still in recovery. It would be a long recovery, never a full recovery, but he was not going to accept that. There was a jerky electricity in his movements and he kept looking all around him, his eyes collecting the sights the way a magpie crammed its beak full of the bread put out for all the birds. The sloping streets, the patched-up castle. *His* images.

As if he thought the town could help heal his bones: the idea of living in an old stone town under a medieval fortress. Right *under* the castle, *part of* the castle. Fused into a fairytale.

'You know what?' Betty said. 'This pisses me off.'

It had been her idea, after they'd walked away from Nunne, actually to give some serious thought to starting a bookshop.

OK, it was crazy. They were closing down on every high street in the country. Like Nunne had said, e-books were strangling the second-hand trade. But e-books were boring, and a sufficiently seductive shop, given over to a particular theme, in the right location, was always going to pull people in.

And also – she wasn't telling him this – it could be a showcase for Robin's paintings. After the commercial work dried up, all he'd had left had been the paintings and, in a recession, original paintings by unknown artists were among the first items to vanish from wish-lists. Especially paintings like Robin's graphically brilliant but slightly skewed, spiritually-disturbing landscapes, streetscapes, stonescapes. But in Hay, with its international tourists... in the kind of bookshop they'd talked about... well, who knew?

'What I think,' Betty said, 'is we should go and talk to some of the others.'

'The other what?' Robin glanced sideways at her. 'Other damaged bastards?'

'Booksellers. Other booksellers.'

Crazy, but the thought of talking to other booksellers gave him cold feet. *Forget Nunne*, he'd said on the way here, *booksellers are not like grocers and ironmongers. Booksellers, there has to be a hierarchy. Maybe subdivisions for philosophy and anthropology and like that. We'll need to tread carefully.*

His ideas could only have been confirmed by Mr Oliver, peering at him over those academic glasses. Betty really hated it when Robin got treated like the thick, naive American. But, more than that, she hated being used by people pursuing personal agendas.

'There could be another shop available,' Betty said.

'With living accommodation? Near a castle?'

The alley was quiet. The remodelled red chimneys from the castle's second incarnation jutted into the luminous grey sky like cigars from a packet. They walked down past Oliver's darkened window and the next shop they came to had giant cricket stumps painted either side of its doorway and bails over the top, below the name P. T. Kapoor. In the window was an archaic-looking biography of Denis Compton, priced at thirty-five pounds.

The name would mean nothing to Robin, who shook his head in wonderment. Even after years living with an Englishwoman born in Yorkshire, he still didn't get it about cricket.

'All I can say, if *this* guy can make a living...'

'Let's find out how,' Betty said.

Before he could argue, she was between the stumps.

* * *

Robin figured the guy was around his own age, maybe a little older. Stocky, with a dark-stubbled face, deep-set sparky eyes and what Robin figured was an East London accent. His blue and white T-shirt said MUMBAI INDIANS.

'Bleedin' Gareth Nunne, eh?' he said. 'What is it wiv these guys? Truth is, he don't know if Oliver wants to sell. Nobody in the trade here knows, on account of Oliver don't talk to them. Well, me, sometimes, to show he ain't racist, but not often. He finks he's been dissed, is what it is.'

'What's that about?' Betty said.

'How long you got?' He looked at Robin's stick, pulled out a stool for him, looked around for somewhere for Betty, but she shook her head. 'Fing is, he'd never had a bookshop before, new or second-hand. College librarian or somefing academic. Told everybody who'd listen that he'd moved to Hay to be *close to literature*. Yeah, right.'

That was frowned on? Robin looked around the store. The spotlit walls and ceiling were painted different shades of green, the window frame white. A cricket bat hung on chains over the counter which you reached through an alleyway of book-stands, the books displayed face-up. Peeling dust-jackets with guys in caps, killer balls coming at you. Didn't appear to be too much in here that wasn't cricket-related.

'He got fixed ideas on what's literature. Imposes his own value-judgements. No crime novels apart from Danish, no romance post Jane Austen. Who's he bleedin' blame when his business bombs? Everybody but himself.'

'Robin Thorogood.' Robin jabbing a thumb into his chest. 'This is Betty Thorogood.'

'Jeeter Kapoor. Listen, Oliver ever lets you in, whatever rent he's asking, offer him half and make him pay for repairs. He quibbles, tell him you've spent the last few hours talking to half a dozen suicidal booksellers.'

'How do you know we haven't?' Robin said.

'You're still here.'

Robin nodded.

'So how long *you* been here?'

'Erm… free years, just over? Man and boy.'

Betty said bluntly, 'Would you tell us about the suicidal book-sellers?'

Robin frowned. His wife tended to skip the pleasantries.

'Not *all* suicidal,' Kapoor said. 'Prozac does it for a few.'

'You're saying the book trade's in what looks like terminal decline?' Betty said. 'Even here?'

'*Even* here? Where do I start? Internet sales? E-books? Yeah, let's start there. Back in the day, if you couldn't find a book on account of it being out of print, you came to Hay, had a fun day combing fousands of shelves, and even if you didn't find it, you'd come away wiv another half-dozen what took your eye. Now… almost noffing is out of print, and one click delivers it to your device for peanuts. Ain't even second-hand. No germs.'

Robin sighed.

'So you think we may be taking a… small risk?'

'Depends how desperate you are, mate.'

Kapoor strolled over to a coffee machine, began messing with it.

'Look, can I…' Robin fished around for a tactful question, then his hip twinged. 'How do you make a living from, like…all this?'

Kapoor tweaked a smile. Robin put up his palms.

'Sorry, I didn't mean—'

'Nah, nah, fair question. Answer is, this is *niche*. You prob'ly wouldn't know, coming from a baseball nation. Don't need whole books to explain baseball, pamphlet, maybe.' Kapoor nodded at the computer on the desk. 'Good portion of my trade's in there. Mail order. Internet sales. Autographed copies. You get test cricketers passing frew town, none of 'em gonna walk past this shop. And I know what they all look like and I'm ready wiv the pen. You ain't got their book, you get 'em to sign old programmes, anyfing.'

'So how much value's a signature put on a book?'

'Varies from a couple of quid to a hundred. Depends who it is. How often they sign. Or if they're dead by now. Lot of my stuff goes abroad – all the big cricketing nations.'

'You're the only cricket bookshop?'

'Only one in Hay, mate, and masses of stuff to go at. Biogs, real and ghost-written, back copies of Wisden, facsimile back copies. Then you got the specialist stuff, scientific analysis of bowling techniques, spin ratios. Also cricket novels, cricket poetry, vintage cricket annuals for kids. And cricket video on the side. No end to it, mate.'

Robin surveyed the racks.

'*A Hundred Great Cricket Jokes*?'

'Volume One,' Kapoor said. 'Ran for fifteen years until nineteen eighty. Full set, depending on condition, can fetch up to ninety quid. Another seventeen sets in the stockroom, job lot, firty quid. Small tip: only display one. Suggests rarity value.'

Kapoor stood back, looking at Robin.

'You're gonna be feeling your way, yeah? You need advice, you ask anybody. Well, almost anybody. What I'm saying, Hay ain't about competition. Not that kind. Not now. Even the old-timers're well pleased to see a new bookshop, long as it ain't too shit or too cheap. Your visitors're buying into the whole package. What's left of it. Used to be over forty book dealers in Hay, back in the day. And that was only yesterday. Am I telling you stuff you know already?'

'Uh…'

Kapoor peered into Robin's face.

'So, your niche. Trust me, a niche helps. Nobody wants their nice cricket library in a bit of plastic tat you gotta keeping charging up.'

The coffee machine started to babble and hiccup.

'OK,' Robin said. 'We have a niche.'

Kapoor smiled.

'Weird stuff, yeah? Witchy books, Teach Yourself Cursing.'

Robin felt himself going red, also felt Betty's tension, which was rare. They'd told nobody. *Nobody.*

'Hey...' Kapoor lifting up his hands, like in some Indian benediction. 'No cause for panic. Bloke here seen you hanging round Oliver's shop and recognized you. You got some sympaffy, mate, leave it at that.' He looked down at Robin's stick. 'You still do that stuff?'

'Like, you're saying if we open a pagan bookstore we're gonna encounter fundamentalists waving their crosses and calling down reprisals from a vengeful God?'

'Here? Unlikely. *Highly* unlikely.'

'I mean you're Indian, right, you'd know all about this stuff. Sacred cows, elephant gods? Ganesh, Kali the destroyer with all the arms?'

'Born in Brentford, mate, but, yeah, my people have many indigenous gods.' Kapoor did a little guru-type bow, gestured at a framed and signed photo of an Indian-looking guy in shades and a white cap. 'But while I'd be the last to diss the deities of my ancestors, when did Ganesh get a hundred test centuries?'

The card underneath the picture said *Sachin Tendulkar.* Robin had never heard of him, but he was getting the point.

'Coffee?' Kapoor said.

'Thanks. Thanks, um, Shiva. You did say your name's Shiva?'

Kapoor threw up his hands.

'Stone me, you can't get away from it, can you? *Jeeter.* Short for Paramjeet. Try fitting that over a bleedin' shop doorway.'

Robin seemed happier. Danger sign. He'd just been told the second-hand book trade was in possibly terminal crisis and they'd be gambling on a niche, but he looked happier.

He's found a possible mate, Betty thought warily. A guy who, on a slow day, he can walk out of the shop and trade insults with.

'You knew he wasn't called Shiva, didn't you?'

'Who, me? A naive cripple from a land where they play base-ball and chequers instead of chess?'

They were walking along Castle Street, the main shopping thoroughfare in Hay. Betty saw food shops, fashion shops, an antiques' shop and an outdoor pursuits shop selling canoes. A chemist and a jeweller's which had a long-established look about it.

Robin, meanwhile – he gave Betty a commentary on all this as they walked – saw streets laid out like the fingers of a grey glove below the castle. A marketplace that sloped away from its curtain wall. A small statue with a crown high up on the gable end of a bookstore. A little structure with stone pillars like a Greek temple. Everything crowded, intimate. Once a walled town, most of the walls gone now, but still a town that was all old, just different periods of old.

And a handful of bookshops, of course, though possibly fewer than either of them remembered.

And one Betty didn't remember.

'Hey.' Robin started to cross the narrow street, calling back over his shoulder. 'Lemme just check this out.'

It was, at first glance, another bookshop, but it had more than books in the window. Behind the guides to the town and the castle were posters and certificates. One said *Hay Order of Chivalry* beside a picture of a man on a horse. A small flask was labelled *Royal Tipple*. There was also a picture of Henry VIII with no beard, a different face and glasses.

A red robe hung in the window. It had a fleece trim, like the one around the rim of the crown, which seemed to be made of thin, bevelled copper with a scattering of what looked like glass scabs. Robin pointed at the orb below the crown.

'That's gotta be out of a toilet! Am I right?'

'It's an old ballcock, Robin.'

Betty glanced up at the sign. The shop was called The King of Hay. In the centre of the window was the King's autobiography.

Richard Booth, *My Kingdom of Books*.

The man on the book cover wore the robe and the tin crown and carried the orb made out of a cistern component. Books were piled around him. In the background you could see part of the castle and the foothills of the Black Mountains.

'I'm going in,' Robin said.

'No...'

Betty was grabbing for his arm, but it was too late. She stood uneasily in the open doorway, listening to him talking to a woman and a bulky man of mature years who occasionally grunted. Robin was nodding at the crown.

'It really safe to leave that in the window? All those jewels?'

'Hmph,' the bulky man said. 'Could be right. Might not be easy to find another poodle collar.'

His laugh was the kind of laugh you rarely heard any more. *It's a guffaw*, Betty thought, as Robin took down a copy of *My Kingdom of Books*.

'This second-hand?'

'Bugger off,' the bulky man said.

Robin came out grinning, cradling the book he'd bought at full price, and the future was spinning in Betty's inner vision and not all of it – she'd have to admit this – was optimistic.

4

Needs

BEREAVEMENT APPARITIONS WERE the most common and least-alarming of all reported paranormal phenomena. The recently dead husband pottering translucently in his greenhouse, the much-loved cat on the stairs.

Seldom scary. The cats you were inclined to leave alone. They seemed happy enough and didn't leave gutted mice on the doormat.

Close relatives seeing the ghosts of known people... this was usually comforting, one of the mechanisms of mourning. You would try and explain it, you'd offer comforting prayers. Then you'd do what you could to help it all fade into a warm memory.

More complicated were the guilt-trips, remorse externalized. Perhaps the dead person had been neglected, unvisited or even abused. Usually, the person reporting the sightings was in need of counselling.

Merrily had spoken to other Deliverance ministers who thought virtually all bereavement apparitions were down to psychological projection.

Understandable, but a bit patronizing.

'You don't disbelieve me, then,' Sylvia Merchant said. 'You don't think I'm deranged.'

'Certainly not.'

'In which case – *two* questions here – do you believe I actually saw what I've described to you? And do you believe that what I saw was the spirit of Alys Nott?'

What *was* this?

Merrily tried to sit up straight; the chair wouldn't let her. It was as if it was pointing her at the depression in the pillow on the empty pale-green bed. A dent which, obviously, might have been made by Sylvia Merchant, reverently lying on her companion's bed. As anyone might do, at some time, in these circumstances.

'Well… as we met for the first time less than half an hour ago,' Merrily said, 'and I can tell you're not looking for platitudes, it would probably be irresponsible for me to give you an unequivocal answer. The truth is I don't know.'

'Perhaps,' Ms Merchant said softly, 'you would want to consult a psychiatrist before forming an opinion?'

This was well out of the box. You listened, you comforted, you explained. You didn't expect to have to explain *yourself* before you started. The way this was going, she'd be quietly asked for a written estimate.

'In a case of apparent demonic possession, I'd be *obliged* to consult a psychiatrist. Otherwise, I'd be unlikely to go near one.' Time to turn it round. 'What do *you* think you saw?'

'But I *know* what I saw. I know *who* I saw.' Said in a calm, explanatory way, no stridency. 'It was not a dream. It was not an hallucination. It was not some by-product of sleep-paralysis. I am not a stupid woman.'

Merrily nodded.

'Has it happened since? Anywhere else.'

'It's happened twice more. No, three times.'

'Is there a pattern?'

'No. Once was in town. I saw her reflection, very clearly, in the window of a restaurant we used to frequent. The third and fourth times were like the first. In the bed.'

When they kept coming back… that was when an unease set in. As an indication of survival, once was enough, maybe twice to make it less easy to dismiss as imagination. But the third time…

'How clearly did you see her, Ms Merchant?'

Never once had she said, 'Call me Sylvia'.

'As clearly as I see you.'

'And – sorry if this seems a ridiculous question – but was the duvet disturbed? As it would be if someone was lying under it?'

'I think I'd have noticed if it wasn't. If it was just a smiling, disembodied head, that would be the stuff of trashy horror films, wouldn't it?'

'Mmm… possibly. When you say—'

'And I feel her presence. That's most of the time, wherever I am.'

'That's… not unusual.'

'The visual manifestation…' Sylvia Merchant was still, unblinking '… that is clearly harder for her to achieve.'

An expert. Oh dear. It was never a good thing when, instead of feeling sympathy, hand-holding, looking for ways to make it seem less like a haunting, more like a reassurance, you were continually made aware of the surreal nature of the job.

'Erm… when you said her eyes were without light…'

Did you mean she looked as if she was dead?

Ms Merchant waited. Merrily drew breath.

'Ms Merchant… why did you want me to come today?'

'Because I'm a Christian. Because we're both Christians. Because we're members of the Hereford Cathedral congregation.'

'Well, yes…'

'And because I would expect someone in your position to have had considerable experience of the earthbound dead.'

Merrily stared at her.

You don't really want me at all, do you? You want a bloody medium.

'Ms Merchant, you're… clearly familiar with a certain terminology.'

'I've read widely. I've been head teacher at schools where Christian worship was observed. Something now frowned on. My attitude to this was, I suspect, one reason I was offered early retirement.'

'Mmm. The way things have been going for quite a while. Look, can I...? You keep referring to Alys in the present tense. As if you're not sure she's gone.'

'Of course she isn't gone.' Faint lines of disapproval were deepening either side of Sylvia Merchant's mouth. 'That's what I've been trying to convey to you.'

'You... obviously don't want her to be gone.'

'She needs me. As I've needed her. On a number of levels. She very quickly became the best secretary, the best assistant I'd ever had. And then the best friend.'

Apart from the traffic, silence. Ms Merchant had reached a point beyond which she saw no reason to continue.

'She died quite suddenly,' Merrily said.

'Very suddenly and unexpectedly. Didn't want to go. Robbed of nearly half a life. She didn't – and doesn't – want to go.'

'I'm sorry, but... it's not easy for you to know that, is it?'

'I do know. It's entirely clear to me.'

'Although you must also recognize, from your reading, that it's not... natural.'

'And how do *you* know *that*, Mrs Watkins?'

God. Never before, in a bereavement situation, had she faced a theological inquisition.

All she could give was the stock answer.

'All religions take the view that the spirit, after death, moves on. Wants – and needs – to move on. Sometimes... there might be problems of withdrawal. For example – and I'm not qualified to express an opinion on this – but if Alys thinks your life will be unliveable without her, she might be held back. It could be up to you to help her.'

'I intend to help her.'

'And... I can help you to do that. If you like.'

'And what would you advise?'

'Well... there are situations – and this is far more common with parents who've lost children – where the child's room is preserved as a shrine. Which is understandable, but not, long term, a good idea. The shrine should be… in the parent's mind. Where the nature of it will usually be changed by time. Whereas the bedroom shrine will only come to resemble a museum.'

'The bed.'

Sylvia Merchant was on her feet. She was very tall.

Merrily said, 'An empty bed… waking up to an empty bed… keeping an empty bed in the same room…'

'You're saying I should get rid of Ms Nott's bed?'

'I can help you… if you like… to move it into another room?'

'Why would I want that?'

'She didn't die in it, did she? She died in hospital. You could sell the bed. Or give it away. There are places always looking for good furniture.'

'It is not an empty bed,' Ms Merchant said.

Merrily said nothing. The shadow fronds of a willow tree in the garden wavered on the lemon wall above the beds. She felt constricted in the typist's chair. Had the chair always been here, or had it been brought up after Alys Nott's death?

'I don't understand, Sylvia. Why *did* you want me to come? Why me?'

'Because I'm a Christian. Because we're both Christians. Because there was no one to pray for her when she died. I'd like you to pray for her now.'

'I'm sorry. Of course I will.'

Prayers. She could do that. No formal ritual at this stage. You could devise your own, as mild or as explicit as you felt necessary. The prayers would be for peace. And afterwards you might leave written prayers behind. Simple lines which could be uttered like a mantra. And then there might be further visits. Aftercare. And, gradually, the atmosphere would change.

Or it should.

'Here?' Merrily said. 'Now?'

'If you wish.'

'Do you think I could alter the positioning of this chair?'

Sylvia Merchant smiled.

'It won't. That's the position Ms Nott had it for years.'

'Right.'

For a moment, Merrily found it hard to draw breath and sprang up, too quickly, from the chair.

A moment later, the chair creaked.

God.

Sylvia Merchant's eyes were alight.

'Now,' she said, 'we are all here. The three of us.'

5

Fix it

THAT EVENING, ROBIN read the book, Betty read the tarot.

Outside, kids were yelling and neighbours mowing their tidy, right-angled lawns, the ones that hadn't been turned into extra parking space for their goddamn people-carriers.

This bungalow – Robin despised it – was attached to another one and built on an estate near Kington, fifteen or so miles from Hay. Pink-brick suburbia made all the worse for having empty hills tantalizingly on the horizon.

After supper, the sky reddening, they lit a fire in the small woodstove they'd installed to save on oil, and Betty sat on the rug near the legs of Robin's chair and felt the excitement around him like ground mist.

'See, this guy... a legitimate hero.'

'Another one?'

'This is the real thing,' Robin said. 'This matters.'

He hadn't been sure if the man he'd talked to in the King of Hay shop – older than the man on the front of the book – had actually been the King of Hay and hadn't dared ask. Robin was strangely shy with people he thought he might admire. But now he was halfway into the autobiography and sure on both counts.

'I just didn't know the half of this. You hear about the King, you think it's a pisstake. Which, OK it was. Until it became *majorly serious.*'

He stared into the stove, the flames still yellow. Robin saw the stove as an essential energy source, like all the books on their shelves, soon to be turned into a different kind of energy.

Betty thought the King of Hay had just looked like some over-weight, ageing bloke, detecting no obvious charisma, but...

'OK... tell me.'

Richard Booth – later Richard Coeur de Livres – had grown up at Cusop, the strung-out village just on the English side of Hay. Back in the early 1960s, when Hay was a run-down farmers' town, sinking into an economic ditch, he'd bought the old town fire station for seven-hundred pounds, opening an antique shop there.

'But his business took off,' Robin said. 'Like *really* took off... when he switched to second-hand books.'

Booth loved books and books seemed to love Booth, and it was a slow explosion. In the years that followed, he opened bookstore after bookstore, building the town an international reputation as the place where you could find a book on anything you wanted, without paying through the nose.

Other book dealers moved in, and Booth bought the castle – part medieval, part mansion house, Jacobean through to Victorian – which also got filled up with books. Pretty soon, Hay had became a unique town with a whole new economic basis, a level of self-sufficiency unknown, not only in these parts, but anywhere in the UK.

'Books had become like the *currency* of Hay.'

'Well, yes,' Betty said. 'That's nice, but—'

'Nice? It was magic! And not in a pretentious way, because he wasn't some nose-in-air, asshole-scholar type. At one stage, the books that *nobody* wanted, he even sold them as fuel... for burning?'

'Would Mr Oliver be happy about that, you think?'

'Oliver didn't fit. Kapoor said that. Oliver was too Establish-ment. Booth's Hay was *outside* all of that. He'd kick-started the economy of a town that was stagnating, and it was pulling visi-tors again – book tourists. OK, in a small way at first. Calls it *trickle-tourism*. The town doesn't get swamped, it just builds steadily. But then the big guys get interested – the national chains, the Welsh development agencies, the Wales Tourist Board. Offering the kind of big money grants which your average entrepreneurs just grab and run with, milk the agencies for all they can get then move on when the grants dry up. But that…'

Robin was on the edge of his chair cushion, his hair in spikes.

'…was precisely what Booth did not do. Sees these agency guys with their chequebooks and their government support and their big shit-eating smiles, and he's like, *FUCK OFF!*'

Betty grinned. It was at times like this that Robin was able to forget his smashed pelvis, his wonky spine. She laid her head against his knees as he described how, as part of a battle to keep the town entirely local, beat off the national chains and the government agencies, Richard Booth and his supporters had decided that Hay, this ancient once-walled town which sat right on the border of Wales and England, should declare itself independent of both.

And that he should be its king.

Sure, it had started out as a kind of joke. There were Hay passports and HAY car-plates, and King Richard was bestowing honours on supporters, giving them Hay titles. Attracting the kind of free worldwide publicity that his powerful enemies on the tourist and development boards would've had to pay out millions for.

A sharp elbow in the ribs of the Establishment. A defiant finger in the face of the organized politics.

'Guy's a goddamn genius.'

Building on the fame, a father and son team from a neighbouring village, Norman and Peter Florence, had started a small festival of literature which, at first, Richard Booth opposed on the basis that it was promoting new rather than second-hand books. But within a few years – because things *happened* here – it was pulling in the best part of a hundred thousand people to hear the world's greatest writers and thinkers. Finally winning Booth's blessing around the time Bill Clinton had arrived in a smoke-glassed limo to address the world from a huge marquee in the grounds of Hay Castle, calling the festival the Woodstock of the Mind.

And when the crowds went home and the tents came down, it was still this small, once-walled medieval town that sold cattle feed and local honey between the second-hand books.

'But now something's slipping away?' Betty said.

'Like everyplace. Greedy bankers, idiots in government, the Internet collapsing high streets. Then the King's health breaks down and he doesn't get to spend as much time here. The castle goes on the market, and now it's in the hands of a trust which may or may not pull it together. And the ideas that took the town on to a new level are just… running down.'

'So it needs… us?'

Oh God. Robin was viewing his possible encounter with the King as a sign of converging destinies.

'Needs people with commitment to more than their own bank accounts. Needs reconnecting to its energy-source.'

This was Robin, seeing everything in mystical terms. Betty thought it would have been so much easier if they'd come here a few years ago, before they'd bought a farmhouse with a ruined church on it and Robin's body had been smashed by falling masonry.

'We should go back,' Robin said. 'Gotta be some other place for rent.'

'Let's wait awhile, see what happens.'

'That's what you had from the tarot?'

Betty said nothing. Although the tarot was just points of reference, a way of seeing what, deep down, you already knew, it still scared Robin.

'Could be like old times,' he said. 'Like the first apartment.'

The first apartment was when he'd followed her home to the UK after they'd met at a Wiccan international moot in Salem, Mass. Robin attending as an exhibitor of artwork for pulp fantasy novels, Betty as… well, as a witch. A sublime witch,

Robin used to say, with hair like a cornfield in the warm days before the harvest, telling her how he'd felt his whole being drawn into a vortex of obsessive love... and something more, something epic and mythological that he could evoke in gouache and coloured inks but would never understand.

The way Betty saw it, him following her home to England, embracing paganism, had been like going to live in his own artwork. Which was fine, until the lucrative Lord Madoc series had suddenly been terminated and the other cover-artwork it had brought in began to tail off in the wake of a betrayal that made you realize that no religion run by human beings should ever be trusted.

'Of course, we were young, then,' Betty said.

'We're still young.'

'What's left of us.'

'OK,' Robin said angrily, 'we'll stay here. You can aspire to three days a week on the checkout and I can sit on my sorry ass trying to paint over the sound of lawnmowers and... and life grinds on.'

It was a matter of supreme irony to Robin that he now had an actual sorry ass.

'OK, we'll go tomorrow,' Betty said.

The entry to Back Fold was facing them next morning as they came out of the parking lot, but they ignored it, heading up an adjacent short track that led around the castle and accessed stone steps leading down through its grounds to the marketplace.

At the bottom of the castle hill, there were unattended open-air bookshelves full of cheap books they relied on visitors' honesty to pay for. Used to be books all over the castle itself, Robin told Betty – at least the parts you were allowed into without a hard hat. And down in the town even the shops that weren't bookstores – the antique shops, the jeweller's – all sold a few books as well.

Books had become the town's circulation system. Carrying the energy, the mojo.

'You take out books,' Robin said, 'you're weakening the system. You're inviting, like, entropy. So whatever they do to this castle, books need to be part of it. Crucial.'

Betty looked up at the castle. They were under the heavy medieval tower, with massive oak doors in the portcullis opening. Doors so huge and damaged they could even be original. A shudder took Betty by surprise; a voice from the square stopped her thinking about it.

'Mr and Mrs Thorogood.'

A very dry, very Home Counties voice. Betty turned slowly.

'Mr Oliver.'

'So you're back.' He was in an Edwardian-length jacket, a suede hat with a turned down brim. 'Still looking for a shop? I confess I didn't think you were particularly serious about acquiring a lease on mine.'

'I tend not to do things for laughs.' Robin leaned on his stick. 'Any more.'

'Then I apologize. As you can imagine, there are passing tourists who just get it into their heads that they'd like to be booksellers.'

'Time wasters,' Betty said bluntly. 'We're not.'

'I looked you up on the Internet,' Mr Oliver said. 'I didn't realize you designed book covers.'

'Just did the paintings for them,' Robin said.

This was before publishers discovered Photoshop and no longer wanted to pay artists. He didn't talk much about that.

'Your designs for the Waugh reissues,' Mr Oliver said. 'Coincidentally, we sold one a few weeks ago. Alec, not Evelyn.'

Betty smiled, recalling how, when Robin had first been offered these Waugh covers, he'd asked her if Alec and Evelyn were husband and wife.

Mr Oliver said. 'We… began by specializing in literary first editions but, sadly, there are not as many collectors as there used to be. Nor, indeed, as many bestselling literary writers.'

Betty saw Robin's mouth opening, probably to say something

like, *fuck literary, just go with the flow*, and shot him a warning glance. Robin shut his mouth, went loose.

'Look,' Mr Oliver said. 'I don't know how much time you have, but… ah… there may be a basis for discussion.'

All right, it wasn't in totally great condition. There was some damp in the walls, and damp wasn't good for books. Caused foxing – was that the term for the brown marks on the edges of pages? But damp could be dealt with… eventually.

Betty said. 'If we decided to go ahead, how long would it take to draw up a lease?'

Mr Oliver's hands opened out.

'Drawn up already, Mrs Thorogood. Just a question of your agreeing to the terms.'

Interesting. When did that happen – before or since he'd checked them out on the Net? Robin was trying to catch Betty's eye, but she kept looking at Mr Oliver, choosing the best time to hit him with Kapoor's suggestions about rent and repairs. She pointed to the stairs.

'Perhaps one more look at the living accommodation before we go away and think about it?'

Upstairs, it looked… *OK*. The rooms were not huge and the windows were small, but it was clean and the taps worked. The whole building had evidently been a barn at one time, and the upstairs was the loft. Must have been converted to living accommodation quite some while ago; there was a small fireplace, probably early twentieth century, another upstairs, now sealed off. Pity, it was cold up here.

Too cold? She went still, slowed her breathing. Robin must have seen her arms drop to her sides; he raised an eyebrow.

Betty shook herself.

'So has this ever actually been living accommodation for you, Mr Oliver?'

Mr Oliver said he and his wife had a house on the outskirts of the town. Clearly it *had* provided living accommodation for someone in the not-too-distant past – note the replaced wiring, the extra power points, the TV aerial socket.

'It's a bit… compact, isn't it?' Betty said. 'We'd have to put some of our furniture in store. Or sell it.'

'I will admit,' Mr Oliver said, 'that I never thought of anyone actually living here. Wouldn't deny that life could be a trifle cramped.'

'For a while, anyway,' Robin said. 'Until we make enough money to turn upstairs into more book rooms. You ever think of that?'

'As I say, Mr Thorogood, our original plan to pursue what you might call a literary purity proved to be incompatible with the times. And the business tended to consume too much of *our* time.'

'It'll come back,' Robin said unconvincingly. 'Quality always prevails.'

'One hopes. I could have sold the shop last month as a… body-piercing establishment.'

Mr Oliver smiled grimly, letting them out. In the alley, an old lady turned round.

'You smelled him yet?'

She was in one of those ankle-length stockman's coats, unwaxed and worn back to the webbing. Mr Oliver sighed.

'Good morning, Mrs Villiers.'

It was the tweed cap she had on that ID'd her – the little old lady he'd seen last time they were here, walking up the alley whistling, making him feel good. She jerked a thumb at Mr Oliver.

'Reckons he don't smell nothin'.'

'Like what?' Robin said.

But she just walked away, looking back over her shoulder, leaving them with a cracked grin with black gaps.

'One of the charms of Hay,' Mr Oliver said drily, 'is the number of *characters* one finds here.'

Mrs Villiers stopped.

'Dickhead,' she said.

Robin smiled happily. You wouldn't get that on the street in Bath or Cheltenham.

As they walked away, Betty said something about them accepting there'd have to be sacrifices. Robin stared at her in the alley, knowing that making sacrifices wouldn't mean like coming down from Michelob to Budweiser. Nor would it involve a white cockerel, a knife and a full moon. Usually, something less bloody than one and more painful than both.

'We'd need more stock,' he said. 'I figure our stuff will fill about half the shelf space. Not much more than what's left of his. We need to check out some car-boot sales.'

They'd discussed this. Charity stores and boot sales were always full of books that might roughly qualify as pagan-oriented. They had just over two-thousand pounds saved to spend on more stock. Not be too many signed first editions there, but New Age pulp would fill a few holes.

'Bets,' Robin said at last, 'were you… getting something? Upstairs?'

One thing you needed to know about Betty, she never claimed to be psychic any more. She just had feelings about places. It wasn't a sixth sense, no such thing as a sixth sense. It was just about paying attention to the other five, getting them working in concert. Which most people rarely did, if ever.

That was her story, anyhow.

'I just think,' she said, 'that we might have some work to do. To make it ours.'

'Ours? Rather than…?'

'Rather than… someone else's. I don't know. Forget it.'

Hardly the first time this had happened. These things, Betty would say, they want to play with you, and it's very rare that anything good comes out of it, so you don't get drawn into the game.

This was when they'd broken with Wicca and begun to avoid anything with any kind of organisation or hierarchy. When paganism, for Betty, had become no more than a viewpoint. If you started seeing it as a stepping-off point, she'd say, you'd just step into a situation with people who wanted a piece of you. Or into a mental-health crisis.

But right now he wanted to know. He wanted her to feel as good about this place as he did.

'Whose?' Robin said. 'Ours rather than whose?'

'Dunno.' She was looking steadily ahead of her, but not seeing what he saw: the brick, the stone, the patched stucco. The solemnity of her expression indicative of some interior process beyond explanation. 'Anyway. Doesn't scare me any more.'

Something else she'd say: never let it scare you. That's what it wants.

'Whatever it is, we take it on.' Betty came out of it, shrugged. 'We fix it.'

6

Formless conceit

HAVING PRAYED SHE wouldn't wake up in the middle of the night, Merrily woke up in the middle of the night.

Encased in cooling sweat, still hearing the metal-framed typist's chair creaking gently in a corner of the bedroom.

Not this one, of course. No chairs in this bedroom. She'd moved last month to a far smaller one in the north-eastern corner of the vicarage where the leaded window would catch the first light as the dawn chorus opened up.

Still a couple of hours to go before the blackbirds began. The panes in the window were blue-black. The softly stated certainties of Ms Sylvia Merchant, head teacher, retired, retained control of the dark.

Because I would expect someone in your position to have had considerable experience of the earthbound dead.

Actually, no. It came down to one experience, in this house. On the third staircase leading to the attic which Jane had claimed for her apartment.

She hung on to it, an anchor now. It had begun with the sense of an unending misery which, for an instant, had been given vaguely human form before becoming a minimal thing of pure, wild energy.

That was it. Lasting seconds. Maybe not even one – who knew how long an instant was? Events were expanded by the mind according to their significance. This one had persuaded her, months later, to say yes to an extra role in the diocese, a job which handed you the keys to a repository of collected shadows.

The dictionary said:

Exorcist: one who exorcizes or pretends to remove evil spirits by ritual means.

Or something like that, suggesting that you could still qualify as an exorcist even if you only pretended to do it. Even if you thought it was bollocks.

And the Church… Merely by introducing the replacement term, Deliverance, the Church had been backing away, softening it, erasing the shamanistic overtones, making it sound more like a social service, a token nod towards the boundaries of belief… and leaving a handy escape route, because who, in all seriousness, could, in this day and age, accept that people and premises could be psychically disinfected through a priest's petition to that increasingly formless conceit known as God?

Those blokes down there – solid, stoical, middle-aged priests. I can tell you four of them won't go through with it. Out of the rest, there'll be one broken marriage and a nervous breakdown.

This was Huw Owen, in charge of C. of E. and Church-in-Wales Deliverance courses, now her self-appointed spiritual adviser. Whether you chose to dismiss it as pure delusion or the product of some brain-chemical cocktail, it was, Huw said, still capable of rotting the fabric of everyday life.

A movement next to her.

'Dark night of the soul, Lol,' she said. 'I collect them, as you know.'

Had her thoughts been loud enough to wake him up, too? She reached for his hand.

Lol said, 'You want to – as they say – talk about it?'

'Thought you'd never ask.'

Lol had slipped across to the vicarage from his cottage in Church Street, just on twilight. Jane was spending the last weekend of her last school half-term at Eirion's parents' place near Abergavenny. Jane and Eirion had been down to Wiltshire to check out the Bronze Age dig where it looked like Jane would be starting her gap year in July, skivvying for archaeologists.

And in her absence... well, everybody in Ledwardine must surely know about Lol and the vicar by now. Just that not everybody approved, and some of them were the most constant members of an unsteady congregation. Which made her, on top of everything else, a hypocrite.

'So Sylvia Merchant sends for me – that's what happens, we get *sent for* – to confirm what she *wants* to be the truth. And if it goes against centuries of established theology, well, anything can be changed these days, if you don't like it much. And if *God* doesn't like it... well, we created him, we can uncreate him. Up yours, God.'

'*That* dark, huh?' Lol said. 'Poor soul.'

'I should be unfrocked.'

'You are.'

'Oh yeah.'

'So you went along with it.'

'Mmm. Did the prayers.'

'With the two of them?'

'Don't think I had a choice.'

Huw Owen's First Law of Deliverance – or it might be the second – was never to leave a disturbed environment without administering a blessing. What he told his exorcism students after the story of the woman who seemed like a liar and then killed herself.

'Actually, I didn't.' Merrily sat up in bed, naked before God. 'I asked for release. For both of them. Can't remember the actual words, but that was the essence of it.'

There was a mauve tint to the square panes of old glass. Later than she'd thought.

Lol said, 'How did she take it?'

'I don't know. I kept my eyes closed.'

The implications were vast and terrifying. If you didn't think

47

it was delusion or brain chemicals. If you thought there was a possibility that you were more than a social service.

She leaned into him, slid back down into the bed.

'Actually, I'm not sure she took it very well. She was a head teacher. Used to calling the shots. Maybe that's why she liked having Alys Nott around. A secretary for all eternity. And, presumably, Alys liked that too.'

'Doesn't matter one way or the other, now, does it?'

'I don't know. Do I have responsibility to what remains of Alys?'

'Hell, no. Definitely not. I don't know much about theology, but I'm guessing she's well out your sphere of influence now.'

'Out of the mouths of babes and songwriters... bugger.' She pushed back the duvet. 'I need a wee. Do you want a cup of tea, or...?'

It was chilly, for May. She pulled her bathrobe from the back of the door. She was replaying what Sylvia Merchant had said.

Her eyes were without light. And I wasn't sure she could see me.

Alys Nott held in some limbo. Trapped and blind.

'You know that night? When I thought I saw something on the stairs to the attic?'

He'd been here that night, though long before they were an item. Downstairs on the sofa while she was upstairs, getting speared by the pure wild energy. He'd been the first to see her, afterwards.

'You *had* seen something,' Lol said. 'Nightmares don't have that effect.'

'But, given the state I was in at the time, to what extent was that a subjective experience? I was looking for answers, and that's how the answer came. Was that a case of the subconscious mind translating something into an image? I don't know. I still don't know how any of this works.'

'You know more than most people.'

'I've read a lot of books about paranormal phenomena, mysticism, occultism. I've studied case histories. I've observed other people's spiritual crises, but I still don't know how much I can accept. I could be self-deluded. I could be a charlatan.'

This was how you thought in the darkest hours.

'Actually,' Lol said, 'there's something I need to tell you...'

She turned, the robe half on. Because it was still before dawn, the devil's time, she felt queasy with trepidation.

PART TWO

JUNE, end of

My Cabinet was picked in five
minutes in the pub. Most were
wearing jeans and there was a high
proportion of lorry drivers.

Richard Booth
My Kingdom of Books
(Y Lolfa, 1999)

7

Sad case

THE NOISE OF the waterfall was like mass excitement, but not in a good way. Bliss was thinking of football frenzy before a grudge game. Wincing at a jagged memory from when he was a young copper in Liverpool, getting his wrist broken on a barricade at Goodison Park. He'd loved it then, the Job. Really hated how long that wrist had kept him off the streets.

In retrospect, it was bugger all, a broken wrist. Fully fixable. Bliss could've wept.

He was unsteady and locked an arm around one of the young trees growing out of the steepening bank just before the rushing water went into its lemming dive. On a warm day it might even be nice here, dappled sun through big trees, white splatter like a vanilla milkshake. Not today. Not with a dead man down in the pool.

He saw one of the divers heaving himself up on to a rounded rock-shelf, mask on his forehead. Grinning up at Bliss.

'Wanna stay put there for a bit, boss? Should we call for risk assessment?'

'Piss off,' Bliss said mildly enough. 'Left me wellies in the car, that's all.'

How much did the diver know about his condition? How much did any of them know? He looked down into the pool and felt dizzy. The diver and his mate were at the water's edge, below the fall. Apparently it was deeper than it looked, this pool.

Bliss glanced back the way he'd come and saw two rapid

streams, side by side. *Shit.* Hands linked around saplings either side, he leaned forwards, his neck inclined until the two streams coalesced into one, and he straightened up.

'Just get him out, eh?'

Back in Hereford, he'd seen Terry Stagg exchanging a look with Darth Vaynor – why would the DI want to drive all the way out to the rim of Wales for a body spotted in a pool, likely a routine drowning?

Why *had* he? He could've just told them he was taking an early lunch, gone out and sat in his car till the numbness subsided.

Terry Stagg had been smiling thinly, probably thinking Bliss was trying to put some ground between himself and acting DCI Twatface Brent, who'd been running the show while he was in hospital and Annie Howe still working out of Worcester. Well, fair enough, he wasn't exactly best mates with Brent and better Staggie thought that than nurture any suspicions about the dangerous brightness of office lights.

Bliss gripped the trees. The truth was that it went further. He couldn't take the city at all any more. It came at you mob-handed. Sensory overload, bit like this frigging waterfall.

He'd been thinking it'd be some peaceful stagnant pond in the middle of a field, but no, the pool was right next to the lane and filled up by a mini cataract shooting almost sheer from the tarmac's edge, white foam harsher on the eye than a fluorescent tube and a noise like you were inside an espresso machine.

The diver raised a hand to his mate, lowered his mask and slid into the pool. Bliss took a long breath and edged towards the falls, tree to tree. There was a crash barrier at the side of the road; to reach the falls in safety you had to cross a bridge, follow the stream through a field and then negotiate the bank. Worse and worse.

After a while, the diver came up, in no apparent hurry.

'Just an old man, boss.'

You could hear the disappointment. Bliss inclined his head,

reducing two pools to one. It seemed squalid down there now, like a broken stone lavatory in perma-flush. He even thought he could see the body, half under a projecting rock. It seemed to be moving. But then, in his state, everything bloody did.

'That's a shame,' he said, 'but how about we *still* bring him out, eh?'

Yeh, he got the inference. Old people would often wander out into the night. In winter, hypothermia would get them. In summer, they might fall into a pool. With drowned old people, the suspicious-death meter tended to drop below the police concern threshold. He'd take one look and leave them to it. Maybe drive into Hay and sit over a coffee in the ice cream parlour, deal with his blood sugar.

The rattle of a vehicle made him turn his head, the sides of his vision squeezing in like an accordion. Billy Grace's old Defender was reversing into the entrance of the nearest big house. This valley was full of big houses, mostly hidden away behind mature trees. Cusop Dingle. He'd never been here before and he probably wouldn't need to come back, ever.

'Try not to damage him, eh? We don't know anything for certain yet. Bring him up to some level ground, for the doc.'

Only seen one drowned person before, a child, again back when he was a young scally, not long before he did his wrist on the barricade. Little kid brought out of a grotty canal, laid on the bank next to the old bike frame his foot had been wedged in. Bliss had had to tell the parents. First time. That night he'd been ready to put his papers in.

One of the three uniforms was waiting for him on the edge of the field, slim, freckly, red-haired girl.

Bliss said, 'The dog walker thought there was some blood, did I get that right?'

'Well,' she said, 'that was what he *thought*. On one of those sticky-out shelves of rock? Long washed away though now, obviously, sir. But then, if the gentleman fell from the other side... that is, went over the barrier from the road...'

'If the dog walker saw blood on the rocks, it suggests he was on the scene not long after the old feller went in.'

'I suppose. This was not yet six, still pretty dark down here amongst the trees.'

'Early risers,' Bliss said. 'The SOCO's friend, your dog walker.'

The numbness was in his forehead, travelling down the left side of his face. He started to sweat.

'We have a possible name, sir. The chap recognized his hat. He wore a distinctive hat, with like a brim? It was wedged... down there. In like a crevice?'

'Gorrit? The hat?'

'Bagged, sir. Anyway, I've just been to his house. His back door's unlocked, nobody home. He lived alone. His name's David Hambling.'

'*He* have a dog?'

No, sir.'

Bliss nodded. Sometimes people got themselves drowned going in after a pet.

'No suggestion of dementia, sir, according to the neighbours. Even though they reckoned he must've been getting on for ninety. If not more. Could be a suicide?'

'Worth the effort at ninety? Morning, Billy.'

Dr Grace, maybe twenty years older than Bliss, was striding over in his blazer and his old-fashioned gumboots, neon teeth whiter than the water. Mother of God, when even Billy's frigging teeth hurt your eyes...

'*Francis?*' Billy contemplating Bliss with his chin tucked into his collar, all faux puzzlement. 'Something I haven't been told?'

'Been advised to get more fresh air, Billy.' Bliss turned to the uniform. 'What's this river called, again... um...?'

'PC Winterson, sir. Tamsin. It's not actually a river, it's the Dulas Brook. Just a bit swollen with all the rain. It's supposed to mark the actual border between England and Wales. Another few metres, this'd be one for Dyfed-Powys. Sir—'

'What are you—?'

Bliss spinning round so fast he stumbled. Billy Grace was looking him up and down. Actually *up and down*. Another frigging expert feeding him through quality control. He walked – carefully – right up to the doc, leaving PC Winterson, thanks to the water-roar, just out of earshot.

'I'm not your patient, Billy,' Bliss said tightly. 'All right?'

'By virtue of being still alive after a savage kicking?' Billy beamed. 'Just about?'

'Piss off.' Bliss backed away, raising his voice. 'As it happens, doctor, this sad case is unlikely to interest me any further. Just an old feller. So, in the absence of anything iffy, I'll probably be leaving you in the capable hands of Tammy here.'

'Tamsin, sir. Sir, there's one other thing. Something we found in his kitchen?'

'Porno DVDs? Bomb-making kit?'

'Cannabis, sir.'

'Really.' Bliss blinked. 'A ninety-year-old dopehead?'

'Not *exactly* unheard of, Francis,' Billy Grace said. 'Occasionally prescribed by some of my more liberal colleagues for its analgesic qualities. And, of course, more often *self*-prescribed. Though I think if you're suggesting the old boy might've toddled down here high as a bloody kite—'

'You'd be able to tell?'

Billy shrugged

'Immersion cases are almost invariably problematical. Even simple drowning... ridiculously hard to prove.' He walked down to the stream's edge, where you could see the waterfall and most of the pool. 'Might've died through the shock of hitting cold water, or natural causes, precipitating the fall into the pool.'

'Only if he was sitting on the barrier at the time,' Bliss said.

'Or wandered in from this side, across the fields.'

'Yeh, I suppose.'

'And there's some other things, actually sir,' Tamsin said to

Bliss. 'Probably nothing to do with, you know, what's happened… but a bit, you know…'

'Things?'

'Funny things. Oh God—'

Tamsin shook. Quite suddenly, the body had come up between the two divers, like an old inner tube, water sluicing through a jacket that might once have been white, froth like bubblegum around the mouth. Bliss winced, turned away and stumbled slightly in the mud.

Billy Grace caught hold of his arm, frowning, then steered him along the stream's edge, away from PC Winterson, the corpse and the waterfall roar, the old bastard diagnosing aloud.

'Occasional apparent difficulties with balance…'

'Piss *off*!'

'… and a slight, residual slurring of the speech perhaps discernible only to those of us who've known you for some years. Still getting the double vision, are we, Francis?'

'Just gerroff my friggin' case.' Bliss dragged his arm away. 'How about you confine yourself, Dr Grace, to suggesting whether this looks like an accident, or suicide – or if there are complications. Other words, did he fall or was he dumped?'

'You're a fool to yourself, Francis.'

'I've been cleared by the medics.'

'And does one of them owe you a favour, perchance?'

'Up yours, Billy.'

Bliss steadied himself to walk back to PC Winterson. She seemed smaller. Sometimes his vision was like looking down the wrong end of a telescope.

'You said funny. Funny how, Tamsin?'

'Funny peculiar, sir. Seemed *very* peculiar to me. At least—'

'Was it you who found out about this?'

'Yes, sir. I've a friend who lives here, and the man with the dog… theirs was the first house he came to after he saw what he thought was a body in the pool. So she rang me, and I reported it and then came here with my friend and I realized there was nothing we could do, and she saw the hat and she was like, Oh God, it's Mr Hambling. So I went up to his house, and the door was unlocked and—'

'Tell you what,' Bliss said in an urgent kind of despair. 'Show me.'

8

No strings

When she put down the phone, an emphatic echo clanged in the air, as if something had shut her out.

This phone was good at finality: 1950s black Bakelite, heavy as a small barbell. A present from Jane. Useful for keeping the bills down, the kid had said – you couldn't wait to hang up.

That was when she *was* a kid.

In the scullery office, silvery early light was draped in the window overlooking the narrowest part of the garden and the churchyard wall. The scullery ceiling was supported by a sixteenth-century beam, gouged and pitted, the colour of old tobacco. Too big for the job now, it had probably been central to whatever the vicarage had been in its young days.

She'd never thought about that before. Never had time.

Guessed you'd be up, Jane had said just now, on the phone. *I'm just, like, ringing to see if you're OK?*

Merrily telling her she was every bit as OK as she was last night, when Jane had last rung. Asking what the weather was like down there in West Wales.

Crap, but that's all right. They can't get started anyway. Still waiting for the geofizz.

Merrily smiling to herself, knowing how long the kid had been waiting to talk like an archaeologist. Smiling to herself because there was nobody else to smile to. There'd been a change of plan. Jane had gone for the West Wales dig instead of Wiltshire because they'd agreed to take Eirion as well, for a month.

The only difference was it had meant leaving a week earlier. Not a problem for Eirion, who was at university. Not a problem for Jane who'd missed her final two weeks at high school... and thus the appalling Prom.

Slight problem for Merrily.

Back to the kitchen and into the main hall, to the front door, past the framed print of Holman Hunt's *Light of the World*. Housewarming present from Uncle Ted, the head church-warden, to whom she'd been a disappointment, a neglecter of the parish. Here was Jesus Christ with his lantern, outside the kind of weathered old door you found here in Ledwardine, his eyes baggy with sorrow, compassion and a hint of – what – disillusion? Disappointment? Him too?

Avoiding the eyes, she went out and stopped herself from locking the front door behind her. This was Ledwardine. Whoever locked their doors in Ledwardine?

Everybody, now.

A wave for Jim Prosser, cutting the string on the morning papers dumped outside the Eight Till Late – Jim, who kept announcing that he and Brenda were getting out, going back to Wales, somewhere bleak and stony where no incomers came in demanding lychees and fresh figs.

On the edge of the market square, now, opposite the crab-like, oak-pillared market hall, mostly used these days as a bus shelter. Nobody sheltering there from today's intermittent rain. The cobbles glistening muddily on the square, old guttering dribbling around the roofs of the black and whites.

Ledwardine: an old slapper who could look after herself. She'd be there when they were all long dead, probably looking much the same despite the efforts of various developers and the whisper of money slid under council tables.

Not yet eight a.m. Merrily crossing Church Street to Lol's terraced cottage, letting herself in to an empty hush, no bleeps from the answering machine. When Lol was merely out, temporarily, you'd walk in here, and the draught when you shut the door would cause a shivering of strings from the Boswell.

But the guitar stand was abandoned, an upturned V of black metal, empty padded rests. No vibration. No strings.

Picking up the mail from the mat: all junk. Fuel-saving offers, insurance deals. Carried them through to the recycling bin, which had been made by a firm called SimpleHuman.

Jesus, if only. She'd be doing this day after day. And next week, she was on holiday. A lonely holiday she couldn't get out of.

In front of the cold stove in the inglenook, she came close to weeping for a moment before scowling it away and opening a window to let in some street sounds. What she wasn't going to do again was wander upstairs, lie on Lol's bed and sob into his pillow.

Jane would have told her how daft and pathetic she was being. But Jane had driven off with Eirion Lewis, the two of them looking like a grown-up couple. *Eirion, yeah* – Jane on the phone to Neil Cooper, the archaeologist – *my partner. Partner?* Jesus wept, at which stage did Eirion become her *partner?* They were *kids.* Could never have called Lol her partner. A loose, casual, cowboy word, no real commitment involved.

No strings.

When she got back, Ethel was mewing in legitimate protest; if Jane had been here, she'd have been fed by now.

'Sorry, Ethel… sorry, sorry, sorry…'

She forked out half a tray of Sheba, the expensive stuff, the special treat food, and then made herself some breakfast, honey and toast. Tried to eat it sitting at the refectory table and suddenly had a picture of herself as if from above, CCTV from the ceiling: one small person at one end of a long, communal table.

The vicarage was vast. It had seven bedrooms, two of them used as stockrooms for the gift shop in the vestry. Maybe she should start taking in battered wives, asylum seekers…

She was stupidly relieved when the old phone jangled and she had to carry the plate through to the scullery office, half a slice of thick toast and honey clenched between her teeth.

'You didn't come in yesterday,' Sophie said.

'Oh...'

Monday. Yesterday had been Monday. Traditionally a vicar's day off, hers always sacrificed on the altar of Deliverance, the little extra job. Monday was the weekly meeting with Sophie at the gatehouse office to go through the Deliverance database, reply to any queries from parish priests, many of whom found this aspect of their role distasteful and couldn't unload it fast enough. Also, to see who might require aftercare. What Uncle Ted called neglecting the parish. But if it wasn't for the little extra job she'd probably have seven parishes by now and he'd be lucky to see her every other week.

'Yes, well, something...' Putting the plate on the desk, dropping the toast on it '... something came up. Sorry, Sophie. Could we possibly make it this afternoon?'

Sophie would be arranging her chained glasses to consult the diary.

'The Bishop should be on the train to London by then, so... yes, I suppose so.'

Small clink: the glasses rejoining the pearls on Sophie's chest. Her primary function was as Bishop's lay secretary, so the Bishop was always going to come first. Actually, that wasn't true; with Sophie, the Cathedral came first... although this was possibly a metaphor for something more amorphous at the ancient heart of Hereford.

'Good. Excellent. Thanks.' Merrily picked up the slice of toast, bit off a small piece. A good day to get out of here. Maybe they could grab some lunch in Hereford, her and Sophie. 'Erm... anything I need to know about, meanwhile?'

Sophie would never ring out of pique, just because a meeting had been missed.

'It'll wait.'

'No…' Call it intuition. 'Go on…'

'You're probably not going to like this, Merrily.'

Merrily put down the toast.

'It's Ms Merchant, isn't it?'

'Must've rung very early this morning. Evidently exasperated at getting an answering machine. As if we ought to be operating a twenty-four-hour service.'

'And Ms Nott? Ms Nott is still with her?'

'If I play the message to you now, you might want to consider your options on the way here.'

Sophie must have had the message already wound back. Ms Merchant's voice was as low and calm as ever but carried, in Merrily's head, like a barn owl's screech.

'Mrs Hill, I'm afraid your young woman didn't do what I wanted her to do. In essence, Ms Nott is not smiling any more.'

Merrily sat down.

'I thought this would come.'

This was how the working day began.

With a blossoming madness.

9

Old habits

FROM THE DOORWAY, Betty watched Robin sleeping in the chair, sprawled diagonally like some spent warrior, in the only position his wounds would allow. He'd been growing his hair again. She recalled the day he'd found a small tuft of grey, attacked his Lord Madoc tresses in disgust.

But he was asleep again, that was the main thing. The past two nights he'd lain awake, stricken with back pain and anxiety: oh, this was all a mistake, the shop would fail; in this bleak new age of atheism, paganism was passé.

If it had been meant, Robin said, they would've sold the damn bungalow.

Yes, that was a bummer. Betty had set herself to cleaning and rearranging and making the bungalow look good for the market and not too scary. Taking down the framed star-charts and the green man, lifting the goddess from her niche behind the door and packing her in straw in a wine box.

In just under a month, five couples had been to view the place. None of them had stayed long. Yesterday, the estate agent had phoned.

'Mrs Thorogood,' he'd said, tentatively, 'if I could suggest… have you thought about perhaps finding somewhere to store your books?'

Good point. You never thought when you lived with them day to day, but books on pagan magic seldom came with muted covers.

The supermarket had given her dozens of strong cardboard boxes. They'd spent all morning packing up all the books which would fill the truck maybe ten times before they were all gone.

But the shop in Back Fold was nearly ready for them, with a new midnight blue ceiling on which Robin had painted a full moon and stars in formation. It was starting to look right.

Even if didn't feel right. Why? Why, why, why?

Betty went quietly into their small bedroom with the mobile, sat on the end of the bed and made her call.

'I don't understand,' Mr Oliver said. 'You think I'm hiding something?'

Betty saw she'd left the bedroom door open a crack and got up to shut it. Thin walls, cheap doors; voices carried in the bungalow. In Robin's up-and-down state, best not to involve him in this. Not yet, anyway.

'You said you bought the shop as a retirement business but found it too time-consuming.'

'That was...' Mr Oliver cleared his throat '... perhaps an over-simplification.'

'And yet, by all accounts, you weren't doing much business at all. I'm sorry – just passing on what I've heard... from a number of sources.'

They'd talked to nobody apart from Paramjeet Kapoor, but if you had good reason to believe something was true, it was morally acceptable to pursue it. *Morally.* Funny how this had become increasingly important to her. In pagan theologies, morals, if they played any part at all, tended to be naive and simplistic.

She heard Mr Oliver drawing a long breath.

'Mrs Thorogood, these people, booksellers... they're not what you think they're going to be – not what I expected, certainly. And the worst kind of gossips. This town's full of gossip. My wife hasn't been well, that's why we've had to keep closing the shop for days at a time.'

'I'm sorry,' Betty said. 'You couldn't find anyone else to work there part time?'

'You can't just have someone on a string. They want something solid, need to know which days they're working.'

'You see, we didn't ask to look at your books – business accounts, I mean, anything like that, because our business would be different. But what I—'

'You'd have learned nothing meaningful. All shops are going through a difficult time.'

'I was also told…' Another guess '… that the shop had changed hands quite a lot in quite a short period.'

'That's not uncommon in Hay. Never has been. Not everyone adapts easily. It isn't London and it isn't Oxford.'

He'd sounded as if he'd hoped it would be. Even Robin wasn't that naive.

'And presumably you're only offering the shop for rent because you've tried to sell it?'

'Anyone in the town would have told you – and I expect they did – that it was for sale for several months.'

'You said – which I thought was very honest – that nobody else had wanted to actually live there.'

'That's not *exactly* what I said, Mrs Thorogood.'

'Is it possible that these premises have… a reputation?'

'Goodness, what *have* those people—? It's an old building, it's not in the best of condition. And it can get cold in the winter. That's why we're not overcharging. If there are any underlying problems with the plumbing or the electrics that I'm not aware of, you may be sure they'll be put right as soon as I'm notified.'

'That's not really what I meant. Are you aware of anything that happened there in the past, which might have cast—?'

'Like what?'

'Something that…' *Careful now.* 'Something which might be thought to have left… an atmosphere?'

It could be a smell. Mothballs might bring on an image of an old woman moving around, counting the dresses in the wardrobe, a sense of sadness, regret, missed opportunities. Most people could do this if they spared the time, and the more they did it the stronger the sensations would be, the more vivid the images.

'Mrs Thorogood, if you're asking what I think you're asking, I've heard that some poor chap once hanged himself in Back Fold, but not on my premises. That's the only unnatural death I've heard of here.'

'Who was there before you?'

'It was an antique shop... well, more of a junk shop. Already empty when the agent took us to view. I thought that in turning it into a bookshop again I was doing something to reinforce the foundations of Hay.'

'Why had it closed?'

'Why do any of them close? I was told they needed bigger premises. Mrs Thorogood, I'd be most displeased if any unfounded rumours were to spread. And just to be absolutely clear, when I said no unnatural death, I meant people. More or less the whole of Back Fold had a single purpose at one time. Slaughter.'

Betty said nothing.

'Of animals,' Mr Oliver said.

'When was this?'

'Until comparatively recently, I believe. Seems to have gone back *many* years. Centuries. It would have been the castle abattoir. Right below the walls, so there'd always be fresh meat close to hand in the event of a siege or insurrection.'

'Perhaps that's it,' Betty said. 'We're vegetarian.'

She watched Robin shifting uncomfortably in his sleep. There was a time when he'd slept like a dog slept, growling delightedly in pursuit of rabbits and squirrels.

She sat down on the sofa opposite his chair in a modern living room which, when they'd moved in, had had an atmosphere of anger and bitterness. If the middle-aged couple who'd sold them the bungalow weren't divorced by now, Betty would be quite surprised.

Not that she'd ever tried to find out. She'd consulted some people and certain books and got down to softening the place. Making sure she and Robin hadn't slept in the so-called *master bedroom*, which had become his studio, a place where he could safely fight with himself.

She'd looked in there this morning while he was taking a shower and found about a dozen photos of Hay taped to the walls, the basis for some watercolour sketches on a side table. All the pictures had been taken from Back Fold, mostly from low angles, looking up at the castle and the crinkly red chimneys of the Jacobean mansion which the medieval building had nurtured like a big cuckoo chick.

Robin did most of his work on a trestle table, but now the table had been removed, the trestles used to accommodate the sound part of a broken oak floorboard Robin had found in a reclamation yard. He'd sawn off the splintered end and gone to work with a plane on the surface, until it was ready for the black paint. Now it was a sign, waiting to be varnished. A sign that looked as if it had been a sign forever.

Thorogood Pagan Books.

She wondered if there'd be enough light for a studio. Pictures not as good as Robin's best were on sale for hundreds, even thousands in Hay, drawing on an international market, tourists who'd fallen in love with the booktown, who wanted a piece of Hay on their wall. Why not an alluring Thorogood nocturne, woolly lights against softening stone? She could see Robin's paintings eventually stealing window-space from the books.

A foothold to something better. As long as there were some books... enough to keep him in the system.

Robin's eyelids jittered like moths' wings, his eyes opened.

'What's wrong?'

'Nothing,' Betty said. 'Everything's going to be fine.'

Later, when Robin went back to work on his sign, Betty took the laptop into the bedroom and Googled antique dealers in Hay. Began emailing them, one by one, asking if they were the people who used to have a shop in Back Fold.

As the sun went down behind the pink-brick estate, she opened the oak chest in the corner, where the goddess lay in her box, along with the Green Man and the tarot cards, the remains of her crown of lights head-dress and a box of candles.

She found a bent green candle, the size of a courgette, set it down in a tray in the window, and concentrated.

Old habits…

10

A better place

THE CITY OF Hereford seemed to be dying, the way a venerable tree died, from the centre outwards – long-established businesses left to rot while councillors turned away to nurture their doomed, peripheral shopping mall, hand-feeding it with taxpayers' money badly-needed elsewhere.

Most people were saying that, but nothing came to save the city.

Still, it was one of the few English cities where, in the absence of high-rise offices and flats, the oldest buildings were still dominant. The spired All Saints Church, on the corner where Broad Street met High Town, was probably packing in more worshippers these days, Merrily was thinking, than at any time in its history.

Except that they were coming to worship lunch. Half the church was a restaurant now, part self-service and not expensive enough to deter vicars. She'd followed Sophie to the upstairs gallery overlooking the business end where a ghost was said to play the organ.

Something authentically medieval about having lunch in a still-active town centre church. Merrie Englande. If you looked up from your table, you could see a little carved wooden man with his legs in the air, flashing his bits from the ceiling frieze.

'She rang again,' Sophie said.

'What, since this morning? It's been nearly a month. She hasn't even returned my calls.'

'She's probably not entirely rational, but she *is* clearly distressed.'

A man at the next table was telling his woman companion that Hereford needed to take its lead from towns like Ludlow and Hay-on-Wye and attract more tourism and high-quality independent retailers with whom the Internet could not compete. Sophie unwound her silver silk scarf.

'The point of contention is Ms Merchant's continued insistence that she didn't ask you to get rid of her partner.'

'I wouldn't use those words, would I?'

'I told her I presumed you'd offer prayers aimed at guiding Ms Nott to a better place. But it seems clear that Ms Merchant's idea of a better place is… her bedroom.'

Merrily poured sparkling water into two glasses.

'I thought it was sentiment, grief – entirely understandable. I offered to help her move the second bed into another room. Which was very much the wrong thing to say.'

'I suppose,' Sophie said, 'one can understand why immediately disposing of her partner's bed might make her feel in some way disloyal. And yet the very presence of the bed might, on first waking, with one's senses a little befuddled…'

'You come out of a dream, your mind's holding an image. It's projected into an empty bed. She really wasn't open to that kind of explanation. As for keeping that chair in the bedroom…'

'The very symbol of a secretary. I'm not sure I particularly like what that implies.'

'I'm not sure whether it's just morbid or, as you say, a bit sinister. What does she expect from me now? She tell you that?'

'Not in a way that was comprehensible to me.'

'When she said Ms Nott was not smiling any more, did you get the idea that was more a reflection of the way *she* was feeling? Or that the image had gone?'

'She wouldn't be drawn. And it wasn't my business to do that.'

'How well do you know her, Sophie? She said they both came to services at the Cathedral.'

'Didn't really *know* either of them, but I remember them, vaguely. Tall woman, quite formally dressed, and a smaller woman. Younger, I think. Quite plain. Demure – although that might be with hindsight.'

'Boss and secretary.'

'You *might* think that.'

'You see, at first, I had the impression that what Sylvia Merchant wanted from me was simply reassurance that what was happening to her was quite normal. That she wasn't deluded. I told her how commonplace it was. That there was nothing to worry about. And then it all slowly became... *ab*normal. She started asking questions about me that went beyond the usual pleasantries. She knew about what we do. She'd gone into it. But clearly what we do... wasn't what she wanted.'

'I'm assuming,' Sophie said, as lunch arrived, 'that, in normal circumstances, this would have begun and ended with prayer.' She looked up at the waitress. 'Splendid. Thank you.'

Merrily waited until they were alone again, apart from the wooden flasher in the ceiling.

'Far too early to suggest anything like a Requiem Eucharist. Which, under the circs, would not have been exactly welcomed.'

'So, did your response... differ in *any* way from the normal?'

Something here she wasn't being told. Merrily looked for Sophie's eyes but they were lowered over her feta cheese salad.

'I may have formed the impression that, rather than arranging a delicate parting of the ways, I was being asked to bless a... oh God... a continuing relationship? She was saying Alys Nott was with us in that room. The dent in the pillow. The chair which, shortly after I'd stood up, creaked, as if someone else had sat down...'

'Eerie.'

'I need to see her again, don't I?'

'I think not, Merrily.' Sophie still didn't look up. 'The Bishop happened to be there when I was dealing with the call and asked me what it was about. His opinion was that this was something in which, ah… in which it was better that Deliverance should not be involved.'

'Bernie said that? Better for whom?'

'Better for you, certainly. Better for Ms Merchant, in the long term. And – presumably – better for poor Ms Nott. So I'm afraid I had to call Ms Merchant back and tell her that I'd forgotten you were on holiday. And that another priest would come to see her.'

'*What?*'

'Didn't have a choice in the matter.'

'Who?'

'Likely to be George Curtiss.'

Cathedral canon. Large, bearded, well known for diplomatic skills.

Bloody *hell.*

'Merrily…' Sophie was looking up at last, cutlery abandoned. '… your role, surely, is primarily as an adviser on the paranormal. In most cases an adviser to the clergy.'

'But once I'm involved—'

'Once it becomes clear it's a *mental health* issue, some form of delusional grief, it might require an entirely different approach. Let it go, Merrily. You need a holiday. You need to spend time with Jane.'

'What exactly did Sylvia Merchant say to panic Bernie? Because I can't imagine, from what you've told me so far…'

Sophie's eyes narrowed.

'We'll talk about it back at the gatehouse.'

11

Without comfort

MISTAKE. THE GATEHOUSE office was Sophie's domain. Sophie's eyrie at the top of a narrow staircase, overlooking Broad Street and the Cathedral Green.

'So… Laurence,' Sophie said. '*Did* he go, in the end?'

Merrily looked out of the window, an irritable rain bubbling the glass, smudging the people crossing the Green with their heads down into the weather.

'Yes. He went. I think he wanted me to say don't do it.'

'It was the right thing, Merrily.'

'To get away from me?'

'To get away from the village.'

Sophie still had her short camel coat on, open but with the collar turned up against her crisp white hair. An unspoken protest about the heating being off in the gatehouse office. Her gloves lay on the desk.

She was right, of course, about Lol, who'd arrived in Ledwardine on the run from the horrors of the mental health system, coming through with the help of the late Lucy Devenish, wise woman of this parish, whose cottage he'd bought after her death. And then, as his relationship with Merrily had deepened, had been increasingly nervous of leaving the village. It wasn't agoraphobia, but there was probably a name for it.

'How long's he away?'

'Five weeks, give or take. So that's four more. I mean, you're right. He was like a plant in danger of becoming potbound. And the money angle, of course.'

With free downloads starving the recording industry, the only way a musician collected a worthwhile income these days was by going back on the road. Not that Lol cared much about money but, if he wasn't making any, his confidence would evaporate. Not good, for either of them.

'Did I tell you Danny Thomas had gone with him? Gomer's partner. Fulfilling an old dream. Well, the dream was Glastonbury, actually, but playing second guitar for Lol… is a start.'

She'd told Lol he should do it for Danny. What she hadn't told him yet was about Jane. She pushed her chair back, away from the Anglepoise lamp. Sophie had switched it on, ostensibly against the unseasonal dimness; it was starting to look like the preliminary to an interrogation.

'So at least you'll be able to spend more… mother and daughter time with Jane, before she goes on her gap year… excavation.'

Sophie edged the lamp a little closer to Merrily, waiting, lines of concern making her face more priestly than any lay person had a right to look. Merrily gave up.

'All right. It didn't go quite as planned. Should've been an excavation down in Wiltshire, in August. But then she was offered a place on another one, in Pembrokeshire, which meant that Eirion was able to go with her. Which is good because these digs have a reputation for, erm, impropriety. So that's worked out quite well, too. For everybody. Almost.'

'And that's when?'

Merrily followed the progress of an elderly couple under a golf umbrella, through the rain to the cathedral porch.

'They left yesterday.'

'Oh, I *see*.' Sophie steepled her fingers. 'So *that's* why you didn't come in.'

'Seeing her off. Making sure she had everything she needed.'

'Laurence on tour, Jane in a Pembrokeshire trench. You're on your own. In that vast old vicarage.'

'Me and the cat.'

'Which doesn't strike me as conducive to a recuperative frame of mind.'

'I'm a grown-up, Sophie. Less afraid of ghosts than I used to be.'

'I wasn't thinking of ghosts. I was thinking of—' The phone rang. Sophie picked up. 'Yes, she is, but she's in a meeting. Can I ask her to call you back when she comes out...? How are you now, by the way? Glad to hear it.' Sophie sniffed. 'Goodbye.' She put the phone down, glaring at it. 'Didn't expect your friend Bliss to be back at work so soon, either.'

'Oh. You sure he is?'

'I don't know. He seemed to resent me enquiring about his welfare. He wants you to call him back. On his mobile.'

Bliss. His mobile. Just like old times. Bliss on the Gaol Street police car park so as not be overheard by Annie Howe or whichever senior officer had him on a short leash.

'Anyway, you can do that later.' Sophie pushed the phone away. 'I'm sorry to sound as if I'm bossing you around, but after working with the clergy for over thirty years and seeing what's happened, all too often, even to the most balanced of priests—'

'Sophie—'

'And that was in the days before multiple parishes and falling congregations. And without the extra spiritual and emotional burden of people who believe themselves paranormally afflicted.'

'I'm not cracking *up*.'

'If you knew how many times I've been told that by people trying to steer a vehicle without brakes. Look at Martin Longbeach.'

'Martin Longbeach lost his partner. He had a breakdown, had to give up his parish...'

'Having also lost his faith.'

'*Mislaid* his faith. And I'm not going to be smug enough to say I'd have held on to mine if anything had happened to Jane and Lol at Brinsop. And that's— Since you bring it up, that's another reason I can't postpone the week off.'

77

'What is?'

Oh, this really wasn't likely to go down well, but she had to know sometime.

'Martin Longbeach is standing in for me.'

'Assure me you're joking,' Sophie said.

'He needs to get back in the saddle. For a trial period. When Jane was offered Pembrokeshire, I thought maybe I could join Lol somewhere, but then Danny's with him, and wives and rock music don't—'

She felt her face colouring. *Wives?* Where the hell did that come from?

Sophie didn't appear to have heard.

'Let me get this right. Martin Longbeach is taking over your services?'

'And the rest. The original idea was he'd stay at the vicarage with Jane and me, and we'd go off during the day, but I'd be available to talk things over in the evening. So if he was experiencing any strain or felt he couldn't go on...'

'I'd assumed it would be Canon Callaghan-Clarke.'

'She knows about it. She agrees with me that Martin's a good guy and a good priest. She thinks it's... that it could be a good idea.'

'So now this... this leaves you and Longbeach *living together*?'

'Sophie, he's *gay*...'

'How bad can this get, Merrily? You're taking a week off, but you're not going anywhere, for the purpose of nursemaiding a notorious neurotic. You do know what Longbeach *did*?'

'I know what he's *said* to have done.'

'He should leave the area.'

'Well, I actually think he'll be a better priest if he stays here and works through it.'

Sophie drew breath.

'You exasperate me, Merrily.'

'Evidently. In which case, perhaps now would be a good time to tell me exactly what Sylvia Merchant said about me.'

Sophie didn't move.

'Sylvia Merchant is not in her right mind.'

'It's a big club. Come on, Sophie...'

'She told me the whole atmosphere of the bedroom had altered in the aftermath of your visit. That she was left – are you prepared for this? *Isolated, deserted and without comfort.*'

'And you...' Merrily halfway out of her chair '... you didn't think it was important to tell me *that*?'

'I told you I believed she was disturbed.'

Merrily pulled the cigarette packet from her bag, realized where she was and pushed it back.

'What else?'

'She said you... behaved as if her friend was an evil spirit. She seems to think you were determined to, as she put it, exorcize Ms Nott.'

Merrily twisted away. The window overlooking Broad Street and the Cathedral Green was grey with mist.

'You may as well have it all. She then asked what procedure she might follow if she wanted to file a complaint. Now that isn't—'

'Against me, personally?'

'Or the Church. It wasn't clear. But it isn't going to happen.'

Merrily pulled her bag from the desk, stood up.

'Merrily, do sit down. It's an irrational complaint. George Curtiss will clarify things for her. Make her see sense.'

'And the Bishop didn't see fit to talk to me first?'

'No time. Had to catch his train to London. He'll be away for three or four days.'

'Taking only emergency calls. Sure.'

'Look it's absolutely no reflection on you. He knows you'd never overreact to that extent. He simply doesn't see it as a Deliverance issue, that's all. Not now.'

'Or not something he wants me to handle. Too sensitive. Meaning politically sensitive.'

'Exorcism's been on thin ice for several years now,' Sophie said. 'Still in favour in some parts of the Vatican, but you won't find any corresponding enthusiasm in the C. of E. at present. But then you know that. Merrily, you're—'

'I know. Tired.'

Clutching her car keys, she stood in the dampness, looking blankly around the Bishop's Palace yard. *Had* she parked the Volvo here or left it in King Street?

Her gaze had passed twice over the black Freelander before she remembered it was hers. This had happened twice before; she'd come rushing out of somewhere, absently looking for the old Volvo with its familiar dents and its rusty scabs, the Volvo that was two weeks traded in, on the advice of a reliable garage guy, friend of Gomer Parry. It had felt like putting an elderly relative into a Home.

She sagged into the Freelander, feeling absurdly tearful. Everything was changing, all the certainties in her life. Lol going back on the road, what if that triggered some old impulses: booze, dope, groupies? OK, not the Lol she knew, but she hadn't known him back in the days when he was almost famous.

And she was tired of subterfuge. Having to hide from Sophie that it was actually Sian Callaghan-Clarke, the Archdeacon, who'd discreetly asked her to accept Martin Longbeach as a holiday locum. *Keep an eye on him, but don't let him know you're doing it.* Was she expected to grass him up if he did anything unstable, in or out of the chancel? And if she didn't?

Leaving the palace yard under the archway, she wondered if the Bishop wanted her out… out of the psychic sector, anyway. Periodically, the C. of E. would attempt to shrink its exorcism role: an embarrassing anachronism, sometimes dangerous, rarely politically correct. Untraceable reports and memos submitted to the shadowy guardians at Church House. Huw Owen had warned her enough times.

All politics now, lass. Women bishops, gay bishops, cross-dressing bishops, sheep-shagging bishops… I've nowt against any of it, it just didn't used to be what they like to call an Issue. All the Church does now is react to the whims of a society that's lost all awareness of itself and thinks arseholes like Dawkins wi' a string of degrees are possessed of actual wisdom. In the old days, society used to react to us.

Huw laughing like a maniac, stretching out his legs, shoeless feet exposed to the open fire at his rectory in the Beacons until, as usual, his socks had begun to smoulder.

I reckon we have one advantage, lass, folks like us... though it's also a disadvantage. Most of the clergy still believe in a God, of sorts, but most of the general public... they believe in ghosts.

12

Cripple

BETTY HAD LEFT Robin painting tree shadows on the shop walls between the bookcases while she shopped for food in Hay.

The sun was out, tourists on the streets. Book tourists. You could pick them out by the shabby-chic clothing, bum bags and back-carriers for babies, some of the men in Bohemian wide-brimmed hats. All kind of middle-class neo-hippy, and Mr and Mrs Oliver looked more like tourists than locals.

They were coming out of Jones the Chemists, one of the oldest businesses in town, Mr Oliver stuffing packages into an old Waitrose bag-for-life.

'—right then. If I go and pick up the rest and see you outside Shepherds in say an hour?'

Crossing the road arching his neck in his purposeful way. When, half an hour later, Betty saw Mrs Oliver – long skirt, summery bag on a sash – walk into the ewe's milk ice cream parlour, she followed her in, introduced herself.

'And when are you opening?' Mrs Oliver said.

She was comfortably plump, hair short and near-white. Diamond earrings, sharp eyes, gardener's tan.

'This weekend, probably,' Betty said. 'We're a bit nervous. Not having had a shop before.'

'I'm sure you'll do well,' Mrs Oliver said.

'Yes, we… hopefully.' She looked round. The dominant colour in here was green, an arboreal haze over everything. 'Are you fully recovered now?'

'From what?'

'I'm sorry, your husband said you'd been… not well.'

'*Did* he?'

Betty said nothing. Discomfort hovered. Then Mrs Oliver seemed to relax, and her eyes lit up like coals in a stove when you pulled out the damper.

'I'm Hilary.'

'Betty.'

'I'm glad we've met. Now, listen. You mustn't be put off by James's failure. Running a bookshop in a recession seems to require a level of enterprise that he lacks. We came here on a romantic whim – *his* romantic whim – for a weekend a few years ago, when he was convinced he'd seen Martin Amis having coffee with Andrew Motion, while he was still Poet Laureate. James's… pavement-café-society moment. After that, he just *had* to live here.'

'And open a shop? Bit drastic?'

'My dear…' Mrs Oliver did an unsmile '… James is one of those people who need to *buy in*. Move as quickly as possible to the centre of things. No use Martin Amis popping in for a browse and a coffee if he doesn't become James's close friend.'

'And has he?'

'Never been seen since. Nor Motion. Though I can't deny that you *do* see authors here. They say every notable writer comes at least once, out of curiosity.'

'I've heard that.'

'Gets to the point, as I say, where you're imagining you've seen someone and you actually haven't. Ah, that's so-and-so! It isn't, but you think it *is* because this is Hay. I saw Beryl Bainbridge once. There she was walking amongst the open-air shelves at the honesty bookshop under the castle walls in her grey, fitted coat and a scarf and gloves. Not a face you'd think you could mistake, and I thought, I know, I'll ask her if she'd mind signing some of her books. But it couldn't have been. Her—'

Someone pushed past the table, dislodging it and causing Hilary Oliver's coffee to spill. She frowned.

'Terribly sad. Her obituary was in the *Guardian* the following day. I suppose what I'm saying is that this is one of those places where people become prone to delusions of one kind or another. Like this ridiculous business of the King, which began as a joke decades ago and doesn't go away. He was pointed out to me once. I couldn't take it on board. My God, his *trousers...*'

Hilary Oliver shuddered.

'Will you still stay here, Hilary, now there's no business?'

'Well, we do have quite a nice house, with a big garden. And friends who like to come for weekends. We'll probably have to stay until such time as James convinces himself it was a worthwhile exercise. He's talking about standing for the town council. Ridiculous – town councils in this part of the world are *nothing*. No powers. Small-time talking shops. On reflection, I suppose he'll quite enjoy that.'

Betty licked her ice cream, thoughtful. What had seemed quite funny at first was suddenly acutely depressing. It was how you didn't want ever to wind up: purposeless. Looking for a reason.

'But at least you're out of the shop,' she said.

'No we're not. We still own it. We had an opportunity to sell the premises and he refused. Two approaches. Both backed away when James demanded they sign a document committing them to preserving it as a bookshop. Perverse. He was held up to ridicule in some quarters because he would only sell *good* books. He said if we weren't dependant on it for a living, we should feel obliged to stand up for what he saw as Literary Quality.'

'That's... kind of admirable, really. Isn't it?'

'My dear, it's bloody silly, precious and guaranteed to fail. I have to say he wasn't terribly pleased, at first, when he found out the kind of books you were proposing to sell, but at least they're books. In the end, he simply refuses to be seen as betraying what he calls the defining quality of the town. But... he's out of it. I know he likes to say it was my health that was suffering, but it was his. I'll say no more.'

Betty said, 'I wondered why you hadn't developed it upstairs, opened up more book rooms. Something we can't do, of course, or we wouldn't have anywhere else to live.'

Hilary's chin retracted, eyes widening.

'You're not proposing to *live* in those upstairs rooms?'

'We don't really have a choice at the moment.'

'James didn't tell me *that*. I mean it's all so… small and…'

Betty waited. What else had James failed to tell her?

The old woman who whistled traipsed past the door in her long coat.

'Anyway, you're young. You have the energy.' Sounded like she hadn't been told about Robin's condition. She looked at her watch. 'James will be coming back soon. Did you want to talk to him? About health?'

'Er… perhaps not. Perhaps you can both drop in and have a look over the weekend. See what a mess we've made.'

'We'd love to. But it won't be a mess. I sense in you a level of determination neither of us possesses.'

Maybe she meant a level of need.

Robin had left the door open, but the paint cloths over the shelves were enough to convince passers-by they weren't open yet for business.

Except for Gareth Nunne. Wedged in the doorway, blocking Robin's light.

'Feel responsible for you now, you bugger. What kind of idiot takes any notice of an old fart with his business crashing round his ears?'

'A desperate man, Nunne,' Robin said. 'A desperate man.' He put down his palette of acrylics, dropped his brush in the water jar. 'You realize it's gonna look better than this. We're barely started here.'

Gareth Nunne pulled the sheets off a couple of shelves.

'Better how, boy?'

'Tidier, for a start.'

'Tidy?' Nunne reeling back, like he'd been pepper-sprayed. 'You don't want bloody *tidy*.'

Robin grinned, first time today.

'Tidy,' Nunne said, like he was addressing a small kid, 'looks like you know what you're selling.'

'We know *exactly* what we're selling.'

'Of course you do. I'm just telling you it en't good to *look* like you know. If you're wearing a suit and all your shelves are beautifully ordered and it looks like every book's been assessed and valued, you're buggered. What you need are subtle hints of chaos… confusion… incompetence. You don't wanner blow it like Oliver, come over as *clever*, when what your customer wants is stupid. Some vague, booky type who don't function in the real world. Your customer's looking for a bargain. Wants to think he's put one over on you.'

Nunne pulled down Wells's guide to the sacred magic of gemstones.

'Say your punter's bought this for peanuts and he's real chuffed, and he tells you it's a first edition. You go, "First edition? Is it really? Well, well. I never noticed that. Good heavens, you got a bargain there, all right."'

'And that works how?'

'It's a sacrifice. They've got you down as an idiot, and that means they'll come back.'

'Uh… right.'

'However,' Gareth said, 'if you're *buying* second-hand books different rules apply. You go, "Well, of *course* it's a first edition – there only ever was one edition, and if people didn't want it first time around, they're not gonner want it now. Only way it'll sell is as part of a set. Say fifteen quid the lot?"'

'You tried to pull that one on me.'

'Aye, and leased bloody Oliver's shop for him. Jesus.'

Nunne beamed at Robin. His port wine stain shone. Then he was serious.

'Don't get me wrong. We're not in competition, yere, like your

Waterstones and your Smiths. It's about getting people into *the town*. The town's one big bookshop. All the rest, the fashion shops, the antique shops, the art shops, that's just the support. When it ceases to be the support and starts to dominate the book trade… that's when Hay will fall, boy.'

He probably didn't mean it to sound as portentous as it did.

Outside the ice cream parlour, a man was crouching on the pavement, taking pictures of the castle, across the marketplace.

'Not really what one would call a *romantic* ruin, is it?' Hilary said.

You couldn't argue with that. Some medieval castles were beautifully stark, like sculptures made by the hand of God. This one looked like a ruin inside a ruin. Repeatedly smashed and burned, patched up, rebuilt, reformed, abandoned again. And now it just hung around, Betty thought, like some huge, shambling, schizophrenic psychiatric patient in the care of the community.

Maybe Robin related to the castle as a fellow cripple.

Cripple. He liked that word.

'The keep,' Hilary said, 'is supposed to have been built by a huge woman. Matilda. Or Maud. Or something.'

Betty had Googled it. The origins of the castle, as much as she could find. Matilda, or Maud, had been the wife of a Norman baron, William de Braose, who ran most of the southern Welsh border in the twelfth century, the reign of King John. William had been known as The Ogre after organizing the massacre of several Welsh leaders he'd invited to dinner at Abergavenny Castle, twenty-five miles or so from here.

'Built it on her own, do you think?' Betty said. 'Or did she just brief the contractors?'

'No idea. I suppose it's partly legend. Matilda was eventually starved to death by King John, apparently. Not here. Somewhere. Perhaps I'm oversensitive, but I find none of that romantic.'

Hilary Oliver turned away from the castle. As perhaps, Betty sensed, she always had.

"Scuse me." The man with the camera was on his feet, approaching Betty. 'This is rather cheeky of me. Taking some shots for a tourist guide, and I need a figure to stand in front of the castle. Would you mind?'

'Me?'

'Only be middle-distance. To give the picture a sense of scale.'

Never liked being photographed. Native Americans thought it captured your soul. But then she thought about Robin.

'OK, then.'

'Very kind. If you stand there in the centre of the square, away from the cars...'

He took several in the end. Her looking at him, her looking up at the castle. She felt awkward, but he seemed professional and harmless enough – dumpy, bearded, middle-aged guy. And she knew that Robin would go, Hey, connection! You arrived. You're part of the scene. You're *part of Hay*.

'If you give me your address,' the photographer said, 'I'll send you some copies of the brochure when it's printed.'

'It's OK, honestly,' Betty said. 'Don't worry about that. I'm sure it'll be pointed out to me.'

They always promised you copies, but they never arrived.

And giving her address as Back Fold had an element of finality she was still unsure about.

13

Protocol and courtesy

'DAVID HAMBLING,' Bliss said.

'So how are you, now, Frannie?'

'Better than David Hambling.'

Merrily thought about this.

'He's dead, right?'

'All right, considerably better,' Bliss said. 'How did you know he was dead?'

'I just... know the way you approach things.'

She'd gone out without her mobile again, had to wait until she was home to call him back. Answering service. She could wait. She'd done some ironing and sketched out Sunday's sermon on the general theme of bereavement. *Sermon.* Never a favourite word. One dictionary definition employed the verb *harangue*. How long would a haranguing vicar last these days? Little female pulpit punk screaming hellfire. They'd take you away.

See... already talking to herself. *And* bloody well forgotten that, with Martin Longbeach in the pulpit, she didn't even need a sermon. God, she was losing it. Stress. Quite glad when Bliss had called back just before seven p.m.

'How much you know about Cusop, then, Merrily?'

Sophie had been right, his speech was a little slurry, Mersey mud reclaiming its own.

'I know where it *is*.'

An insignificant left turn, just as you were about to cross the Welsh border into Hay-on-Wye.

Bliss said, 'Your patch?'

'Certainly in the diocese.'

'Separated from the Dyfed-Powys police area by two or three fields and the Dulas Brook,' Bliss said. 'Right on the rim. The brook actually marks the English border. Learned that today.'

'New knowledge always makes a day worthwhile.'

'Something wrong, Merrily?'

'Nah, just a bit... Go on. tell me something else about Cusop Dingle.'

'You can't see Hay at all from there, close as it is. Too low. Can't see much of anything, really. Funny kind of place. Secretive. Lorra trees. Would you like to see it?'

'You're asking me for a date?'

Merrily sat down, put an elbow on the scullery desk to take the weight of the phone.

Bliss said, '*Have* you heard of David Hambling?'

'Not sure. Was he a priest?'

Small laugh from Bliss.

'If you can spare the time, I'd like you to take a look at Mr Hambling's library. As a person with knowledge of what we might call the spiritual underside.'

'Satanist?'

'Half-eleven all right?'

'Sure. Why not.'

'I wouldn't keep you long, it's just— Sorry, did I get that right? you just agreed without an argument and having to clear it with the Bishop?'

'I did.'

'Bloody hell. Well. If you know where the Cusop Dingle sign is, follow it and just keep driving till you see my car.'

'Is it possible there's something in Cusop I need to know about?'

'Might be.'

'Only it has a church and a minister. Should I mention it, out of protocol... courtesy, even?'

'Nah, I wouldn't. Not at this stage.'

'Frannie, you don't know what protocol and courtesy *mean*.'

'Yeh, well, had trouble with a lorra words since I had me head kicked in.'

'I did wonder how that was going? In fact I even Googled *brain-injury*, which is something I don't normally—'

'Merrily.' Bliss's voice was suddenly wound tight. 'Brain *stem* injury. Different. How's Jane?'

'Gone away for gap-year therapy. How did he die, this man?'

'Found in a pool below a waterfall. Probably drowned. We don't know for certain yet.'

'Cusop has a waterfall?'

'Several, apparently. Least, the brook does.'

'Don't have to inspect a body or anything, do I?'

'Eleven-thirty, then,' Bliss said. 'Ta ra.'

She sat staring at the phone. Would she have said yes with such alacrity if the Bishop – and even Sophie – hadn't gone behind her back over Sylvia Merchant? Courtesy and protocol. A two-way street.

No call that night from Jane or Lol. None expected. Jane had already rung four times in just over a day – what did that say about both of them?

She left it till after ten, when she knew he'd be in, and called Huw Owen in the Brecon Beacons. No answer. No answering machine. Didn't try again. What did she really expect him to say about Sylvia Merchant? What could you really claim to do for these people when even the dictionaries had their doubts?

Merrily went to bed too early, a last-light sheen on the landing window, a brown fog on the oaken stairs.

On your own. In that vast old vicarage.

Who knew how old the vicarage really was? Three centuries, four centuries, five... more? You'd need to carbon date every oak beam even to make an educated guess. She'd gone up and down these stairs tens of thousands of times, knowing the house was empty but also knowing that Jane would be home before nightfall. And also, in the past year or so, that Lol was in his cottage at the bottom of the cobbled square.

Coming back from the bathroom, it was like being the only guest in a drab old hotel. One of the bulbs in the landing light had expired a couple of nights ago and now the walls were the colour of worn leather and she was unusually aware of her footsteps. It was oppressive in the way it had been when she and Jane had first moved in and she'd had recurrent dreams of the house being even bigger than it was, with a forbidden extra storey. Also vividly bloody dreams of her dead husband, Sean, Jane's father, who had died in a motorway crash with his other woman.

Did she actually like this vicarage? It was impressive. Lots of period features.

No, not a lot, really. Amazing it had survived when the Church was flogging them off all over the country, putting the clergy into former council houses. She suspected the reason it hadn't happened here was Uncle Ted, senior churchwarden, retired solicitor with an extensive portfolio of stocks and shares, who'd been known to bail the parish out more than once and thought a showpiece black and white village like Ledwardine deserved a seventeenth-century seven-bedroom mausoleum for its vicar to freeze in.

Merrily spun round, shivering in her T-shirt and pants, gazing into the night-blue squares of the leaded window. A small black shadow flitted in front of her into the bedroom.

Me and the cat.

Some people said cats were drawn to negative energy. Ethel mewed. Merrily bent and picked her up, put her on the rug and climbed into bed.

After a few minutes she got up again, went across to the window which overlooked the village lights, said a small, neutral prayer for Ms Merchant and the soul of Ms Nott and went back to bed.

There was a small bump and squirmy movements between her feet.

Ethel. Hopefully.

14

A hollow in time

BLISS LOOKED SOMEHOW askew, walking uneasily like a soldier conscious of roadside bombs. A defensiveness behind the sloping smile.

Not brain damage, brain *stem* damage. Different. Google said some functions impaired, but not mental capacity. Not for too long, anyway. Usually.

'Frannie.'

'Ta for this, Rev.'

Mid-morning in Cusop Dingle might have been early evening somewhere else. Wet, white sunlight was strained through the canopy of heavy trees hanging over the black Freelander, Bliss's Honda and a small police car in the opening of a track leading across the bridge to some hidden house.

More people lived down here than you'd think. A few cottages edged the narrow lane but the bigger houses were set back on higher ground enclosed by dripping trees. Full of shady glades on a sunny day but in weather like this it was, Merrily thought, quite a dark place.

She pointed up the track, which curved away into woodland.

'It's up there?'

'No, this was just the only place for us all to park without blocking the road. If we shurrup, you can hear the falls.'

Following the sound of water-rush, she peered down over a roadside rail. Jutting shelves of rock, foam. The clear pool below was bound to be deeper than it looked.

'Another bloke was drowned there years ago,' Bliss said. 'And someone once drove a car through the fence above it, but narrowly escaped. So it's got form.'

'This is a *suspicious* death, Frannie?'

'Well, *I'm* suspicious, but it's like a disease with me.'

Not suspicious enough on the night he'd stumbled into an illegal cockfight in a sweaty cellar below the Plascarreg estate in Hereford. Getting his head trampled into the sawdust.

Bliss said, 'What?'

'Nothing.'

Yesterday he'd even snapped at Sophie – *snapped* at Sophie.

'And he's a bit unusual, our man,' Bliss said, 'as you'll see. Which makes his death by apparent drowning open to a little extra scrutiny. Humour me, Merrily.'

He set off under tree canopies heavy as tarpaulin then crossed the lane to another track, leading uphill into more woodland.

'Where we going, Frannie?'

'Not far. Norrin these shoes.'

'You in charge now, at Gaol Street?'

'Not exactly. There's Brent. Acting-DCI *Dr* Brent.'

'You have coppers now with doctorates?'

'My guess is he gorrit online. Sixty dollars from the University of Dry Gulch, Arizona.'

The track curved round, the ground rising quite steeply out of the dingle. Bliss took a breath and started to walk again, faster, as if to prove he could. Merrily caught him up.

'So do *all* more-senior officers have to be your adversary necessarily? Is it part of the job description? Because Annie Howe—'

He stopped.

'She's back in Worcester.'

'I mean I know you were never exactly best mates but, when you were hurt, she did seem… concerned to an unexpected degree.'

'Probably concerned I might recover.'

'Everybody changes, Frannie. That a castle tump?'

'What?'

She pointed towards the top of the track. It was over the hedge, a low, green mound, flat-topped.

'No idea,' Bliss said.

'You don't want anybody to think you're unfit for frontline duty, right?'

'Who's saying that?'

'Nobody's saying it.'

'I *look* unfit?'

'You look… I dunno, really.'

'Had the medicals. Passed with flying— Passed, anyway.'

'When?'

'When what?'

'When did you have the medicals?'

'Last one a couple of weeks ago. More to come, but—'

He stumbled slightly, hissed, walked on, his face taut, his thinning hair cut close.

'I meant what time of day?' Merrily said. 'Only I was reading how people with your kind of injury feel tired more quickly, so if you were seen earlier in the day—'

'Mother of God! You gonna friggin' stop this at some point, Merrily? Pray for me in your own time.'

Bliss had stopped at a stone gatepost, a bit taller than he was. There had once been perhaps a lion or an eagle on top, but it was just a crooked projection now, like a broken thumb. Another post, about ten feet away, had been reduced to a stump. A track between the posts led down into thickets and a copse and, presumably, the brook. Merrily looked for gables, tall chimneys.

'The house far away?'

'No distance. The reason you can't see it, it's a bungalow.'

'With pretensions?'

'I'm told there used to be a big Victorian farmhouse on the site, demolished years ago. At a time when farmers got to preferring less maintenance and oil-fired heating.'

'But I take it this David Hambling wasn't a farmer.'

Bliss said nothing, waved her between the gateposts.

It was nice to feel wanted.

In the clergy, you spent many hours in the homes of the recently dead. While drawn curtains, or any marks of mourning, were no longer exactly commonplace, there was an atmosphere you came to recognize: a sense of quiet, sober unreality, a hollow in time.

But this wasn't like that.

A tidy fitted kitchen, pine units, bottle-green roller blinds, spotlamps on a lighting track. Light ochre walls that looked sunny even on a day like this. There was milk and sugar on the dresser with a packet of chocolate digestives, a bottle of red wine, a copy of the *Radio Times* opened to last Sunday's TV. This was the room of someone who had... just popped out.

She thought of that comforting homily, often read at funerals, about the dead person being only in the next room.

There was a young policewoman waiting for them.

'Merrily, this is PC Winterson. Tamsin, Mrs Watkins is here in a consultative capacity. So this is between us, right?'

The girl was nodding quickly, evidently flattered at being included. Bliss was like that, oblivious of rank and pecking order. You were his mate till you let him down. He pulled out a chromium-framed stool and sat on it.

'*I* think... we might help ourselves to a pot of Mr Hambling's tea. Would you mind, Tamsin, if it's norra terribly sexist request? Could *mairder* a cuppa.'

Tamsin smiled, took a stainless steel teapot to the stainless steel sink. She was pale and freckly, ginger hair tied back with a rubber band.

Merrily remembered the first time Bliss had asked her to take a look at someone's house. Specifically two white walls of photos of women, now dead. *You're looking at his inspiration. These are the ones he wishes he'd done. The ones he wishes he'd got to first.*

Deceptive, in the end, but he wouldn't have taken liberties there with the teapot.

'Is this… any kind of a crime scene, Frannie?'

'Not that we know of.'

'Mr Hambling – how old did you say?'

'Over ninety. Which is one reason why nobody but me and Tamsin's thinking of crime. Yet.'

'No relatives, Frannie?'

'May take some time to get them up here. He had a wife, from whom he seems to have been estranged but not divorced. And who we think is now dead. We also think he's gorra daughter… somewhere. But Tamsin's the expert, Tamsin's local to the area and therefore in possession of that distinctive Welsh border character-trait where you drip-feed information gradually in case you're talking to an enemy. Taken me friggin' ages to gerrit out of her. You were born on a farm at…?'

'Dorstone, sir.' Tamsin was blushing to the roots of her pulled-back hair. 'Near there. Few miles from here. It's where I live. But I had this friend from school who lived at Cusop, and I used to spend a lot of time here, and she told me, way back, about Mr Hambling. How kids used to dare one another to sneak up and… well just dare to come here, really.'

'Because…?'

Bliss waited. He evidently knew the answers to all these questions, wanted Merrily to get them first hand.

'Stupid, really. It seemed stupid at the time, but we were all reading like Harry Potter in those days? We wanted to believe it could be like that. In real life?'

She looked at Bliss, who nodded, good as saying, *Don't tell me, tell her; she gets paid not to laugh at this shit.*

15

Catered for

TAMSIN SAID, 'I just assumed it was because he looked like one. And because it was supposed to be haunted up here.'

The bungalow overlooked Cusop Dingle on one side. Another offered a view across fields to the castle at Hay-on-Wye, the lesser-known side, the part that was more like a mansion on a hill.

This bungalow, unusually big, solidly built of brick and stone, was itself on a small promontory surrounded by decaying outbuildings inside a half-circle of oak and thorn and yew trees. Another stream was frothing over shallow rocks below it and down to the dingle. But it was an ordinary enough bungalow, surely no more than fifty or sixty years old.

'How old would he have been then?' Bliss asked.

'Seemed like out of the Old Testament at the time. Or Charles Dickens? With his white hair, white whiskers. From a distance, it was like— I remember thinking, it was like a halo, all around his face. He'd've been eightyish, I reckon, but he was pretty sprightly. Chase you off. And catch you. Sometimes.'

'And was he nasty? When he caught you? Or... nice?'

'He never caught me. Well, I never went that close. Too spooky for me up yere.'

Merrily said, 'Why do you say that?'

'They used to say you could see like strange... lights? My friend reckons she seen it once. Like the countryside was lit up from inside? It was only for a fraction of a second. Like one of those… like a UFO experience. Nothing to say it was anything at all to do with Mr Hambling, except it was near his house. I'm just telling you this 'cos the DI said to tell you everything, no matter how daft it sounded.'

'So just part of local folklore,' Merrily said.

'Don't know how far it went back. I probably wasn't born before Mr Hambling was here. My friend, she asked a bloke and he said she wasn't the first to see it, the light. It's just something you can't confirm one way or the other. Sorry.'

'Mrs Watkins,' Bliss said, 'specializes in peculiar tangents.'

'Your parents know about all this?' Merrily said to Tamsin. 'Did they tell you off for being silly?'

'Or maybe *warn* you off?' Bliss said. 'In case he caught you.'

Tamsin shook her head.

'I never heard any adults mention Mr Hambling, to be honest. Not until I started talking to them last night. People I'd known since I was a little girl.'

'When he caught kids,' Bliss said, 'was he… unexpectedly friendly, perhaps?'

'Not that I heard. They said he could get a bit annoyed if he'd been interrupted.'

'Doing what?'

'I don't know. I mean, I think I know where you're going with this, sir, but I really don't think there was anything like… that. Like, it's not as if we didn't know about it going on, even as country kids – there was this bloke we were all told to keep away from, but he was quite young. He moved to Abergavenny, where I think he got nicked finally for kiddy-fiddling. Besides, my friend, when we got older, she used to say she… that she thought Mr Hambling was well catered for in that department.'

'Which department?'

'Women, sir.'

Bliss raised both eyebrows.

'You haven't told me about this, have you, Tamsin?'

'No sir.' Tamsin didn't blush this time. 'I was getting round to

100

it when you went to look for Mrs Watkins. Situation was that David Hambling, he used to have quite a number of visitors, and some of them were women. Quite young women. Well, compared to him.'

'When was this?'

'All the time. I mean, still. I thought I'd better check before saying anything, so I phoned my friend at work, and she phoned her mum who said there was one here like a few days ago?'

'One what?'

'A young woman. Well… young*ish*. Thirty-five? Driving a red Audi. My friend's mum reckons they did his shopping for him.'

'There's no car here, is there?'

'He's never had one. He liked to go everywhere on foot. They reckoned he'd walk miles at one time, up into the mountains, along the Wye. Like I said, he must've kept himself very fit. But if he needed to go any distance, there'd always be someone to take him.'

'All strangers to the locals?'

'I think so. Not that he wasn't friendly with local people… he was. He'd help them out, do things for them.'

'Like?'

'Well, he… he like knew a lot of old things that doctors don't do any more. Like if you dislocated a bone he could put it back? And he knew about herbs. He could take away headaches. And people who were run-down, he'd get them going again.'

'That's interesting,' Merrily said.

'And they reckoned if you'd lost something important he could find it sometimes. But he wouldn't take money for any of it. All he asked in return was that they should respect his privacy. And not talk about it.'

'Somebody obviously talked about it to you,' Bliss said.

'Yeah, but I reckon that's only 'cos he's dead. It's a funny place, Cusop, sir, people's privacy does get respected. Like the King of Hay, *his* home's in Cusop. His family home, but I bet not many people know exactly where it is. Lot of people who run things in

Hay, they live in Cusop, 'cos it's separate. No estates down yere, and most of the houses are secluded. And the Dingle, it's a dead-end – far as cars go anyway. You get to the end, you're near enough in the mountains. Somebody once said to me it was like a bottle. You put the stopper on and nothing gets out. Sorry, sir, you prob'ly didn't want all this.'

'No, carry on, Tamsin, you're doing really well here. So nobody recognized any of the women who came to see him?'

Tamsin looked uncertain.

'It's possible they *did*. But not 'cos they were local. They recognized them from other places. Newspapers and television. Well, famous people do come to Hay, don't they? Writers and TV people and politicians. So it's not that much of a big deal. With the women, people used to be a bit scandalized by it, at one time, but not any more. It was more like, you know, good luck to the ole devil, kind of thing. That's the impression I got.'

Bliss said, 'When you say they brought his shopping...'

Merrily followed his gaze around the kitchen, past the Stanley oil-fired cooker and the big fridge/freezer to another door and three rows of shelves with branded items and jars and pots.

'That's where Tamsin found his dope, Merrily. In a jar conveniently marked *herbs*. I never asked, Tamsin, but what led you to it?'

'Just the smell, sir. In his study... his library. Unmistakable, really.'

Merrily said, 'He smoked dope?'

'Or he entertained people who did,' Bliss said. 'Me first thought was who's his dealer? Was he linked into the kind of people who wouldn't think too hard about nudging an old feller into a pool and robbing his gaff? But there's over six hundred quid in a wallet in his desk. You couldn't easily miss that.'

'So you're thinking he had his cannabis or whatever delivered with the groceries?'

In a guilty way, she was starting to enjoy this. It was calming to be hanging out with working coppers. Their needs were so much simpler. She turned to Tamsin Winterson.

'Tamsin, I'm still not getting this. Why exactly *did* kids think he was a wizard? Apart from the herbs and bone-setting.'

'Well… they look through windows, kids, don't they?'

Tamsin looking a little sheepish.

'Was there anything particularly odd or unexpected about the way he died, Frannie?'

'Not expecting much from the PM. He had a head wound, which might've been from a bump on one of those big shelves of rock at the bottom of the falls. Was he attacked here, then towed down the field and thrown in the pool? We don't know. Nobody would think that was likely.'

'So why are you convinced somebody killed him?'

'I'm *not* convinced and I'm still looking for a reason. With all the fences and stiles involved, it wouldn't be easy unless there was more than one person. Or did he go to the pool with someone who then pushed him in? Or clobbered him and then pushed the body in? We've done a little house-to-house, yielding no sightings. We've had a SOCO skim this place. Although there's no obvious reason to regard it as a crime scene.'

'You need witnesses.'

'Dog walkers,' Bliss said. 'We need more dog walkers.'

Tamsin brought them tea in some rather classy stoneware mugs. Milk, sugar in a bowl.

'Just the job,' Bliss sipped. 'Earl Grey, too. You've gorra big future, PC Winterson.'

'In CID, sir?'

Bliss set his cup down on the worktop, tilted his head, exposing his spreading thin patch.

'That's the way you're thinking?'

'It is, actually.'

'Well,' Bliss said, 'I'll bear that in mind, Tamsin. Not that I get listened to much.'

'Thank you, sir. Sir—'

'Tamsin, how about you just call me boss? The usual mode of address in the casual, freewheeling world of CID. Also, I friggin' hate *sir*.'

Tamsin nodded seriously.

'Sir, I don't— I don't want to give the impression – boss – that Hambling had like a harem. Obviously, I'm not qualified to say. Sometimes, apparently, there'd be a few cars in quick succession, with both women and men in them?'

'An orgy?'

'His coven, they used to say. I'm told.'

'Lovely. That's a very evocative word.'

'And there's one other thing. I haven't been able to check this out properly, I only got it this morning. Sometimes, people visiting Mr Hambling would park up at the church?'

'Is that close?'

'Just at the top, past the castle mound. Not far to walk, and there's good, flat parking. The night before Mr Hambling was found, there were cars parked up there. More than usual.'

'How late was this?'

'Don't know. I had it from an old lady, and she don't stay up very late. There's nothing to say… I mean, they could've parked there for any reason. But…'

'But there could've been a gathering at his house in the hours before he died.'

'It's possible, isn't it?'

'Anything's poss— What are you smiling at, Merrily?'

'Nothing.'

What if the David Hambling affair was just a kite being flown by a young, rural copper looking for a step up? You noticed, over time, that Bliss tended to reserve his impressive range of sardonic put-downs for senior officers, was never patronizing to underlings. You could tell he liked this kid.

Bliss picked up his cup, made for the door next to the fridge/freezer.

'You want to say a little prayer first, Merrily? Before we enter the inner temple?'

'Not just now, thanks.'

'Boss...' Tamsin was blushing again. 'This is just so I've told you everything, right?'

'There's something else?'

'The lights I mentioned? I'm just telling you what this old lady said. Just so you know.'

'Yeh, yeh, not gonna hold it against you, Tammy.'

'Tamsin, sir. Boss. She said it was like a flashgun going off, back in the days when they went pop, only there was no sound, just everywhere lit up white. Only like in negative, where the dark things are light. That's what she said. And she said it felt... unearthly, kind of thing. As if you were seeing through the land. Anyway, that's—'

'And she saw this when?'

'The night before Mr Hambling was found. Through her bedroom window just as she was going to bed, so before midnight.'

'Right,' Bliss said.

'She thought it was like an omen. Though that was obviously after she'd heard about Mr Hambling. She's quite a well-spoken old lady. I can give you her name.'

'We'll have a think about that,' Bliss said. 'The temple's through there, Merrily.'

'You keep saying temple?'

'What do I know?' Bliss said.

16

The unknowable

SUDDEN SUN HAD pushed a bar of light through the crack between grey velvet curtains, bringing out the glow in two vast rugs. They looked kind of Zoroastrian. Men with curious waist-level wings, cauldrons of fire.

'Mmm,' Merrily said. 'Looks like the kids weren't far off.'

Bliss walked over to the mahogany desk by the tall window. All a bit churchy, but it didn't seem to be an altar.

'He *was* a wizard?'

'How about we don't use that word.'

Floor-to-ceiling darkwood bookcases lined the walls. Deep shelves, shadowed but you could see they were full. In the few spaces between the bookcases, there were small pictures. Black-framed drawings or engravings, all figurative, and all the figures were naked. And active.

Bliss pointed up at the ceiling. The two oak beams crossing it looked older than the house.

'Could be replacing supporting walls. I reckon this might be three rooms knocked into one.'

Merrily turned to where a dozen plain, darkwood chairs had been arranged in short rows. Freestanding wrought-iron candle-holders stood behind them, layers of wax on the candle trays showing they were not merely decorative. A sweetish scent weighted the atmosphere. Incense rather than cannabis.

'Don't see it as a temple, though.'

'Why not?'

'Well, unless...' She bent and pulled back a corner of one of the rugs. 'No... just floorboards. A temple would be designed to some strict geometric format. And it would have a magic circle. A protective circle. And generally there are black and white squares on the floor.'

'So what's this?'

'It's what it looks like – a library. And a lecture room. Or it might have been used for group meditation. And yet...'

Shallow niches either side of the long window housed small statues. On the left, an Egyptian woman with a thin staff and an ankh. Isis? On the right, what was almost certainly the Virgin Mary, hands raised. Curious.

'Yet what?' Bliss said.

'Have you looked elsewhere in the house? In the barns? For anything resembling a temple?'

'The other rooms are what you'd expect. Plainish bedrooms, two bathrooms, the kitchen, which you've seen, and a little study. The outbuildings all have holes in the roofs, old bales of straw, a rusting tractor... What was he – a witch, warlock? What do they call it these days?'

'I'll need to have a better look at the books, but I think this is something more... academic. You're probably looking at ritual magic.'

'Which means?'

'How many weeks have you got? It's a formalized system – in fact, several formalized systems – with origins going back far further than contemporary witchcraft. As far back as ancient Egypt. Possibly.' She nodded at the statuette in its niche. 'I think that's Isis – Egyptian goddess. Can we draw back the curtains then I can see some of these books?'

'Little switch, near Tamsin's elbow. Thank you, Tamsin.'

'Well,' Merrily said, 'that's nicely done, isn't it?'

Velvety light in all the bookcases now displaying thousands of volumes, some clearly old, leather bound. You'd never get Jane out of here.

'I could look at some of this stuff and think this guy was a collector, possibly a dealer.' She put out a finger without touching the faded ochre spines of a set of four. 'This looks like it could be Israel Regardie's original publication of the rituals of the Hermetic Order of the Golden Dawn. You know about them?'

Bliss said, 'There's an early David Bowie song...'

'Well referenced, Frannie.'

Tamsin, standing in the doorway, looked a little mystified. A great oak door, possibly from a church, hanging open to the windowless inner hall linked to the kitchen. This room could be in a different and older house.

'The Golden Dawn was Britain's most famous nineteenth-century magical order, involving people like W. B. Yeats, the poet, and Aleister Crowley, the Beast 666. Its rituals were all very secret, until Regardie blew the lot in these books in maybe the nineteen thirties. There was a row about it. And I'm thinking this edition could be worth an arm and a leg.'

'So Hambling could've been dealing in this stuff?'

'Well, no... probably not, because... look, lot of new editions. Lot of paperbacks. Reprints. You can get some of these for ninety-nine pence in The Works. And they're stacked alongside the expensive stuff. This is a working library, isn't it? Alphabetical.'

Crowley in quantity. All the well-known ones, *Magick in Theory and Practice*, the *Confessions*, the novels, *Moonchild* and *Diary of a Drug Fiend*. And others she'd only heard of: *The Book of Lies, The Book of Thoth*. Bound copies of magazines and journals, like *The Equinox*.

Above, in the Bs, were Helena Blavatsky's *Isis Unveiled*, Alice Bailey's *A Treatise on Cosmic Fire*.

And some oddities.

'More than just a magical library.' Merrily pulled out a book. 'The autobiography of Richard Booth, the King of Hay?'

Next to it, two novels by Beryl Bainbridge. On the shelf above Crowley, several books by Bruce Chatwin, travel writer and novelist. Who'd spent time in the Black Mountains, so maybe that accounted for him.

Tamsin said, 'Should I make some fresh tea, boss?'

'Yeh,' Bliss said. 'That'd be good.'

When she'd gone, Merrily shut the oak door.

'So which of you really thinks there's more to this than an old man falling into a pool – you or Tamsin?'

Bliss smiled. It was still lopsided, and there was a red scar under his left eye.

'And how bad *are* you? Really. No bullshit, Frannie.'

Bliss wiped a hand across his mouth as if he'd been punched.

'Could be better. Tunnel vision when I'm tired, which isn't good, driving-wise. Double vision, when I look down without bending me head, whether I'm tired or not. Which means I don't go up ladders in case I start missing steps on the way down by treading on the one that doesn't exist. Offered surgery to correct the eyes, but they couldn't guarantee it'd work, and apparently if it didn't it might be friggin' *wairse*. So I said it was improving all the time.'

'Who knows the truth?'

'Couple of people. One of whom could shaft me bigtime with West Mercia if we ever fell out. And someone who only knows what he can actually spot with his bits of kit. What he can't detect, I haven't told him.'

'Frannie, you're a—'

'Fool to meself, yeh. But I think you can understand why I wouldn't wanna spent me days knocking around a house that sooner or later Kirsty's gonna get half of. If not the lot. First week out of hospital, I'd just sit down and pass out in the chair.'

'You're over that?'

'Still gorra phobia about it. That and bright lights. Rooms like this – gloomy – are good. Powerful lights do me head in, so if I wound up with a friggin' desk job I'd need an office with subdued lighting. Which'd probably contravene some Health and Safety shite to stop you tripping over the waste bin. Worst-case scenario is semi-permanent sick leave. That well-known euphemism for scrapheap. Not gonna happen, Merrily. Just need to stay in the saddle till it turns the friggin' corner.'

'That's like walking a cliff edge.'

'And if you look down you see all these pointed rocks. Only double.' Bliss found a sickly laugh. 'Good days and bad days, Merrily, and a bad day is how I wound up investigating a small drowning at Cusop Dingle. Dull morning, office lights, head feeling like it belongs to some other bastard. Small drowning? Ha. No such thing as a small drowning. Just gonna check it out.'

Merrily let her face fall into her hands.

'Excuse was a dead drug dealer we pulled out of the Wye up towards Mordiford. Turf war thing. You get inventive when you've something to hide. And I gerra bit of leeway, being a damaged hero, and Brent had a day's leave. And then... bugger me if it doesn't get interesting. Tamsin shows me the dope... and all this. Kid thinks there's more to it, and nobody else is likely to – the coroner's officer wasn't impressed. Be nice if the kid was right, wouldn't it?'

'And useful for you, under the circumstances. Where's she based?'

'Peterchurch. Last of the village copshops, about nine miles from here. The short-sighted suits are gonna close it down soon. So – bottom line, Merrily – this is not a temple, but Mr Hambling could actually have been a... what?'

'Magician?'

'And what's that mean outside of fairy tales?'

'Magic is... the science and art of causing change to occur, erm, in conformity with will. The late Aleister Crowley's definition.'

'But he was a friggin' fruitcake.'

'He just liked to mix business with pleasure. Extreme pleasure.'

She inspected two of the framed drawings on the wall. They were both explicitly sexual. One, which looked as if it had been photocopied from an illustration in a book, was a rough and fibrous, coital tangle of threshing limbs. Underneath was written: *Man is matter and spirit, both real and both good.* The other involved several figures with exaggerated genitalia, both male and female, the kind of drawing done by a dirty old man with a stub of a pencil and one hand in his pocket.

'Also looks like Hambling was holding meetings here. Giving... intimate lectures?'

'Intimate?'

'I mean to small, exclusive groups. He wasn't advertising it, was he? There are groups that meet to meditate together. Like prayer groups only... more esoteric. That Crowley description about causing change to happen through focused will power... the changes they're looking for are mostly in themselves. They want to increase their level of consciousness, they want heightened awareness. Contact with other spheres of existence.'

'Psychic powers, in other words.'

'People who follow a religion, like Christianity or Islam, have faith that there's something beyond normal life. A magician wants to *know*. To know the unknowable.'

'About Hambling,' Bliss said. 'He wasn't Hambling.'

Merrily pulled out one of the chairs. It was solid, had a straight back, no arms. Good chair for meditation. She sat down, keeping her gaze on Bliss.

'You're saying the body in the pool was someone else's?'

'I'm saying David Hambling was an assumed name. Only learned that this morning when the coroner's officer was here with Hambling's solicitor. Who's been his solicitor for many years and his father before him, so very solid.'

Merrily said, 'Was he Lord Lucan?'

'You're being bloody frivolous this morning.'

'Demob happy.'

'His name was Peter Rector. Before he came here, he was living in a farmhouse up in the Black Mountains where he ran educational residential courses. And not in cookery.'

'I see.'

'Another thing we've learned is that he's left most of his money… to one person. To whom he was not related.'

'Ah.'

'Who I was thinking you could have a word with. On the basis you'd get more out of this person that I would.'

'Bloody hell, Bliss, you go on about people like Tamsin taking ages to get to the point—'

'Just to draw a line under it. Or not. Don't look at me like that! If I'd had the balls to tough it out under the lights in Gaol Street neither of us would be in this position. However, if it turns out there *is* something suspicious which I, having come all the way out here on a whim, have somehow failed to uncover…'

'Egg on face?'

'The full Spanish omelette. But unless Billy Grace's PM reveals something iffy, I'm in no position to take it much further after today, anyway. There's certainly no basis on which I can legitimately approach the beneficiary.'

'You said he was running his courses in the Black Mountains?'

She pulled a book from the shelf, next to Richard Booth. *Hills of Vision: a history of religious life in the Black Mountains* by R. H. Beynon. Sorry… the beneficiary?'

'Everybody'll know about Rector by tonight, Merrily, so nothing classified, but we might have a few days on the identity of this person. Someone I'm not acquainted with, obviously, but, more significantly, nor is Tamsin. Despite living in the next village.'

'One of the women who did his shopping? His dealer? Oh—'

A piece of paper had fallen out of the Black Mountains book. She bent to retrieve it.

'Actually, this is someone,' Bliss said, 'who I believe is known to you.'

'Oh good. Maybe he can lend me some money to get Jane through university.'

'*She*, actually.'

'Can't be anybody I know well. In fact I can't think of anyone I know in Dorstone or any neighbouring village.'

'I don't think Hardwicke even qualifies as a village.'

Tap on the door. Sound of crockery wobbling on a tray.

Hardwicke?

'Oh my God.' Merrily stared at Bliss. 'Not *her*...'

Bliss shrugged, looking helpless. It made sense now. She'd tie him in knots.

God, the way you just walked into these situations. Merrily, exasperated, opened *Hills of Vision* to slip the paper back inside, saw what was on it, recoiled.

'Frannie...'

They intercepted Tamsin with the tea, took the tray, with the book and the paper, back into the kitchen. Laid the paper on the worktop under the window.

It was a photocopy. A black and white photo occupying the middle of a single piece of A4 copier paper folded in two.

Bliss didn't touch it.

Merrily said, 'Do you think she's dead?'

'I don't know.'

The picture was grey and grainy. It was a photo of a woman seen from behind and from above.

At least, the narrow shoulders suggested a woman. Her head had been shaved, but not carefully, leaving some tufts of hair and a lattice of blood trails. And on the skull, the way skinheads used to have it done and maybe some still did, a crude and bloody swastika.

Under the picture, a single hand-printed line. Felt pen, it looked like.

It said,

What will you do now?

17

Putrid

Robin looked out of the sitting room window, down into Back Fold.

'Only drawback here, is what you see. Or don't see.'

What you saw were the modern buildings opposite, housing an opticians and some other stores that were not exactly historic. What he hadn't realized before was that Back Fold was only half medieval. What you couldn't see from the bookstore was the castle.

'Downside of actually having the castle wall as your own back wall. You wanna see the castle, you gotta go open the bathroom window, stick your head out.'

'Or perhaps,' Betty said, 'you could just pop downstairs and out of the front door and... wooh, a castle!'

Yeah, what the hell. He hauled the rolled-up rug they'd brought into the middle of the room, and they both unrolled it. Only a plain rust-coloured rug, but it gave the room a new warmth.

Betty stood in the centre of the rug.

'Only real problem is that we can't have a fire.'

'We have fireplaces.'

'Two,' Betty said. 'Ground floor and here. However, if you go outside, walk up the castle drive to the point where you can look over the wall and down on this place, you'll see a plain, slate roof with no stack, and no aperture through which smoke may be released into the air.'

'Huh?'

'Check it.'

They went downstairs. No need to walk up the castle drive. Even from street level you could see the roof was all slates, no chimney. The castle's curtain wall rose just higher than its apex. Had this been the original wall? Probably, in some form. No reason why it shouldn't date back at least to the twelfth century when the castle had belonged, like most of the southern border castles, to the de Braose Family.

'Shit,' Robin said. 'You're right. Wonder if there's a planning law to prevent us installing a small wood-burner and shoving a neat flue up between the tiles? This is like when we make so much money we buy the place from Oliver.'

Betty gave him a smile. He was in optimistic mood today. He'd chosen a bedroom for his studio.

The phone beeped.

'You leave a message for me? Tom Armitage, Salisbury?'

Betty said, 'Sorry, you're breaking up. Can you hang on?'

She pointed at the phone, conveying to Robin that she needed a stronger signal, and took it to the top of the alley, watching Robin going back into the shop. Hadn't said a word to him about her call to Mr Oliver or any of this.

'That's better.'

'Sounds exactly the same to me,' Tom Armitage said.

The size of his website suggested he was thriving in Salisbury, which doubtless still had a good percentage of residents who could afford antique furniture. He asked Betty who exactly she was.

'I'm a bookseller.'

'In Hay? Are there any left?' His accent wasn't local to Hay. Or Wiltshire, come to that. He sounded posh, a touch cavalier. 'Booth still there? Indefatigable old bugger. Luck of the devil. When he's gone – if he ever consents to go – he'll be seen striding the battlements with his tin crown under his arm. What's the problem, Mrs Thorogood?'

'We're opening a book business in your former premises. In Back Fold.'

'And?'

'I was interested in who might have had it before. Its history.'

'Because?'

'Basically, because I'm a nosy cow.'

Tom Armitage was silent for a moment. Betty heard a semi-distant sawing in the phone, somehow not a sound you associated with antique furniture. She saw Jeeter Kapoor outside his shop, talking to the old lady who whistled.

'Trouble with me,' Armitage said, 'is that as long as everything's ticking over nicely I tend not to ask too many questions. That, of course, is one of the things about me that irritates the hell out of women.'

'Luckily, I'm very accommodating.'

'We must meet one day. Are you a divorcee?'

'Not yet.'

'I see. So he's off at last, is he?'

'Who?'

'Jamie Oliver.'

'We're renting it. From Mr Oliver.'

'Ah. And somebody told you bad things about the shop, did they?'

'Are there bad things?'

'Way I see it, the only reason you'd be talking to me, well out of town, is not wanting someone to know you were asking. Now that could be Oliver, in which case, fair enough. A smug git. I can tell you we more or less used it as a store room. We'd have big items in the window and if anybody was interested there was a phone number to call.'

'Who had the place before you?'

'My old man, actually. This was when Booth was getting into the papers as King of Independent Hay. Idea of that appealed to my dad, so he sold his business down in Essex, came up there, bought a big place and accumulated other bits of the town over the years. Of which Back Fold was one.'

'When was this?'

'Early nineties.'

'And he bought it from…?'

'Bloke who'd been there about a year and, if my old man was interested, was selling it off cheap. Because… ah, this might be what you've heard about. There was a chap who dealt in ancient comic books – war comics. We kept finding pages under floorboards or lining shelves. Stormtroopers with bayonets, screaming *Die Englisher pig!* Which he did, apparently.'

'Who did?'

'The guy who sold the comics.'

'Died?'

'Overdid it with the drugs.'

'Oh.'

'Look, I don't… I don't know the details. Except that he apparently wasn't found for about a week.'

'Where?'

'Well… where he lived.'

'Over the shop?'

'I suppose.'

'I see.'

'Which is the only bad thing I've heard connected with that shop. But we all have to die somewhere, don't we?'

'Can't have been pleasant,' Betty said, 'for whoever found him after a week.'

She was looking at the whistling old lady, who sounded angry with Jeeter Kapoor.

'If you en't seen it,' she said, 'you got no right to say it en't true.'

'All right.' Kapoor had his hands up. 'So it's true.'

'Pleasant?' Tom Armitage said. 'No, it wasn't, apparently. Place probably needed fumigating. They said you could smell him for… quite a while afterwards. In fact – oh hell, if you want the truth, an implausible amount of time afterwards. See, anything goes a bit putrid in a cupboard now, you'll be wishing I'd said nothing.'

'People who OD on drugs, they're often a bit disturbed.'

'I wouldn't know, Mrs T. Like I said, I seldom ask questions.'

'Not uncommon in the antiques trade, I'd guess,' Betty said.

'Oh, you *are* a caution. Are you beautiful? You sound beautiful.'

'Face like the back end of a Renault Megane. When you sold it to James Oliver... did you tell him about the history?'

'There *is* no history, for heaven's sake! If some chap had gone berserk and slaughtered his entire family there, I'd've felt obliged to mention it, but nothing *happened*. So a guy OD'd on something. Commonplace end in those days. And Oliver was such a superior sort of fellow – agreeing a price and then coming back with a lower offer, saying he'd found something wrong – that I probably wouldn't have told him anyway. Look, I'll break the habit of a lifetime and ask: has something scared *you*? Have you smelled anything?'

'I don't get scared by this kind of thing,' Betty said.

'Good for you.' He sneezed. 'Sorry... bloody sawdust everywhere. Look, all I'd say to you is that places like that tend to become a refuge for people on the run. I don't mean from the police or anything, but from something drastic in their lives – broken relationships, bereavement, unexpected job-loss. Not always happy people, that's what I'm saying. And they tend not to stay long. I'd guess that shop's been an unhappy stopgap in too many lives. So nobody's ever bothered to make it look or feel good. How's that?'

'Very convincing. Thank you for telling me. Do you know the man's name? The man who died?'

'No. Don't think I ever did. Look, must call in on you next time I'm up there on a buying expedition.'

'I'll look forward to it.'

She shut down the phone. The old lady was stumping towards her, florid-faced.

'He don't believe nothing.' Peered closer at Betty. 'I bets you do. You got the look. You go there, just on dawn, you'll see.'

Betty didn't smile.

'Where?'

'I just *said*. Where the *brook* comes in. You go down where the brook comes in. But don't bloody take him. Bloody Pakis.'

Betty said, 'Can I just…? You asked Mr Oliver if he'd smelled something.'

'What?'

'In the shop.' Betty pointed. '*That* shop.'

The old lady said, 'You smelled him yet?'

'The man who died?'

'You smelled him yet?'

'No, but—'

'You will.'

And she was off, hands rammed into the pockets of her stockman's coat, Kapoor watching her, trying to smile.

'You get used to Tessie.'

'Who is she, exactly?'

'*Exactly* – I dunno. All I know is she's got what you'd call a chequered reputation. Married a rich old bloke called Mr Villiers decades ago when she was a young fing. Landed one of them tall terraced houses, bottom of Castle Street. When he snuffed it, they reckon she drank his money away and now she lets out rooms. She also sees fings. She's harmless.'

'So who did she see… where the brook…?'

'The Dulas Brook. Where it enters the Wye. Little beach down by the sewage works. Don't ask.'

'What about the smell?' Betty said.

'*You* brought *that* up.'

'I know. Jeeter, might she be talking about the man who died here? Drug overdose? Not found for a week?'

'Shit,' Kapoor said. 'Who told you that? We agreed not to say noffing.'

'Who did?'

'Few of us. Not till you was settled, anyway. Not that it means anyfing, but nobody wants to fink of a niffy corpse in the building. He was just a junkie, far's I know, and it was years and years ago. So any smell…'

119

Betty said. 'Do you know his name?'

'Jerry. I *fink*. He's one of those faces the old-timers mention in passing and glance at each other meaningfully and if there's somebody like me around noffing else gets said. But the idea of some old hippy haunting the place… Or his pong. Do me a favour.' Kapoor paused, looking at her. 'You don't feel uneasy here, do you?'

Well, yes, she did, and not only in the shop. Even in the town centre, now, she sometimes had the feeling of being watched, and not just as a pair of nice legs in a short skirt. Not stalked exactly, just watched. Carrying somebody's lingering gaze around like a clammy miasma, the way it had happened years ago, before Robin, with the high priest of a coven she'd left pretty quickly.

'Of course not,' Betty said.

18

The word

WHEN SHE GOT in, the phone was ringing.

'I nearly cried off, Merrily. Nearly rang you and said I couldn't do it after all.'

Plump, comfy Martin Longbeach. As was.

Oh God.

'What brought that on, Martin?'

'Couldn't sleep hardly at all last night. I was thinking I should get out altogether, move to another part of the country. East Anglia, Cornwall. Where nobody's talking about me.'

Inevitable that, sooner or later, this was going to come up.

'All they're saying,' she said, 'is that you had a bereavement and a subsequent breakdown.'

Forgive me.

'But then I thought, how often do you and Jane have a chance of some days out together?'

Might have been a good time to tell him about Jane not being here, how the situation had changed. She didn't.

'Anyway. Friday morning be all right to bring my stuff, Merrily?'

'Or you can move in then. Whatever's best for you.'

'That would be good. You've been very kind to me, Merrily.'

'Listen, I'm not coming on Sunday, Martin. You're on your own.'

Better all round if she wasn't there to listen to his sermon. If he was planning to unload something on the congregation, she'd rather be out of the village.

Unload something on the...?

Oh, Jesus wept. Merrily clapped a hand over the mouthpiece of the Bakelite phone, took a deep, deep breath. In Martin's particularly conservative part of Herefordshire, no matter how far this faded into history, it would never be a laughing matter. Nor here, except possibly in the saloon bar of the Ox. To which you could only hope the intelligence had not yet permeated.

One way or another, next week was not going to be easy.

She stayed in the scullery and rang Huw Owen.

No answer. She leaned back in her curved captain's chair. Even Ethel was out. The silence in the vicarage was like earwax. She switched on the computer and Googled Cusop Dingle.

Wikipedia said it was a single track road once known as Millionaire's Row because of all the big houses. It ran alongside the Dulas Brook, with its many waterfalls, into the foothills of the Black Mountains, and had been home to the notorious Hay poisoner Herbert Rowse Armstrong, the only English solicitor ever hanged for murder.

Which was a long time ago. To go back even further, she looked up Cusop in Jane's much-thumbed copy of Ella Mary Leather's *Folklore of Herefordshire*, first published in 1912. As always, more illuminating, if you were the kind of person who specialized in peculiar tangents.

> Fairies have been seen dancing under foxgloves in Cusop Dingle within the memory of some now living there.
>
> Not far from Hay Station on the Herefordshire side there are some rocks overhanging a brook which flows into the Wye. Fairies or 'little people' formerly lived in these rocks and in the haymaking time used to provide dinner for the haymakers in the adjoining fields. But once a haymaker took away a knife; after

this the fairies never came again, although the man
took the knife back.

The last line almost adding a nice touch of credibility. A Welsh
Border farmworker would be well miffed with himself at ruining
a source of free meals. Less cosy was a mention, four pages later,
of Cusop as a place where people believed in the
will-o'-the-wisp, Mrs Leather quoting a certain Parry, of
Kington, in 1845.

The *ignis fatuus* or exhalation termed Will-o'-the-wisp
or Jack with a lanthorn, which is sometimes seen in
churchyards or marshy places in summer and autumn,
was considered by many old inhabitants in this
neighbourhood, when the author was in his infancy, to
be a kind of device of the evil spirit to draw human
beings from the road they were pursuing into some
frightful abyss of misery; and there leave them
without any hope of regaining the enjoyment of
happiness in the land of the living.

Will-o'-the-wisp had more recently been explained as marsh
gas, a phenomenon not, presumably, confined to marshes.

You just never heard about it, though, did you? Though
someone drawn to peculiar tangents might well, on reading
about a *frightful abyss of misery*, picture a deep waterfall pool
with a dead man in it.

'David Hambling,' Huw said when he called back. 'No. New one
on me.'

She could almost see him in his chair in the stone rectory,
sinking lower as more stuffing leaked out. Welsh born, brought
up in Sheffield, returning as ordained minister. There might
even be a low fire, as summer didn't much like the Brecon
Beacons and this was hardly an effective summer.

Merrily said, 'How about Peter Rector?'

There was a pause.

'He'll be dead now.'

'Yes. He is. That's what I said.'

'We're happen at cross-purposes here,' Huw said. 'The Peter Rector known to me must've been dead years.'

'Well… the post-mortem results aren't through yet, but this one, as I understand it… less than two days? Believed to be over ninety years old. Would that fit?'

'Aye. It might, too.'

'White hair and beard. Large collection of mainly esoteric books. Smoked cannabis.'

'And living in… where did you say?'

'Cusop Dingle. About a mile out of Hay-on-Wye, on the English side.'

'And how long's he been there?'

'Don't know exactly. Could be anything over twelve years. He lived very quietly, didn't have a car. He had friends who did his shopping. His neighbours didn't know much about him but seem to have respected his privacy. He was known as a healer, a bone-setter and possibly a dowser.'

Huw's laugh carried a yelp of astonishment that was rare. You could hear his chair scraping on the flags as he stood up.

'Small world then?' Merrily said.

'Smaller than I'd reckoned possible. You do know about his activities at Capel-y-ffin?'

'In the Black Mountains?'

'Aye.'

'No, I don't. Just that he was running educational courses.'

'Long time ago. Over thirty years. You'd've been a kid. Everybody thought he'd gone abroad. And he were just a few miles away? Beggars belief. I'm looking at the map now. Cusop – got it. Nowhere else in the country, I reckon, where you'd get such a change of landscape, climate and culture in… six miles? As the crow flies. You know about his books?'

'I saw them. A roomful. A big roomful.'

'No, I mean, *his* books. Rector's. The ones he wrote.'

'He wrote books? I never even thought to look. Bookwise, it was all a bit overwhelming.'

'I'll tell you what,' Huw said, 'while I get my head round this, why don't you look him up on the Internet? I'll call you back.'

'All right, but I'll just tell you one more thing. He's left his house and contents – which, depending on how much land goes with it, could be worth the best part of a million – to Anthea White.' She paused. 'Get your head round *that.*'

'Athena?'

'The Witch of Hardwicke. Frannie Bliss is trying to persuade me to talk to her with a view to finding out why. The kind of people he was mixing with. What was happening at Cusop. And yes, I *have* told him I'd prefer root-canal surgery without the anaesthetic.'

'Intriguing, though, lass. Give us an hour, and I'll try and equip you for the ordeal.'

Five minutes later, with Peter Rector entered into Google, Lol called.

He was in a motel outside Carlisle. He didn't sound gloomy, exactly, but he did sound tired. He was expressing dismay at how much had changed since he was last on the road. Merrily was resisting the urge to ask if he was getting regular meals.

Regular meals – she should talk.

'So much more music in pubs now,' Lol was saying. 'Bigger towns, where they get lots of gigs, they carry on talking and drinking. You're just a distant soundtrack to their night out. It's the more remote places where they actually listen. They've travelled further, so they listen.'

'So you're doing OK?'

'More than OK, I suppose. Doesn't seem right.'

Merrily said nothing. How could a man who'd been so comprehensively crapped on over the years be so pathetically grateful?

'Anyway,' he said, 'I'm bored with me. Seeing too much of me. You and Jane, how's, uh… how's that going?'

'Erm…'

Merrily transferred the phone from one hand to the other. She hadn't wanted to but, under the circumstances, there was no way of avoiding spelling it out.

'Not a problem, though, it really isn't. I can try and beg some time off when you get back.'

'Except that you're on your own. On holiday in an empty house.'

'Well, it's never *totally*—'

'How about you *don't* mention the presence of God. It'll just make me want to ask you to marry me, again, put the old bugger's nose out of joint. Abandon the rest of the gigs, square things with Danny, hit the long road home.'

'Through the darkness and the rain.' She felt her voice floating away. 'Like in some old movie.'

In the tradition of which, about twenty miles from home, in blinding rain, he'd be involved in a shattering collision with an exhausted lorry driver who didn't know the road and…

Oh Christ, stop it. She gripped the phone with both hands. *Rationalize.*

'OK, you're right. It feels a bit odd. There *is* that rattling around feeling. Until Saturday. When Martin Longbeach arrives.'

Short silence.

'Forgot about that. You and Martin.'

'Who *is*…'

'Gay. I realize that.'

'And not in a good state, losing his partner. Everybody says it's easily controlled these days, but that's not always the case.'

'Martin's not got it, has he?'

'Don't think so. So why was *he* spared, all this self-laceration. And I…' Hard to stop her voice speeding up '… don't want him thinking he's being supervised, or on suicide watch, so, bottom line, can I live in your house?'

'What?'

'Your cottage. Can I live in it?'

'Blimey.'

'Not if you don't want me to.'

'Drink out of my cups? Light my stove if it gets cold?'

'I'd bring my own logs.'

'Bathe in my bathroom?'

'Bring my own soap.'

'Um… sleep in my bed?'

'And eat your porridge, yeah.'

'Well, that… that should be… that would be OK.'

'Good.'

'OK… well, you've got the key. Just one thing…'

She waited.

'You have to promise not to wash the duvet cover afterwards,' Lol said.

Emerging from the scullery, she felt feather-headed. Couldn't be sure how he'd phrased the bit about asking her to marry him, convinced that even though he'd said *again* it was actually the first time the M word had ever passed between them.

She was still sporadically smiling, in an appallingly stupid, trembly, girly way, when she was sitting at the computer, clicking on links to Peter Rector, and the word *Nazi* came up.

19

Small obsession

HERE WAS A man who wanted to be in the Rolling Stones: long black hair with a few grey tufts, clean-shaven, generous Jaggeresque lips in a loose, amiable smile. A face deeply scored by experience but lit up by big, brown owl-like eyes – the eyes of somebody who was either preternaturally wise or doing a lot of drugs.

But this was the 1970s and Peter Rector must have been twenty years too old to be in the Stones, and there seemed to be no more recent images anywhere.

The biographical detail was scant, his age nowhere apparent. He appeared on several occult sites. His books were not available on Amazon but Abebooks had links to a few second-hand copies, mainly at eye-watering prices.

Notably *A Negative Sun,* a dense study of the mysticism at the core of Nazi Germany, published in 1969.

Which had changed his life, she learned as the phone rang.

Huw said it was about Himmler and the SS and the occult roots of the Aryan dream. Explained as never before... at the time.

'As a young lad, Rector were in the war. Captured by the Germans at Tobruk. When he wound up in a prison camp in Poland, the camp security happened to seize a book on ritual magic that one of Rector's girlfriends had posted to him from Cambridge.'

'So his interest in this stuff goes back a long way,' Merrily said.

'Almost lifelong,' Huw said. 'Parents were Cambridge professors, father a theologian. Peter Rector grew up in a house full of religious tomes, and the ones that interested him most tended to be on the occult fringe.'

'Where did you learn that?'

'He wrote occasional articles for magazines. Some of them are reproduced on the Internet. He said he was very keen to serve in the Middle East to get into Egypt… investigate the pyramids and the Sphinx and the birthplace of Hermetic Magic. Hadn't counted on winding up in a German POW camp, but that were a blessing in disguise. The deputy commandant, one Kurt Scheffler, had SS links, strong esoteric leanings and nobody amongst his fellow officers genned up enough to hold a meaningful discussion with. So he has Lieutenant Rector brought in for questioning.'

Thus, Huw explained, had begun a friendship that was to transcend the armistice and lead, after Scheffler's death, to Peter Rector's seminal exploration of Nazi sorcery.

'You had a lot of time on your hands in a prison camp. They'd sit up half the night, him and Scheffler, discussing the magical symbolism of King Arthur's Camelot, Madame Blavatsky and the Theosophist movement. Most of it starts wi' the Nazi interpretation of Blavatsky's bonkers evolution theories suggesting fair-haired Aryans were the purest strain of humanity. Arising in the last days of Atlantis.'

'I know. I *think*. All the rest of us came from polluted strains caused by, erm…?'

'Having sex wi' monkeys, aye. Scheffler had academic and SS contacts in Berlin, and he'd obtain books and documents which he showed to Rector. Who was jotting it all down from memory. If Berlin had found out, Scheffler would've been pulled out of Poland and shot before you could say Heil Hitler, but they got away with it. Happen Scheffler thought he were making a convert.'

'Was he?'

'Who knows?'

Merrily was remembering a TV documentary she and Jane had watched about Heinrich Himmler's SS stronghold, the dramatic castle at Wewelsburg, organized around his Aryan take on Camelot and the Knights of the Round Table, the quest for the Holy Grail.

'Rector spoke German?'

'He did by the time the war ended.'

'You wouldn't think mixing with the enemy would go down all that well with his fellow prisoners.'

'Oh, I think it would, lass. Nights drinking schnapps in the German officers' quarters would give him a lot of useful details to pass on to the escape committee. Anyroad, end of the war, Rector emerges with a goldmine of incredible history and a stack of useful contacts. Moves back to Cambridge where it takes him twenty years, on and off, to turn it into a book. Widely acclaimed as a seminal work on magic and the Master Race. Wasn't written in a sensational way and it wasn't full of strident condemnation. Which was what caused some confusion later.'

'So you've read it?'

'Years ago. Gives you a vivid understanding of how occult theories came to justify the mass extermination of Jews – small hairy men, inferior species polluting the gene pool, all this. You can even understand why they saw Hitler as an avatar, a god incarnate with a mission to guide mankind into the next phase of the golden age or some such crap.'

'You sound... surprisingly impressed.'

'It's compelling. He intended it to be. It's shown from the Nazi perspective, rather than just... look at these bloody crackpots. And he does it that way because that's how he received the knowledge. While it was happening. While it was convincing men like Scheffler. While it was white hot.'

'So what were Rector's actual views? *Did* he have Nazi sympathies?'

'He said not, after the war, when he got accused of it. What he said to the Germans is another matter. It got him through it, anyroad. And it made him a lot of money when it was over. Goes back to university, studying theology and ancient history. Lectures for a while, joins a number of occult fraternities. Meets Crowley in his heroin days, Israel Regardie, Kenny Grant, Austin Spare.'

'There's one of Spare's… erotic cartoons on the wall at Cusop.'

'Good mate of Rector's, by all accounts. Maverick, even amongst his occult peers. Died in the sixties.'

'So why are Spare and the others remembered more than Rector?'

'Hard to say. Unless, after being suspected of Nazi sympathies, he deliberately courted obscurity. Seems to have given a few lectures to boost sales of *Negative Sun* and then moved on. Never wrote about Nazism again, despite offers from publishers. Went to ground. Here.'

Seemed Rector's parents had a farmhouse with some land between Capel-y-ffin and Hay Bluff. A second home; they'd loved it there because it was all so different from the flatlands of Cambridgeshire and the Fens. Summers at the cottage, all the long holidays. So, while Peter wasn't born there, he and his siblings had done a lot of their growing up in the Black Mountains.

'Where there's a tradition of odd events that he must've shared with Scheffler on those long night over the schnapps,' Huw said. 'You'll've heard of Father Ignatius.'

'Established an Anglican monastery up there? Around the turn of the twentieth century?'

'Rector's old man'd written a paper on him. Father Ignatius being the name adopted by an ordained C. of E. minister called Joseph Leycester Lyne, fanatical Anglo-Catholic. The monastery's up there to this day, spooky owd place. Better known now, mind, as the home of the artist Eric Gill, who set up his own community in the nineteen twenties. Great sculptor, mad Catholic, colourful sex life involving his daughters. Summat in the air up there.'

'So we're actually talking not far from Cusop.'

'As the crow flies, about six miles. He inherited his parents' house up in the mountains. This was the nineteen seventies, his escape from the taint of Nazism. He'd written two more books on magic by then, nowt to do wi' Nazis, but none of 'em sold like *A Negative Sun*. Sod's law.'

'So people did think he was actually a closet Nazi?'

'It were all a bit of a mess.' She heard the groaning of old leather as Huw stretched in his chair. 'It came out he'd sent a chunk of his royalties from the book to Scheffler's widow. Doing the right thing, as he saw it, and you can understand that. But you still had a lot of anti-German feeling in Britain, even in the seventies, and, aye, he were perceived by some as still being too close to it. I see him as just a very learned, erudite bloke who were a bit naive. And, like I say, he'd moved on.'

'So he *was* – I mean the kids at Cusop had it right – he was a magician. Or just someone with an academic interest in it?'

'Oh, bloody hell, more than an academic interest. Lot of popular demand, them days, for mystical experience, wi' the drugs and the psychedelic music. He found a way to continue his studies and his… experiments… and make a good living from it. He rebuilds his life, up in the Black Mountains, in his fifties. Sets to work on the owd farmhouse, opens up outbuildings for self-catering accommodation. Converts the biggest barn into what today you'd call a conference suite. Lectures, workshops. People were taught meditation exercises, sent out into the hills to try them out. Strong vibes in the hills above Hay.'

'Like an ashram?'

'Aye, a Welsh ashram. *Transformation* – that were his buzz-word. He called it the Centre for the Transformation of Mankind.'

'There's modest.'

'It were the seventies, Merrily. You thought big. For Transfor-mation, read altering your state of consciousness, discovering your psychic potential. Exploring the Inner Planes, as they liked to say. Whatever you liked, except owt that stank of Nazism. He pulled a lot of celebrities into the mountains. Writers. Actors. Musicians.'

'So how did he wind up as a recluse in Cusop Dingle?'

'Couldn't tell you. Until you told me he'd been found in a pond, I didn't even know he were there. He was supposed to've gone abroad. All I knew was the Centre for Transformation got wound up in the mid-eighties, not long before I came down here, and he'd sold the farm to an adventure-holiday firm. All over.'

'Right. Huw...' She was curious. 'How come you know so much about Peter Rector?'

'Good question. I... I suppose I encountered him in my... quest, if you like, for summat else. Small obsession, Merrily. Listen, I'd love to take this further, lass, only I've a bunch of Deliverance rookies at the chapel till weekend. But if you want to meet me up there Saturday morning, you might find it enlightening.'

'First day of my so-called holiday.'

'We'll do that, then. I'll see you at Capel around ten. At the little church.'

'OK. I'll be there. Thanks, Huw. Erm... one final thing... was Miss White involved in Rector's activities in the mountains?'

'I don't know. You going to ask her?'

Merrily said nothing. Athena White. The use of words like *bête noire* might be a bit excessive when applied to a woman approaching eighty, last seen in a wheelchair. A retired spook – possibly – whose tiny frame enclosed a monstrous intellect.

'In an old folks' home, in't she?'

'The Glades at Hardwicke. Next place up from Cusop. Quite an upmarket home. Always maintains she's able to live happily in a place like that because of her rich inner life. Always been blatantly contemptuous of me.'

'If she were that contemptuous,' Huw said, 'she wouldn't talk to you at all.'

And he was gone, before she'd had a chance to ask him about Ms Merchant and Ms Nott.

But then, what could he have said?

She hadn't mentioned the photocopy, either, because Bliss had told her not to discuss it directly with anybody.

Like he said, it told you nothing. Could have been a copy of a picture from a book. Some Holocaust horror.

Part of Rector's research, maybe – she hadn't known then that he'd written books. The female, photographed from behind, was unidentifiable, the picture so grainy you couldn't say with any certainty that it was a female. The words could mean anything.

What will you do now?

Who? Rector himself? It had been hand-printed on the photocopy.

Why had the copy been kept in that particular book? No possible connection with Nazism there. It was mainly about medieval monastic life.

Impossible, without tests, Bliss said, to say how old the copy was, either. It had been flattened in a hardback book in a shelf unit protected from the light.

For the moment, Bliss had said, might be best just to put it back.

But keep it in mind.

And then he'd photographed it with his phone.

Merrily switched off the computer and went upstairs for a suitcase. Couldn't get the image out of her head. Couldn't lose it. The way it had come out of a book she'd pulled out almost at random.

What *was* random?

20

Transition

AFTER DARK, SHE carried the first of two suitcases of clothes, toiletries and food across Church Street to Lol's cottage.

The silence of the living room – no bleeps, no strings – felt softer, no longer dispiriting. Merrily switched on the wall lights and the ceiling shone a vibrant orange between chocolate beams. It felt like – *be careful* – coming home.

She fell back into the sofa, thinking about Peter Rector's room, with the Zoroastrian rugs, the erotic drawings, the books on ritual magic and some not obviously related subjects. In her mind, the room now had an atmosphere of intense serenity so ingrained it was like a perpetual hum. Until you shook a photocopy from a book about religious life in the Black Mountains.

She'd only been once before to Capel-y-ffin, on a late-winter's afternoon, finding it remote and bleak, residual snow caught like pockets of plaque in the teeth of the rocks.

She wondered about Bliss and the physical problems that were blighting his working life and could still end it prematurely. Had he thought of trying natural therapy? Would he have the patience? Could she help in any practical way?

Shoulders fitted into a corner of the sofa, Merrily stretched out her legs, with a guilty sense of detachment. Could never quite achieve this state at the vicarage. Living, as it were, over the shop, in a too-big house that had to be a refuge, twenty-four/seven, for anybody troubled.

Nobody yet knew where she was. Only Lol. She listened to his voice in her head, thought of the M-word, a pleasant pre-sleep lethargy setting into her leg muscles.

No time for this. She rolled off the sofa to tug one of the suit-cases up the stairs to the bathroom, unload soap and flannel, toothpaste, electric toothbrush, deodorant, towels, underwear. Zipped up the case to take home with her and refill. Maybe one more trip before bedtime – didn't want to keep going back to the vicarage next week to trouble Martin Longbeach for essen-tial items she'd left behind.

Standing in Lol's doorway, she felt held in an odd, airless state of transition. Neither here nor there. It was not a particularly warm night – there'd been none so far this summer – but at least the rain was holding off and the cobbled square was mellowed in the yellow-pink glow of the fake gaslamps while a flat, waxing moon dangled like a medal above the church steeple.

Six cars and two Land Rovers were parked on the cobbled square. The council was trying to turn it into a mini pay-and-display car park, and the village was fighting it. Quite right, too, if the Council was prepared to wreck tourism for short-term gain. Visitors hated an unexpected charge in some olde worlde village. It created ill-will against a community which had done nothing to deserve it.

Always some battle in Ledwardine, probably no bad thing.

Ochre lights burned blearily behind the leaded mullioned windows of the Black Swan. She'd have to go across there tomorrow, tell Barry she wouldn't be at the vicarage next week but Martin Longbeach would. And then she'd have to tell Gomer Parry, who could perhaps keep an eye on Martin because... well, who knew?

When she was locking Lol's front door behind her, there was a movement on the square: someone in a long mac and a hat coming out of a grey car on the edge of the cobbles, walking over to the market hall to stand uncertainly by one of its corner oak pillars, looking across at the vicarage.

Merrily paused. The man moved slowly across the cobbles,

still glancing up, after every couple of paces, towards the vicarage where the security light was splintered by overhanging trees. Merrily stepped quietly back into the shadow of the Church Street terrace.

There was something about that walk that wasn't...

Oh God.

The figure had passed under one of the fake gaslamps, and she'd seen white hair, long neck, cheekbones so high they looked painful for the skin. She'd seen Sylvia Merchant, now decisively crossing the road to the vicarage, vanishing under the moon-dappled ash tree beside the gate.

Bloody hell. Sylvia Merchant coming to visit? Normal reaction would be to walk boldly over, invite her in for a cup of tea and a chat. Ask her – diplomatically, at first – where exactly she'd got the idea that a few prayers constituted an attempted exorcism.

But there was Sophie...

... had to call Ms Merchant back and tell her that I'd forgotten you were on holiday.

George Curtiss, Cathedral canon, was supposed to have gone to talk some sense into Sylvia Merchant. Diplomatic George. What had happened to that idea?

Merrily slipped back inside Lol's cottage, shut the door and returned to the living room, keeping the light out. Watching from the window, opening it slightly, in time to pick up, from across the silence, the echoing *thock, thock* of a knocker on old oak.

Evidently, Ms Merchant had been given reason to think the vicar was *not* on holiday. But if she wanted to talk, rather than file a complaint, why didn't she phone first?

After a couple of minutes, Ms Merchant emerged from under the trees and seemed to be talking to someone, rather crossly. Nobody there, of course. Nobody on the square except Ms Merchant, her coat hanging open, the end of the belt swinging.

Mutter, mutter.

Ms Merchant stood looking around the village square. The only sounds were the distant hiss and thump of the juke box in the Ox, down the bottom of Church Street. Normality.

For a shivery moment, Merrily was reminded of Big Weale, the Mid Wales solicitor whom Eileen Cullen, the nursing sister from Hereford Hospital, had sworn she'd seen emerging from the hospital mortuary, where his dead wife lay, followed by... an *indistinctness*. Big Weale had been very dangerously disturbed. Probably nothing like that happening here. People *did* chat to the recently departed. Nothing wrong with that. Part of the process of letting go.

Ms Merchant didn't immediately return to her car but walked a few yards up to the church lychgate, looking up at the moon over the steeple. Stayed there for a couple of minutes before presumably deciding, by the absence of interior lights, that Merrily wasn't in the church either, then walked back to the square.

The light from a fake gaslamp, as she passed under it, showed she was smiling, rather grimly, as she unlocked the car with the bleeper and then went around to the passenger door and held it open for the empty air.

PART THREE

The night sky looked pale and
strange. Reflected in the window
I saw a glimmer of flame...
'Join the ranks of the homeless,'
remarked a hippy standing next
to me.

Richard Booth
My Kingdom of Books (1999)

21

An extremely brief affair

'AND WHERE, PRAY, is Robinson today?' Miss White asked sweetly. 'Are you an *ex-item*, as they say? Has he tired of your piety and your wearisome soul-scouring and found himself a new home between the thighs of some cheery little whore?'

She was crouching behind her Zimmer like a cat in a cage. None of the other residents was in this particular lounge. Occasionally a wizened face would peer around the door at the far end of the room and then vanish when it discerned the occupant.

'Athena,' Merrily said, 'I'm awfully afraid that… Robinson is working. But he sends his…'

'Regrets? I doubt it.' Miss White was sitting in a strong, supportive armchair with the Zimmer in front of it. She peered over the frame, curious. 'You didn't call me Anthea. You must want something. How exciting. What've you brought me?'

'Left your chocolates with Mrs Cardelow to share among the other old ladies.'

Poor Mrs Cardelow, who, on arriving at The Glades, must have thought her worst problems would be linked to dementia. As distinct from a malevolent, alien intellect in a bushbaby's body.

Miss White's eyes narrowed. Was she wearing heavy mascara or were they just becoming more satanic? Merrily pulled out one of the harder chairs and sat down a safe distance away, her black hoodie unzipped to expose the pectoral cross.

'So… when will you be back on your feet? I thought people were supposed to do a fair bit of walking after hip replacement.'

'Never walked anywhere without a specific purpose, Watkins, as you know.'

'I thought that *was* the purpose.'

Miss White scowled.

'Felt compelled to discharge myself soon after surgery. No one warned me that the art of being a patronizing little shit is now part of the core curriculum at medical schools. On which basis…' She lifted the Zimmer to one side, exposing her cuddly mauve jersey dress '… I suppose I should greet you like a breath of fresh air.' She sniffed. 'No, that's not right, either. Never mind. Why did you leave my chocolates with Cardelow?'

'Mmm…' Merrily looked out of the window, across the grounds to the Radnor hills, dark with impending rain. Actually she had the overpriced Belgian chocs in her bag. 'If what I've heard is correct, you can now afford to buy your own. Also the finest thirty-year-old malt.' Turning back to Miss White. 'In quantity.'

Taking care not to smile. It was a gamble, but the odds were very much against the old vampire bat ever lowering herself so far as to ask how Merrily knew about the Cusop inheritance.

'Watkins, I should say at the outset that if you've come about your pathetic steeple fund or the… parish orphanage, or some such—'

'Wouldn't be so crass, Anthea. I've come about Peter Rector. A man even older than you. Whose mental decline can only be measured by the way he's disposed of his assets.'

You didn't drop your guard and you didn't give an inch. But her palms were moist and she had to clear her throat.

'Hard as it is for me even to frame the question,' she said, 'does this mean that you might have been the, erm, love of his life?'

Miss White frowned, but her voice was tiny and kittenish.

'Try harder.'

'All right. Ruling out the possibility of some enormous, back-dated blackmail payoff, we're probably looking at something that would take a long time to explain to someone without an extensive knowledge of the dark arts. Closer?'

No reply.

'Of course, you don't have to tell me anything. Or even the police.'

'Watkins, you wouldn't *dare* deprive me of the pleasure of demoralizing a detective.'

You had to accept that even the appearance of an Armed Response Unit fanning out across the lawn would elicit no more from Miss White than a faintly scornful smile. But now, quite suddenly, she was serious.

'Seems to me, Watkins, that the only way you could know of my... well, you might think of it as good fortune, but at my age it's no more than a tedious responsibility... is, indeed, from the police. Who aren't yet ruling out the possibility that Peter Rector was murdered. Yes?'

'Yes.'

'And who, perforce, must now dip their clomping boots into unfamiliar waters. So some superintendent approaches his masonic brother, the Bishop of Hereford, with a view to obtaining some assistance from his appointed "advisor on the paranormal"...'

'*No!* Hell... the Bishop's not even in the Masons...'

At least, not any more.

Merrily pulled her bag onto her knees.

'Do they allow smoking in here, Athena?'

'Of course. They also allow the snorting of decent-quality cocaine and a limited amount of oral sex. Help me up. We'll go outside.'

The lawn slanted down to a golden row of laburnums and a teak bench, with a dedication plate, on which they sat, with the Zimmer alongside, as the smoky clouds crept up on them.

'One cop,' Merrily said. 'A friend. No inquiry. Just suspicions. And I'm not even at work. I'm on holiday.'

Miss White peered at her from a corner of the bench.

'Do I believe you?'

'I'm a Christian.'

Miss White turned away and gazed, through a gap in the trees, at the modest grey twin-bell tower of Hardwicke Church in the middle distance and the hills of Radnor on the other side of the hidden Wye.

'Very well. I'll go this far with you. I'll concede a difficulty in accepting that my friend Peter Rector died as a result of what the coroners used to call misadventure.'

'How long have you known him?'

'Forty years.'

'Did you see him often?'

'Saw him hardly at all.'

'What bothers... some people... is that Mr Rector seems to have had visitors only hours before his death. I suppose it could save a lot of trouble if you were able to explain to me, so that I can explain to my friend, what they might have been doing there.'

'And did some nosy neighbour report that one of them was on a Zimmer?'

'Not that I know of.'

'That's probably because I wasn't there. So how would I know about his possibly apocryphal visitors?'

'Well, maybe you wouldn't, but I was thinking you might know why he was living there, under a spurious name, and... essentially, I suppose, what he was up to.'

Athena White adjusted herself on the bench.

'Let's be clear about something. There are – always have been – things I know about but can't discuss. Any more than I could, in my former occupation, break the Official Secrets Act.'

Merrily didn't really know what her former occupation had been, other than that it had included a period at GCHQ, the government communications centre at Cheltenham. You assumed it involved ciphers and the linguistics of espionage. But for all anyone really knew she might have been Head of Accounts.

'I take it you know why Mr Rector left you his house and contents and… all his money?'

'Not *all* his money. He has a daughter in Canada or somewhere. She'll get half the money. And of course I know why I've been left the house. I also know I'm not obliged to tell anyone. And I won't.'

'And who will *you* leave the house to?'

'That's an interesting point. And pertinent. I don't yet know. But to return to the first part of your original questions, I imagine he moved here for the same reason he moved to Wales. Now he's dead, I can admit that I first encountered him while on secondment to the Security Service during the early seventies.'

'MI5?'

'Call it what you like if it gives you a *frisson*. There were worrying elements of neo-Nazism around at that time, even down to the pathetic little urban skinheads with swastikas tattooed on their skulls. Rector's book was quite subtly written, from the wartime Nazi point of view, to show how magical thought – even when corrupted, or perhaps *especially* when corrupted – could damage the physical world. Some factions found it terribly exciting in a contemporary sense.'

'Neo-Nazis?'

'Rector's book was a considerable influence on extreme right-wing activists. It suggested there was what you might call a dark energy just waiting to be tapped into again. It suggested he knew even more than he'd put into the book. We needed to know – to begin with – who his sources were and to what extent the… darkly inspirational effects of the book were intentional. I was asked to… look into him. Chosen, I suppose, for my knowledge of… certain allied matters.'

'So your employers knew about your interest in the esoteric.'

'Well, of course. Would've been futile to try and conceal something they could, occasionally, use in the national interests. In this instance, it amounted – initially – to little more than attending Peter's lectures and working out where he was coming from.'

'And that was…?'

'Oh… Peter Rector had a great developed talent for what one might call magical empathy. He could project himself into other people's consciousness, see through their eyes. Whether you want to believe this was simply the application of advanced visualization is up to you. It's something which, in future years, he was able to pass on to pupils – especially writers – with considerable success.'

'You're saying that when he wrote the book he was allowing himself to empathize with the Nazi shamans or whatever—'

'Precisely. Entirely factual material, but the presentation was a creative exercise. Never entered his head that he'd be seen as a sympathizer. By the time I was following him around he'd become a latent hippy, growing his hair, and experimenting with hallucinogenic drugs. He was giving talks and interviews about Nazi occultism only because his publishers were making him. And for the money, of course. He was also becoming alarmed about the kind of people who were pursuing him.'

'Pursuing?'

'Writing long letters to him, waiting for him after his lectures. Tracing him to his hotel. Sitting next to him on trains. My own masters, of course, by this time, were now far more interested in *them*. Which is how I came to befriend him.'

'You were told to.'

'Well, of *course* I was told to. He just wanted to run away, but the service was keen for him to stick around and quietly encourage these individuals so that they could be identified and kept under surveillance. My job was to get him to cooperate.'

Well, well…

'You'd have been about… my age, then?'

'I would imagine.'

And doubtless very sexy.

'And, erm… did you succeed?'

'For a limited period. And, before you ask, I have no intention of going further down that particular thoroughfare.'

'Heavens, Athena, you were a *honey trap*?'

Miss White gazed into the hills, expressionless.

'Remove that foolish grin from your face,' she said, quite mildly, 'before I'm compelled to slap it. It was never going to be a long-term thing. Peter hated playing a double game and hated, even more, having to associate with these wall-eyed maniacs in their leather coats.'

'But he rather liked you.'

Miss White sighed.

'In that sense, it was an extremely brief affair. A certain mutual respect remained, however, and we kept in touch, mostly by telephone. We, as they say, *looked out* for one another. When he moved to the mountains, he asked if I'd like to be involved in his study centre. I declined. The thought of all those ghastly people in search of spiritual fulfilment… besides, I knew it wouldn't last. These things never do.'

'But when you retired, you came here.'

'Some years *after* I retired, I came here. I like the air.'

'Do you remember when Rector came to Cusop under the name David Hambling?'

'Of course I remember. It was about a year after he phoned me one night and said, "Why do they keep coming back? Why are they doing this to me?"'

22

Worm in the apple

'YOU MEAN THE Security Service?' Merrily said. 'On his back again?'

The laburnums were aglow under a sky now an ominous sage-green, Radnorshire rain clouds sailing in. But it was still warm, no breeze.

'Good God, no,' Athena White said. 'Peter Rector was no more than a curling file in the bottom drawer by then. I'm talking about the vermin with swastika tattoos in their armpits and shrivelled paperback copies of *A Negative Sun* in their back pockets.'

'What were they doing?'

'They were turning up on his courses. Didn't have far to come either, some of them. This was the era of young people fleeing into the countryside to set up smallholdings. The Welsh Border being one of the cheapest areas of southern Britain to buy into and reinvent yourself. Get a cottage and an acre of scrub for a few thousand. Live off the land. Self-sufficiency, small is beautiful.'

'Was it?'

'Hardly ever. It was usually damp and gloomy, and everything died. And amidst all the silly little hippies you'd find a more sinister survivalist element with primitive weaponry. And these deranged followers of the Aryan left-hand path.'

'I didn't... actually know about that,' Merrily said.

Warily.

'You'll find them on the Internet to this day. Probably the one named after Peter Rector's book. OSIS – the Order of the Sun in Shadow. Its central premise was that mankind evolves only by acts of extreme violence. Its targets were the usual Jews and gypsies, sundry foreigners and those it describes as *The Detritus* – people deemed to be a drain on society, whether unwilling, unfit or too old to work. I'd qualify as a prime example. Accept voluntary euthanasia or we'll have to kill you.'

Maybe it was an effect of the colours of the sky but Miss White's cheeks looked drained and sunken. She'd always been the old woman in the poem who dressed in purple, living on her wits and her witchery. Merrily glimpsed cracks in the protective layers, felt her inner rage and the terror of its containment in an old lady's body.

'They were actually here? On the ground?'

'Out there.' Miss White pointed past the bell tower to the misting horizon. 'Living in their remote farm-workers' cottages in the wilderness. Or up in Shropshire and Montgomeryshire. Perhaps in emulation of Hitler and Himmler in their rural retreats, looking down over mountains and forestry, drawing inspiration from the haunted hills and the legends. Dismal little fantasists.'

'How many of them?'

'Mere handful, I expect, but two hate-driven individuals on the Internet can be a virtual army. It's what kind of influence they have. The power of their steaming rhetoric.'

'What did they want from Rector?'

'Some of them clearly wanted him to be their leader. He still had cachet. The more obvious ones who appeared up at Capel – identifiable by the kind of questions they asked at the end of his seminars – were given their money back and unceremoniously dispatched down the mountain.'

Merrily sat back, shaking her head.

'Athena, either I'm not getting this or there's something you're not telling me. If they were on his courses, presumably they'd realize he wasn't preaching Nazism. What was he doing up there that might lead them to suspect that he wasn't a lost cause?'

They leaned into their separate corners of the bench, the Zimmer between them.

'All right,' Miss White said. 'How much do you know about what's become known – rather disparagingly, I suppose – as chaos magic?'

Not much, actually, but she could bluff for a while.

'Free-range sorcery?' Merrily said. 'Pick 'n' mix?'

'For a person of the cloth,' Miss White said, 'you can be a frightfully crass little woman.'

'Thank you.'

'Although, I will admit to finding some of it – or at least the way it's handled – to be superficial, haphazard, disrespectful and dangerous.'

'Let me work this out. It's a practice that rejects what you might call the confining disciplines of the past by following, in the most liberal sense, Aleister Crowley's maxim, *Do what thou wilt shall be the whole of the law*. Cabala and Catholicism, druidry and freemasonry, witchcraft, yoga, dianetics... if it works, toss it in the pot?'

'You're halfway there. Halfway to Peter Rector's discipline, anyway. And discipline is the operative word. Performed correctly, what we're talking about is the *most* disciplined form of magic. Bringing elements of different traditions together successfully requires a very sure touch.'

'I can imagine. What I *can't* imagine is why?'

'It's product based. A means to an end. The means tailored to the desired result. For example – during the war, a magical defence system was set up by Dion Fortune and a few others, based in Glastonbury. It had one central aim, which was to keep Hitler off British soil. A psychic wall erected around us. But *within* that central premise, different operations were mounted to challenge specific developments in the war. Now I'm not saying too many different occult methods *were* used to this end, but it was a project to which the principles of what we now call chaos magic might well have been applied. You identify *exactly* the result you're after and you decide which combination will best achieve it. Yes?'

'Has a weird logic,' Merrily said.

'However, it also gets carried away with the need to break rules. From the heretical merging of religion and magic comes a general breach of taboos. The energy of the perverse. You see where I'm going with this? Perhaps you don't.'

'Not sure.'

'You don't. All right… the Order of the Sun in Shadow write on their websites of the necessity of breaking human taboos, pushing the mind and body beyond accepted limits of behaviour. Performing acts regarded by society as hideous, in order to align themselves with perceived dark cosmic forces. The sublime shock of breaking civilization's constraints releasing them into the next evolutionary stage.'

'Satanism, in other words.'

'Satanism only exists in the theology of your fundamentalist friends.'

'I don't have any fundamentalist friends. Let me get this right. I think what you're saying is that the practices of modern extreme right-wing magical groups is developed from the same source as chaos magic, as practised by Peter Rector. Did he ever follow the other path?'

'I think I'd have to say not intentionally. But he nevertheless pointed the way, and would never recover from the guilt.'

Miss White supported herself on the Zimmer, her small, pointed chin on her arms.

'I suppose what was worrying Peter the night he phoned me was the possibility of a worm in the apple. Someone studying or helping at the centre undercover, as it were. A disaffected follower of what he'd perceived to be the Rector philosophy. Perhaps using techniques he was learning there to expand the parameters of his own negative theology. Poisoning the pond, essentially. Peter couldn't prove it, but was increasingly conscious of things going wrong. Arguments. Dissent. A clouding of the atmosphere. When something's functioning on a rarified level, it doesn't take much to tip it the other way, and even if the problem's expunged the equilibrium is never quite restored.'

'What was he doing up there that was harmed?'

'Not for me to say.' Miss White wiped a dismissive hand through a ball of frantic midges. 'The ironic thing is that Peter Rector's writing had shown these people how to present it in a far more... honourable light. In their terms. Thus, for example, the so-called Detritus are seen as acceptable victims for blood sacrifice or ritual execution. Performing a human sacrifice is viewed not only as ethnic or social cleansing but as a form of initiation.'

'But surely it never—'

'Never happens? How do we *know* that it never happens? All right, evidence of a human sacrifice would lead to a police hunt on a frightful scale. But if some denizen of cardboard city, some anonymous doorway-sleeper – some *detritus* – were to disappear... who *would* know?'

No answer to that.

'They also dislike Christians. Your turn-the-other-cheek primitive socialism, your creepy humility, your abhorrence of violence, the delusion that love conquers all. If you're ever unfortunate enough to encounter someone following this path, you'll see a person who, endeavouring to reach a new level of humanity, has effectively jettisoned all the finer qualities of this one.'

'OK, I get the point.'

'I'm not sure you do. It vaguely parallels the way a psychopathic serial murderer is often shown to have begun with small animals. By the time he progresses to human beings, the act of killing has become almost routine, and he's looking to raise the bar. He'll kill with abandon, increasingly at random, believing himself invulnerable. But if there's magical ritual involved, the impulse will be fuelled by what *you* would call psychic energy so that the act is done in such a state of higher consciousness that—'

'Please...' Merrily put her hands up. 'I'm getting it.'

There was a silence.

'He had a breakdown,' Miss White said.

'Rector?'

'When I say breakdown, you couldn't begin to understand the profundity of it. I mean a *severe* psychic breakdown. Periods of days without sleep... vivid hallucinations causing bouts of inner self-mutilation. At its core, a conviction that he'd been the tool of the demonic. Crying out in the night for a cleansing death. If he hadn't been among the right people he *would* have been dead, or spending the rest of his days in the psychiatric system.'

'And this was... when?'

'Around nineteen eighty, maybe a year or two earlier, I don't keep a diary. No one spoke about it. The Centre puttered along in his absence. Frenzied activity behind the scenes to hold him together, to dispel what was seen as a psychic attack.'

'By whom?'

'Names would mean nothing to you, but he had enemies, as you can imagine, people who felt he was betraying them. When he returned, still shaky, he wound it all up very quickly, sold the property to some adventure holiday company, left the country for a while. Came back a year later. With a sense of mission.'

'To Cusop?'

'To Cusop. To throw himself into what he considered his last redemptive project.'

Merrily waited, felt the first spots of lukewarm rain.

'And you really can't say what that is.'

'No. It was his magical baby, and he believed it was working. Spectacularly.'

'His Cusop group – these were the people who'd helped him through his breakdown?'

'Mainly.'

'And nobody else knew he was here.'

'He didn't drive. Banked via the Internet. Changed his appearance. Walked the hills and along the brook and the Wye, but rarely went into Hay where he might just have been recognized.'

'But everyone knows now.'

'Yes.'

'And they'll know about you, Athena.'

Miss White smiled sadly into the midges.

'I wonder if he even thought of that. He hadn't seen me in years. I wouldn't let him. I was off the map. Out of the picture. Just a voice on the phone. I realize he'd have an image of me as I was. Quite a bit younger than he was. Invulnerable.'

Merrily saw Aphrodite in a miniskirt. Pert, sharp, outrageously clever, consciously mysterious. Even now, that kittenish voice on the phone...

'Are you... also inheriting whatever it is? His project?'

'Not your business, Watkins.'

'He's not left you everything for old time's sake, has he?'

No reply.

'You don't want it, do you?'

'How do you know *what* I want?'

'You're afraid, I think,' Merrily said.

'I shall never...' Miss White turning on her so quickly that her dyed black hair danced like a nest of snakes. 'I shall *never* be as frightened as you are. In a state of constant terror that your whole life might be a sham. Clutching at delusions of pathetic poltergeists because if *they* don't exist how can something as huge as God be more than a fabrication?'

'*Miss White!*'

Merrily turned, grateful. A woman in an overall had appeared on the terrace behind them. Looked like Mrs Cardelow, proprietor of The Glades. Athena White ignored her. Mrs Cardelow cupped her hands either side of her mouth.

'It's going to rain! Do you need any help?'

Miss White rose up gripping her Zimmer. Held up one hand, displaying a contemptuous middle finger. The woman may have shrugged. She went back into the house.

'I still don't really know what you are,' Merrily said. 'I don't know if your peculiar abilities, given the presumed, clandestine nature of your former occupation, amount to nothing more than advanced psychological, manipulative… tricks.'

'And you never will,' Miss White said.

She was calm again. The rain was falling in slow, deliberate blobs. The Radnorshire hills had vanished. Merrily didn't move.

'I thought it was his profligate imagination,' Miss White said. 'Succumbing at last to the pressure. I thought he was deluded, still bent on his rack of self-recrimination. Now I think he might have been right. I think there has been death. Killing.'

'Where?'

'Not far away.'

'When?'

'I don't know.'

'That isn't much help, Athena.'

'I don't *know*, you silly bitch. I don't know where or by whom, but I think someone died before the Centre was closed down, and I think he felt responsible for that. And I do not dismiss the possibility that Peter Rector was murdered the other night. Executed. They like to claim certain places, you see. As portals where the energies they're seeking can be drawn down. Or up. Places of sacrifice.'

'Do you know who they are?'

'The Order of the Sun in Shadow? I knew who they *were*. The leaders, anyway. They weren't difficult to trace. Virtually advertising for members at one stage. That's why I can't see them as involved. But you see it's a virus. Its adherents are encouraged to seek recruits. Having broken their own barriers, they're instructed to find others over whom they have dominion, until they too transcend the abhorrent. And so it goes on and on, like some noxious chain letter.'

'In theory. In fantasy.'

'Fantasy,' Miss White said, 'is a material. I prefer to spell it with a ph... as in phantasm. Phantasy is a material with which magic works. Ponder that, Watkins. Now go and tell your police friend.'

'He'd think it was bollocks.'

'Well then...' Miss White smiled bleakly. 'There you have the eternal dichotomy.' She looked up into the rain. 'We should go in.'

Merrily stood up. Held the Zimmer frame steady.

'Get away!'

'Sorry.'

Miss White looked up, her mascara starting to run.

'That pool... has a reputation. Did you know that?'

'Has it?'

Merrily zipped up her hoodie over the pectoral cross.

It's got form, Bliss said in her head.

'Watkins...' Bluing knuckles gripping the handles of the Zimmer. 'Never thought I'd say this, but keep me informed.'

'Which of us would that help, Athena?'

'I can't tell you what you don't know, but I may be able to confirm what you think you might.'

'I think I see.'

'Good,' Miss White said.

23

Victims

STANDING ALONE IN the centre of his bookstore – *his* store, for Chrissakes – Robin had a panic attack so sudden it was like an altered state of consciousness. Spinning around on a terrifying carousel of half-filled, crooked shelves, his mouth dry, his brain turned into a wrung-out sponge.

Holy shit, what were they *doing*? They'd hired a hovel in which to sell their souls.

He looked around for a chair and there wasn't one. He'd forgotten, once again, to bring a goddamn chair, and the only desk they had was too big, so they needed a new desk to sit at and take the money and discuss stuff with the customers. In two days there would be customers. Or not. Either way, in two days the sign would say *open*.

Robin pressed the tips of his fingers into his forehead, began to breathe very rapidly, each breath going like an old steam train starting up: *fuck, fuck, fuck, fuck, fuck...*

Two days left. Too freaking days to get this place fit to open. No going back now. He'd designed small posters for The Most Mysterious Shop in Hay, taken them round to the newsagents and anyone with a noticeboard. They'd have a proper, formal opening when there were a whole lot more books, flag it up over a much wider area. Maybe even invite the King to perform the ceremony. Saturday – this was gonna be half-assed, but if they didn't make some kind of start the holiday season would be over.

All Betty's fault. These days, he only suggested stuff so she could talk him out of it. Betty, who right now was back at the bungalow, showing people around so they could sell it at the bottom of the market again. If this failed they'd be trapped in the rural poverty band, and he was horrified by the speed it had happened. An easy rental agreement, Landlord and Tenant Act, 1954 and before it even went through they'd been given access to measure up, test the lights, the plumbing, and Robin had come over, day after day, each time hoping it would look different.

And it had. Each time, despite the starry ceiling, it had looked a whole lot worse.

Worst of all, he didn't like being alone here, now that he couldn't run any more. He stared at the wall, the doorway to the kitchen and the stairs. The wall was solid, the doorway a shallow open space with musty air, which his imagination at once filled with some black, Lovecraftian needle-toothed denizen of chaos. He could've painted it for you in gouache, his medium of choice back in the days when he was *seducer of souls, guardian of the softly lit doorways.* The days before graphic artists been driven out of business by tightwad publishers and Photoshop.

The flash of anger took him to the door. He'd bring in another box of books. More shelves in here than he'd figured. In his head, all the shelves had been bulging after three truckloads had gotten unloaded, but whole boxes of books seemed to fill no space at all. Even though it seemed so cramped in here, the books had gotten swallowed. All his beloved books. The books he hated to sell – what kind of a start was that?

The truck was wedged into the corner, where the top of Back Fold merged with the track to the Castle across the road from the big parking lot. Loading, right? He'd put a sign to that effect on the dash. It also said, SAD CRIPPLE AT WORK.

The rain was holding off, and he stood and gazed across the cars on the scenic parking lot, all laid out like shiny-back molluscs on a beach, over to the sweep of the hill which hardened into the Black Mountains. Not black at all, and the view made his spirit rise a tad. So much here to paint.

He tossed his stick into the truck's box, let down the tailgate and hauled over one of the book bags, a black bin liner. They'd actually found more books than expected, close to a couple thousand, some rarities, kind of, but he wouldn't bring these till Saturday morning. Dragging the bag of books until it tipped over the tailgate, Robin squatted down. If he could get underneath it…

'*Shit!*'

The binsack had split. He tried to hold the books in, but the bastards were spilling over the road. Robin stumbled and the pain ripped into his hip. *Oh fuck, fuck, fuck…*

'Hold on, boy…'

A man was under the sack, taking the weight. Robin leaned back against the cab, breathing hard. The guy had the sack back on the truck. Bent to pick up a few of the books and then gathered the whole mess into his arms.

'You OK?'

''Cept for feeling like a dick.'

The guy who'd rescued him was much older, a tall, narrow man in a drooping tweedy jacket and a flat cap, hands behind his back, head tilted, peering.

'Mr Thorogood, I think.'

Robin looked up, blankly at first, into a half-remembered, half-moon face. Then the past was around his shoulders like a greasy old coat.

'Jeez,' he said. 'You shaved off your moustache.'

Dumb response, but despite all the hours the guy had spent by his hospital bed, he couldn't recall the name. Pretty clear now, though, why the whole damn town had access to his and Betty's history.

'Jones,' the guy said. 'Gwyn Arthur. Former detective superintendent of this parish and others either side of Brecon, and now… after an undistinguished but sporadically interesting career… retired.'

'What are you doing here?'

'I live here. People do. Even old plods.'

'Hell…' Robin shaking his head. 'My apologies. Only, anyone connected with that particular stage of my life…'

'I can imagine you'd want to wipe us all from your memory. A bad time, boy. You caught the attention of a fanatic in need of a target. My greatest regret that we were unable to put him away for peculiar offences. But when no one will testify… hands are tied.'

Robin recalled Jones in the orthopaedic ward, murmuring questions in his mild, West Wales rumble. Recording all Robin could tell him – not enough, evidently – about the ordained minister who'd aroused hatred against Betty and him while abusing women in the name of God.

'Where's he now?'

'Ellis?' Jones followed him into the store, arms full of leaking bin liner. 'Over in your homeland, last I heard.'

'One good reason never to go back. So you're out of it, now, huh?'

'Should've gone abroad, boy. Retired to Spain like the criminals. My wife wouldn't. Too much family. Well, hell, I said, they'll visit. No good. So I bought a share in a bookshop. Just to feel useful.'

'It working?'

'Crime fiction. A popular misconception, it is, that policemen despise it. Why should that be, when the police always win? So… there we are. Serve in my shop two days a week, rest of the time prowl the streets, seeing too much. All very sad, Mr Thorogood.' He smiled, clapped Robin gently on the shoulder. 'Should've seen the way things were going with that man, long before we did.'

'Nobody saw,' Robin said. 'Nobody outside of the valley.'

'In this area, the past is like the ditches… well overgrown and full of rusty old barbed wire.' Jones was looking around the store. 'Shop all right for you, is it?'

'Yeah, it… it's OK. Gets us started. Just dump them anyplace.'

Gwyn Arthur Jones let down the sack. Murry Hope's *Practical Celtic Magic* and *Myths and Legends of the North American Indians* by Lewis Spence fell out onto the concrete floor.

'Lot of paperbacks, Mr Thorogood. Unless it's something like a vintage green Penguin, you can't make much on paper-backs, I'm finding. Rarely collectors' items, so people buy the e-books instead.'

'Well, thanks for those encouraging words.'

'No, no… you just need more hardbacks. And a reputation for collectors' items at reasonable prices. Like the cricket boy next door.'

A wave of tiredness washed over Robin.

'We're haunting boot sales and charity outlets. Checking out dealers who might pick up books along with furniture in house-clearances.'

'Well.' Jones stood with his hands behind his back, looking up at the rubblestone wall above the main shelves. 'Anytime I can help you, you let me know. All right? With the shop or… anything else?'

Glanced at Robin, like he was waiting for him to speak. Robin dug out a wry smile.

'I've a police pension,' Jones said, 'so it's no more than a diver-sion for me now, an escape. But I'm thinking it's serious for you. And your good lady? She's well?'

'Sure. Um… I guess it was you told Kapoor. About me and Betty?'

'When I heard you were taking that shop, I told him I knew you, yes. As well for people to know you were the victims, that's what I thought. Was that wrong?'

'No, that's… thanks.'

'Remember what I said.'

'We're gonna be OK,' Robin said.

'Of course,' Jones said.

* * *

The retired couple from Coventry who came to view the bungalow this morning had been taciturn, appeared incurious. They clearly disliked all the fitted bookshelves, were quietly critical of the garden where Betty grew herbs and Robin struggled to keep the lawn down.

And yet... within an hour of them leaving, the agent was on the phone. They'd made an offer: three thousand less than the asking price. A glow spread through Betty like alcohol. Even Robin had expected to have to come down at least five K.

'Perhaps you can tell them we'll think about it,' she said coolly.

Taciturn and incurious were no bad things, sometimes. Neither of them had asked why a squat, green candle was burning in the window in full daylight.

'If I'm honest...' The agent sounding a bit resentful. 'I doubt you'll get a better offer.'

'One of us will get back to you,' Betty said.

Call it a feeling.

Betty looked over to the window, where the candle was burning low enough, now, to see the jagged end of the front door key embedded in the green wax.

He started to rearrange the shelves with more books face out: *Natural Magic*, *The Book of English Magic*, *A Witch's Bible*.

If one in three books was face out, he reckoned he could fill all the shelves. Also, they needed to think about getting some of these signed by the authors. Famous pagans. Jeez, how many famous pagans *were* there these days? Gerald Gardner, Alex Sanders, Doreen Valiente – all dead.

Days ago, he'd brought his old Black and Decker and some wooden steps. He shook out some wall plugs into his hand, wondering if they'd be deep enough to plug the outside wall, take big enough screws to hold the sign up:

Thorogood Pagan Books

That seemed so feeble now. It needed a cooler name, more enigmatic.

Too late. Everything was too goddamn late.

Robin lugged the sign outside. Damn. Gonna need a second pair of steps, so he and Betty could hold it up from either side of the doorway. He went over to the cricket shop, see if Kapoor had any.

Kapoor looked suspicious.

'You OK up a ladder?'

'Sure.'

'We could get some guys.'

'I don't know anybody.'

'I'll get Gore,' Kapoor said.

'Gore?'

'Gwenda's guy. You know Gwenda's Bar?'

'Not sure.'

'Dead centre of town, opposite the clock. Actually, I was finking... you need to meet people, don't'cha? Few of us fetch up there most nights. We meet up to bemoan our lot, as Connie Wilby likes to say.'

'Wilby?'

'Veteran bookseller. Long established. You wanna meet some other whingeing booksellers, come over to Gwenda's tonight... say nine? That convenient for you?'

'I get to bring my wife?'

'Good idea. Course, the first fing they'll tell you is to rip up the lease and run like hell.'

Robin grinned. Then he didn't.

'Kapoor... seriously, *is* there anything we aren't being told?'

'Like what?'

'Like about the store? The cop was here. Jones? Crime books? Guy who told you how I got to be a cripple?'

'They don't use that word any more, Robin.'

'Cripple's what I am. It's like you can't touch a black guy for calling himself a nigger.'

'I'll work that out later. What did Jones say to wind you up?'

'Nothing. He just kept looking around the place. And not much at the books. Like he knew something and didn't know whether he needed to tell me or not.'

'You're too sensitive, mate.'

'That's Betty,' Robin said.

'What is?'

'OK, I realize you don't believe in this shit, your god being a guy in cricket pads—'

'Nah, nah, that's different, innit?' Kapoor came out from behind his computer. 'My gran, she was... she'd tell you fings and she was... most times she was on the money. More fings in heaven and earth, all that. I don't knock noffing, mate.'

Robin stared down at his feet. He used to like discussing this stuff.

'Betty picks up memories. Vibes. Back when I was in one piece, she got something we'd discuss it. Now... I dunno.'

'Seems to me that ain't how it works, mate. Else she'd've foreseen a bleedin' wall coming down on you. Let's get that sign up, eh? You can put a cloth over it till Saturday. You don't wanna leave fings too late.'

'Maybe it's already too late,' Robin said.

Kapoor was back towards the end of the afternoon with a crop-haired, close-bearded guy in his thirties. Wore a Welsh rugby shirt and carried a short orchard-type ladder under an arm.

'Same size as Oliver's?'

The guy had like an army officer's voice. He looked up at the gap where Oliver's sign had hung.

'Bigger, but it oughta fit,' Robin said. 'But it's pretty damn heavy. It's oak. I'm just hoping it isn't gonna drag out any stone.'

'Should be OK.' Guy's hand came out. 'Gore Turrell. You want to do it now?'

'You don't mind?'

'Jeeter said you had a drill. Masonry bits?'

'I guess.'

Robin went back into the store, found the drill, lugged out the sign. It was heavier than he remembered. Was the storefront even gonna take this kind of weight?

'Hmm.' Gore Turrell stood looking up, his hands on his narrow hips. 'Let me get some more steps.'

'Anybody can do it, it's this guy,' Kapoor said.

Gore Turrell was gone no more than five minutes, returning with a toolbag, the steps under his arm. Kapoor extended a hand like a TV host.

'Bookseller, bartender, builder, carpenter...'

Gore grinned.

'Patronizing bastard.'

They set up two pairs of steps either side of the doorway, a little uneven on account of the way the ground sloped. Gore Turrell drilled four holes in the oak sign, two either side, and plugged the walls. Then he went on the higher steps with a screwdriver and some long screws, Kapoor on the other end holding it up, getting it aligned, Gore calling to Robin on the ground.

'That about right for you?'

Robin looked up, felt a tremor.

Thorogood Pagan Books

Jeez, they'd arrived. Part of the town. And, more than that, part of the castle. The castle of Richard Coeur de Livres. Book-heart. Though from down here, the renewed red chimney stacks of the Jacobean extension looked like a modern affirmation of the castle's original military purpose: a row of bullets in a magazine.

He'd never thought of it that way before. He felt a momentary dismay, but what the hell?

'Yeah,' Robin said. 'Thanks. Thanks, guys.'

'They reckon the King had a handful of blokes like this,' Kapoor shouted down. 'It was how the new Hay was made.

Miles of bookshelves sawn and hung by local craftsmen. Makes you feel inadequate, don't it?'

'I *am* inadequate,' Robin said.

Turning away so they wouldn't see the terror on the face of a guy who knew nothing about bookselling and was too crippled to go up a ladder. Jesus, in a life full of false starts, this could be the—

He heard Kapoor's cut-off cry, a scraping of wood on tarmac that turned into a near screech as he swung round, saw the ladders swaying then toppling, Kapoor on the ground, the oak sign coming down on him like a falling tree.

24

We shall come again

BLISS WOULDN'T TALK about it on the phone, not even in the car park. After work, he came over to Ledwardine, running crookedly through the rain, from the vicarage where he'd left his car.

'Forgot you were on holiday at Lol's.'

It had gone quite cold; Merrily had lit the stove. Bliss looked around Lol's living room.

'Not too bad, as holiday homes go. Nice stereo. But then I suppose he would have, in his trade.' He sat on the edge of the sofa, upright, as if he was still afraid of suddenly losing consciousness. 'So we have a problem, then, do we?'

'I'm trying not to overreact, but...' She put coffee in front of him. 'Yes. I think so.'

'Makes me manic, this stuff, did I tell you?'

'You may have done.'

'Suggests you want me not to underreact. Interesting.' He sipped, put the mug down. 'Let's take it from the start. The woman who stands to collect... let's say over a million... is not exhibiting conspicuous signs of... what? Joy... gratitude? I don't know how excited they get at that age.'

Merrily dropped into the armchair near the stove.

'This is a woman you normally can't get near. She tells you no more than she feels you deserve, in between the barbs and the insults. She doesn't want you to like her. Or – even worse – pity her.'

'That's what I'd heard.'

'From whom?'

'You, probably.'

Merrily sat down with a glass of water and told him all of it. All of what she'd assured Athena White he'd dismiss as bollocks. Solidifying the story with what she'd learned about Peter Rector from Huw Owen. Putting it all together for someone else gave it a cohesion and credibility that she hadn't expected.

'These neo-Nazi cults,' Bliss said. 'I've come across a couple over the years. Not round here, up north. The situation is, in Germany, Scandinavia, these guys are bad news, all tooled up. Over here, usually a disappointment. Tends to be some little twat with a swazzie tattoo, a reedy voice and a mountain bike.'

'So what about the photograph? The woman with the bloody—'

'Merrily, as we agreed, we've no way of knowing if that's something or nothing. It's certainly not enough to launch an inquiry.'

'When we found it, we didn't know there was any connection between Rector and Nazism, and now we do.'

'Yeh. Thanks to you. I asked you to check out his place and, as it turns out, I did the right thing. So, yeh, now we know he was the inspiration for our friends with the reedy voices and the mountain bikes. But did he really move back over the border because he was scared of these buggers? I don't see it.'

'Maybe he'd just had it up to here with their attempts to bring him back into the fascist fold. I don't know, either. I don't think Athena's saying he was scared exactly. He just didn't like the way they kept showing up at his place in the mountains. Where he wasn't able to screen the people signing up for his courses. Not as easy then as it is now.'

'It's not enough, is it?'

'If you put it all together...'

'Yeh, but that's not how we work, the police. We don't collect many points for preventing the hypothetical. All right, occasionally it blows up in your face, and you all look like dicks. What I'm saying, I do appreciate what you've done, but...'

'This is the payoff, is it?'

'Heard from Billy Grace this affy. He says Rector drowned. There was a cut in his head, but nothing too damaging. Probably scraped on a rock, as we thought. No complications, nothing requiring further investigation. Maybe his hat blew off into the pool and he was clambering over the rocks trying to reach it.'

'He seem to you like the sort of ninety-odd-year-old man who'd go climbing over rocks to get his hat back?'

Bliss sipped his coffee.

'End of the day, Merrily, like I say, while we don't like mysteries to remain unsolved, we don't go out of our way to create them. Can I have another spoonful of sugar in this?'

Merrily went into the kitchen, replaying Athena White in her head. *They like to claim certain places... As portals where the energies they're seeking can be drawn down. Or up. Places of sacrifice.*

Mystical drivel. Bliss was right, of course. It was a different language. When she came back with the sugar bowl and a spoon and another mug of water for herself, he was rubbing stiffened fingertips hard into his brow and didn't look good.

'Frannie, do you have anyone at all you can, you know, call on? At home.'

'I'm fine.'

'You're not, though, are you? What if things get difficult? However much you play with words, it's still a head injury. Unpredictable.'

Bliss looked furtive. Really, *furtive* was the only word that came to mind.

'Gorra friend,' he said gruffly. 'Comes weekends, mostly. All right?'

'Oh. Woman?'

'Maybe.'

'You can't tell?'

Chances were, a cop. *Someone who could shaft me bigtime with West Mercia if we ever fell out.* Absolutely no use asking him; he was already steering the conversation into a different lane.

'Another reason to gerrout of Gaol Street was in case I inadvertently told Brent he'd been fast-tracked up his own bum. Like you said, bit of a tightrope. Merrily, I'm grateful for your help, just don't want to waste any more of your time, that's all.'

Merrily lifted Ethel on to her knees.

'Athena White, the thing about her, as we know, she worked in some capacity for the security service. Just happened to be studying the cabala over lunch in the park instead of *The Times* crossword. All I'm saying, she's not some New Age airhead. If Athena White's on edge, I think that's cause to worry.'

'About what? Rector's dead. Do we have a specific other person to get anxious about? Miss White herself?'

'Don't know.'

'Let's just keep an eye on it.'

Merrily nodded. What could she say?

'I've got one more thing, Frannie. Arranged to meet Huw up at Capel-y-ffin on Saturday, hopefully to get an idea of what Rector was doing up there. *He* thinks I'll find it significant, anyway. And seeing I could be on holiday from tomorrow, when my locum moves in...'

'Merrily... have a rest.'

'If anything starts looking dangerously rational, I'll let you know.'

Bliss finished his coffee.

'If anything dangerously rational happens, you won't need to.'

Half an hour after he'd gone, she was still staring into the reddening stove. You started out doing a small favour for Bliss, finding out, within a day, that there was something here that probably needed pursuing, and then he was backing off.

But *you* couldn't. You didn't need rationality. Rationality was not your remit.

The cat jumped down, and Merrily stood up, finding she was shaking, the image of the woman's slashed skull as vivid as when it fell out of a book about religious life in the Black Mountains. What struck her now was that it hadn't been a professional-looking picture. It was a *snap*.

Didn't know whether it was rage or fear or a sense of helplessness, but it sent her out of the front door on to the empty square.

Needed to go to the vicarage, anyway. One more night to pick up the mail and check the answering machine before it became Martin's responsibility. She went back for her keys.

The mail amounted to one item. Postcard. Picture of Hereford Castle from across the river.

Dear Ms Watkins,
After learning that you were <u>not</u> away, as I was told, we came to call on you.
We shall come again.
Yours sincerely,
Sylvia Merchant

We shall come again.
She read it again. We *shall.*

This was getting both ridiculous and borderline nightmarish. The answer might simply be to ring Ms Merchant, go and see her if necessary, tell Sophie and the Bishop about it afterwards. Or maybe, as a first stage, ring George Curtiss, see what he'd learned.

She came out of the vicarage drive holding the postcard away from her, between two fingers, as if it was contaminated.

Footsteps behind her.

'You all right, vicar?' Gomer Parry said.

25

The quiet

THE SKY HAD cleared, setting up a rare soft evening. Sandy light on the town, shadows deep as clefts in rock, and Robin was aware of a strange sense of seaside. In a coastal town, you could sense the sea even if it wasn't in view – that constant hidden pressure.

Only here it wasn't the sea, it was the river after which the town was named and which had become a secret presence, barely visible even from the castle hill.

It occurred to Robin that virtually nowhere in the town of Hay-on-Wye could you see the Wye from the ground and he was aware of no sign anyplace that pointed you to it. A whole street of stones had been built centuries ago with its back to the water. Even the road bridge crossing the river into Radnorshire was accessed through not much more than a slit between buildings.

Crazy. This was *the Wye*.

Watched over by castles and abbeys and cathedrals. And Hay didn't want to share it. This symbolized everything he didn't understand about Hay, which was…

…almost everything. He'd realized that, leaning on his stick while the easy-going Gore Turrell was fixing up his shop sign with no hassle at all, and Robin had thought, *It's too soon. We're not ready.*

A split second before the wooden steps skittered on the sloping ground, and Kapoor lost his footing and crashed into the road, the steps coming down on top of him. If they'd hadn't, he'd have taken the full weight of the sign and he'd be dead, his skull smashed, blood running down Back Fold.

The cold overcoat of foreboding had slid back around Robin's shoulders. Paganism dealt in portents. How clear did you want your omen?

What if Kapoor had died?

And he hadn't even thought to offer to hold one of the pairs of steps he couldn't climb himself to see they were steady. Asshole. Liability. At the end of it, he'd been shaking more than Kapoor, his hand still unsteady around the phone, half an hour later when he was calling Betty.

Betty was doing business. He'd phoned to ask what time he could pick her up, bring her back to Gwenda's Bar to hear the wisdom of booksellers. She was waiting for a call from the agent who, in turn, was awaiting a call from the people who'd been to view the bungalow. He knew that, at some stage, she'd sell the bungalow, at whatever price. Betty was practical, pragmatic, while he was... don't ask.

When the mobile bleeped again, the day was thinning and the candle in the window had melted down, so that the serrated edge of the Yale key was actually visible inside the hot wax.

'I don't know what you told them, Mrs Thorogood,' the estate agent said, 'but I passed on the information that you were considering their offer and – and I can assure you this doesn't happen often these days...'

Pause for effect. Betty's thoughts were stilled. She'd given up three hours ago, deciding the people from Coventry must have shrugged and walked away. A thousand more suitable properties were on offer in the area; if they couldn't get a cheap deal, why would they bother?

But now the agent was calling from his home.

'They came back ten minutes ago. They liked all the book-cases. And they liked the fact that it hadn't been tampered with. Seems all the other similar houses they'd looked at had had their front gardens paved over to provide more parking space. Or there was an extension or a terrace for the barbecue. Things like that.'

Betty smiled.

'They offered within five hundred of the asking price.'

'Gosh,' Betty said.

She felt far away.

'Someone up there is on your side.'

'Evidently,' Betty said.

'Congratulations. I don't get to say that very often any more.'

'Thank you,' Betty said.

When she went back into the living room, the front door key was projecting from the candle like a blackened finger bone with a tiny flame on the end.

He never did find the river.

Wound up back on dusky Castle Street, walking down to where the Gothic clock tower stood, centuries younger, Robin guessed, than the buildings around it but bestowing its own sense of the medieval. A circle of wan light in the clockface, the weather vane puncturing a cobalt sky. Around the tower, squares of yellow and orange light were appearing in stone and whitewashed buildings, with the castle's shadowy crust up behind.

Robin stood on the edge of the terraced area, near the Granary, where he'd eaten earlier, alone. Across the junction, discreetly recessed, dimly but enticingly lit by a wrought-iron hanging lantern, was Gwenda's Bar.

The clock said it was gone half-nine. He hesitated. Circumstance had flattened the old confidence, which he now saw as brashness, unlikely to endear an American to the Brits, whether he was trying to sell them a house or a second-hand book.

A long shadow met his own.

'Strange, quiet evening,' Gwyn Arthur Jones said, like they'd

174

been standing here together for hours. 'Always distrust quiet, see, in a town.'

'Not good for business?'

'Unless it's police business.' Jones looked across the street 'Gwenda's, is it?'

'Kapoor suggested I called in.'

'Makes sense, boy. A booksellers' drinking hole waiting to happen, for many years, and now it has.'

'I was thinking it had been here since forever.'

'Couple of years, that's all. An example of how new people can become accepted very quickly, if they learn the rhythms. Nothing too fancy. Nothing too posh.'

That old Gareth Nunne patter.

'Booksellers' bar,' Jones said. 'Walked in, with her boyfriend, and hit the Hay zeitgeist, as they say. The worse bookselling gets, the more gets spent at Gwenda's. Anything happening, you hear about it first in Gwenda's.'

'I guess they'll've heard about how Kapoor was nearly killed fixing up our sign.'

'Boy's all right, I'm told. Bar the odd bruise. Were you hurt?'

'No. This was someplace else, he'd sue my ass. All my fault for wanting an oak sign I was never gonna be able to fix up myself. Then I'm just... like standing there, watching it happen.'

'Hardly be expected to throw yourself at it, in your condition.'

'That's the whole point. I'm a goddamn curse.'

Gwyn Arthur was shaking his head, wearing his 2H pencil-line smile.

'But it's done?' he said at last.

'Me and Kapoor finally held it up between us, the sign, and Gore Turrell took most of the weight.'

'Strong boy. Comes from swimming in the Wye and running all the way up to Lord Hereford's Knob before breakfast. Only outsiders do that, of course, as you know.'

'Not me.'

'No. I'm sorry. I meant no offence. Anyway, you're installed. Your name is up there. You exist.'

'Yeah. I exist.'

Jones was a strange guy. Robin watched him walking away, bent forward like some curious goblin, occasionally glancing to one side or the other like he was looking for a reason for the silence.

26

Nemesis

Bliss still agonized, week-to-week, about whether she'd come back.

The Friday night vigil. Although sometimes it'd be Sunday. Or Wednesday, occasionally. He'd be sitting, just like he was now, in his stripped-back living room, on the cheap sofa he'd bought to replace the quality sofa Kirsty had taken. One eye on the clock, although he knew she rarely appeared before dark and British Summertime was why it kept getting later.

Week after week during his so-called recovery period, he'd be sitting here waiting for the darkness or going up to the bedroom, watching through the window for the white BMW which would usually pull in some distance away, down near the kids' playground.

He'd watch her getting out, shouldering her bag, that aura of official business around her, those sharp, impatient glances to either side before approaching the modern house he'd never liked, on a pencil-box estate in Marden on the Hereford flatlands.

Oh God, Annie...

Always wondering if this was going to be the night when the white car wouldn't come and he'd just carry on waiting here until he fell into an uneasy sleep and woke up into some steely new day when he and Annie would be history.

Secret history. Mother of God, for years, he hadn't even liked the way she looked. *A metal coat-hanger with tits*, Terry Stagg had said. It was clear that Stagg still had no suspicion about Howe and Bliss. Nobody did. It was laughable. You could do a briefing on it for the whole of CID, in simple, witness-statement English, and they'd all look at you like you were insane.

It could only ever make sense if you'd been there on a winter's night, coming up to Christmas, when they'd dug something smelly out of Herefordshire local government. *They* had. Him and Annie, suddenly finding they were a double act. Connecting, feeding each other. Then coming back here, that night before Christmas, glowing with *result*, to the house recently vacated by Kirsty and the kids. Electricity.

Bliss loved replaying in his head how neatly she'd folded her clothes before fitting herself into his bed for what he'd thought was going to be a one-night stand that neither of them would ever talk about, least of all to one another.

And then six months had gone, seven months, and they still had a dangerous secret. Only coming close to exposure after the cockfight fiasco, when he'd discharged himself from the hospital, walking like a drunk, his eyeballs ringed with blood, and she'd driven him out to her flat in Great Malvern and taken two weeks off to hold him together. The nearest either of them had come to commitment, and he still didn't know how it had survived. They were both so—

A short, formal tapping on the back door. Bliss jumped up from the sofa. Hadn't even heard the car. Had he fallen asleep again, without feeling sleepy? He drew a long breath against the creeping numbness down his left side.

The tone of the knock was enough, and it wasn't yet sunset. He stumbled through and opened the door, and there she was in her long, pale mac, the strap of her overnight bag over a shoulder, and then his mobile blew the evening apart.

A farmer voice. His heart sank. Never happy with farmers.

'Inspector Bliss, is it? I'm sorry to bother you. Robert Winterson, it is.'

'Sorry, who?'

'My sister's Tamsin – PC Winterson?'

'Oh, right… Tamsin, yeh.'

'I'm at my dad's farm. Where Tamsin lives, with my parents? Only, she was gonner to babysit for me and my wife tonight, and she didn't turn up. So I rang my mother, and she en't heard from her. If she's doing overtime or some'ing she always rings her mother.'

'Right.'

'We left it a bit, because she don't like anyone from yere bothering her at work. And then we called her mobile. No answer.'

'When was this?'

''Bout an hour ago? I know that's not long…'

'Could be there was no signal where she was,' Bliss said. 'You know what it's like round there. How did you get my number, Mr Winterson?'

'It was on her laptop. Everything on her phone she copies into the laptop in case it gets lost or stolen. My mother says she's been working for you. Nights and that.'

'Nights?'

'Been out till late the last two nights. So you don't know where she is?'

Bliss was unsure how to handle this. When he was a young copper living at home he'd often tell his ma he was working late on a case when he was really out with his mates or some judy. Didn't want to drop Tamsin in it if she had some unsuitable feller on the go.

'Well,' he said, 'she *has* been checking on a few things for me, but… you're sure she's not on nights?'

'My mother's sure.'

'Look, if I hear from her I'll get her to ring you ASAP.'

'Thank you, Inspector. She's been… quite excited, kind of thing, working for you.'

Except she hadn't been working for him, not really, had she?

'She's a good girl,' he said. 'Enthusiastic.'

'She is.'

'Tell you what,' Bliss said. 'Could you give me your phone number and your mother's? And do you happen to have Tamsin's mobile number?'

Should've taken it down when he gave her his, but he'd never figured on it being necessary.

'Sure to,' Robert Winterson said. 'I'll find it now.'

Annie drew the curtains across the window. Bliss called up Tamsin's phone.

Annie said, 'Do I know her?'

'You might've seen her if you were up this end.' Tamsin's phone was switched off. 'Red hair, freckles, serious-looking. She was checking out a few things for me.'

'On what?' Annie took off her mac, folded it carefully over the back of the sofa. The coat-stand had been Victorian; Kirsty had taken it before he'd changed the locks. 'Not the bloody drowning?'

'They're all talking about that, are they?'

He'd given her the full background over the phone. No secrets from Annie Howe any more. It felt weird.

'They couldn't care less about the drowning, just you.'

'In *Worcester*?'

'In Worcester, I get phone calls from Gaol Street questioning your mental health. Not in so many words, but you get the idea.'

'Brent?'

'Calls me more often than he needs to. He doesn't like you at all. And, as he thinks I like you even less, he talks to me without inhibition.'

'That must be fun.'

'You'd doubtless find it fun.' Annie sat down on the sofa, loosening her pale blond hair. 'I don't. Can we light a fire?'

'It's June, Annie.'

'Who'd guess?'

This well-concealed domestic side of Annie, he liked that. He found kindling and a copy of the *Hereford Times* and got down on his hands and knees on the hearthrug.

Annie said, 'Do I understand from that phone call that you're pursuing the drowning on an extra-mural basis?'

'Actually I'm not. Not now.' Bliss put a match to the paper. 'Nor had I instructed Tamsin to pursue it.'

'And you'd given her no reason to think that if she happened to come up with anything it would be gratefully received?'

He looked up at her. She was in jeans and the striped sweater he loved because she'd been wearing it on the electric winter's night. A little crumpled now, and he loved it even more.

'You're saying you think I led her astray?'

'Not deliberately.'

The kindling caught and crackled. Bliss spread out a few lumps of coal from the scuttle.

'She told me she had her eye on CID.'

'And I expect you told her you'd do what you could.'

'Not in so many words.'

'In your current condition, that might be the next best thing to a promise.'

'She's not daft.'

'How old?'

'Twenty-one, twenty-two.'

'There you go. A young copper with the faint possibility of a murder on her doorstep. She knows she wouldn't be playing much of a part in the investigation if there was ever a need for one, but she's thinking what's it going to do to her CID prospects if she's missed something under her nose. That didn't occur to you?'

Bliss hefted the scuttle and slung the rest of the coal on to the flames, Annie wafting coaldust away from her face.

'How long's she been missing?'

'She's not *missing*, she just hasn't rung her mum. Let's not over-react. When're you coming back to Gaol Street?'

'Keep telling you, I don't want to come back. I don't want to be your boss any more. Can you understand that?'

Bliss sighed. Strangely, it didn't matter to him that she was his superior and probably always would be. Could never see himself getting higher than DI, though he could see her making ACC or better. But it didn't matter, and that surprised him.

'What might she be looking into?' Annie said. 'I mean, if she wanted to come up with something that would impress you.'

'Annie, she's in the back of some young farmer's Land Rover. She's just using me as an excuse for staying out late.'

'You don't know that, though, do you?'

'All right. It's conceivable she might be looking to identify possibly the last person to communicate with Rector. A woman, aged about thirty-five who was delivering his groceries. And possibly his dope.'

'His dealer?'

'I'd be more inclined to think somebody who deals with a dealer on his behalf.'

'All I'm saying is, if cannabis found in the home of a man of ninety-odd was enough to make *you* think there might've been something untoward... well, who knows how her mind's working?'

'She'd've told me.'

'Maybe she wasn't sure. Just the way you weren't sure about what was happening on the Plascarreg, until—'

'All right!'

'Who else knows about this?'

'Nobody. Well, apart from Mrs Watkins.'

He saw Annie's head go back against the sofa, eyelids coming down, lips tightening.

'The forensic priest. And she comes into this... how?'

'As a consultant,' he said.

'Oh, a *consultant*.'

'I needed an expert opinion on whether Peter Rector was involved in anything iffy. Tamsin said the local kids, of whom she was one not that long ago, thought he was some kind of wizard. Their word. Harry Potter generation. Maybe somebody saw his library, which involves a huge and expensive collection of occult books. And some erotic drawings.'

'You only told me about the cannabis.'

'I didn't think you'd be impressed with the library. There were apparently gatherings at his place involving people the kids liked to call his coven. So I was thinking unbalanced people, maybe doing more serious drugs or hung up on some crank cult thing. I'm thinking what if it involves anybody... underage? I was thinking individuals who, for some arcane reason, might want to drop him in a pool.'

'And what did Ms Watkins have to say?'

'She said that while there was no evidence of a temple or whatever on the premises he was certainly some kind of active practitioner of... something. She was gonna try and find out if anything was known about him. Exorcists are well genned-up on what you might call the spiritual byways. Trouble is, once you follow one you wind up in places where, because no obvious crime's been committed...'

'The police and the CPS are not equipped to function. And Watkins *is*?'

'She can sometimes translate it into a language we can understand, that's all I'm saying.'

Annie gave him a level look.

'So what *are* you going to do about PC Winterson?'

'Hope to God she comes back before bedtime. Otherwise, I wouldn't know where to start.' He sat down in the armchair opposite her. 'You're not making me feel good about this.'

'I'm sorry. You're probably right. She'll be out with some man, or her phone's run out of juice.'

Bliss leaned forward, hands on his knees.

'Half an hour ago, I was wondering if I'd ever see you again. Like this.'

He felt tears behind his eyes. Shut them fast, shaking his head. What the fuck had happened to him? He was a friggin shambles.

When he opened his eyes, Annie's severe face had softened, or seemed to, in the lamplight.

'Oh, *I'll* keep coming back. I think you're my Nemesis.'

'That a basis for a relationship?'

'Nearest I've ever come to one,' Annie said. 'Go on. Do what you have to. Ring Winterson's brother back. See if she's home and, if not, get some details. Without alarming him.'

Bliss nodded, groping for his phone.

27

Orange spine

David Hambling? Peter Rector? Capel-y-ffin?

Gomer Parry was shaking his head, pulling out his ciggy tin before remembering they were in the Black Swan. He pushed it back into his old tweed jacket, scowled.

'Can't be doin' with them Welshies, see, vicar.'

Merrily tilted her head to one side.

'But you *are* Welsh.'

'No, *them* Welshies. Some Welshies is all right, not much different to the rest of us. But *other* Welshies... Oh hell, keep your distance, vicar, that's my view of it.'

Gomer's bottle glasses were reflecting milky light from the panes of a small mullioned window in the lounge bar. His cap lay on the table next to his cider, his carrier bag from the Eight-Till-Late at his feet. She'd been absurdly grateful to see Gomer.

'And it en't about the ole language, vicar, don't you go thinkin' that.'

'Right.'

Some things were better left alone. It was probably a plant-hire issue: somebody quibbling over the bill for a complex system of drainage ditches and tarnishing, in Gomer's eyes, the reputation of an entire region.

'But you worked in Hay, did you? That's Wales.'

'Oh hell, aye. Mabbe ten years on and off, sure t'be.'

He was smiling dreamily, glasses misted. Radnorshire-born, from farming stock. Gomer Parry Plant Hire dating back long before he was living in Ledwardine, digging Merrily's graves and cutting hedges on the side.

'So does that mean…?' She thought of a book found unexpectedly in Peter Rector's esoteric library. 'You ever actually work for Richard Booth, Gomer?'

'Ha!'

The whole bench rocked, Barry, the proprietor, looked across from behind the bar, his eyepatch lifting, Gomer holding down his frenzied white hair.

'You ever see that little tin plate I had on the side of the ole digger, vicar?'

'Don't think so.'

'Gwynneth One, it was, or mabbe it was Muriel. Damaged in the fire at the ole depot. Never got round to replacing it. The tin plate, this is.'

'What did it say on the tin plate?'

There was a half-chewed matchstick between Gomer's teeth. He took it out.

'*By Royal Commission,*' he said.

'The King of Hay.'

'Worked for him for years. Good times, vicar. Sometimes I even got paid. Well, thinkin' back, you always got paid, one way or another. Even if it wasn't in actual money. What you gotter understand about the King, see, is he was… what's that word for all over the place?'

'Never mind, I think I know what you mean. Oh… chaotic?'

'Exackly! And he never looked the part. Well, that was part of the joke, ennit? Belly out over his baggy pants, glasses on crooked kind o' thing. Talks for best part of an hour and you never made no sense of a word of it. But you knowed there was sense *there*, see. Just that you wasn't smart enough to get it.'

'I've heard that.'

She remembered Fred Potter, from the Three Counties News Service, saying how difficult radio and TV reporters had getting a usable soundbite from the King of Hay. Like he was speaking in tongues sometimes, Fred said. He could cover four separate issues in the space of a sentence that had more alleyways than Hay itself.

'He en't what he looks, see,' Gomer said. 'And yet he is.'

'Duh…'

'Educated down Oxford, they reckons, but he don't give a toss for fancy qualifications. "Gomer," he says – and you knowed he wasn't bullshittin' – "Gomer, give me fifteen fellers with doctor's degrees for one o' of the likes o' you." See? Real wisdom that is, vicar. Wait for a bloody graduate to cut your blocks, you'll freeze to death.'

Rarely so effusive about anything, Gomer. Merrily just sat there, nodding, letting it all come out, stowing away nuggets. Local knowledge. She must have shopped in Hay a hundred times but she wasn't *from* there. She was outside the orb, connections missed, dots unjoined. And she hadn't been around here in the years when Hay was the most exciting town on the planet, all because a chaotic bloke in trousers that might have seen better years had declared independence.

'Some'ing in the air, vicar. At the time, you was thinking what a load of ole wallop… but looking back you was proud to be part of it. You din't say, "Oh, that en't my department kind o' thing, I just does plant-hire." You said, "All right then, Richard, gimme a couple o' days I'll figure out how to do it." Never worked on a castle before, see, but, hell, there's always a first time.'

'What did you do at the castle?'

'Ground to be cleared, ole stone to uncover. And other stuff I don't talk about.' Gomer tapped his nose. 'Handful of us worked as the key-retainers, kind o' thing. He made that town the best little bloody town in the country – *both* bloody countries! And the bloody ole councillors and politicians, English and Welsh gnashing their teeth on account of what they had to pay for, bigtime, the King got for nothing.'

'You mean through all the publicity he attracted?'

'And because folks liked what was happenin' there. All the famous folks as flocked in. I seen that Marianne Faithfull once. Her was there a good while, on and off. Tidy bit of— Anyway, there was a sorter magic at work, you could feel it. You'd think the King was all washed up one week, facin' the bankrupt court, all the bloody hestablishment vultures hoverin' around, claws out… then he was bloody back.'

'But now he's lost the castle.'

'I reckon he never quite got a grip on the ole castle,' Gomer said. 'We all done what we could, but we all knowed it was goner takes bloody millions to make it safe.'

'Safe? The masonry?'

'They wasn't safe together, that castle and Booth. Falled asleep one night, left a big ole tree trunk in his big ole fireplace. Bloody place catches fire. Hell of a mess. It was like…' Gomer rubbing his hands together, thinking. 'En't my place to ponticate, see, vicar, but it was like the ole castle was the only place din't like what he was at. Didn't like gettin' loaded up with books. He resented it, that ole castle, he was about war, not readin' books. Know what I'm saying?'

'I suppose.'

'Load o' books got burned that night, mind, sure to. Get you another drink, vicar?'

'No, I'm fine, thanks, Gomer.'

'Gonner be a bit quiet for you. Janie away, Lol away.'

'Bit of bad timing,' Merrily said.

She'd left messages for Canon George Curtiss, but he hadn't rung back. In the end, when the mobile chimed, it was Sophie, calling from home. She took it on Lol's sofa, curtains open to the last light.

'You're not going to let this go, are you, Merrily?'

'Would you, if you'd been accused of what, in most jobs, would be classed as unprofessional conduct?'

'George isn't sure if he's permitted to talk to you, given that a complaint *may* have been made. Which seems…'

'What?'

'... silly, but George likes to tick boxes that don't exist. He made an appointment to see Sylvia Merchant, turned up at the appointed time and there was nobody in. The next time, he didn't ring, just went to the house at Tupsley, in civvies, quite early in the morning, and she had to let him in, claiming she'd been confused about the time for their first meeting. But, essentially, George got nowhere. He says she was very polite, quite pleasant. And entirely unhelpful.'

'You've spoken to him?'

'The Bishop's spoken to him. Ms Merchant said she hadn't yet made up her mind what action to take. She said she needed thinking time.'

'Part of which was spent coming here.'

'When? What did she say?'

'Night before last. She didn't say anything – not to me, anyway. I was across the road, just leaving Lol's cottage, when she got out of a car and walked over to the vicarage, knocked on the front door. I didn't approach her, just watched. She then went to the church, presumably to see if I was there. The point being that she obviously knew I wasn't on holiday. In fact... that was what she said on a postcard that I found behind the door tonight.'

'She *wrote* to you?'

'It says she'll be back. It says *we*'ll be back. And I don't think she was referring to her solicitor.'

'I don't understand.'

'She seemed to be talking to somebody. But she was quite alone. I think you know what I'm saying.'

'Oh, *God*.'

'She mention Alys Nott to George?'

'She wouldn't talk to George about her bereavement. He told the Bishop she didn't appear to be unduly distressed. Very pleasant and almost cheerful. Brave face. Didn't want to talk about you, either, as I say. However... did you happen to notice her bookshelves while you were there?'

'I didn't even get into her living room.'

'George says they were all reference books – film guides, a book on opera, regional guides. Books for consulting rather than reading for pleasure. And a whole row on psychic subjects. George said his eye was drawn to a familiar black and orange spine.'

'I see.'

The Deliverance Study Group's handbook on exorcism. Not exactly easy to find.

'George suspects she obtained the book to see for herself the procedures you ought to have followed.'

'*Did* follow!'

'Of course,' Sophie said. 'I'm sorry.'

But the damage was done.

28

Report it

BLISS HAD BEEN here before. Hated it.

Not Dorstone. Other places, three of them, all in the years before he came down to Hereford. Bigger places, with more people to disappear.

All of them in summer, as it happened. One had been the home of the kid who drowned. Missing for a night before they found him, and Bliss remembered the overcrowded living room, all the helpful neighbours swelling the anxiety until the critical moment when it all went down around the mother's arid wail.

That had been on a former council estate on Merseyside, this was a farmhouse at the end of a pitted track with wooded Dorstone Hill behind it. Still at the arse-end of the day, but all the lights were blazing, as if someone thought Tamsin might be out there and had forgotten where she lived.

Annie parked the BMW on the edge of the field, close to the entrance to the yard.

'Better not come in with you.'

'I know.' He was struggling into his jacket to cover up the baseball sweater with the big, cheerful numbers on the chest. Just grateful she'd driven him out, knowing what he was like at the wheel when it got late. 'You're not here.'

It was a sagging, rubblestone house, quite low, not very big. The man standing in front of the porch was wearing an unfarmery light suit. Robert Winterson, dressed for a night out with his wife that never happened. He held out his hand to Bliss and they shook under a domed security lamp projecting from the side of the house, showing Winterson to be about forty, thickset, close-cropped hair.

'Like I said…' Bliss turned his back on the light. 'I don't want you to start gerrin too worried. Not yet.'

'It's my mother, it is. She's the baby of the family, you know? My mother never wanted her to be in the police, see. Not the way it is now, women doing the full job.'

Bliss saw a woman's face at the nearest window, all the lights on in there, walls, ceiling, table.

'She's a clever girl, and she's a good copper. There'll be a reason for this.'

'Of course,' Robert Winterson said. 'Course there will. I feel bad about bothering you.'

'Hell, no, you did the right thing.'

'Anyway, we got Kelly yere,' Robert Winterson said. 'She insisted on coming over.'

'Kelly?'

'Kelly James – Tamsin's mate? From Cusop?'

'Sorry, yeh…' Sometimes he wanted to kick his own head in. 'Good.'

When he'd called back, Robert Winterson had said this Kelly had rung the farm, expecting a call from Tamsin that hadn't come.

'Mr Winterson, about Kelly, could you do us a favour? There's things I need to know, questions I need to ask, but I don't want to distress your mother by asking them in front of her.'

'You want me to get Kelly out yere?'

'Exactly. Thank you.'

Kelly James was in a baggy white YFC hoodie, looking even younger than Tamsin, golden curls like a baby.

Conspicuously pregnant, eyes aglow with tears.

'I just did what she told me. I was only trying to help. It's all my *fault*…'

'We could all say that, Kelly. Just… take your time. When exactly did you call Tamsin?'

'Must've been about half-six?'

'And what did you tell her?'

'Told her I'd seen this woman. Near Mr Hambling's house? She'd asked me if I seen the woman again, could I let her know.'

'When was this? When you saw the woman.'

'After I came home from work. Four? I go home early now, what with…'

She'd lowered her voice, covering the bump with both hands, like she didn't want the baby to hear and develop a prenatal anxiety problem.

'Where do you work?'

'In Hay. I work for my Uncle Geoff, he's an accountant? When I get home, I've been going for a walk, with the dog. Get some… fresh air and exercise.'

'And you went up by Mr Hambling's house.'

'Not that far. I don't go that far. I went by the church, as far as the ole castle. The mound, earthwork jobbie? And that's where I seen her. Standing on the mound. Really still. Like some monument.'

'And this was definitely the woman you'd seen before, going to Mr Hambling's place.'

'With a cardboard box. Groceries type of thing. Bottles sticking out.'

'What's she look like?'

'Tallish. Posh-looking. Fairish hair, up in a scrunch at the back. You could tell she was posh, the way she walked. Head in the air kind of thing. She had classy boots on.'

'She see you?'

'Dunno. Mabbe. I was a bit excited, see, so I just like turned round and walked back with the dog, and I could see this car on the church car park?'

'What sort?'

'Audi. Dunno what model, but it was red. Well, I hadn't got the mobile with me, I was only out for a short walk, so I just kept saying the number over and over again so I wouldn't forget it, and then I went home and called Tamsin. It was her day off, so she's at home, and she said she'd come right away.'

'So she took down the number.'

'Yeah.'

'Tell me exactly what she said.'

'She said, "I'll report it," and then she said "I'll come out." And I'm like, "What do you want me to do?" And she said, "Nothing. You stay there." She said, "I'll ring you later."'

'And then what happened?'

'I don't know. I just… did what she said. Nothing.'

'You didn't see the red car again? Or the woman?'

Kelly shook her head.

'You can't see the road from our house. I'm like, Oh please don't come down before Tamsin gets yere. In my head, kind of thing. And then when I didn't hear anything after about an hour I thought I'd better go up there again, and there was no sign of anybody. And I waited another… don't know how long, and I rang her mum.' Kelly started to cry. 'Left it too long, didn't I?'

'You'd no reason to think there was anything wrong,' Bliss said. 'Did you?'

He looked back at the house. Two faces at the bright window now. He hated this. Motioned Kelly further away from the house, under a Dutch barn with a tractor and trailer in it.

'Who did Tamsin say she was going to report it to?'

'Just said she was gonner report it.'

'Right,' Bliss said. 'This car number. I don't suppose you remember it do you?'

'I put it down. Soon as I got in. Put it in my phone.'

'Good *girl*—'

Kelly was fumbling out her smart phone.

'She's gonner be all right? *Is* she? It was just one… posh woman. If it'd been a bloke… but it wasn't.'

'She's probably doing a bit of investigating, Kelly. Things she wasn't sure she could tell you about.'

'Did she not phone you?'

Kelly's shoulders shaking.

'I'm sure she intends to,' Bliss said. 'She probably just… hasn't had a chance.'

When the duty sergeant at Gaol Street, Gerry Rowbotham, came back, they were parked in a roadside picnic place past Hardwicke Church, just before the junction. Like a courting couple, Bliss thought bitterly.

Except for the mobile phone clamped to his left ear, the gathering anxiety.

'Claudia Cornwell,' he repeated and spelled it out, Annie writing it down. 'And it's Plas Gwyndwr, with a W. Near Talgarth. Thanks, Gerry. Just say the postcode again.'

His mouth was dry and he was going numb all down his left side, to the waist. He'd been through his phone for texts, emails, anything. He'd avoided meeting Tamsin's parents. Nothing to tell them, nothing that wouldn't make it worse, couldn't face the cups of cooling tea, the untouched biscuits. Plus, their situation wouldn't be eased by watching a senior copper struggling to stay upright, blinking in the lights, slurring his words.

'All right, Gerry, listen, can you ring whoever's been at Peterchurch today, find out when they last heard from Tamsin. I know it's her day off, but somebody might know. And if she's got any close mates in the job. But, most important, find out if she's also done a PNC check on that reg. and when. And come back to me.'

'Francis,' Annie murmured. 'Just report it.'

'How far's Talgarth from Hay, Gerry, ten minutes? Fifteen?'

'I'm really not trying to pull rank,' Annie said, very low and urgent, 'but I'm saying it again. You have to report this.'

Bliss nodded, put up his hand, then got both hands round the phone, his forehead banging inside.

'Gerry, listen… this could be nothing. This could be a complete false alarm, but Tamsin Winterson's brother rang me and they can't find her and they can't raise her on her mobile. She was last heard from trying to trace that car. No known offence involved, no suspicion of any offence. As I'm only about fifteen minutes away, I'm nipping over there, have a word meself.'

'It's Dyfed-Powys area, isn't it?' Gerry said. 'It's in Wales.'

'No need for them to be involved. Yet. Let's keep this low-key, might be nothing. Just call me back ASAP.'

When he came off the phone, Annie was hissing like a punctured tyre. This really was not like the December night when they'd been working together, off the meter.

'Annie, what am I supposed to friggin' do? Nobody else knows enough to talk to this woman.'

'The central issue…' Annie slumped back hard in the driver's seat, both hands tight on the wheel '… is you have a missing person. Yes, I can see a small advantage in your talking to the woman, rather than anyone else, but I can also see you dropping yourself very deeply in the shit if this escalates.'

'A missing woman. A missing adult. We don't overreact any more, do we, if it's norra kid?'

'It's a *police*woman, for Christ's sake. A very *young* policewoman.'

'Off duty. And no reason for them to think she's in any danger. And she's gonna be embarrassed as hell if there's a simple explanation, like… like she thought she was babysitting *tomorrow* night. Could be that simple. And she wasn't exactly gonna report back to Kelly, was she, on police business?'

'Do we even know she *went* to Cusop?'

'Annie, we don't even know she left the farm. Her mother was in Hereford, shopping, most of the afternoon, and her dad and her brother were out picking up a second-hand trailer. Last time they saw her was lunch.'

Annie stared through the windscreen towards a placard in

front of the hedge across the main road. It was advertising some philosophy event in Hay. It said, *How The Light Gets In.*

'Please?' Bliss said.

'Francis, you may never be able to pay me back for this.'

Annie started the engine, put on the headlights.

29

Nail bar

'Slaughterhouse area, see.'

'What is?'

'That's what it was. Back Fold. The town abattoir. Back Fold ran with blood. Echoed to the sounds of bellowing.'

'When was this?'

Robin laid his glass down, dismayed.

'*I* dunno,' Gareth Nunne, the human barrel, said. 'Within living memory, more or less. Some people's memory. Likely my dad's. He's eighty-nine.'

'I'm vegetarian,' Robin said.

There was a short, hollowed-out period of quiet and then enough laughter to blast all the glasses off the bartop. Robin found he was also laughing. Had to have been an abattoir some-place in a farmers' town. No bookstores back then, maybe a newsagents that sold books on the side.

The way Gwenda's Bar did. Under the tawny lantern light, you walked down this widening alley of crooked bookshelves, all books priced at a pound, before you emerged into this oak-panelled parlour, which smelled like pubs used to smell, and the embrace of laughter.

The panelling was chipped and stained in places, shabby-chic, without the chic. About twenty people were drinking real ale and local wine, served at fat farmhouse dining tables with chips and gouges in them. The bar was like a butcher's slab, lit by globular frosted lanterns, teardrops of cracked yellow light.

Robin, meanwhile, was lit by most of a bottle of something from a Welsh vineyard.

Would've been churlish to keep refusing. They were nice people, even Gareth Nunne who'd tried to rip him off and wound up inspiring him. None of them what he'd been expecting, still figuring that the stringy entrails of his meagre knowledge of the book trade would be exposed on Gwenda's rugged bar and publicly picked over by experts.

Her name was Gwenda Protheroe. Someone said she used to be in the theatre. Sometimes she served behind the bar, sometimes just sat on a tall stool, wearing a little black dress and a wry, sympathetic smile that was kind of sexy in a momsy way. Not long after he'd walked in here Gwenda had told him the bar was an attempt to restore the way rural pubs used to be in the old days – parlour pubs, someone's living room where ale was served. Like the Three Tuns in Hay used to be before it was done up, back when it was run by someone universally revered called Lucy.

Not actually that long ago, apparently, but a rough old parlour pub wouldn't be economically viable now, which was why this had become a wine bar, also serving coffee and food. But Gwenda said this was just one small retro development. In other areas, Hay was in danger of going *badly* wrong.

'I hear there was a woman with plans to open a nail bar there,' she said now.

'Where?'

Gareth Nunne looked up from his cloudy beer.

'In the Back Fold shop,' Gwenda said. 'Oliver's shop – Robin's shop. Seriously, a flaming *nail bar*.'

'What, like carpentry supplies?'

'You're an old fool, Gary,' Gwenda said fondly.

Just a trace of a London accent there. Gareth Nunne smiled into his beer, his port wine stain skin blemish laid around one eye and down into his left cheek.

'And what,' he said, 'did Mr James Oliver say to that, Gwennie?'

'Well, I've heard several versions, but some might've been made up, so I won't pass them on. Yet.'

Nunne turned bleary eyes on Robin.

'He know what kind of books you're gonner be selling?'

'Leave the boy alone,' Gwenda said. 'He doesn't need to worry about that.'

'No, come on, what did you tell him, Mr Thorogood?'

'Uh…' Robin shrugged. 'I just said books. General books.'

'So you didn't mention *The Teen Witch Style-guide—*'

Robin threw up his hands.

'Aw, you just *had* to pick on that one. It's a book I did some creepy Goth drawings for, is all. They dumped a dozen copies on me.'

'Get off his back,' Gwenda said. 'A bookshop's a bookshop. Teen witches are fine by me. Not that you find them much any more.'

'Period value?' Robin said.

'There, see, he's learning.' Gwenda smiled at him. 'So you've been an illustrator, then, Robin?'

'Gwenda, sweetheart.' A murmur. 'This is the man who gave form to Lord Madoc.'

It was Gore. Welsh rugby shirt, white jeans.

Gwenda looked blank.

'The *Intergalactic Celt*?' Gore said.

Robin gazed uncomfortably into his glass. Gwenda raised a forefinger.

'Hold on, those the books you used to collect when you were a kid? The warrior chappie with big hair? Great pile of them down the bottom of your wardrobe?'

'I know it wasn't really aimed at kids,' Gore said to Robin. 'But I was a precocious reader. Man, I wanted to *be* that guy. What happened to him?'

'He finished,' Robin said tightly. 'The writer adopted a new pseudonym and started something else that didn't need an illustrator.' Felt his fingers forming fists. 'The way no one seems to need one any more.'

'That a fact,' Gore said.

He had his hands curled around Gwenda's shoulder, like doing a massage. Jeez... they were an item? Gwenda and Gore, who had to be fifteen years younger?

'Cover designs get done in-house with Photoshop and other... similar money-saving devices,' Robin said. '*Talent*-saving devices. The days when commissioned artwork was part of the creative process, when books were illustrated by legends like Mervyn Peake, that's history. The days when you'd do a full-size painting for a book or an album sleeve, and the original was worth good money... that's *over.*'

Robin unclenched his fists. An uneasy silence had broken out.

He swallowed some wine. His face felt hot. Mistake. Hadn't intended for this to surface. Not so soon anyway, because it was one explanation of why he'd felt driven to open a bookstore. And what kind of bookstore it had to be. And he'd been sitting on this, thinking it was gonna make him look stupid.

'I take it you don't like publishers very much, then, Robin?' Gwenda said gently.

'It's... one reason why we're here. We came over one day, and I'd just been kicked off of what I'd figured for a long-runner, replaced by some kid with an Apple Mac, and I'm feeling pissed because I love books, and... and I'm thinking second-hand, that doesn't do publishers any favours.'

His face felt redder than Gareth Nunne's birthmark. Looked up to find Nunne giving him a level stare that was not unfriendly.

'No need to apologize about that, man. Not yere. You're right. We're no good for publishers, and they know it. They love the Hay *festival* to bits – good publicity for new merchandise. But they don't like the town so much. Or us. Specially us. They say they do, but they bloody don't.'

Jeeter Kapoor was pulling out a stool, sitting down at the table opposite Robin, refilling Robin's glass.

'Be better for publishers if all our stock got bleedin' pulped.

Better if we all got closed down, replaced by one big book-chain branch that only sells new and shiny.'

Robin looked up at the globes of light, a line of them like planets. Felt that everybody in here was tuned in now, waiting for him to say something. Somebody started to clap, and it got taken up. Somebody patted him on the back.

'Finish the bottle, Robin,' Gwenda said. 'On the house.' She looked around, meeting eyes. 'Well, he is, isn't he?'

'What?'

'Starting to sound like one of us.'

Robin glanced from face to face, unsure whether they were winding him up. He heard a throaty laugh, turned and met the eyes of Connie Wilby, a comfortably heavy, elderly woman with a shop in Lion Street. She lit a cigar, the smoke drifting into the inglenook beside her.

'We started asking customers if anything had gone wrong with their e-book readers. Or if they'd been accidentally broken or dropped in the bath. And could they pass them onto us, in exchange for free real books. And we put them all together and we all brought hammers one market day and battered the guts out of them. An e-book massacre. Great fun. Great therapy. Luddites? We're not Luddites, Mr Thorogood, we're bloody aesthetes. Four bookshops shut down last year, replaced by shoe shops and frock shops and number five – but for you – would be a bloody nail bar.'

Gareth Nunne sank some beer.

'You smell it in the air sometimes, boy.'

He burped. Robin looked at him. All he could smell was the rich smoke in the air around Connie Wilby. The smell of old pubs. She pulled from her pulpy lips the slender cigar she was puffing in blatant contravention of the law of the land, and gave Robin this lavish smoke-wreathed smile.

'Never been banned in the Kingdom of Hay, Mr Thorogood.'

'The beginnings of decay,' Gareth Nunne said,

'Huh?'

'What you can smell.'

'We gotta stop it,' Robin said. 'We gotta *fight*!'

His fist in the air like freaking Che Guevara. He was halfway smashed. His head sang, the yellow lamps were fused into a sweating necklace of light and somebody was talking about a drowned old man, a floater in a waterfall.

'And that was Peter Rector? Thought he was dead and gone years back. Peter Rector out at Cusop? All these years?'

'Gone now. Peter bloody Rector.'

Robin saw Gwyn Arthur Jones coming in, dipping his head under the hanging lantern, silently taking a seat at Connie Wilby's table. Taking out a pipe and tobacco, saying nothing.

'You got any Lord Madoc novels in your shop, Robin?' Gore Turrell said, an arm around Gwenda's waist.

'Dozen, maybe.'

'Consider them sold.'

'Naw... no way. You fixed our sign.'

'It was an honour,' Gore said.

Robin felt his eyes fill up, struggled to his feet.

'Think I could use some air.'

30

Blowtorch

So, ok, he was not *exactly* smashed, but far from sober, he'd admit that. No fit state to drive and that truly was a problem, the truck being their only vehicle. No way he was getting pulled over, losing his licence for at least a year.

So getting home tonight – not a prospect.

But, Jesus, there were times he might've cared more.

It was nearing midnight, a waxing moon and stars on show – not much light pollution from Hay, no traffic, no people. When Gwenda's bar had closed and his drinking companions had gone home, Robin had walked the empty sloping streets, up and down stone steps, across cobbles, for over an hour, intent on clearing his head.

But his head had only filled up with the town. Starting with the Gothic clock tower, starlit, moonlicked, a fairytale touch like out of the Pied Piper of Hamelin. Otherness.

He limped away from it, up a steep street to where the road divided, the junction watched over by the small statue in the apex of a building. He now knew this was Henry, first of the Tudor kings who'd passed this way after landing in West Wales, en route to his destiny.

More narrow streets, more hanging signs, and the next thing was the Buttermarket, like a Greek temple, with its locked iron gate. And then the sign which said *Bear Street*, bringing to mind an old photo he'd seen in one of the history books of a poor dancing bear brought into Hay as entertainment on market day.

The bear began a fractured dance, like in an old silent movie shot against stone walls, streetlights and the obsidian mirrors of darkened windows. Robin backed away, half closing his eyes, the town and its isolated lights breaking down into blown-up pixels of colour.

He stood his stick against a wall, opening out his hands, letting himself dissolve into the pattern. Trembling in that emotional place where, if things were good, your senses could sometimes soar. Nothing to do with Betty's condition, this was a painter's thing, beginning with an intense desire to discover, translate, *interpret*.

Feeling yourself into a place. He'd known it in the country-side, at dawn and twilight, but never in a town before. Couldn't afford to paint it like Hockney did in Yorkshire, using several canvases fitted together, so he'd make do with a single sheet of white-primed hardboard on which images would be overlapping, details of Hay coalescing or superimposed one over the other. One glance, and you'd take in the whole town, sublimi-nally. The town on a hillside, streets which had seemed parallel but in fact curled, one into another. He'd looked at them on a large-scale map and seen that the centre of the town actually formed a heart-shape, roadways like veins wound around it.

He followed a wall to the market square, directly under the jagged cliff-face of the castle, and it was here that the twinge had taken him, curling around his spine. Unable to move until it began to fade.

But it was in these moments of ebbing pain that his vision had begun to burn again, only so much more fiercely, like a blowtorch stripping everything before it, whole centuries crum-bling away like worn stucco and he was close to crying aloud in this kind of atavistic ecstasy, as if the hours he'd spent in Gwenda's bar had been a kind of initiation and now the town itself was admitting him.

Into its heart, the heart of Hay.

Was this possible?

Back under the clock tower, quivering inside, Robin sat on the edge of the terrace below the Granary. To his right Barclay's Bank, to the left Golesworthy's country outfitters. The bank was the only representation on this street of a national business. There were two or three other banks in Hay, but no chain stores that Robin had seen so far. A medieval town holding out against empty progress.

Betty said calmly in his ear, 'Do you know how much you've had?'

'Too much.' Robin abandoned his original plan to say it was wine from a Welsh vineyard, how potent was that gonna be? 'And I don't see any cabs. And if I did, we'd have to get another cab in the morning to collect the truck. I fucked up.'

'No kidding.'

'In our position, do you turn your back on people who wanna make you feel welcome? Bottom line is I now know a whole bunch of booksellers.'

'Better get a room somewhere, hadn't you? Book into a hotel or a B and B.'

'What?' Robin changed ears with the phone. 'No *way*.'

'*Yes.*'

'You know what all that costs in this town in high summer?'

'It doesn't matter. Listen—'

'There's a coat and some old sacks in the truck.'

'You can't sleep in the bloody truck!'

'No, but I can take the stuff into Back Fold. Roll up some of the old curtains, make a pillow.'

Pause.

'Not a good idea.'

'It's not cold, Betty. And this is my fault. And, like... why would it not be a good idea?'

'Because I'm not there. And you have injuries. And you're pissed.'

'Just beyond passing a breath test is all. My senses are all functioning. In overdrive. I walk fine... fine as I ever walk. Not gonna be a prisoner of this. I can fit a key in a door. And the point is I have to do it. It's right.'

'You don't have to do it at all. We've sold the bungalow.'

'Huh?'

'They came to look, they made an offer.'

'Jeez! How much?'

'Even first time round, it wasn't a bad offer, but—'

'Did they confirm it? Did they sign?'

'I said we'd think about it and they—'

'There'll be others. Nobody takes the first offer. If we hold out, we can maybe get closer to the asking price.'

'They came back not long afterwards with an offer of very nearly the asking price. Did you get that?'

'I...' He clamped the phone hard to his ear. 'You're saying...?'

'It's a done deal, Robin.'

'Holy shit!' His head had gone back, his eyes raised to the clock tower, and its face was a warm moon. 'We're... we're saved! We can make this business *sing*.'

'So book into a hotel,' Betty said.

He felt tears on his cheeks, like the dew of a new morning. It was turning around. All in a few hours. Home. They were home.

'I love you, Bets.'

'Listen,' Betty said. 'The Black Lion do rooms. They're probably still open. Or the Swan. Celebrate. Get a good meal or something.'

'I don't have enough money.'

'Do it on the bloody debit card! What this has done, it's bought us some time, Robin. We have time to get it right. *Please.*'

Robin was walking up the street in a giddy euphoria, up from the clock tower towards the market square. An eccentric arrangement, the clock tower actually below the market square so if you wanted to know the time you had to go seek it out, peer around corners.

Weird. He loved it.

'Listen,' he said. 'Did I tell you we got the sign up? Not easily, but when you need help, these guys just appear.' Not telling her what nearly happened; it hadn't happened, and it was his fault anyway. 'So how about we open tomorrow? Just open the doors, see what happens? Knowing that when the deal goes through we can buy a pile more books.'

'Yes. Whatever. Meanwhile, book into a hotel, Robin. This is about letting go. Get a good night's sleep, come home early tomorrow and I'll be ready to go back with you, and we'll talk on the way.'

'OK.'

He walked raggedly under the statue of Henry Tudor, to the castle wall. Beyond it, the remains of the medieval keep was gazing jaggedly down from the highest point of the town. The hole where the portcullis had been was crudely boarded up. Like a wooden gag. He looked away, carried on past the war memorial, along Castle Street, where several shop windows had posters opposing plans by some supermarket giant to move into Hay, wipe out all the small food stores, clothing retailers, household electrical dealers. Bring in the big and the bright and the shiny and the new, piss all over the old.

Robin had a blurred memory of Connie Wilby, who'd spent the whole night smoking cigars in contravention of the law of the land, taking him on one side, telling him why *big* and *bright* and *shiny* and *new* were words with no meaning for the Hay economy.

'You still there, Robin?'

'Yeah, I'm here.'

And he *was* here. Standing in the entrance to the alleyway called Back Fold.

'Get some sleep,' Betty said.

Hay Castle was lofting up in front of him, moonlight-vast, all of its ages fused together by the shadows, the chimney stacks like the backs of hands turned black.

Different place at night, nobody else living this end of the alley. Jeeter Kapoor was with his wife and kids in a ground floor apartment in one of the new stone-clad blocks across town.

Robin carried this old UK air-force greatcoat he'd brought from the truck, the coat so stiff with age and disuse it almost stood up by itself when he put it down, along with three cleanish hessian sacks and a flashlight, to the door of Thorogood Pagan Books. He leaned his stick against the door to fumble for his keys, and there was a sour smell all over him, and...

'Brekkin in, is it?'

Hell, she could move silently when she wasn't whistling.

He held up the key and Mrs Villiers backed away from it like it was some kind of talisman for warding off old drunks.

'En't dead yet then?'

'I'm sorry?'

Mrs Villiers did this kind of liquid chuckle. She had these small, round, monkey eyes.

'Thought you was, boy. Thought you was dead.'

'Huh?'

He saw a screw-top wine bottle poking out of a pocket of the long, frayed coat.

'Cherry don't do it n'more.'

'No? Mrs Villiers...' Robin tried to focus on her through the fumes. 'Who we talking about? Who did you think I was?'

'Put her up at my place one night, for free. I sez don't you go there no'more, see.'

'Whadda you mean? Who?'

'I sez one day you won't come out.'

'Who?'

'And her di'n't. Was it you? Was it *you*?'

'Listen,' Robin said, 'whatever you're saying, I think I need to know this stuff. Talk to me.'

But she'd gone. She moved fast, Mrs Villiers. He stood staring down the alley until the whistling came curling around the chimneys like ribbon.

He carried the stiff greatcoat and the sacks up the wooden stairs to the sitting room. There wouldn't be room to eat in the back kitchen downstairs, so they'd brought a pine table and some chairs up here. What they hadn't brought – one for the removal van – was the sofa. *The* sofa. Just like they only had one bed. The only two items you sleep on, and they'd be the last to arrive.

He went through to the first of the two bedrooms, divided by a blockboard partition which he was sure would disintegrate like a wall in an air raid if you lightly applied a shoulder to it. Not a stick of furniture in either room. The low rooms up here, you could tell they must once have been no more than a loft, maybe a hay store for animals waiting to die.

Back Fold ran with blood. Echoed to the sounds of bellowing.

Robin inhaled massively. He couldn't stay here.

But, more than that, he couldn't leave. They had... hell, they had a business to start tomorrow.

Would have to be the bathroom, with its shaving bar which lit up mauve when you pulled the string. No mirror, only a grey-white wall, a basin and a lavatory. The bath ran the length of the opposite wall under a small, square window the one where, if you put your head out, you could see the castle.

He went back to the living room, pulled all the flat cushions off the dining chairs. Back in the bathroom, he tossed them in the bath with the sacks spread on top then shambled over to the lavatory and took a piss, standing to the side so the shaving light would show him where the bowl was. A bronchitic cough when he pulled the chain – or maybe that was him – before the water came coughing out.

He eased off his jacket and rolled it up as a pillow, trapping it under an arm. Unlaced his trainers but kept them on, as he pulled the string to douse the depressing mauve light, before climbing unsteadily into the cushioned bath.

Standing there, putting off the moment when he'd have to try and lie down. Turning around to lean over to the small square window and its view of the castle's curtain wall and the sloping roofs rammed into it, to a stripe of sky and moonlight like crumpled chocolate-foil left on the stone. Behind it, the castle itself, invisible in the night, maybe dreaming of the old nights of blood and fire.

He turned away from the window, sinking down, in hurting stages, into the bath. Dragging the greatcoat over himself, like a rough sleeper in a high-street doorway, folding his body on to the side that gave him least pain – a close contest at the best of times.

Telling himself he'd had worse beds. Would've handled this no problem back in the day, when women eyed him in the street, with his long, dark pagan hair and his wide pagan grin made dangerous by a black stubble which now featured sad, pointillist dabs of white. Looking like the warrior he could never be.

He contrived to fold himself into the enamel bunk, drawing up his knees. Thinking himself back into the warm, pixillated streets and the soft lights. Everything bathed in a pinkening mist as he fell thickly asleep.

Whenever he awoke in pain, he shifted a little and sank back into the sleeping town letting go like a spirit in warm air with no reassembled bones to slow him up. Down Back Fold into Castle Street, and then the market square, under the cliff face of the castle, down to the clock tower, into High Town, Lion Street, Bear Street, history unfolding, the pink deepening until the heart of the town, blood-red now, became his own heart, swollen, throbbing and twisted, as if his chest had been opened, his ribs parted to let someone's fingers start feeling in between the arteries, gripping the organ like a soft orange and... *ah no...*

He awoke fully this time, gasps torn out of him like rags, as he heaved himself up too quickly in the clammy bath, his face creamed with sweat, his nose and throat thick with mucus, a familiar agony jagging up his left leg as his eyes opened into cold early light, which...

... was not the early light. The high window was black as the bottom of an old grill pan. Nothing out there, no birds stirring. The only light in the glass was reflected from the room, and it was razored and sporadic, like fork-lightning.

Fearfully, Robin let his head turn to the wall above the metal basin, where the shaving bar, the one he'd extinguished with a tug on its cord, was sputtering like a dud firework.

It terrified him.

He rolled over the side of the bath. Lay jackknifed on the boarded floor, all the ruined bones grinding in his back and hips and groin. Looking up to see the monkey eyes between the chips of purple from the shaving light, and the crackly old voice coming out of the static amidst the electric spittle in the air.

Thought you was, boy. Thought you was dead.

31

Treats

TEN MINUTES OUT of Hay, Bliss's fingers softly drumming on the dash, they were in Talgarth, shelved into the base of the Black Mountains like some Alpine resort, only without the wealth. Main roads meeting here, new junctions, a bypass, but the satnav woman had sent them into the town.

And then out again by a side road, the lights dwindling and Annie's angular face withdrawing into shadow. Well, he knew she wasn't happy about this and, yeh, he was feeling bad about involving her, she had a career, status, reputation. In her place, he'd be playing it entirely by the book. Hugging the frigging book.

But it was already too late. They were given sixty yards warning of a narrow sharp left, and then the satnav woman was signing off. Tall trees either side and high wrought-iron gates hanging open. Annie stopped between them, looked at Bliss.

'Yeh, all right,' he said, 'I don't like it either.'

Annie said nothing, drove slowly, on full headlights, between the gates into a steep dirt track that became a tarmac driveway, curving just too perfectly up a tamed hill. The beams found wellingtonia and monkey puzzle trees, and three storeys of muted lights.

'Bugger me,' Bliss said. 'Who put this here?'

'The Victorians, it looks like.'

Could've been a hotel, but it evidently wasn't. Annie pulled into a forecourt under a pillared veranda as twin vaults of calm light were directed over them from up in the ivied walls. She switched off the engine.

'Not on the breadline, then, Claudia,' Bliss said, as his phone rang. '*Gerry.* What kept you?'

'Here's the score, Francis. Tamsin Winterson hasn't been in contact with Peterchurch since she was last on duty. Her best friend in the force, Emma Green, South Wye, hasn't heard from her since last weekend. And it seems you're the first to do a PNC check on that number. We're still trying to track Tamsin's phone.'

'Listen, Gerry, I'm here now, Talgarth, so I'll have a word with this woman. You wanna call Tamsin's parents? Who's in charge tonight?'

'Inspector Ford's here. I'll put him in the picture.'

'Tell him I'll ring him when I've finished here.' Bliss killed the call. 'So what now? If Tamsin never followed up that number, what did she do? Did she go shooting up to Rector's place? Did she confront this woman?'

'Don't go in hard,' Annie said, 'just to show you aren't impressed by the conspicuous wealth.'

On the forecourt, Bliss saw a grey Land Rover and a low, red car with four smoky rings on its driver's door: Audi Quattro.

This undoubtedly was the place, and she was in. He felt in his inside pocket for his wallet and his warrant card. Somewhere in the house, a dog barked gruffly.

'*Oh for—*'

No wallet. Wrong jacket. Everything he did, or thought he'd done, now, it was all check, check, check. If he forgot to check, he screwed up.

'Take mine.' Annie Howe unclipped her bag. 'Just make sure you cover up the picture when you flash it.'

'Thanks,' he said. 'Thanks, Annie.'

'And if you're not out in forty-five minutes...'

She put a hand on his arm. He couldn't see her face, didn't know if she was serious. When he tried for a smile, it felt like there were lead weights attached to the skin over his left eye.

* * *

The front door was up some steps, at the end of a porch the size of a small chapel, and the woman who opened it was younger than he'd expected.

'Sorry to bother you so late. DI Bliss, West Mercia CID. Are you Claudia Cornwell?'

Maybe not. She had curly hair and an emerald nose-stud. Also a Dobermann standing beside her, silent and watchful.

'Police? Is there a problem?'

Local accent.

'There might very well be a problem,' Bliss said. 'Is Ms Cornwell in?'

'If you wait there, I'll see.'

'Actually, she is.'

A wholly different woman's voice coming from behind him. A low, but not exactly hesitant voice from Off. He turned slowly until he could see her in the floodlights at the bottom of the steps.

Both of her. Bliss hissed, bent his head until the images coalesced. She was wearing a light tweed jacket, black jeans pushed into the expensive boots. Brown hair was pulled back and held together by one of those big crocodile clips.

'You did say police?'

'Sorry to bother you this time of night,' Bliss said, 'but I do need to ask you some questions.'

'No problem.' She came lightly up the steps. 'I've been out at a meeting. You're on your own?'

'My colleague's in the car.' Maybe the BMW helped. 'Nothing too contentious. Won't take long.'

'All right.' She glanced at Annie's ID and then moved past him into the house. 'This is Michelle, my nanny. Come through.'

Quite a big woman, though not fat. He followed her into an entrance hall less baroque than he'd feared, although the central staircase was impressive. Four pairs of wellies, adults and coloured ones for kids, were lined up behind the door.

'What did you say your name was?'

'Bliss. Francis Bliss.'

'Ah.' She turned, gave him a small and quite pleasant smile. 'Would you like some coffee?'

'Not just now, thanks.'

'It's all right, Michelle.'

The nanny nodded, moved away. The Dobermann stayed, still watching Bliss until she patted her thigh, said 'Prospero... come, Pros,' and the dog loped off behind her and didn't look back.

The room Claudia Cornwell led him into was plain and used-looking. Off-white walls, a cream rug on bare boards, a brass standard lamp, a drinks cabinet and a big, patched teddy bear on a lumpy, chintzy sofa.

'Do take a seat. A proper drink?'

'No thanks.'

'I won't tell anyone.'

'Alcohol does me head in this time of night.'

'Ah... of course.'

Like she understood. People like her always had to have understood, Bliss thought. He sat down next to the teddy bear.

'Plus, I'm in a bit of a hurry,' he said. 'The thing is... I believe you might've had dealings, tonight or this afternoon, with one of my colleagues.'

'I doubt it.' She looked amused. 'Always drive terribly carefully, Inspector, especially at night.'

'This is a young policewoman. Out of uniform.'

'So how would I know she was in the police?'

'Ms Cornwell...'

'I'm sorry. Where was this?'

'Cusop. Probably.'

'Cusop?'

'Near Hay-on-Wye. Close to the home of the late David Hambling. Or Peter Rector, as he was formerly known.'

Claudia Cornwell sat down, unbuttoned her tweed jacket,

looked steadily at Bliss from under eyebrows heavier and darker than her hair.

'Tell me, are you fully recovered now, Mr Bliss?'

Bliss said nothing, kept himself still. At least the lamp wasn't bright.

'And – if you don't mind my asking – what are you doing here? Are you allowed to operate in Dyfed-Powys territory?'

'You're not my Euro MP or something, are you?' Bliss said.

Claudia Cornwell laughed. It was annoyingly musical. Bliss waited. Maybe it was as well Annie had stayed in the car. Annie hated being wrong-footed, even more than he did.

'Sorry for that,' Ms Cornwell said. 'I'm a criminal barrister. We've never met – South Wales circuit, mainly – but I know quite a lot about you. Some of which I would have used with considerable relish were we to have faced one another at Worcester Crown court. As we surely would, had Victoria Buckland not changed her plea to guilty.'

'Jesus,' Bliss said. 'Vicky's brief?'

'Was to have been. I was quite looking forward to it. I so enjoy a challenge. Yes, the eleventh-hour change-of-plea was a very wise decision, but I'm sure we'd all have had a lovely time.'

'Would've been great,' Bliss said. 'Long as you didn't get her off on a techie.'

She looked into his left eye.

'Victoria's friends made quite a mess of you, didn't they?'

'I'm better than I look. And I'm guessing that's given you enough thinking time, Ms Cornwell.'

Claudia Cornwell rose and went to the drinks cabinet, took down a half-empty bottle of Laphroaig.

'Don't mind if *I* have one, do you? Calm my nerves at being grilled by an expert. Sorry – not trying to patronize you. What's the issue with your young policewoman?'

'PC Winterson. Tamsin.' Bliss watched her eyes. 'Lives not far from Cusop.'

'I doubt I've ever met her.'

'She's been assisting me, as a local girl, with an inquiry relating to Mr Rector's death.'

Claudia Cornwell unscrewed the bottle, releasing peat musk. Poured an inch of the whisky into a crystal glass and sat down.

'You want to keep this casual, I imagine?'

'Meaning what?'

'You're not on duty, are you? Obviously got your girlfriend in the car.'

Bliss said nothing.

'I promise you, you'll get far more out of me if I don't have to watch what I'm saying.'

'You're very savvy, Ms Cornwell.'

'I haven't done anything wrong, and I've never met PC Winterson. I'm merely trying to help you in the best way I can, Francis.'

'You haven't spoken to her on the phone?'

'No.'

'Or been aware of her trying to contact you?'

'No.'

'Or anyone from the police, in the context of Mr Rector.'

'No.'

'Ms Cornwell...'

'Call me Claudia, we're not in court. '

'Claudia, I'm here because Tamsin Winterson's missing. She wasn't on duty, and there might be quite an innocent explanation for this, but...'

'But as she's a serving police officer you're obviously concerned. So what are you asking?'

'I'm asking myself – and now you – if the absence of Tamsin Winterson could be in any way connected with the as-yet-unexplained death of Peter Rector. Of course, if Tamsin turns up at first light and says her car broke down miles from the nearest mobile signal, you may never hear from me again.'

'Yes, but, Francis...' A helpless smile '... why am I even being associated with the possible disappearance of your officer? I'm very sorry to hear about it, and I hope you find her safe and well, and yes, I did *know* Peter Rector, but—'

'Thing is, Claudia, you've been seen twice in the vicinity of Mr Rector's home. PC Winterson had been told you were there today and she was on her way to ask you a few questions. On the basis that it's possible you were the last person to see Mr Rector alive.'

'When was this?'

'When you appeared to be delivering certain… provisions?'

Claudia Cornwell sat back, cradling her whisky glass and then shaking her head wearily.

'All right. Yes. That might, indeed, have been me. If I'd been to London, I'd bring Peter occasional treats from Fortnum and Mason. Items not so easy to obtain in this part of Wales. Or possibly any part of Wales. Or… his part of England. I was very fond of him.'

'When you say treats… would they perhaps include items *not* available from Fortnum and Mason?'

'You mean cannabis?'

That was bloody quick.

She said, 'He wasn't an habitual user, and it was entirely for personal use. It played a very occasional role in his work.'

'With respect, Claudia, that's what they all say.'

She met his gaze.

'Oh, I don't think they do.'

Bugger. You didn't just say things fatuously, for effect, to a barrister.

'You could well be right,' Bliss said. 'I'm not exactly an expert on his other activities. Not yet, anyway. How long have you known him?'

'Years and years. I was brought up not far from here, and he was a friend of my parents.'

'You don't sound local.'

'Went away to various schools and then Oxford. I can sound alarmingly local when I want to.'

'Why were you standing on the castle mound at Cusop late this afternoon?'

'It's… Look, it's somewhere we used to walk, Peter and I. I obviously couldn't get into his house, so it's where I went to say goodbye. I've what looks like a longish case coming off towards the latter part of next week, so may not be able to attend his funeral.'

Bliss nodded. He wondered what form her goodbye had taken.

'Actually, I didn't stay long,' she said. 'To be quite honest, it didn't feel comfortable.'

'In what way?'

Claudia sat up, easing her jacket off.

'Do you really want to go into all this?'

She tossed the jacket on to the sofa between Bliss and the teddy. She was wearing a white silk shirt, two or three buttons undone, revealing a pendant, a gold disc with some kind of symbol on it. Might be something like a St Christopher medal. Or might not.

Bliss looked at his watch. He had half an hour before Annie might start getting restive.

'You know what, Claudia?' he said. 'I think I need to.'

32

Plea of insanity

BLISS CALLED Robert Winterson from Annie's car, parked on a double-yellow in the centre of Talgarth.

'The police are here,' Winterson said. 'We're going over it all again. Nothing you got to tell me?'

'Afraid not, Robert. I've spoken to the woman Tamsin told Kelly she was looking for. Drew a blank. She didn't do anything to check the car registration number she had from Kelly. I'm sorry. And listen, Robert, if they want to search the farmhouse and your house, don't be offended. It's a formality they've gorra observe.'

'They done that already. They wanted to know everywhere she went. Well we din't know – she used to go running on her days off, to keep fit, up in the hills, everywhere. To keep fit for her job.'

Something choked off in the background suggested Tamsin's mother had clocked the expression on Robert's face. Bliss bent his head, his right hand wrapped tightly in the unfastened seat belt. No worse side of the job than this.

'And I'll stay very much in touch,' he said. 'Anything you think of, please come back to me at any time.'

'Mr Bliss, my mother would like a word.'

'Well, I do need to… Of course.'

Bliss squeezed his eyes shut.

'Inspector Bliss…'

'Mrs Winterson, can I just assure you—'

Mrs Winterson said, 'I just wanted… I just *need* to ask you if you can tell me if she's… do you *know* of any actual danger she might be in?'

'No, I don't. Not at all. And I… I know it's daft to say this, but I don't want you to worry, 'cos we're gonna find her.'

'She was very excited to be working with you,' Mrs Winterson said.

Bliss's head was hammering.

He said to Annie, 'I'm sorry. I'm really sorry for gerrin' you involved in this.'

'You'll need to go in and make a report.'

'I know. But how much is gonna be *in* it?'

He pulled down the sun visor against the sodium street-lights and told her everything this time, all the details. It took about twenty minutes. Annie sat back, letting down the side window.

'Not exactly what I wanted to hear,' Annie said. 'And there's hardly time for a considered opinion. But my feeling is that if you went babbling on about an old woman from Hardwicke and… satanic neo-Nazis… well, I know how I'd react.'

'Yeh. What I thought.'

'Francis, I'm trying to *help*. People like Mrs Watkins get paid – albeit a pittance – to listen sympathetically to this kind of drivel. We get paid to lend half an ear on the occasions when someone's trying to enter a plea of insanity.'

Bliss nodded. Annie started the engine.

'My feeling is that it would only complicate the search for Winterson by diverting attention and manpower from where they need to be focused.'

'I'm forced to agree.'

'There's no evidence that Winterson's disappearance is in any way linked to the non-suspicious drowning of a man in his nineties. You should have walked away from that before you did, but I understand why you didn't. And you obviously shouldn't be back at work, but that's a side issue. Right now, someone needs to find Winterson's car, her phone, her friends, boyfriends. Search her parents' farm outside and in, and… well, you don't need me to tell you.'

Bliss nodded. Rich Ford, the uniform inspector, rang.

'Jesus, Francis, she's a relation. Well… her dad's the wife's cousin, kind of. She couldn't be hiding something from the family, I suppose? Personal problems?'

'She *could*, but I don't see it, Rich. She'd promised to babysit for her brother, and she struck me as a conscientious kid.'

'All right,' Rich said. 'Let's not bugger about. You can leave these situations too long. We need to put the troops in. I'm going to have to wake somebody up, talk to headquarters.'

'I only wish I could think of something more expedient.'

'This bloody drowning, Francis…'

Bliss took a breath.

'What that comes down to is that when she was a kid, her and her mates used to make up stories about Rector. He was eccentric, he was known to have an interest in the occult and he knew about herbs and fixing dislocated bones. Tamsin thought the circumstances of his death might be worth a second look. It was her own backyard. Talk to Kelly James, she'll tell you what she told me. She took down the registration of a car belonging to a woman Tamsin thought might be the last person to see Rector alive. Tamsin said she'd look into it, and that seems to be the last anybody heard from her. I've talked to the woman. The woman says she's never seen her.'

'And this is a barrister? Has she prosecuted for us?'

'Works Wales, but she was gonna defend Buckland.'

'Must be good. Or desperate.'

'There you go.'

'Looked at from another angle,' Rich said, 'what we have is a missing girl in the countryside. Day off, out of uniform, all kinds of bloody animals out there these days. And she's a copper. She'll know how we're likely to react if she goes off the map, and how much that costs.'

'Yeh.'

'You'd better come in, Francis. We're going to need some paperwork from you.'

Annie flicked him a glance.

'Good. I wouldn't risk embroidering it any further.'

She was driving back through Hay, all quiet lights, empty streets. Midnightish.

'We think we know what's going on out there,' Bliss said. 'Could be we don't know the half of it. You ever think that?'

'No, I don't. Things we used to consider bizarre, not much of it gets concealed any more. There's even some kind of grouping of pagan police, for heaven's sake. No Witchcraft Act any more. Less contentious than being in the Freemasons.'

'Like your dad?'

Charlie Howe, one-time head of Hereford CID. Disgraced. Annie didn't even reply.

'As it happens, Claudia said she could tell me the names of two senior police officers who were into it,' Bliss said, 'and at least four who're witches. Though she talked about witches in slightly superior tones, like coppers talk about traffic wardens. Norra lorra mental training required, just turn up, light a fire and get your kit off.'

'And she believes it actually *works*? A famously intelligent woman. QC-material?'

'She said it works on its own terms, whatever that means. She says it's a wonderful discipline. If you're the type of person for whom the physical world is, as she puts it, insufficient for a rounded life.'

'You could say that of the average churchgoer.'

Which Annie wasn't. Calling her a sceptical agnostic would be coming down on the liberal side.

'Difference is,' Bliss said, 'that your average churchgoer is told to put his faith in God and stay out of the boiler room. People like Peter Rector and Claudia... if there *are* other spiritual levels, they want to know how it all works. The hidden mechanics. Where they can fit their spanners.'

He could still hear Claudia's voice, very reasonable, explanatory, like she was addressing the jury as equals. Saying she was quite sure there were lots of things she didn't know about Peter Rector but she could assure Bliss that all her dealings with him had shown him to be, essentially, a lovely man who'd *harm none*, as the witches said.

Annie drove past the big car park, down and over the bridge into England.

'Strange,' she said. 'I'd taken against that woman from the first time I met her.'

'Claudia? I thought—'

'Mrs Watkins. Women priests – that whole thing made me angry. Women who wanted to be priests, I thought we were bigger than that crap. But the night when you were taken to hospital she was unexpectedly helpful, and I realized she was getting her head around aspects of human behaviour that were a complete mystery to me.'

'Different side of the brain, Annie.'

He let his head fall back, under the engine hum. A long night with too many bright lights. They were right. He shouldn't be back. Should've stayed at home with a bunch of dvds. If something had happened to Tamsin Winterson because of something he'd failed to process, how would he live with that when they put him out to grass at barely forty?

'Coming to say goodbye to Rector,' Annie said. 'That doesn't sound convincing to me. What was she *really* doing there?'

'She wasn't exactly being surreptitious about it. Driving openly to Cusop in a bright red car, putting herself very visibly on top of an earthmound.'

'Do we know she was actually alone there? How many students did Rector have?'

'Five or six she knows of.'

'So he was running courses at Cusop for fee-paying acolytes. She provide you with a list?'

'Didn't ask for one. No real reason to. But, like she said, she only knew what Rector wanted her to know, so there could be more of them. Which would explain what Tamsin picked up about what locals were calling the coven. And also why there's no temple. He wasn't performing rituals, he was conducting tutorials.'

Annie turned right again, for the Golden Valley and Hereford.

'Francis, I really can't take a chance on being seen taking you into Gaol Street. We'll have to go via Marden and you can pick up your car. Will you be all right with that?'

'Sure. I just want Tamsin found and all this over with.'

'Try and sleep,' Annie said.

'You're going back to Malvern?'

'I can stay at your place, if you like.'

'You're better going back to Malvern. Keep your head down. Sorry about the weekend.'

'You're not talking to Kirsty here, Francis.'

Bliss smiled, eyes closed, reminded of why, even if it was strongly discouraged, a relationship with another serving officer could work well. Whenever he'd buggered up a weekend for Kirsty she wouldn't speak to him till the next one was looming.

Another twenty minutes to the house at Marden, to pick up his car. The BMW growled quietly.

The countryside around them was dark and loaded. Nobody phoned to say Tamsin Winterson was OK.

Part Four

… artists, poets and visionaries
have found this place a place
where 'Prayer is valid'… where
the veil between the visible
world and the invisible has worn
diaphanously thin.

Fr. RICHARD WILLIAMS,
Parish priest, Hay-on-Wye
on Capel-y-ffin

33

The N-word

MERRILY WAS THINKING that if she hadn't been expecting Martin Longbeach, she wouldn't have recognized him, when he arrived around eight a.m.

'I know,' he said. 'But I'm fine, I really am.' He handed her an oil bill and a subscription copy of *Private Eye*. 'Postwoman gave me your mail at the gate. Saw the dog collar, I suppose. Safe pair of hands.'

His laugh was like a knife scraping a plate.

'Of course they are,' Merrily said at the vicarage door.

Hoping the unease didn't show. Even his hands looked pale. She remembered when he was tubby and camp in an innocent comedy-vicar way, screening shrewdness. He must have lost two stones, maybe more. His monkish face had acquired lines, his eyes looked like bruises as she led him into the vicarage kitchen, Ethel watching from her spare basket.

'Not allergic to cats are you, Martin? She'll be wandering over here when I'm out. Likes to hang out with people.'

Martin Longbeach shook his head, bent to scratch Ethel under the jaw. Ethel craned her neck into his finger.

'If you think this is not going to work,' Martin said to the cat, not looking up, 'I'll go quietly. I really don't deserve friends like you.'

'Now don't start that,' Merrily said. 'Please.'

Well, they weren't exactly friends. Met him perhaps four times, knew more about what he'd done since his breakdown than anything from his earlier life.

'Took a holiday last week,' Martin said. 'Except it wasn't.'

'I know quite a bit about holidays that aren't. Still, not been great weather, has it?'

'Perfect for my needs. I took a cottage for a week, in Mid Wales. A mile from Pennant Melangell, the shrine of St Melangell. Every day, I walked to the church.'

'Always useful, remote churches,' Merrily said, remembering. 'That primitive, Celtic... thing.'

'Barefoot.'

'Oh.'

'Every day.' The scrapy laugh again. 'Fasted for five of them. Nothing except spring water.'

God...

'Do you think that was, erm, a good thing, Martin, on your own? That is, presumably...'

'Oh, quite alone, yes. That was the idea. Giving Him an opportunity to make away with me. See? In the end, I was forced to realize it was all self-pity, Merrily.'

'Were you?'

'The great revelation, by the grace of God and a dozen big bottles of Aqua Pura. You can't die of self-pity, I don't think. Rage is something different, but equally despicable.'

Don't. Just *don't*, Martin.

'Why don't I show you your room?' Merrily said.

She'd prepared one on the western side, from which the church was not visible, only the bottom end of Church Street where it sloped to the river bridge. A small room. Jane had painted the walls pale blue, the ceiling midnight blue. A copper oil lamp, electrified, stood on an upturned painted chest by the bedside, and the wardrobe was light pine.

'Calms the fevered brow just to be here, Merrily.'

'Bathroom next door. I'll show you how things work in the kitchen later. And there's an iMac in the scullery. You're OK with that?'

'Perfectly.' He looked down at the duvet cover, an old one, much-washed, but the only alternative was pink. 'We didn't even live together, you know.'

'Look, Martin, you don't—'

'It was a celibate relationship. *Technically* celibate. Not so much because Daniel had HIV, but because the spiritual side of it had become more important for both of us. Or so I told myself. We prayed together every day. And because it's no longer an automatic death sentence, his death was... it knocked me bloody sideways, Merrily. I felt we'd been unjustly punished... *for trying*. You know? Trying to be good Christians – in everyone's eyes. This is quite a conservative area in some ways. Well... most ways, really.'

'Where are you from originally, Martin?'

'Me? Cardiff.' Pronouncing it like a native, *Cairdiff*. 'So, thinking you're doing your best to be virtuous, trying to be a good Christian – sin of pride, do you think?'

'Not necessarily, no.'

'When Daniel died... I just gave in to an all-consuming rage. You'll've heard some of it, anyway. I think you need to hear it all from me, really, before you—'

'No!'

Didn't need to, didn't want to. Was that wrong, unfeeling?

'Martin,' she said desperately, 'can I ask your advice? Not being patronizing or anything, I do actually need help. This...' She took from her jeans the postcard of Hereford Cathedral from Sylvia Merchant. 'This is something that also relates to bereavement. In, perhaps, a potentially... quite negative way.'

She read the message on the card, explained its background. Standing in the window, from which you could see Lol's cottage.

'These women,' he said. 'I'm assuming a long-term relationship?'

'Though I don't think they lived together until she retired. And there's no certainty that it was anything more than companionship. But... that's not my business.'

'Boss and secretary,' Martin said.

'A long, working relationship. I was thinking two desks in the same office, twin beds. Continuity.'

'In Victorian times,' Martin said, 'some wealthy women – and some not so wealthy – would have a personal maid. To cater for *all* their needs.'

'So I gather.'

'But what did she want from you?'

'I don't know. Thought I did. She went directly to Sophie, saying that she'd been seeing her companion after death. I thought she wanted some reassurance there was nothing unhealthy or worrying about that. And that Ms Nott, having provided evidence of an element of survival, could now go on to find… you know, eternal rest? Not quite the case. Apparently.'

'Did she ask you to try and stop it happening?'

'Thinking back, she didn't ask me anything. She just reported it. She apparently wanted advice. I played it by ear. As you do.'

'And when she says *we…*' Martin waved the card '… I presume she means the two of them.'

'She's either… well, there are several possibilities. She's deluded… she's pretending, she wants *me* to think Ms Nott might still be around, or…'

'Or Ms Nott *is* around,' Martin said.

'Yes.'

'Or the other possibility, Merrily, is that she *wants* Ms Nott with her, and by visualizing her there…'

'There's a word for that. I think it's the N-word.'

'I believe it is, yes.'

'But… even if we're prepared to believe that a retired businesswoman is ready to give in to what she may not realize are necromantic urges to keep a dead person on a lead…'

'She's a regular churchgoer, you say?'

'A cathedral-goer.'

'Yes.' Martin nodded. 'I suppose the worst this reveals is a lamentable ignorance of the rules of exorcism and deliverance.'

'I think…' Merrily put a finger over her lips then took it away '… a deliberate misinterpretation.'

'Which prayers did you use?'

'Well… nothing that might sound ritualistic. I busked it. As cosy as I could make it, without insulting her intelligence. Ms Merchant is not a particularly cosy person.'

Martin lowered himself to a corner of the bed.

'I don't know what to say. I mean, are you consulting me as a recently bereaved person… or as a homosexual?'

'As a priest, of course, with a knowledge of exorcism.'

Martin smiled. He'd done the course with Huw, even if he'd probably never been called on to do the business.

'There's always been gay clergy,' Merrily said. 'Did anybody make a thing of it? It's a point Huw Owen makes. As soon as you turn something into an Issue, everyone starts to overreact. The Church never handles Issues very well.'

'Men like me,' Martin said, 'we don't help. I'm a stupid, emotional person, Merrily, which I hope is nothing to do with being gay. Rendered temporarily insane by grief and rage, I… got drunk.'

Merrily nodded, resigned to it now.

'On wine. On communion wine – quite deliberately – in the vestry. Helplessly, mindlessly, angrily drunk.'

'I didn't know that bit.'

'Only the next bit, eh? In the chancel.'

'Only, as you say, the, er… next bit. Some of it. Possibly.' She looked beyond him out of the window, down the street in search of inspiration. 'What can I say? We've all screamed at God, in the night. And I think… I suspect… I know… priests scream louder.'

'Bit more than a scream, Merrily.'

Could be the hardest shrug she'd ever forced. She heard the phone ringing, the extension in her bedroom two doors away.

'Get that… please,' Martin said.

She shook her head. Let the machine pick it up. No more excuses for avoiding this.

'A priest having a breakdown,' she said, 'losing his faith, it's never pretty, is it? You didn't make a secret of it. You confessed all to Canon Jeffrey Alexander, the diocesan school-sneak. I'm tempted to think that was entirely deliberate. You sought him out, the way, erm, Christ sought out, erm, Judas Iscariot. Not that I'm...'

'No more lives left, Merrily. That's the bottom line.'

'Anyway,' she said. 'The other reason I'm telling you about Ms Merchant and Ms Nott is that, as that card warns, she's planning to come back.'

'And not, I imagine, on her own.'

'And you'll be here.'

'Well,' Martin said. 'There's challenging, isn't it? You want to be involved?'

'If I happen to be around.'

'Take them on together, is it?'

'Won't feel outnumbered, will she?'

Both of them giggling creepily, like maladjusted kids in front of a juvenile panel.

'I'll bring my cases up, then.' Martin Longbeach opened the bedroom door, then stopped. 'You know that feeling of being on the brink of madness you get sometimes in this job?'

'All too well.'

'I used almost to like that,' Martin said. 'Once. Now go and check your answering machine. It's not going to be for me.'

It was Huw Owen, who'd tried to reach her at Lol's, left a message on both machines.

'Two of the trainees had to leave early, so we wound up the course last night. Don't suppose you can do Capel this morning, by any chance? Around eleven at the little church? Feller I'd like you to meet. All a bit heavier than I'd figured, lass. Let me know, anyroad.'

Couldn't see why not. She called him back. He wasn't there. She left a confirming message on his machine.

So. That was it, then. She'd be out of here sooner than she'd figured. By the time she was back from Capel-y-ffin, Martin Longbeach would be the Vicar of Ledwardine.

Loose ends? She switched on the computer to check if there were any files she needed to email to the laptop, noting that the latest bookmarked reference was the most recent website for OSIS – the Order of the Sun in Shadow.

The site was called Dark Orb. She'd scanned it once and found it all so lurid and extreme – *a new aeon dawns in a sky of glistening blood* – that she'd wondered if it wasn't all an elaborate joke.

Anyway… not the best night-time reading for a paranoid priest. She wiped it.

34

Niceties

Acting-DCI Brent said, 'You don't look well, Francis.'

The Renault Clio was at the bottom end of the car park where the spaces were marked out for coaches. The Clio was old and scratched and forlorn. Bliss felt as close to tears as when his Irish gran died.

'Long night,' he said.

He coughed, turning away, looking blankly across the car park to the recycling bins. The sky was mercilessly white. He'd snatched just two hours' sleep in his car and by the time he was back, *this* had happened, changing everything.

Hardening it up. No longer the possibility of a night with a boyfriend nobody had known about.

'Her phone was in the side pocket,' Brent said. 'Dowell's got it. Not revealing much, last I heard. When she's finished, she can go to Cusop with you. As you seem to know your way around.'

Bliss said nothing.

Iain Brent, PhD. *Ph frigging D.* Smooth-skinned, light-haired, gym-toned. Five or six years younger than Bliss, probably younger than Annie Howe. Brent thought he was clever, on account of all the certificates saying he was. Pretty soon it would be like the army, highly educated twenty-two-year-olds from some cop-Sandhurst starting out with the rank of inspector. That would be the day he quit.

'Some issues we'll need to discuss, Francis,' Brent said. 'But not now. We still need to find out exactly where Winterson's been, who she's spoken to in the last couple of days. Can't afford to skimp on the basics.'

The basics. Yeh, you could probably trust Bliss with the basics.

'If you think it'll help attending the briefing, you can do that first,' Brent said.

Twat.

Hay police station was small and grey and stuffed down a back street, no more than a couple of minutes' walk from England. Too small and not enough parking space for an operation on this scale, so Dyfed-Powys had fixed it for them to use the Hay Community Centre, also grey and even closer to England. Bigger, though, with chairs and tables for the incident room and a field alongside.

DCI Brent would be based here. Just in case this turned into a murder inquiry. Just in case, with the car being found in Hay, the Dyfed-Powys cops from Brecon tried to muscle in, grab too much of the action.

'We need to talk to all known friends and relatives of Tamsin,' Brent said to the assembly. 'In this case, unusually, we don't have far to look. Who were her best friends in the police? And, before that, at college. I'm sure some of you will have ideas. The situation may change but, for the present, Inspector Ford's our office manager. So let's keep him, and his assistant, Alison, very busy.'

Extra computers were being carried in. The bar was opened for coffee. Outside, the troops were gathering. No smiles, no black humour.

'Next briefing at twelve,' Brent said. 'Unless there's a development that alters things.'

Bliss was hovering outside, waiting for Karen Dowell, when the first TV people arrived, the reporter and cameraman in separate cars. The reporter came over.

'Excuse me, are you with...?'

'*Liverpool Daily Post,*' Bliss said.

Brent came out of the community centre with DI Watts, from Dyfed-Powys, who were being friendly, under the terms of the cross-border crime initiative. Happy to let them use Hay as an operational base, but Brent wouldn't be happy until it was clear that he'd be SIO, no matter how far into Wales this went.

Watts was older and balder and heavier than Brent. The TV cameraman shot them, as Karen Dowell wandered over to Bliss.

'DCI's on unfamiliar ground, boss. I was convinced he was going to ask about a translator.'

'Into what?'

'If there was the slightest possibility that some Welsh people, even though they all speak English, might prefer to communicate in their own language...'

'In *Hay*?'

'He likes to observe the political niceties,' Karen said, 'as you know.'

'Yeh, I could almost believe that. Nothing from Tamsin's phone?'

'Nothing obvious. They're ringing all the stored numbers now, but, essentially, no business on that phone since she talked to Kelly James. The phone was in the car, and the car could have been here all night.' Karen took in a long breath. 'Doesn't look good, does it?'

'That car needs a good going-over. Did she drive into Hay and park it, or did somebody else?'

'Couple of locals say there was an old blue Nissan truck parked a couple of spaces away. May have been there for most of last night, but gone by the time we got here.'

'Basically,' Bliss said, 'there's no evidence that Tamsin even left Dorstone. Last people to actually see her were her own family at about two p.m., after lunch. She hadn't said where she was going or what she planned to do. But apparently it wouldn't be the first time she'd taken work home, if you see what I mean.'

'Would that necessarily be your drowning? Could she have been working on something else?'

'Worth considering. I think we can take it she didn't cross paths with Claudia Cornwell, so it could be that she didn't even go to Cusop. Still, let's do it thoroughly, like the man says. If I've missed anything, I don't want anybody else finding it.'

At least he could still talk like this in front of Karen. A mate. Either Brent didn't know this or he did know it and didn't want any mate of Bliss's too close to him, reporting back.

They walked up the hill towards the car park, a long traffic queue forming because the cops were restricting access to the car park and also questioning people, in search of anybody who might have parked there yesterday.

Karen pulled out her car keys.

'Go in mine?'

'I look that bad?'

'We all know you're not out of the woods yet, boss.'

'*All?*'

He was still wearing the baseball sweater with the big numbers, was unshaven, and his left eye kept half closing. Not comfortable, but not life-threatening.

'No,' Karen said, 'not all, just a few of us. I can see why you decided it was better to get back in the saddle, I'd probably be the same, especially with *him* around. Just don't tire yourself out too much, is all I'm saying, because he'll pounce on anything.'

'Yeh.'

'And I don't care what anybody says, we'd be better off if Annie Howe hadn't gone to Worcester. Could be a cold bitch, but you knew where you were with her.'

Bliss said nothing. The big car park was just round the corner and up the hill from the community centre. Karen was parked near the top, the little Renault Clio cordoned off at the bottom. Karen pointed beyond it towards the foothills of the Black Mountains.

'That's Cusop, just there, see. Those big houses in the trees? Easy walking distance through the fields.'

Shielding his eyes, Bliss saw movement across there. Bunch of uniforms already doing the walk, like soldier ants. Dogs and sticks. And after that, it was big country time, chopper terrain. In case she'd been injured or collapsed on a run up there. The last hope had been that Tamsin would arrive for work as normal this morning, having spent the night with some bloke.

'Karen, what's she done? Farm girl. Knows her way around. What can she possibly have *done*?'

He kept getting images of her in her perfectly pressed, spotless uniform, the thin red hair, the freckles, the solemn expression. Call me boss, he'd said, as if she already had a foot inside the CID room.

Didn't usually get emotionally involved. It didn't help.

Maybe he *wasn't* out of the woods.

35

Cold history

THEY SAID THAT if you drove west from London, the Black Mountains would be the first actual wilderness you encountered. Probably true. Living in Hereford, in the river valleys, you were unaware of them for much of the time. Unless you were a hiker or a fell runner or a member of the SAS, you really didn't know your way around the high ridges and exposed summits with arcane names that weren't on the road maps. Didn't know your Black Hill from your Cat's Back.

A secret wilderness, Merrily was thinking, and destined to stay secret because no road crossed the mountains from England. Capel-y-ffin wasn't much more than a mile over the Welsh Border, but it still took over half an hour to get there from the Hereford side.

Along the Gospel Pass. The best road, not to say the only road, twisting roughly north–south through the mountains. So called because legend said St Paul had been this way, maybe St Peter, too.

How remotely likely was it that Middle-Eastern Biblical icons would have travelled this route? Seemed more likely the stories had been invented by the monks at Craswall Priory in the north or remote Llanthony Priory to the south, in the days when monks knew all there was to know about everything, and needed money.

Still, if St Peter and St Paul *had* been this way, chances were they'd still recognize it. You forgot what kind of road this was, how many times you had to pull into the hedge, as it climbed and climbed, like a vein up an arm, to let oncoming all-terrain vehicles through and a few ambitious tourists.

She was late. There'd been a hold-up in Hay, some problem on the car park. Already late getting away from the vicarage with having to show Martin how the kitchen worked while resisting, one more time, his determination to explain – *oh God* – the circumstances of his sacrilege.

But he was OK, really, was Martin. Nothing wrong with being vulnerable, insecure, paranoid. If it came to it, he was likely to get more out of Sylvia Merchant than George Curtiss had.

She held the Freelander on the handbrake at an awkward junction. Craswall? No, couldn't be. She followed the twist to the right and came out on the road to Hay Bluff, a sheep-shorn plateau with vast views. Popular with walkers, a meeting place for hang-gliders and probably the last place offering safe, level parking before Capel-y-ffin.

Two empty cars and a Land Rover, lined up alongside the stone circle by the roadside. A pagan statement on the Gospel Pass, if not much of one; it was ragged and irregular, only one stone of any size, bent over like a lonely gravestone beside a pool of brown water. From here, the road was only going to get worse.

Unlikely this was going to be worthwhile, now. Any obsession of Huw's would be interesting, but Bliss… she was feeling, with hindsight, a bit annoyed with Bliss.

That's not how we work, the police. Not many points for preventing the hypothetical.

But then, quite suddenly, hypothetical was no longer the word.

The CD player in the Freelander was playing up, kept cutting out, so she'd had the radio on, and the ten o'clock news had it as second lead.

'*Police on the Welsh Border have begun a major operation to find a twenty-two-year-old policewoman missing from her home*

242

in Herefordshire. More than a hundred officers from two forces are involved in the search for PC Tamsin Winterson, who...'

What?

Merrily braked, reversed back to the stone circle, while a policeman, not Bliss, was saying Tamsin Winterson was a capable officer with a good knowledge of the area, but...

She sat and stared out over God knew how many counties and then pulled the phone from the dash and called Bliss.

'Let me call you back,' Bliss said.

'I can't wait for—'

'Five minutes.'

She couldn't go anywhere because you couldn't rely on a parking place or a signal after leaving the Bluff.

Tamsin? Was this some appalling coincidence? How often did police officers just disappear? Why this one? Why now? The dizzying views before her were across the lower hills of Radnorshire, Herefordshire, Shropshire. She looked over her shoulder, to where the soiled sky lay like a gloved hand on a long thigh of naked mountain. A helicopter in the distance.

The phone chimed.

'Where are you?' Bliss said.

Meaning was she on her own?

'Hay Bluff. I said last night that I'm supposed to be meeting Huw Owen. Have you—?'

'No,' Bliss said. 'Nothing. I was gonna call you... at some point.'

'You think this...?'

'Merrily, I don't know, do I? It might be totally unconnected. We... they found her car a couple of hours ago, on the car park at Hay.'

'Oh, hell... I passed it, wondered what was happening. Nobody saw—?'

'Nobody saw anything. Nobody saw her getting out of the car, but it could've been in the middle of the night. And there's a little gate at the bottom of the car park accessing an endless network of footpaths. Miles of them. Up into the mountains to where you are. Lorra ground to search.'

'You have any idea why she might've… gone off somewhere?'

'No. And then there's the possibility, not so remote, that when the car got here it wasn't Tamsin at the wheel.'

'That sounds even worse.'

'Yeh. That is worse. I can guess what Brent's thinking. He's thinking Tamsin, out of uniform, just another nice-looking girl, only this one's going to places where nice girls don't go on their own. And maybe some creep chats her up or just spots her somewhere quiet and goes for it.'

'It's not impossible, is it?'

'No.'

'She's just a kid,' Merrily said.

'She's a serving police officer.'

'That's what you keep telling yourself.'

'Yeh.'

'In between wondering how Tamsin being missing could possibly be connected with the drowning of an old wizard.'

And wondering, too, no doubt, if all this would be happening if he hadn't come back to work until his wounded nervous system could cope with bright lights.

The grey sky was visibly moving in, and she was feeling exposed between the empty cars and the broken relics of cold history. Would a woman come up here alone, when it was even quieter? Well, yes, maybe, because the country *wasn't like that*.

If you didn't think too hard about, say, the couple who'd been shot dead on the Pembrokeshire Coast long-distance footpath and all the bodies dumped in ditches and the rarely publicized increase in rural organized crime.

'In all honesty,' Bliss said, 'I don't know how it could possibly connect with the man in the pool, and it could be I'll be the only bugger even asking the question. Cross-border inquiry now. Brent's moved in with the Welsh, and I'm just a spare prick at a wedding. Me and Karen's in Cusop, which I'm convinced still has things to tell us, but I'm buggered if I can think what they might be. Coppers don't go missing like this, Merrily, it doesn't happen.'

'I liked her,' Merrily said.

Liked? Past tense? For God's sake…

'Keep me in the loop,' Bliss said. 'I have to get back.'

You came round the corner from switchback hell – tight bends, risky roadside drops, cynical mountain sheep shaving the stubbly grass – and then the lane dipped and the stony landscape softened into a tunnel of trees. And there, close to the roadside, about eight interminable miles from Hay Bluff, was the tiny white St Mary's Church, the *capel*, with its squat, crooked bell tower like the cap on a rusting petrol can.

Not much of a settlement, otherwise. A track opening up into a paddock, a farmhouse across the narrow road. Sheepdogs barking as she climbed down from the Freelander, but no human presence.

The yew trees in the churchyard were whispering about how *ancient* it all was as she approached the porch. The chapel had been built in 1762, dedicated to St Mary in a place of far older worship, doubtless on both sides of the Christian era.

She went in. Some churches, no matter how small, would greet you with a menacing yawn, but this wasn't one of them. This was a galleried shoebox with the sense of sanctuary you only found in remote places. The window at the east end was plain, apart from engraved lettering which said,

I shall lift up mine eyes to the hills from whence cometh my help.

And there were the hills on the other side of the glass, stark and promising nothing as Merrily turned to the altar, thinking about a prayer for Tamsin Winterson.

'Cosy as buggery, eh, lass?'

She spun. He could move quietly when he wanted to, in his old trainers, his frayed and etiolated denim jacket.

'How long have you been here?'

'Bloody hours. What kept you?'

'Traffic congestion. In Hay. There's a missing girl.'

She told him about Tamsin. Huw walked back towards the door where he stood with his hands behind his back, hair like old silage around his bone-yellow dog collar. He stared down at a little sculpted mouse on the font lid.

'Well, that's a bit coincidental. I was going to tell you about another.'

'Another what?'

Huw looked up through the window at the hill from whence might come help. Or not.

'Another missing girl. Two, in fact,' he said. 'I've arranged for this bloke to meet us here in a hour. Local. Knows about Rector and a lot besides. Just gives me time to show you what makes Capel the strangest place I know.'

36

The Wire

MOST OF THE short journey to Hay, Betty was silent. They weren't exactly not talking, but they certainly weren't communicating. Too much had happened inside a single day. And a single night.

She'd been waiting for Robin in the hallway of the bungalow, with the folding table they were taking for a book display. She'd watched him prising himself from the truck at the side of the road, edging up the bungalow's shared driveway with his back to the fence. She'd observed his attempts to look normal, absorb the pain. She'd winced at the stricken grin when she'd asked him,

'So how was the Black Lion?'

'It didn't have you, Bets, otherwise...'

'Now that's odd. Because when I rang the Black Lion they said that nobody called Thorogood was staying there. So, in case you'd checked in with a woman under an assumed name, I described you.'

'Jesus, Betty!'

'And nobody—'

'Maybe it was the Swan.'

'And then I rang the Swan, just in case I'd got it wrong.'

'I... What am I supposed to say?'

'I'm taking it that you slept at Back Fold.'

He looked like he'd been mugged and left in the gutter. Bloody *idiot*.

'All right,' he'd said, 'I slept at Back Fold and I've had better nights. OK?'

She hadn't let it go and got it out of him in the end: for reasons so crazy and convoluted that he must indeed have been very pissed last night, Robin – a man who needed an orthopaedic mattress, for heaven's sake – had *slept in the bloody bath.*

If she hadn't been driving and it hadn't been so bruised, she might have smacked his face.

He'd said that he'd had bad dreams. Somebody had told him he'd be living on the site of centuries of animal suffering and slaughter and he'd had a creepy encounter with a creepy old lady who whistled in the night and he'd had too much to drink, and he'd seen all the changes that were needed in the shop and it had all gotten on top of him and no, he was never gonna sleep there again, not until there was a bed and both of them were in it, OK?

'Robin…' Betty was peering beyond the line of cars. 'What's going on here?' She saw police. Several police cars, police tape, vehicles being redirected, some turned away. 'What is this?'

'No idea,' Robin said. 'None of it was happening when I left.'

A policeman came round to Betty's side window. She lowered it, and the policeman leaned in.

'Did you, by any chance, park here yesterday, madam?'

Robin said, 'I did.'

'Until when?' The cop came round to Robin's side. 'When did you leave?'

'Um… this morning? Half-seven?'

'Can you tell me where you were parked, exactly?'

'I dunno, somewhere down the far end? The place you got all taped off?'

'And you're saying you were here all night?' The expression in the policeman's eyes altered, like traffic lights changing from amber to red.

'Not me,' Robin said. 'The truck.'

'This truck was here all night?'

Betty saw that half the car park had been taped off. The cop pointed to a space on the right.

'Park there, please, sir, and let's have a chat.'

'What about?'

'Just park there. I'll follow you over.'

By the time they were parked, both of them out of the truck, the policeman had been joined by a thickset man in plain clothes, who introduced himself as DS Stagg, of West Mercia Police. They wanted Robin's name and address and the address of the shop. They wanted to know what time he'd parked yesterday and why he hadn't gone home last night. A group of other police had gathered some distance away, watching them. Betty began to get concerned, Robin was just getting irritated.

'The fuck's this about?'

'Please don't swear at me, sir,' DS Stagg said. 'Just tell us why you left your vehicle here all night.'

The police were starting to spread out in a casual half-circle. Betty started to feel a little nervous. Robin was leaning against the box of the truck. He looked awful. He was sweating.

'My husband has orthopaedic problems,' Betty said. *Wrong.* Why would she just say that? Stagg looked at her.

'Were you with your husband last night?'

'I… no. I had to stay at home all yesterday. We're selling our house. I had to show some people round. What's all this about? What's happened?'

'Why didn't you go back home to your wife last night, sir?'

'Because…' Robin closed his eyes on an indrawn breath '… because I guess I'd had too much to drink.'

The cops looked at one another. A fair-haired man in a soft leather jacket was moving close enough to listen to everything. Betty stared at Robin. Robin's smile was strained with incredulity and back pain, his hair sweated to his forehead.

'I figured I was doing the responsible thing, you know?'

'You're saying you were drunk?'

'I'm saying I had cause to believe I was over the alcohol limit for being on the road.'

'Where were you drinking?'

'Uh… Gwenda's Bar? Down by the clock? I was with some booksellers. We're opening a bookstore here.'

'So there are people who will vouch for you being there until… when? What time did you leave Gwenda's Bar?'

'I don't entirely recall. Eleven?'

'And where did you go then?'

'I… just kind of walked around, to sober up? Then I went to our… bookshop in Back Fold, and… No, hell, I came back to the truck.'

'You came back here, late at night.'

Betty listened to Robin explaining how he'd come to fetch an old coat and some sacks to use as bedding, so he could spend the night in the shop. She could have wept. Could tell the police weren't believing any of it, and she was hoping to all the gods that Robin would not even attempt to explain why he was so determined to spend the night in Back Fold.

When he stopped talking, there was silence. He stared hard at the cops, backed up against the tailgate of the truck.

'OK. Let's deal with this. Whadda you think I did?'

'Why do you think we're here?' This was the fair-haired man moving in. 'Hmm?'

'How the fu— How would I know *that*?' Robin spreading his arms. 'When I went home to pick up my wife, it was all normal here!'

'DCI Brent, West Mercia,' the fair-haired man said. 'This is a joint operation with Dyfed-Powys Police. We're looking for a missing person, and we're talking to everybody who might have used this car park yesterday.'

'So whyn't you just say?'

'And your name is…?'

'Thorogood.' Robin spelled it out. Robin Thorogood. That's my wife, Betty Thorogood.'

'So far, sir,' Brent said, 'you're the only person we've found whose vehicle was here all night. For reasons which, I have to say, don't make immediate sense to me. If you thought you were over the limit why didn't you get a taxi?'

'You know how much cabs cost? 'Sides, where do you start looking for a cab in Hay?'

'You look in a bad way, Mr Thorogood.'

'I *am* in a bad way. Some of the time. I have injuries.'

'Injuries you received last night?'

'Oh, sure. I had a couple fights, then I was run over by a—'

'He was...' Betty put herself in front of Robin. 'He was in a serious accident a few years ago.'

'And still has the bruises?' Brent said.

Stagg said, 'I don't see a disabled sticker in your windscreen.'

'I don't...' Robin's face was going red, his teeth were clenched. 'I don't *have* a disabled sticker. If they ever offered me one, I'd refuse it. I don't like to abuse the system. Plus I like to suffer, which I'm doing right now.'

Betty wanted to scream at this Brent that he should know that Robin was a stupid, volatile, arrogant bastard who thought there was some kind of stigma attached to a sticker allowing him to park in convenient places without risk of prosecution. Who actually thought there was a stigma attached to being disabled. *Him* being disabled.

But she kept quiet. Let them find out, if they wanted to. Let them check his medical records or whatever they did.

'You're American,' Brent said.

'Makes ya think that?'

'How long have you been over here?'

'Years. I'm a UK citizen. You wanna see my papers?'

'And you're the owner of a bookshop here,' Brent said. 'Did I get that right?'

'We rent one,' Robin said.

'Where?'

'Just across the road. Back Fold.'

'And you'll be open all day? You'll be there, both of you?'

'All day. Whatever. Who's missing?'

'And why, for heaven's sake,' Betty said, 'would you think my husband would have had anything to do with it just because he left his truck in a car park overnight?'

Brent didn't reply. One really infuriating thing about the police was their belief that asking questions – and how far was this from an interrogation? – was a one-way street.

'You're saying don't leave town?' Robin said. 'You're truly saying that to me?'

'What I'm saying—'

'Ya know what? I always used to be impressed by the British cops. Specially compared to some of the brutalized bastards they allow to police New York. I thought you guys were civilized. Now – no, listen, hear me out – now I think you're watching too fucking much of *The Wire*. And pretty soon no one will ever trust you. And just like in New York, no one will ever talk to you without a lawyer. And that's when this country will lose what little remains of the fucking decency and the fucking charm that made people like me wanna fucking *live here*!'

'We'll probably want to talk to you again, sir.'

'For leaving my truck overnight on a parking lot? Paying the full fee? You wanna see my ticket?'

'You know what I think?' Brent said. 'I think you *were* in a physical confrontation last night. Sustaining the kind of injuries most people might have taken to an A and E unit. Or, if *they'd* been assaulted, to a police station.'

'I'm not fond of hospitals.'

'Or police stations?'

And then Stagg asked Robin, in an almost perfunctory way, if he'd noticed a light-green Renault Clio, which he said he hadn't. They asked him if he'd seen a young woman on the car park. Red hair, freckles, medium height. He shook his head.

Betty started to feel sick.

37

The full Lazarus

HER RIGHT HAND was ruined, as if deformed by leprosy. The edge of the palm was ragged, the fingers had missing tips and the thumb was like a fragment of grey bone, all the flesh stripped away by crows.

There was a lingering pathos in those hands, open to the hills and the low and smoky clouds, as if she were saying, *Please God, no more.*

The white lady. Life size.

'Huw... I've seen this before,' Merrily said. 'In miniature.'

In Peter Rector's house. A plaster copy. Niches either side of the window. Isis on one side, the Virgin on the other. *This* Virgin.

'This was where she's said to have appeared? This is the spot?'

The former monastery, gaunt and Gothic, steep-pitched roof, not as old as it looked, was built into the hillside, wedged between the trees. More recently, it had been a youth hostel and a pony trekking centre. The statue of the Virgin Mary was on a plinth in its forecourt.

Huw looked up to inspect the statue's ruined hand.

'It's been moved. Happen for its own safety. It was back there,' he said. 'In what were called the Abbot's Field.'

They'd left their cars down in the valley, where the newborn River Honddu ran, and walked up, under dripping trees. On the way, Huw had reminded her of the story of Joseph Leycester Lyne, the ordained Anglican clergyman, who had called himself Father Ignatius and become committed to the formation of an order of Anglo-Catholic Benedictine monks. Falling under the spell of the extensive, romantic ruins of medieval Llanthony Priory, four miles down the valley from here, setting out to raise the money to restore it.

That had proved beyond him, Huw said. But what he'd done here had been more than second best. This was a powerful place. He still called it Llanthony. Still went down in history as the Monk of Llanthony.

And this... the white lady... was Our Lady of Llanthony.

Behind her lurked the shadowy ruins of a stone church, below which, Huw said, lay the mortal remains of the former Joseph Leycester Lyne.

'Builders buggered up the church foundations,' Huw said. 'Monastery were a better job all round. Good enough for Eric Gill a couple of decades later. Still intact.'

They walked back towards the wooden crucifix, by the track, at the side of a field.

'Big charisma?' Merrily said. 'Father Ignatius?'

'He had rich followers. Raised a fair bit with his evangelical egomaniac's grand tours. A national celebrity in the late nineteenth century, preaching all over the country, collecting donations and a body of followers who'd become the monks of Capel-y-ffin. And displaying his miraculous powers.'

'Healing?'

'On a Christlike level,' Huw said.

There was a pause. One of those pauses in time. Somewhere above the clouds, an invisible plane ploughed an aerial furrow through a different world and Merrily felt momentarily disoriented.

'I don't bloody know!' Huw threw up his hands like the white lady. 'I don't bloody know, Merrily. Is it all a sham? I don't *know.*'

But clearly cared. *Blimey.* She took a step back. How often these days did Huw express this kind of emotion?

'Truth is,' he said, 'this place has been obsessing me, on and off, for years.'

'You've never talked about it.'

Huw let his arms fall.

'We all need a private hobby. I were still a kid in Sheffield when I first read about this, in one of me mam's old books. Haunted me, at first – I'd've been about eight. Scared the life out of me. But it *stayed* with me. I suppose it were one of the reasons I came back – the fact that I'd been born within half an hour of… a mystery. A *big* mystery.'

He told her a story dating back to 1873 when Ignatius and his followers had been helping to build the monastery. Part of the work had involved lifting huge crates of stones, by means of pulleys, sixteen feet above the ground. One of the crates had unbalanced, tossing all the stones on top of one man, crushing him to death. When the body was pulled out it had been described by a witness as a distorted mass of pulp.

'So Father Iggy gets summoned,' Huw said. 'And an Inner Voice which apparently spoke to him several times in his life instructs him to fetch a bottle of Lourdes water. There's a circle of folks around the body which parted when Father Iggy returned… and *he found himself face to face with the Silence which is unlike all others for it embodies the suspended breath of two separate worlds.'*

'Are you quoting, Huw?'

'*Face to face with silence*? Would I come out wi' that? If you must know, it's from a great slab of overwritten hagiography, *The Life of Father Ignatius,* by his fan club secretary, one Beatrice de Bertouch. I've read all six hundred-plus pages twice and some bits seven or eight times. Which is why I know some of these excruciating slabs of hyperbole off by heart.'

He sounded angry that all this had not been documented by someone more reliably objective.

'Sorry,' Merrily said. 'Go on.'

'*The Monk had come to act,'* Beatrice says, *not to pray. He was, at that crucial moment, God's active and irresponsible instrument.'*

'Irresponsible?'

'Happen closer to the truth than Beatrice intended. She's a bit short on irony. She explains how Iggy kneels down by the corpse, sprinkles it with the water from Lourdes and then – *speaking slowly and emphatically* – he gives it the full Lazarus. After which, Beatrice says *miracle was accomplished. One single and mighty thrill seemed to sweep through every fibre of the shattered frame.* And the next instant he's back on his pins.'

'Well, yes.' Merrily starting to see what he meant. 'If this guy had been a distorted mass of pulp, this is even bigger than Lazarus. I'm guessing the full story only emerged when he'd been back on his feet for some time and all the bloodstained stones had been removed from the scene.'

'This job's making you a cynical little bugger, isn't it?'

'Under the tutelage of a master.'

'Aye. Anyroad, there's a few more stories like that, from when he were on tour. Fair bit of newspaper coverage at the time. If it was a scam, it were well handled.'

'Surely too sensational to be widely believed,' Merrily said. 'Even at a time when spiritualists were manifesting ectoplasm behind lace curtains. Which I suppose brings us to the big one.'

Feeling regretful, Merrily bent and touched the chalky robe. The statue of the white lady was gazing beyond her, through lidded eyes. The sky looked full of rain.

'If you follow her eyes,' Huw said, 'I think you'll get a rough idea where it appeared. The Welsh Lourdes.'

'You hear about it,' Merrily said. 'But not often.'

'Four known sightings back in Father Iggy's day.'

'When was this?'

'Eighteen eighty. One of the monks saw it.' Huw lowered his voice. 'Like a blue mist forming.'

Then he talked about the thirtieth of August, 1880. Eight o'clock in the evening. Some boys from the chapel choir playing cricket with a stick as a bat. A dazzling figure crossing the field: a veiled woman inside an oval halo, hands raised in blessing.

'Being little lads, weren't exactly filled with the holy spirit,' Huw said. 'One of 'em says, I don't like that. If it comes near me I'll hit it with me stick.'

'Bless him,' Merrily said.

The field was still lit up for a short time before the figure had melded with a bush and the hedge and vanished. The monks had kept watch, and the following Saturday the bush had lit up.

Merrily said, 'You believe it?'

'It's the little lads does it for me. Hit it with me stick. I like that. Rings true.' Huw shook his head. 'The put-downs started soon after it came out. There's another contemporary account in a book called *Nunnery Life in the Church of England*, by one Sister Marry Agnes. Sister Marry were a nun in the Anglican community here. Had a bad time at the hands of a bitch of a prioress who, she says, deprived her of food, thumped her round the head and made her lie in front of the church door for every bugger to walk over her into the services. She reckons Iggy did nowt to stop it.'

'That true?'

'Don't know. But she takes him apart in her book, and then, not surprisingly, puts the knife in for the apparitions. Not that she were there at the time, you understand, but she puts forward the theory that the figure was somehow projected on to the mist or whatever by one of them new-fangled magic lanterns.'

'A projector?'

'Balls. They'd be hard pressed to do it now, wi' a hologram machine.'

Merrily smiled.

'You *want* to believe in it, don't you?'

Huw scowled.

'No, come on,' Merrily said. 'You do.'

'Put it this way,' Huw said. 'If this were in Ireland, there'd be a load of tatty giftshops all down the bank. Lady of Llanthony key rings, luminous crucifixes, BVM T-shirts. It's as valid as Lourdes and Fatima and Knock. But the BVM belongs to the

Catholics, and that's a good enough reason for it to get rubbished. Another reason is that all the other chapels round here were Baptist, and them buggers were hardly going to be in sympathy with a bloke who thought Rome had no exclusive rights over the Benedictine order.'

'I see,' Merrily said. 'One of ours.'

She looked around through a fine mist that wasn't quite rain. Thought about Father Ignatius performing his Lazarus routine with *Lourdes* water. As if he knew what the next stage was.

Perfect for Peter Rector, Huw said.

Perfect for what Rector did next.

On the way up to the monastery, she'd given him a précis of what Athena White had told her.

'Up here,' Huw said, 'you can do owt you like.'

38

Take the money

'ONE OF THEIR own,' Kapoor said. 'One of their own goes missing, they go a bit crazy.'

He'd been waiting for them in Back Fold, one of several shop-keepers standing outside their doors in the intermittent rain. All the atmosphere of a dark carnival.

'But why were they hitting on *me*?' Robin couldn't stand still. British cops – this hurt. 'Some kinda institutionalized xeno-phobia? Look at me – I'm still shaking. I thought the bastards were gonna cuff me, toss me in one of those cages, back of a van.'

Robin looked at Betty, but Betty was just staring out the window. They were still not talking much. She'd sold the damn bungalow for good money; should've been a great day. Did she think there was *something in this*? That he'd done something crazy last night?

Well, OK, he had.

And paid for it. A cold psychic rebuke for his presumption. But how could be tell her what he didn't understand himself? How could he come out with this stuff in front of Kapoor?

'You fink they know somefing?' Kapoor said. 'That she was here before she disappeared?'

'Well, of course they know. They found her car.' Robin wiped the air with both hands. 'I'm sorry, I'm sorry, I just...'

'Nah, mate, not last night. I mean when she was in town asking questions about the old geezer in the pool.'

'When was this?' Betty said.

'Wednesday? Yeah, Wednesday night. It was her, no question. Recognized her picture this morning on News 24. Seen her round town a few times, though not in uniform. Wasn't in uniform when she was asking about the pool guy.'

'Where was this, Jeeter?'

'Gwenda's. Where everybody goes if they wanna find out anyfing. Reckon I should tell the cops, case nobody else has? Maybe somebody was like stalking her?'

'Just don't say you know me,' Robin said. 'The guy who parked in the wrong place for too long. And this was supposed to be our first real trading day. How'dya like that?'

'I don't,' Betty said. 'Because we're not opening today. Not now.'

'I'm afraid this isn't going to take very long,' Brent told the midday briefing at Hay Community Centre. 'We're really not much further. We know a lot more places where Tamsin Winterson *might* have been since yesterday evening but wasn't. I think what that tells us is that whatever happened to her happened very soon after she received that call from Kelly James. DI Bliss?'

Bliss, sitting next to Brent at the table opposite the bar, didn't consult his notes. Every time he'd looked down he'd seen double rows of scrawl, and holding up the pad would look ridiculous.

'DS Dowell and me, we've spent most of the morning in Cusop, basically doing house-to-house with PCs Conway and Trickett. Mrs Claire Loudon, who runs a guest house near the entrance to the lane that curves up from the dingle to the church, thinks she saw a small green car, sometime between six-forty and six-fifty last night. Thought it was a Peugeot, but it might have been a Clio. She didn't see it return.'

'So it's important,' Brent said, 'that we concentrate on the car. How it got to the Hay car park, where it was coming from, who was driving it. We've traced the driver of a blue Nissan Navara truck which had been parked all night about twenty metres away from where Tamsin's car was found this morning and… well, there could be more to learn from him.'

He turned to Rich Ford who reported that neither the uniforms on the ground nor the helicopter had found anything in the hills, but all the farmers within a five-mile radius had been alerted. Bliss was thinking of the full statement he and Karen had taken down from Kelly James, who'd been too upset to go into work. And the personal asides: he now knew Tamsin had wanted to be a cop since she was a kid, watching *The Bill* on the box and trying to train one of the sheepdogs to find drugs – a lump of her grandad's pipe tobacco standing in for cannabis resin. This was getting to him, now.

Though not conspicuously to Brent.

Facing Bliss, when the briefing was done, over folded arms, a smugness coming off him like aftershave. Brent had probably never met Tamsin Winterson.

'Francis, we need to deal with this business of the drowned man, Peter Rector. You need to explain to me exactly why you found it necessary to involve Winterson in what seems like a very unpromising inquiry?'

This was a time-waster.

'Iain… as I've stated several times, it was Tamsin who approached me. She lives in the area, she has friends in Cusop, she suspected there might be more to it.'

'Why were you there in the first place?'

'As I explained in my report, I had an hour to spare. A body in a small pool sounded worth a quick look in view of another recent suspicious death we both know about and…' No way round this, now '… the docs – while confirming that I'm quite fit to work – say that exposure for long periods to artificial light might delay complete recovery from my… temporary head injury. So I took a break, which included my lunchbreak, drove out here.'

If Brent ever checked with the docs, he could be stuffed here, but the chance were he wouldn't. Not in the short term, anyway.

'Also, I think it's important,' Bliss said, 'to encourage young coppers to come forward with their suspicions. Don't you?'

'She told you about the cannabis in Rector's house.'

'Yes, she did.'

'And she also showed you Rector's extensive collection of occult-related literature, indicating he might be part of some... cult?'

'Nothing so exciting. It seems to be no more than a study group, which includes the barrister I spoke to last night. Who Tamsin thought might have been the last person to see Rector alive.'

'Rector who was known in Cusop as David Hambling.'

'Having changed his name in search of a quiet life. A best-selling book he wrote forty years ago had brought him... unwanted followers. He was ninety-three years old. After talking to Claudia Cornwell, I've concluded that this very small circle of followers had become more of a support group. Fetching his groceries, his laundry, that kind of thing.'

'Was Winterson convinced?'

'I don't know. But I think we can assume she didn't meet Cornwell yesterday.'

'So nothing obvious here to explain her disappearance.'

Bliss shrugged. Brent leaned back, fingering his chin.

'She seems to have been quite excited at working with you. Hero of the Plascarreg.'

Mother of God.

'She isn't daft, Iain, and she's ambitious, which is no bad thing, is it? She's very solid for her age. Promising. And she isn't gonna believe everything she reads in the papers.'

'Well,' Brent sat up, stacking his notes together. 'Don't want to keep you too long under artificial lights, Francis. Do you need fresh air?'

* * *

Maybe Kapoor had put it around about what had happened on the parking lot. Whatever, it seemed to Robin it was like the town was determined to put things right. Before one, people had started to come in, the few people he knew, to wish them luck on the opening day that wasn't going to happen. Beginning with Gwenda and Gareth Nunne, Gwenda handing Betty a bottle of the Welsh vineyard white, which Robin thought was a nice gesture, but after last night he was glad she'd presented it to Betty.

Suddenly there was like a party atmosphere – yeah, that was how confined the space was. They'd thought about some kind of launch party, but Robin realized that wasn't in keeping with the spirit of the town, which was all about starting low-key and letting something build. And imagine if they'd done that today, crass-bastard pagans celebrating amidst all the tension.

'Lord Madoc!' Gwenda wore a leopard-print dress and a man's hat with the brim turned up. She'd seized a paperback. '*Now* I remember. This is bloody staggering, Robin. I'm going to send Gore over to check these out.'

But Gore didn't come. At least, not before someone else did.

'Listen,' Robin said when he and Betty were alone at last. 'I had an idea. How about we give it a week, let these people sign for the bungalow, and then get out there and spend. Build up stock. Pick up what we can from the charity stores and then I call in some favours with every pagan magazine I ever did free artwork for? I'm thinking big display ads in the Lammas editions. I'm thinking, how would the great Richard Booth handle this?'

Betty just stared at him.

'Well?' Gingerly, he sat down. 'Whaddaya think?'

She wore the smock thing he liked, with that kind of Inca design. Her hair was held back by an Alice band. He so wanted her to be happy. In that moment, he believed they could be happy.

Betty said calmly, 'Either you tell me precisely what happened last night or I'm out of here and I won't be coming back.'

Jesus...

'No...!' Back on his feet, a log-splitter working on his lower spine. 'What are you... what's the matter with you, Betty? You really think me and this girl—'

'No.' She sighed. 'I don't.'

'I'm sorry about last night, I truly am. I had too much to drink, I was so grateful to Gwenda and those guys for letting me *in*, I overindulged, I'm walking the streets in like a daze of... of illumination. And I thought I could top it off by squaring things here. Mentally. Emotionally. Too fast, too soon. I'm sorry. I can't tell you how much.'

Her silence filled the room, breaking him, the way it always did.

'The only female I saw on the streets was the whistling old lady, Mrs Villiers. Who spooked me. Thought I was someone else. The guy who stinks? You know the way she—?'

Betty stiffened.

'What else did she say?'

'She said, "You came back".'

'She thought you were the guy who smelled?'

'She was like...' He had his hands either side of his head, trying to shake out the memory '... like I stunk of what I'd been doing. Something like that.'

Betty said, 'There was a man died here after a drug overdose.'

'*What?* When?'

'Long time ago. They didn't find his body for days.'

'And like, you found this out... *when*? From *whom*?'

'Tom Armitage.'

'And who the f—?'

'He used to own this place. I spoke to him on the phone. I did tell you I was getting a vibe. Didn't know what it was, didn't want to make a thing out of it until I knew what it was. If it mattered.'

'We're not talking to each other, are we? It's like this place is coming between us. Something doesn't like us. It was, like, all over me last night.'

'What was?'

'I dunno, I'm not sensitive. Small things. A light I'd switched off came on by itself. The light was weird. Nothing felt like it was how it should be. Maybe it was me, but being drunk out on the streets, down in the town, that felt good. More than good. Soon as I shut myself in here, bad. Sick. And now I'm thinking this whole thing was a wrong move. If the deal on the bungalow goes through, why'n't we just pay Oliver off, load the books back in the truck, find someplace else… anyplace? Take the money and run.'

'Oh God, Robin…'

He moved towards her, tears coming, and the door opened.

They broke apart.

The doorway was darkened by the thickset detective, Stagg, three uniform cops behind him.

Stagg watching Robin weep.

'Mr Thorogood,' Stagg said, 'we'd like another word.'

'You're kidding,' Robin said.

Stagg didn't reply.

'Four of you?' Robin felt his blood pumping, like he'd cut his wrists and it was dripping down into his hands. 'Four of you would like a word?' He was in severe pain. 'Well, *I'll* give you a word. I'll give you *two* words.'

'Shut up, Robin,' Betty said quietly.

But it was too late for that. He knew it would be. It was almost laughable the way these guys were determined to piss on the party he'd never have. He stood facing Stagg, hands clawed by his sides.

'We'd like to take a look around, if you don't mind, sir,' Stagg said.

'The hell I don't mind! You got a warrant?'

'I think you'll find, Mr Thorogood, that when we're looking

for a person we believe might be at risk… we don't need a warrant.'

He nodded to the uniformed cops and they came in like they owned the place.

39

Convoy

Huw said, 'Well?'

'They're just appealing for sightings of her car.'

Merrily switched off the radio, climbed out of the Freelander.

'Nowt new, then.' Huw nodded towards a small man in a farmer's woollen shirt and a plaid tie, walking down towards St Mary's Church. 'Emrys Walters. Baptist minister. His dad were one of the artisans hired by Eric Gill to tart up the monastery, create a Catholic chapel inside. He raised a hand. 'All right, lad?'

'Ow're you, boy?'

He was older than Huw, probably in his seventies, fit-looking, weathered, short white hair.

'This is Merrily Watkins, Emrys. Vicar of Ledwardine, over the border.'

'Ledwardine. Well, now.' Emrys spoke slowly, shaking hands with Merrily. 'Gomer Parry lives there, that right?'

Merrily smiled, like you did when anybody mentioned Gomer.

'Worked with him down in Hay, years back,' Emrys said. 'He still piloting that great big…?'

Emrys did the motions of steering pulling levers.

'JCB? Oh yes. And digs graves, cuts hedges.'

'Thought I hadn't yeard he was dead.'

Huw said, 'Let's go and sit down, eh?'

* * *

The little church had a steadying air. Pews like park benches under the white walls, the gallery with its wooden rails, the message in the white window about the help in the hills. Huw shut the door and they sat at the ends of separate pews and talked about Peter Rector.

'Never knowed he was back, see,' Emrys said. 'Not a whisper. Cusop, well, that's no distance. Not as I've ever been there, mind.' He shook his head. 'Drownded. Well, well.'

Huw leaned forward, hands clasped.

'When you last hear of him, Emrys?'

'Gotter be twenny, thirty years since left the farm, sure to. We thought he'd gone abroad somewhere, see, and died out there.'

'Common misconception,' Huw said. 'Can I take you back thirty, forty years?'

He got Emrys talking about Peter Rector's return to Capel after the death of his parents and the publication of his best-selling book, with lots of money to spend.

'And he did spend some, too,' Emrys said. 'Done up all the outbuildings – barns, sheepsheds, the lot. Water, electricity. Kept me in work for over a year, on and off. I was still a young man, then, never made no claim to be an expert tradesman, but I gotter say he always treated me with respect.'

Emrys talked vaguely about the residential courses, with Rector as a kind of guru, as they called them then.

'He *looked* like a guru, see, with his height and the commanding way he walked. Long black hair, and those eyes – intense way he had of looking at you. Like he could see through your appearance to the core of you. Not everybody liked that. However polite he was, there were plenty who avoided meeting him in the lane, just because of the way he looked at you. What they didn't understand – he told me this once – was how much pleasure the hills gave him after his years in a POW camp. The air, the freedom.'

'And the earth-power he found here,' Huw said to Merrily. 'The strange energy. The mysticism in the hills. As experienced before him by Father Iggy and Eric Gill.'

'Ah… Mr Gill.' Emrys smiled cautiously. 'Father Ignatius builds the monastery, and he's mostly forgotten now. Gill just lives in it for a while and he's the most famous feller ever lived in Capel. Fair bit a gossip about him, even then, mind.'

'No surprise there, Emrys.'

'Thing was, 'cordin' to my father, he was a real nice feller to deal with. Very English, very polite, real enthusiastic. Made you realize what you'd got, living yere. The ole farmers used to go down to Hay market and feel like they was nothing, *from* nothing – thin ole ground, still covered in thick snow a month after all the rest was green. But Mr Gill, he'd tell you he felt priv-ileged to be yere.'

'Gill was a traditional Catholic, I think,' Merrily said.

Knowing from Huw's expression that this wasn't quite right, but it was too late.

'Oh aye, lass. As traditional as anybody who went to mass in his own chapel and then kept on having sex with his daughters.'

Merrily said nothing, recalling the sinister little-girl voice of Miss Athena White.

… the necessity of breaking human taboos, pushing the mind and body beyond accepted limits of behaviour. Performing acts regarded by society as hideous…

Wondering how Eric Gill had married passionate Catholi-cism with serial incest. Had he really confessed his sin… and then done it again and again? Or had he not quite seen it as a sin? Had he managed to find something profanely sacred in it, something spiritually empowering?

She turned to Huw, raised an eyebrow.

'Aye, I know, lass. If Rector were chaos magic and Father Iggy were chaos religion, Eric Gill… I don't know what you'd call his combination of devoutness, art and incest. But even he couldn't keep it up for long, as it were. Four years, Emrys?'

'Mabbe the winters was too hard, too long. Take some heating, the old monastery. Mabbe the demands was more'n he'd reckoned on. Moved on to what you might call softer climes, I believe.'

'And then Peter Rector arrives,' Huw said.

'Could be Mr Rector's parents was here within a year or so of Mr Gill leavin'. Their farmhouse, that's a couple of miles away, up towards the Bluff, but they used to come down yere to church, and the son he'd go up through the woods to the monastery, to play with the local farm boys.'

'So,' Huw said to Merrily, 'Rector were steeped in the atmosphere here from about the age of ten, all through his formative years before the war. He'd learned about Father Iggy, and the farm lads'd be telling him all the stories about what Eric Gill got up to.'

Emrys said Rector's parents had been interested in Eric Gill's stone-carving and drawings. Emrys's own dad had also learned quite a lot from Gill about carving memorials, and he passed the knowledge on to Emrys, telling him about the man with a posh accent who came out of England and taught you how you make real art out of your biggest natural commodity.

Rector had no talent for stone-carving, Huw said, but he knew about the curious atmosphere of the place, and when he came back, in what you might call vigorous middle age, to claim his inheritance, he'd learned a whole lot more.

'Keen to try out a few things – and what better place than this? Tiny population and all these absorbent hills.'

'I bet *you* fancied this parish,' Merrily said.

'I'd've loved it, lass. But the opportunity never arose, and I ended up further west, where I were born. And this is part of Hay now. Or Hay...' Huw leaned forward, bizarrely excited '... Hay is part of *this*. Feeding off the energy Ignatius found. St Mary's at Hay is probably the only Anglo–Catholic church in South Wales. Incense, bells and whistles, the lot. And pulling in record congregations when all the others are dwindling.'

'But that could be just an inspiring vicar.'

'Could be,' Huw said lightly. 'Could be. Or, if you wanted to be fanciful, you might think summat were drifting down the holy Gospel Pass.'

'Nice idea,' Merrily said. 'Now, is anybody going to tell me what Rector was actually doing up here and how it relates to two missing girls?'

It still took a while to come out.

Emrys said, 'Mr Gill's was an artistic community, see: his own family, Mr Davy Jones the painter and various staff... including priests. Always a strong religious element. Mr Rector's, forty years later, was... well, we all thought that was religious, too, and likely so did he.'

'Nobody really knew what went on,' Huw said. 'They only saw – or thought they saw – some of the effects of it. But you might care to speculate about Rector experimenting with the natural energy, enhanced by the yearnings of Father Iggy and Eric Gill. If I were more of a mystic, I might say that the veil between heaven and earth, between here and there, between one kind of existence and another... you might think what went on up here had stretched it tight as a drum.'

Emrys looked uncomfortable. No wonder the people of the Black Mountains had retreated into the starkness and simplicity of their Baptist chapels.

'Sometimes,' Emrys said, 'Rector's people would walk all the way from the farmhouse to the monastery, before dawn, in complete silence, till they got to the place where the Lady was seen in the eighteen seventies. All arriving in the morning mist.'

Merrily said, 'You saw this?'

'And I turned away, Mrs Watkins. I turned away. For, as the Bible says, I was sore afraid.'

'Who *were* these people? The people who came to study with Rector, and to partake in his... rituals.'

'Rich people,' Huw said. 'Paying to live rough and learn secrets. Famous people – rock stars who wanted summat closer to home than an ashram in the Himalayas. Rector seems to have liked famous people. Creative people. Artists.'

'And writers,' Emrys said. 'They reckon that in the early years of that Hay Festival, when it was held in the town and these writers and poets used to go to the pubs and the cafés, he'd get into conversation with them. Seemed to be able to attract people to him. When you seen him you thought *he* must be somebody you knowed from the papers or the television. Somebody famous. What's the word…?'

'Charisma,' Huw said. 'Just like Father Iggy and Eric Gill.'

'Aye. Same when you seen him walking across the hills… these big, long strides. Like he owned the place. I don't mean in an arrogant way, I suppose I mean like he *knowed* the place. And it knowed him. On some higher level.'

Even in the earthy acoustic of the chapel, this was getting impenetrable. It still wasn't clear exactly what form Rector's residential courses had taken. What he was actually teaching.

'Put 'em through it, mind,' Emrys said. 'The rich folks.'

'Part of the exercise,' Huw said. 'Separate yourself from your normal environment. Be closer to the hard, stony ground.'

'And havin' to mix with the Convoy. Not all of them liked that.'

'Sorry,' Merrily said. 'The what?'

'Convoy,' Huw said. 'You must remember the Convoy, lass. The so-called New Age Travellers. The neo-hippies who went round in customized buses, getting stoned and holding moveable festivals. Mostly along the Welsh border on account of the remoteness of it. Until a law got passed making it illegal for more than two or three to travel around, set up camp.'

'Of course. Yes. Heard people talk about that. Clashes with the police all over the country. Weren't they demanding the same status as Romany gypsies?'

'Farmers mostly hated them,' Huw said. 'Useless scroungers trespassing on private land, burning fences for camp fires. Not popular in the country towns either. Specially in Hay. Every autumn a dozen or so knackered owd buses'd arrive on Hay Bluff – holy of holies for the Convoy – where there were a stone circle they could claim for their own and you could pick thousands of magic mushrooms in the season.'

'Ah.'

'Psilocybin mushrooms. Poor man's acid. You made a brew wi' 'em. Quite effective… I'm told. Anyroad, Peter Rector would involve some of the Convoy folk in his communal activities. His rituals. Which didn't make him many friends in Hay.'

'They'd walk over from their camp on the Bluff,' Emrys recalled. 'Quite a few at first, but in the end it was just a handful who'd come back.'

'Why them?'

'Happen because they were the ones up for owt,' Huw said. 'Nowt to lose. Willing to participate in who knows what.'

'Does either of you know what?'

'Could be looking at enhanced visualization. Various attempts… by ritual and a combined focus – and happen a pot or two of mushroom tea – to bring summat into existence… a *perceived* existence, if you prefer to retain some scepticism.'

'Specifically?'

'Merrily,' Huw said. 'You know what we're talking about.'

'Sacrilege,' Emrys said. 'We turned the other way because he was a friendly man when you knowed him. And he'd brought money into the community.'

Merrily gazed across the nave at the little mouse on the font lid. Thought it might have moved.

'And did she come?'

Emrys Walters, a non conformist minister from some plain, cold chapel, had turned his head away towards the east window, a hand shaking with the memory of something.

'Some folks reckon so. Aye.'

40

Mephista

'I DIDN'T EXPECT that,' Merrily said. 'I didn't expect any of it. How come we never heard about it at the time? Even you.'

Huw looked at her like she'd just come out of an egg, reminding her that these things still happened, or were perceived as happening, day-to-day, and nobody knew this more than they did, the medieval hackers at the spiritual coalface.

'It gets blanked out,' Huw said. 'Even by the Church. A whole level of human experience trashed as loony-fodder – doesn't happen, can't happen, nobody's that gullible any more. Also, this is Capel-y-ffin, where it were blanked out here the first time because it didn't fit the religious order of things.'

They watched Emrys Walters getting into his van in front of the farm where the sheepdogs had started barking. The questions Merrily wasn't sure she wanted to ask were stacking up.

'You met any of the others who thought they'd seen it?'

'Nobody else – not round here – wants to talk about it. They don't know what they saw. They want to forget it. The way they wouldn't have if it hadn't been summoned by a combination of rich buggers and mushroom-heads from the hated Convoy.'

'What did it look like?'

'Accounts vary. Some say grey, smudgy, soiled, indistinct. No more than a discolouring of the morning mist. Others… radiant. I don't know, it's all subjective and I were still up north at the time.'

Emrys's van rattled into life, coughed out blue smoke. He beeped his horn at them as the van pulled away, and they stood at the side of the lane and considered the possibility of Peter Rector conducting a psychological experiment to see if, through meditation and combined visualization, an image of the Lady of Llanthony might be made perceptible again, nearly a century after its first alleged appearance.

Huw stood staring at the clouds.

'And how do you feel about that yourself?' Merrily asked.

'*I* think… that Peter Rector was, at that time, still a darker man. A man who wanted to play with the elements, if he could, and people's minds, which he knew he could. Happen for its own sake, or his own gratification or his own psychic development. I can't see as it'd be for anybody's good.'

'And was this when the girls went missing?'

'You see why it were important for you to know the background first?' Huw said.

The girls had been from the convoy. One was sixteen, the other in her twenties. They'd vanished while the convoy was camped on Hay Bluff, picking mushrooms. Not the most peaceful gathering; there had been regular confrontations with the police, under pressure from the farmers and a proportion of the townsfolk of Hay to move them on.

Generally speaking, Hay, like all towns, didn't like the Convoy people. They came down from the Bluff to collect their state benefits, buy their cheap cider, drink it in the streets. Sometimes there was trouble. Shops banned them to protect their stock.

'And both girls had been to Rector's gatherings?'

'As far as I can ascertain, only one,' Huw said. The younger one. The daughter of what you might call holiday hippies. Owd hippies who wanted to recapture the excitement of their youth, in the Summer of Love. They'd buy an owd bus and join the convoy for a few weeks. Usually they'd be welcomed by the regular convoy, not least because they had more money. Mephista's parents... they were in the writer-and-poet bag.'

'She was really called Mephista?'

'Kind of name hippies gave their kids. Her dad were a free-lance writer who was supposed to be planning a book about life on the road with the Convoy. Her mother took the photos. They might've had the heart to finish it if they'd ever seen their daughter again.'

'Vanished? Just like that?'

'Mephista were a problem. She didn't relate to the New Age traveller thing. She wanted city life, clubs – discos as it would've been then. The parents dragged her along to Rector's place if only to keep an eye on her. They were very keen on Rector – well, you would be if you were doing a book. But then one day Mephista was gone and the older woman, too. The older one came and went a lot, used to get lifts into Hay and might not come back for a day or two. Thought to be on the game. So it would've been a while before they found out she was gone, too. The camp wasn't exactly tightly organized, as you can imagine.'

'Who told you all this?'

'Emrys. Who else? He's a good man. He'd go up and chat to the Convoy now and again, see if they needed any help. They never told him to bugger off. He thought they were generally harmless, happy to be up there out of the way. It's interesting, psilocybin, the mushroom drug, I were reading about that not long ago. Banned now, ranked alongside cocaine, but some experts reckon it's up there wi' Prozac as an antidepressant. A natural antidepressant. If you were a homeless hippy, happen it made you feel less like trash.'

'These girls – neither was ever found?'

'Nor came back. There was a police investigation, but where do you start? Especially if they don't want to be found.'

'If the older one was on the game...'

'I imagine that worried the parents quite a lot over the years. That Mephista might be down in Swansea or Cardiff or Bristol, turning tricks, getting ravaged by hard men, hard drugs. They never stopped looking, the parents. They'd keep coming back – Emrys'd see them in the hills, as if it were at all likely their daughter would show up here again.'

'And Rector?'

'He'd've been checked out at the time by the police. Nothing happened to him. But it all ended soon afterwards, anyroad. Happen it were the missing girls. Anyroad, he went quiet.'

'He had a breakdown, according to Athena White.'

'Oh, a *breakdown*...'

Merrily shrugged. Huw's lined face looked bitter, as if Rector had stolen his private vision and trashed it.

'Farm went on the market and Emrys never saw Peter Rector from that day to this.'

'Not knowing he was just a few miles away. Under a different name. With a beard.'

'Ah, let's go down to Hay, get summat to eat, eh?'

'Wait.' They'd reached the Freelander with its hem of crusty mud. A big dome of a hill blocked the eastern horizon. 'What if he had good reason to think there were bad vibes here? The atmosphere soured.'

'Your mate White's evidently still on his side. Bloody owd witch.'

'I'm not being naive, Huw, but suppose he *had* been infiltrated by some seriously awful people? What I'm thinking, could they have come in through the convoy? Like you said, anybody could join it.'

'Happen.'

'And what if he did have a good reason for... making something happen?'

'What, like introducing Anglo-Catholicism to Hay?'

'Not sure I was thinking of that, but it's there. It's happened.'

'So,' Huw said, 'he finds himself a nice, secluded refuge a few miles away, where it's not quite as cold and you can grow proper trees, surrounded wi' nice, middle-class country dwellers.'

'And begins what Miss White calls his Last Redemptive Project.'

'Redemptive, eh?' Huw sank his hands into the pockets of his ancient jacket, looked down at his trainers. 'To redeem *himself*?'

'Or the area? Where Father Ignatius failed, presumably, and his church collapsed into a dangerous ruin, and Eric Gill got all excited but then couldn't stick it for long. And where Rector himself let the past catch up with him. If you keep on walking from Cusop Dingle, this is where you finish up.'

'And where do *you* go from here, lass?'

'Don't know. Sometimes it all looks like a crooked path that leads nowhere other than Richard Dawkins's back door. Do people like Rector just create a working fantasy? Do we all?'

'Wasn't what I meant, lass,' Huw said gently. 'I meant are you going to tell Bliss any of this?'

'What would that achieve? You really think the police are going to follow it up on the off chance it might point up a reason for somebody to have killed Rector? Thus providing a very tenuous link with a missing girl?'

She looked up into the hills, from whence there were no visible offers of help.

41

Into the hearth

'Name's Robin Thorogood,' Brent said. 'American. A bookseller in Hay. Or planning to be.'

Small group of them on benches in a back room of the community centre, down near the toilets: Bliss, Ceri Watts of Dyfed-Powys, Karen Dowell, Terry Stagg, Rich Ford.

'So what've we got?' Ceri Watts said.

'Circumstantial up to now. However...' Brent started counting off the pluses on his fingers. 'He only lives in Kington, but he was in town all night. Leaving his truck on the car park near where Winterson's car was found. Says he got drunk and – rather than get a taxi home to his rather lovely wife – chose to sleep over his shop. Which, as he's only just taken it on, has no furniture, least of all a bed. I'd have to be extremely pissed to sleep there in any circumstances.'

'And that's it?' Bliss said.

'He says he slept in the bath,' Terry Stagg said. 'Even though he claims to be disabled. His fellow drinkers at Gwenda's Bar have confirmed he was there until eleven-ish, but none of them knows where he went after that. Although two people in the town say they saw him wandering the streets, unsteadily. Like someone who should be in Talgarth, as one put it.'

'Meaning the former psychiatric hospital there,' Ceri Watts said.

For Brent's benefit. Whoever this feller was, Bliss felt a twinge of sympathy, remembering how, just after they let him out of the hospital, he was all over the pavements in Hereford and people would cross the road to avoid him.

'Any previous, Iain?'

'No, but the word is his circumstances have changed quite a bit in the last couple of years, and not in a good way. Soon as Stagg started talking to him, on the car park – just routine stuff, to begin with – it was like he was still drunk. Very obviously lying. His wife was with him, and you could tell she didn't believe him either.'

'Maybe she thought he'd been playing away.'

'And maybe he'd been playing with Tamsin Winterson. And maybe something got out of hand.'

'Big leap, Iain.'

'*You've* taken enough of those in your time, Francis. Something else about Thorogood is that he denied all knowledge of Winterson. Virtually every other shopkeeper – bakers, ironmongers, café and sandwich bar owners and booksellers too – either knew her personally or recognized her picture. It's her local town. People are worried – except for Thorogood.'

'Although, as I understand it,' Rich Ford said, 'he's only been around for a matter of weeks.

'So what's he done with her?' Bliss said.

Brent turned to Terry Stagg.

Staggy had grown this spotty beard, probably to cover up a couple of his chins. He cleared his throat.

'Well, she's not in his shop. It's not even as big as it looks from outside. Books downstairs and a kitchen. Upstairs, living room, two bedrooms, bathroom. Mrs Thorogood said they were planning to move in properly when their house was sold, but hardly any furniture there yet.'

'What did crime-scene think?'

'Not impressed, sir, unfortunately. We went over the place thoroughly. No cellar, no outbuildings, no room for any. It's quite a confined space.'

'And how's Mr Thorogood behaving?'

'Pretending to be outraged, sir, but I reckon he knows what he's fucking done.'

Bliss looked at Brent, sensing a muted excitement there, before turning to Stagg.

'*Done*, Terry? Do I take it we're now of the opinion that Tamsin's definitely dead? Because that's a different kind of search, isn't it? You think this was something random? Or was he thinking, I know, I'll park me truck very visibly next to this girl's car, look for an opportunity to rape her—'

Brent put up both hands for silence.

'Let's not get *too* far ahead of ourselves but, all the same, this is clearly not the most balanced bookseller in the town. I've known longer shots that paid off.'

'So which one's the most balanced, Iain? They're friggin' *booksellers*. It's hand-to-mouth these days. And like Rich says, this feller's not been around the place for long. Is there *any* connection we know of between him and Tamsin?'

'Well, no… and yes.' Brent looked entirely untroubled. 'And you might find this interesting, considering your apparent interest in the late Peter Rector's library. The only connection's the books. The kind of books that Thorogood sells. Terry?'

'It's all he's got in there,' Stagg said. 'Weird books. Witchcraft books. Crank stuff. Reckons he's a pagan.'

'Norra crime, Terry.'

'He's a nutter, boss, trust me, and I'll tell you something else. When we went in there, it was just him and his missus and there was some tension there. Between them. I may be wrong but I reckon he'd been in tears. What's that say?'

Ceri Watts scratched the side of his neck.

'As it happens, I know a bit about this man. Involved in a fracas in Radnor Forest, few years ago. An evangelist guy, Ellis, very much a crackpot himself, took against Thorogood and his wife because they were doing whatever pagans do in a ruined church. All got a bit overshadowed, at the time, by an arrest for an ostensibly unconnected murder in the same area. But it was fraught enough, and that's how Thorogood got his injuries. Now, Gwyn Arthur Jones was SIO on that, and he's living in Hay now, so if you want any background on Thorogood, he's your man.'

'I'll bear that in mind,' Brent said.

You could see him forgetting it before your eyes.

Robin was quiet now, Betty hoping to all the gods that it wasn't relief. She stood in the damp, musty silence, surrounded by all their lovingly collected books which deserved better, and wiped her eyes with a sleeve.

The hardest part had been holding Robin back without this looking like something she had to do all the time.

She was in the tiny kitchen getting a glass of water when she heard Robin calling to her from upstairs. She found him standing in the middle of the rust-coloured rug, hands on his hips. He did that sometimes to ease the pain.

'What the hell...?'

Pale daylight gave the room a greasy yellow patina. A sooted board lay in front of the upstairs fireplace.

'Hmm,' Betty said. 'One of them mentioned that on the way out. It was sealing the chimney off, one of them tapped it and it fell out. Seems we're breaking the law. It's asbestos.'

'Bastards just had to find something, didn't they?'

'We need to dispose of it, but not in a public skip.'

Betty bent and lifted the plate, getting sticky soot over both hands. She just wanted to hurl it through the window. Went on her knees to the cramped fireplace. There was a small pyramid of soot in the bottom and another trickle coming down like black sand in an egg timer. Betty squinted up the chimney.

'Yeah, I know,' she said, 'I'll send the cleaning bill to the police.'

There was a crisping from above, and she backed out fast. Soot was one thing, but a major eruption of dead jackdaws...

She sat back on her heels in the dirt, suspended in an extraordinary moment of crystal *I-am-here* consciousness. What the *hell* was she *doing*? If Robin really was no longer happy here, was ready to take the money and run…

Something fell into the hearth. Nothing dead, only an accumulation of tar. Where it had broken off, she saw a bare patch on the firebricked wall and the edge of something crudely carved there. There was a buzzing in her ears, like tinnitus. Coldness in her chest.

'Betty?'

'Hang on.'

She reached up and pulled off more flakes of tar, brushed the wall clean with the edge of her hand until it was fully revealed.

Maker's mark? Too big, surely.

'Robin, is the phone up here?'

They had just the one mobile.

'In my pocket.'

'Put it on camera for me, would you?'

She scrambled out of the fireplace and went to put on the light. She could see now that the carving on the chimney wall was not as crude as it had looked. Didn't have Robin's finesse, but there was a kind of painstaking precision. It looked old, but it couldn't be very old because brown firebricks like this couldn't have been around all that long.

And which firebrick manufacturer in the last eighty years would have put out a product carrying a swastika?

Of sorts, anyway. Robin handed Betty the phone, and she thrust it firmly up the chimney and took a picture in case it should crumble to dust before her eyes. When she rolled away, she had the impression of a shadow rising as if formed from soot. She scowled.

'Iain, for what it's worth…' Bliss had caught up with Brent in the doorway after the others had left. 'For what it's worth, I think she's a smart girl. And totally committed to the Job. I don't think she's the kind of girl who'd cop off on a whim with some piss-artist bookseller.'

'The vagaries of human behavioural patterns will always surprise me, Francis,' Brent said.

'You being a PhD and all.'

Brent shook his head, kind of pityingly, then it came up, jaw jutting.

'And what about a policeman, Francis? Would she… cop off with a detective, do you think?'

'What's that mean?' Bliss's guy went tight. 'Sir.'

Brent waved it away.

'Don't you need some sleep?'

'And you need everybody you can get,' Bliss said. 'If your bookseller angle falls down, all overtime restrictions'll be off by tonight.'

'If.' Brent headed for the operation room. 'Go home, Bliss. Have a bath, have a shave.'

Bliss walked savagely away, through the main doors, letting one swing behind him. Couldn't remember whether he'd left his car on the field at the back or the big car park. Couldn't believe what he thought Brent had said.

The numbness had taken half his face.

Couldn't find his car on the field behind the community centre. No, he wouldn't've put it there; he hadn't even known they were using it until he'd got here. Bugger. He walked round the building and out of the entrance into Oxford Road, where a woman came up to him, pushing a bike, panting.

'Excuse me, are you with the police?'

She was looking at him, uncertainly, and he realized he was still wearing his baseball sweater with the big numbers on the front. He nodded.

'Only somebody asked me to tell the first policeman I saw. They're saying a body's been found in the river.'

42

Unfinished

WALKING DOWN TOWARDS the clock, they saw shoppers sitting at tables outside one of eateries, some examining books they'd bought, some looking around, aware of something happening that wasn't quite normal.

Under a darkening sky, Merrily and Huw grabbed one of the tables outside the Granary, across from the clock tower. Merrily pulled out her cigarettes.

'OK to smoke here, you think?'

'You'll soon know if it isn't.'

'Huw, they've got better things to do.'

Merrily guessing you rarely saw any police at all, on foot, in the streets of Hay-on-Wye. You wouldn't see this many on a normal day in a city, and they looked more menacing now, more militaristic with all those straps and pouches. Like the addition of a gun for every cop was only one strip of Velcro away.

'So you met her,' Huw said, 'the missing copper?'

'She was very... She *is* very likeable. Very keen.'

Lighting up, she had a vivid mental image of eager, freckly Tamsin Winterson, back in Rector's stone bungalow.

CID, sir?

I'll bear that in mind, Tamsin.

Telling her to call him *boss*, as if she was already halfway there. Oh God, this was awful. She felt like some tourist voyeur in her jeans and T-shirt and a fading grey fleece.

'Doesn't look too good for her, does it?' Huw said. 'Police don't go missing.'

'But with a police officer, they're never going to give up the search.'

They'd stopped their cars at the ruined stone circle by Hay Bluff, Huw pointing out where the Convoy used to gather. Open common land, once a big bus station for psychedelic single-deckers and luminous haulage vans with windows punched in their sides. Fence-post fires, generators for the music, astral travel, courtesy of the psilocybin mushroom. A woman and a girl slipping away into the crazy night, forever.

They'd seen a police helicopter, so low that it appeared almost to be grazing the hills.

'If you want to hold the table, I'll get us summat to eat. Anything in particular?'

'Anything.' She got out her purse. 'But not much. If they still do those goat's cheese open sandwiches... Or whatever's similar.'

'Put that away, lass. I've got a private income.'

'Have you?'

'No. Listen, if you get time, after, go and have a quick look at Father Richard Williams's Marian grotto. You might like it.'

'Oh... the church. Yeah, I will. Might pray for guidance.'

By the time he was back out, with two teas, her phone was chiming. She inspected it. Oh, hell.

'It's Martin Longbeach. I'll have to call him back.'

'Just hope he's not desecrated your church already.'

'What I've always admired about you, Huw,' Merrily said. 'That overwhelming compassion.'

Looked like rain was coming in.

Martin came directly to the point. He said Sylvia Merchant had called in at the vicarage around mid-morning.

'Just like that?'

'She asked when you'd be back. I said you'd be away from the vicarage for ten days. I said – I hope you don't mind – that you were upset about what had happened. She said she wouldn't want that for the world.'

'That doesn't sound like her, Martin.'

'Or words to that effect.'

'So obviously you told her I'd mentioned it.'

'Well, yes. And then I invited her in for coffee and we had a long chat. I told her about Daniel. She asked if I'd… seen him? You know? I said I hadn't.'

'She was, erm… alone, I presume.'

'Oh, yes.'

Merrily saw a policeman talking into his radio and then hurrying away down the street, several nearby shoppers watching him, expelling low, anxious whispers, a sorrowful excitement on their faces.

Oh God. Merrily throwing her concentration into the phone.

'Martin, I'm curious. Did she ever specifically say to you that she was gay?'

'She didn't say she wasn't. The thing is, Merrily, those of us who have never been any other way or sought to conceal it, we don't make an issue of it. The longer I live, the more I think that's the cause of all the ill-feeling, all the dissent. I'm not a gay priest, I'm just a priest. Should there be gay bishops? There always *have* been gay bishops. Just not with a capital G.'

'Funny. Huw Owen makes the same point.' She glanced at him. 'If in a slightly blunter fashion.'

'I suppose it's just the same way, as Sylvia didn't, for quite a while, say she was a spiritualist, although it became clear that she—'

'What?'

'You didn't know?'

'No.'

'Doesn't mean she's one of these people who go to public seances every week. Seems to attend only one church, which is the Cathedral. What she wanted to know – and that, I'm guessing, is what she wanted to approach with you – is whether spiritualism is considered compatible with Church of England worship.'

'She didn't mention this.' The scream of an oncoming emergency vehicle forcing Merrily to switch the phone to her other ear. 'She told Sophie I was treating her best friend as if she was an evil spirit requiring major exorcism. Which was, of course—'

'Merrily, grief—'

'Even allowing for what grief does. I don't understand this. Or why she also avoided discussing it with George Curtiss from the Cathedral.'

A police car went past at speed, full squeal.

'I think she just wanted to talk to you,' Martin said. 'To have an intelligent discussion, one-to-one.'

'About spiritualism?'

'Which we had. An intelligent discussion. And I thought I should tell you, as soon as possible, that she has no intention – nor ever did have – of making an official complaint against you.'

'That's not what she told Sophie.'

'Merrily, it was a cry for *help*. She wanted attention. I'm glad that I was able to give it to her. Permitted to give it. No offence at all to you. She probably opened up to me because I'm gay.'

'And what did you tell her – about compatibility?'

'I told her it was a broad church and we never turned anyone away, but that our belief – or at least mine – was that attempting to maintain contact with our loved ones on the other side of death was unlikely to be beneficial to either.'

'And she said?'

A woman came out of the Granary with their lunch on a tray. Merrily pushed her chair back and signalled to Huw to eat.

'She said there was sometimes unfinished business,' Martin said.

'There's nearly always unfinished business. This is still not making any sense, Martin. You tell her you don't condone communion with the dead, where does this get her?'

'Well, I hope I've made it clear that it's nothing for you to worry about. You're on holiday and you can relax.'

'So you're going to see her again? Unfinished business?'

'She wants me to meet her medium. To make it clear to me, as she said, that there's nothing unhealthy in it.'

'And you're going to—' She waited for another police car to go through. 'You're actually going to *do* that?'

'Can't do any harm. It's not as if I'm going to become a convert. *Relax*, Merrily.'

'Be very careful, Martin. We're both on unsafe ground here.'

She watched the blue lights dispersing oncoming traffic like fly repellent, nobody relaxing here.

43

Weight of bone

NEVER REALLY LIKED to get there first, and it rarely happened, thank Christ, but this was a small town, being on foot an advantage.

If you could call it that.

Bliss had alerted Rich Ford and then followed the woman downhill through the back streets on the English edge of town. She said she hadn't seen it herself; a canoeist in a wetsuit had asked her if she knew where the police station was, telling her his mate had spotted it near the bank. Was it a man or a woman? She didn't know, was pointing now across the narrow main road to a turning alongside a vet's clinic.

It ended at a car park next to a concrete building – sewage works. Then there was rough grass and a beach of pale brown stones sloping into the river, and what looked like an explosion of blood against the greyness of the water and the sky.

'Police,' Bliss said quietly.

Out of breath, forehead numbing, as they parted for him.

'In all his finery,' someone said. 'Rather eerie.'

The sun had gone in completely, and the scene was sombre, a mist of funereal rain draped over the dark trees on the opposite bank. The red was lurid, maybe just a blanket thrown over the body.

And then someone laughed.

Mother of God.

Bliss pushed urgently through.

* * *

Laid out in his sodden robes: the full-length cape edged with fake ermine, held together by a chrome pin. The tall crown of beaten gilt on his head. In his left hand the sceptre made from the ballcock from a lavatory cistern with the small H on top like a tiny version of an old-fashioned TV aerial.

H for Hay.

Bliss was like, 'What the f— What's *this*?'

Two patrol cars, blues and twos, screeching into the concrete car park behind him.

'Don't you recognize him?' a man said gravely. 'It's the King of Hay.'

'Couldn't believe it.' A boy of about sixteen was crouching beside it. 'We had to get him out, didn't we?'

He was wearing a pale blue wetsuit. Behind him, another boy, same gear, and two orange canoes pulled up from the river.

'And you found him where?' Bliss said.

'Just by there.' The wetsuit boy had a Welsh Valleys accent. 'He was floating, he was, not far from the bank. At first, we thought it was a… you know. Well, you would, wouldn't you?'

'Yeh,' Bliss said. 'You would.'

He bent to hold up the bottom of the scarlet cape to reveal a pair of shapeless, too wide, dark grey trousers and scuffed, black lace-up shoes. He used a pen to lift up the bottom of a trouser leg, flesh colour underneath.

Two uniforms either side of him now.

'Jesus, boss, that was a scare.'

'Just a bit odd, Darren. It appears to be the torso of a male dummy from a shop window. But quite an old one. Wooden, in fact. See how the feet are screwed in?'

'You blokes mind moving back just a bit?' A guy pushing through, TV camera on his shoulder. 'That's fine. Thanks.'

'Hold it, pal,' Bliss said. 'We need to be quite sure about a couple of things.'

The cameraman moved back, shooting Bliss, who recognized the reporter with him, Amanda Patel, from BBC Midlands today.

'Giss a minute, Mandy.'

'What *is* this about, Frannie? We thought—'

'Yeh, we all thought. It's a bloody relief.'

Amanda let the cameraman finish recording, from a distance, before turning to the crowd, looking baffled.

'Can anybody... does *anybody* know what this is about?'

'It's the King of Hay,' an elderly man said. 'Someone made a very accurate effigy of the King of Hay, Richard Booth, and sent it floating down the River Wye.'

'It's jolly lifelike,' Amanda said. 'Scared me for a minute. No, really, is it a leftover from a carnival or something?'

'We haven't had a carnival this year. Nor last.'

'I remember when they were going to execute the King, or something like that, for a publicity stunt. But this... I mean it's not really the best time for jokes, is it?'

'You are quite right there,' the elderly man said.

'Can't be the actual crown jewels, can it?'

'I think you'll find they're still in the window of the King of Hay shop in town. But someone's gone to considerable trouble to create facsimiles. And then throws the whole lot in the river.'

'Bit sick, if you ask me. We've got some shots, in case it ever means anything, but...' Amanda Patel shook her head. 'I think I'm going to leave it alone, Frannie. Just looks like bad taste, anyway, with the hunt for Tamsin. And after what happened to that old man at Cusop. Come on, Paul.' She nodded at Bliss. 'Thanks, Frannie.'

The cameraman lowered his camera and followed Amanda Patel, who glanced once over her shoulder, looking uncertain. A kid was leaning over the King trying to pull off his crown.

'Hey!' Bliss was on his feet. 'Geroff!'

'It's glued on, boss,' Darren said.

Like the sceptre was to the hand. No wonder nothing had come off in the water.

'Always factions in Hay,' the elderly man said. 'People who support an independent Hay, other people who think Booth's held up progress by scaring off big business.'

'Some countries they'd have put out a bleedin' contract on him.'

An Asian guy in a Mumbai Indians T-shirt, with a bearded man in his thirties who was looking quite amused, prodding the effigy with his trainer.

'As he isn't seen here as often as he was, I don't see the relevance of a public drowning.'

'Especially not now, when something far more serious is consuming everyone's attention.'

This was a tall man with a half-moon face that Bliss recognized.

'*Hello*, Gwyn. I thought you'd retired.'

'Don't rub it in, boy.'

'What you doing here?'

'As I have to keep telling everybody, I *live* here. Bookseller, now. How's it going, Francis?'

'Going nowhere fast,' Bliss said. 'And this kind of incident doesn't help.'

He'd worked with Jones a couple of times. Shrewd. Deceptively quiet. Called by both his first names because Gwyn Joneses were ten a penny in Wales. He had that look of loss and longing in his eyes, the look that Bliss was dreading one day seeing in the mirror.

'Like so much that happens here,' Jones said, 'it doesn't make immediate sense.'

The boy in the wetsuit came to his feet.

'Leave it with you, then, should we?'

'Yeah, we'll do something with it.' The bearded man looked at Jones. 'What you reckon, Gwyn? Should I dispose of it? Don't want to cause embarrassment for the King.'

'And if it turns up on the television?'

'It won't, though, will it? You heard what she said. If they already have a big story in Hay, they're not going to want a bit of whimsy.'

'Not sure he wasn't actually in England when they found him,' Gwyn Arthur Jones said. 'This is the exact border, I think.' He pointed across the rough grass, where it formed a kind of peninsula between the river and quite a wide stream bursting into it. 'That's the brook, is it not?'

'The Dulas Brook?' Bliss went to the edge, peered down. 'This is where it comes out in the river?'

'The official border between Wales and the other place.' Jones bent to the effigy, fitted his hands underneath its arms and raised its upper half from the stones. 'Not too heavy. No, boy, I don't think we should dispose of it at all.' He looked at Bliss. 'Something here I instinctively mistrust. If somebody wants it in the river, I'd quite like to see it stays out. I've a little room at the back of my shop… all right with you, Francis?'

'How far's your shop?'

'Halfway to the clock. Yellow sign. It's called The Cop Shop.'

'Of course it is.'

'Give you a hand?' The bearded guy lifted up the head and shoulders. 'If I take this end and Jeeter takes the feet we can carry it between us and that way nobody gets soaked.'

Bliss shrugged. The effigy's head lolled, as if it was a real head with the weight of bone, Bliss guessing papier mâché with a thin skein of plaster of Paris, which had suffered in the water. The features were inexact. In the greying, blurring light, it looked like a real face that might be about to try and speak.

44

The mountains and the word

BY THE TIME she was back at the car, it was raining. Merrily had a headache. Found a packet of Anadin in the glove box, just one left.

False alarm, someone had told her and Huw outside the Granary. They'd thought there was a body in the Wye, near where the Dulas Brook flowed into it, but it had turned out to be an effigy of the King. What a bloody mindless thing to do, a woman had said, when the town had its heart in its mouth about Tamsin Winterson, known to many of the folks here since before she could walk.

Merrily swallowed the Anadin. Huw had gone home. This was one of those times when she might have gone home, too, and directly into the church to let it all out, but the prospect of meeting an angsty Martin Longbeach in there, gearing himself up for Sunday's service…

She stood for a few moments in the rain, then made a conscious decision, stripped off the wet fleece.

She pulled her newly waxed Barbour jacket from the back seat and walked out into the rain.

Little lights everywhere. A fairy grotto.

In the middle of the altar, attended by small figurines of the Virgin Mary, a tabernacle held the host under glowing candles and a starry blue dome.

St Mary's, Hay.

Oh, this was the real thing, all right. And yet she felt embraced by the shadows rather than the lights, wondering if she, or any woman priest, was welcome here. It was a broad church, the C. of E. and the Church in Wales, but few of her colleagues had been tempted, not even Martin Longbeach. Not anyone in Herefordshire where Bernie Dunmore wouldn't have touched it with a six-foot crozier.

Not that he could totally prevent it, if some minister wanted it. She knew for a fact that Richard Williams, the Anglo-Catholic vicar, had taken over an average congregation of about half a dozen, and now, apparently, it was averaging forty.

The lure of old ways.

She should be so lucky.

She stepped back, took off her coat and sat in one of the right-hand pews, next to a painted virgin and child.

St Mary's Church, Hay. Another St Mary's Church at Capel-y-ffin.

And Cusop… St Mary's. Marian country. How far did that go back? Did the alleged visions of the Lady of Llanthony have origins pre-dating Father Ignatius? She sat with hands flat on her knees, closing her eyes, and now the scent of incense was powerfully on the air, and she set her thoughts adrift, opening herself to some kind of understanding.

Voices would intrude.

… that Peter Rector was, at that time, a darker man. A man who wanted to play with the elements, if he could, and people's minds…

Like he owned the place… like he knowed the place. And it knowed him.

… what better place than this, where the very air was full of spiritual energy?

When she opened her eyes, it was to the rows of candles alight on the votive stand. How many of them had been lit today for Tamsin Winterson?

Big mysteries that hung like the incense on the air. Small

mysteries ripping families, whole communities apart. Small flickerings of hope.

Before she left, she lit another, with a short, intense prayer, and left her last fiver in the offertory box.

Outside, the rain had stopped, a sputtering sun gilding a corner of the sky. She walked all around the low-lying, squat-towered church, counting the ancient yew trees, shapeless sentinels flagging up pre-Christian origins. The church itself must have medieval foundations, but seemed to have been substantially rebuilt over the centuries. Quite an ordinary church, really, from the outside.

But its site was not.

Coming down from the circular churchyard, she saw its immediate neighbour, a green mound, evidently a castle motte, smaller and perhaps older than the hill at the top of the town where Hay Castle reared, with no church beside it. She followed the sound of water, down a steepening path beside the mound, found a fast-flowing steam dividing it from the church, and a place where the water went tumbling vertically over a small cliff, like a quarry face. She followed the path to where it joined another, found a spring coming out of a rock.

Stone and water everywhere, all this rushing, swirling energy so close to the River Wye but separated from it, the river obscured by trees, a living screen, as if the sight of it might be too much.

She began to tingle in a way that Jane might tingle, at the perception of something powerfully primeval. Oh God, why were all the sudden thrills so pagan-tainted these days?

The sun was burning away the clouds as she crossed a wooden footbridge over the stream, moving away from the church, but there were some old buildings ahead, quite low, and the sound of traffic.

From a short alley between some almshouses, probably nineteenth century, once humble, now bijou, she emerged on to the main road, some way below the Swan Hotel and almost directly opposite the opening of Forest Road, the long and winding lane – the only lane – leading to the Gospel Pass.

For a blinding moment, the main road and its traffic disappeared, and she saw, like a bright ribbon, the ancient connection between the church at Hay and the little oilcan church of Capel-y-ffin, both encircled by yews denoting prehistoric ritual origins, both dedicated to St Mary the Virgin who opened her ruined fingers to the sky.

St Peter and St Paul carrying the word down from the mountains, to Hay.

While at the opposite end of the town, the Dulas Brook, bypassing another church of St Mary, at Cusop, offered itself to the River Wye... so sacred that the town was afraid to look at her. Merrily stood at the side of the road, water glistening on the sleeves of the freshly waxed Barbour.

How the mountains came to Hay. The mountains and the word.

And what else? *What else?*

Walking back into the town centre, she felt, at last, connected. Getting a feel for it. It didn't feel Welsh, but then it didn't feel like England either, and that odd sense of being abroad seemed central to the experience.

But then that was the same for the whole of the border area. It was as if Hay, despite all its incomers, was somehow the quintessence of the border. A kind of alchemy at work here, taking in outsiders and then changing them in its own eccentric image.

And that was good... wasn't it, transformation?

There was a tiny pop inside her head, like a bubble bursting, followed by an acute sense of awareness... not self-awareness, something more objective: a vivid sense of being in a particular place, as if she were watching herself on a film. Probably a state of consciousness that Peter Rector and Athena White could bring on at will; it might happen to her once or twice a year and she was never quite sure if she liked it or not.

Hadn't happened in the church, but it might have been as a result of being in there, the mind-altering qualities of a re-coloured faith. Looking up Castle Street, there was a sense of timelessness, as if the whole area had been chemically preserved. An orange cast on the scene, as the sun peeled back the clouds, like she was viewing it through one of those old cellophane Lucozade wrappers from her remotest childhood. Almost as soon as it happened, it began to fade, but not completely.

She shook herself.

There was a shop on Castle Street called The King of Hay, its windows a little museum of Independent Hay. Richard Booth might have lost the castle and his biggest bookshop, but he was still a presence, which was probably important.

He made that town the best little bloody town in the country, Gomer Parry had said. 'Both *bloody countries!*

Two men were looking into the window, one wearing a T-shirt with a design involving the word Mumbai.

'… you are, boy,' the other man said, 'there's the originals, all intact. Now isn't that odd? Why would anyone go to all that trouble?'

'I fought London was a mad place, Gwyn. Hay, I give up trying to work it out.'

Merrily glanced between them and saw the crown jewels in the window, in all their pound-shop splendour, and was aware of the taller man looking down on her then leaning over to her, with a smile and a murmur.

'You're looking well, Mrs Watkins.'

45

Third-class citizens

Velvet-voiced, quietly cerebral, just slightly sinister. He'd been in charge of what became a murder inquiry in the Radnor Valley. Head of Dyfed-Powys CID at the time. A caretaker role, he'd told her, in the year before his retirement.

'You've shaved off your moustache,' Merrily said.

'So people keeping reminding me. As if there was little more to me than that.' He turned to his companion. 'Mrs Watkins is an investigator for the Diocese of Hereford. We met when she was sent by the Bishop to try and resolve the difficulty between a religious fanatic and the Thorogoods. Mrs Watkins, this gentleman is their immediate neighbour, Mr Paramjeet Kapoor.'

She shook hands with Mr Kapoor, a little confused.

'I'm sorry – where is this?'

'The Thorogoods? Across the road, up the alley.' Gwyn Arthur Jones pointed. 'Set up a little bookshop, the name of which suggests they haven't yet been converted to your faith. Not surprising you don't know, they aren't open yet.'

'How are they? How's Robin now?'

'Injuries *appear* to be under control. More than can be said for his temper, mind.'

'Don't help,' Mr Kapoor said, 'having the cops on his back.'

'What's he done?'

'Wrong place, wrong time,' Gwyn Arthur said, 'and didn't feel a need to justify his behaviour.'

Merrily remembered how Robin Thorogood had taken the

impact of a load of falling stone to save his wife. No Father Ignatius around, then, with his bottle of Lourdes water.

'Erm, do you… do they think Tamsin's dead?'

'Experience tells them this will be the most likely outcome. Sometimes you find the killer before the body. One leading to the other.'

He'd always looked mournful. He was like most people's mistaken idea of what an undertaker was like.

Mr Kapoor said he needed to get back. Not that trade was great.

'It's like people are just wandering around waiting for somefing to happen. I don't know this girl but a lot of 'em do, and it's like family, you know?'

When he'd gone, they kept on walking up the street, Gwyn Arthur observing things in the way of an old-fashioned beat copper, though he must have been at least a detective superintendent when he retired.

'Changing,' he said.

'Fewer book shops? Or am I imagining that?'

'Look there. Antique shop – used to be a bookshop. Fashion shop – used to be a bookshop. Shoe shop – need I go on? The irony is that few of them would be here if it wasn't for the book-shops.'

'Must be strange for you,' she said, 'being in the middle of a big police operation and not part of it.'

'Mrs Watkins, it feels sometimes as if I no longer exist. I have a share in a bookshop, now, specializing in the fictional exploits of detectives who, of course, age very slowly or not at all.'

'Isn't there, you know, cold-case work you could do?'

He laughed.

'Sounds exciting, doesn't it? Like archaeology. Cold case is mainly paperwork, computer work. Rather dull, and you don't get out much.'

They walked along the street of stone shops and offices, tree-less until the jagged shock of the castle, like a gigantic broken ornament on a shelf. They stopped by the war memorial on the square, a pay-and-display car park on all but market days. Well, then... no point in letting an opportunity go.

'Do you remember the Convoy, Gwyn? On Hay Bluff?'

'Strange days,' he said.

'What about Peter Rector?'

'Who drowned this very week.'

'And who was once, I understand, a near neighbour of the Convoy, up on Hay Bluff?'

'Ye-es,' he said thoughtfully. 'He most certainly was.'

'Did you know that Tamsin Winterson was a bit obsessed with the death of Peter Rector?'

She sensed his focus sharpening like a camera lens.

'Well,' he said, 'I do know – having been there myself at the time – that PC Winterson, in plain clothes, was asking questions about Mr Rector in Gwenda's Bar, where information gets exchanged. I wondered at the time if she was in plain clothes officially – sent to milk her local connections – but I'm inclined to think not. There are distinct levels of society in Hay and I would guess she, as a farmer's daughter from Dorstone, was not part of the one that meets in Gwenda's. Booksellers, mainly. Seemed out of place there, unsure of her ground.'

'What was she asking?'

'Trying to find out if anyone in Hay had known a David Hambling, of Cusop.'

'Did *you* know the real identity of David Hambling at the time?'

'No, I did not.'

He looked down at her, eyelids lowered, and she realized she must, serendipitously, be tapping into something here. That he was as interested as she was, if not more so.

'I met Tamsin, you see,' Merrily said. 'The day before she vanished.'

'Did you now?'

'Someone thought I might be able to shed some light on

Rector's world. And she happened to be there at the time. You had to like her. Serious, dedicated. Ambitious in an almost touchingly transparent way.'

She waited.

'Also' he said, 'she was asking about a woman in a red Audi. In the light of her subsequent disappearance, I thought I'd better call in at the community centre this morning to report what I'd heard. Asked if I might speak with the senior investigating officer. I was allotted a uniformed constable who wrote down my statement, asked no questions, and that's the last I heard.'

'He know you were a former senior detective?'

'I didn't make a thing of it, though I rather expected that someone would know. But there we are. Once you're gone, you're gone. I'm... mildly interested in why you should be asking me about all this.'

Mildly was not the word. Merrily raised the bar.

'I was also going to ask if you knew anything about the disappearance of two girls from the Convoy in the earlier nineteen eighties.'

'I think we need to sit down,' Gwyn Arthur said. 'Don't you?'

They found a table in the shadows, and there were plenty of those in Gwenda's Bar. No windows, only yellowy globes and strips of light through the slats of an extractor fan high on a wall. Yes, you could imagine information being exchanged here, possibly even drugs.

She'd never been in before, hadn't even known it existed at the end of this short entry lined, like so many in Hay, with books. Gwyn Arthur had raised a hand to the young, tight-bearded man behind the bar and the only customer, a bulky guy with a port wine stain who Merrily was sure she remembered from one of the bookshops.

It made it easier for both of them that Gwyn Arthur knew Bliss and had even met Huw Owen during his years based in Brecon. Gomer Parry, too, come to that, but everybody knew Gomer.

And oh, yes, he well remembered the ragged, dope- and diesel-smelling Convoy. Who, policing the border in the nineteen eighties, did not?

Not that CID had much to do with it until the girls went missing. The Convoy had been a headache for the uniforms. Gwyn Arthur said Ralph Rees had been uniform super in those days, one of the most decent, humane coppers you could ever have encountered. Ralph had been planning a second career as a vicar, fixing his retirement to get into a theological college in Cardiff before the cut-off point. Never made it – he'd died while Gwyn Arthur was out west. Bloody tragedy.

'Anyway, Ralph was the man in charge of moving on the Convoy, and a professional diplomat couldn't have handled it better. Quite organized, they were by then. One had researched all the law relating to travellers, and he'd appear in court for them – in a dark suit, for heaven's sake, with a stack of law books, though he had no qualifications. He'd negotiate with Ralph, man to man. I think Ralph rather liked him.'

Sometimes the travellers had been given diesel for the vans and buses, just to get them back on the road, keep them moving – even if it was only past the boundary of the Dyfed-Powys police area.

Then, one autumn day, a posse of travellers had gone into the station at Hay to report that two girls had not come home for two nights.

'Just disappeared from the camp, and the Convoy were reluctant to move on until they came back. Well, we thought at first it was just a scam to buy more time. But the parents of the younger girl were virtually camped out at the station.'

'Mephista?' Merrily said.

'Not a name you forgot. The parents were decent people in their way. Old hippies from Brighton. Good-life types. They were frantic.'

'Did you find out anything at all, in the end?'

'We did what we— I believe we did what we could. Probably not enough. The older one, Cherry Banks – I say older one, she was about twenty-three, but she'd been around. Well, mostly around Cardiff docks, to tell the truth. Mixed race, prostitute-and-sailor parentage. Inquiries were made in that area, to no avail.'

'You thought the younger girl had gone off with her?'

'I was a detective sergeant then. Not my place to point the inquiry in any particular direction. My main job was to question everybody in the convoy. Not easy, as some had criminal history, but they couldn't have it both ways. Either we took it seriously, which meant asking some intrusive questions, or we treated them like the third-class citizens they thought we thought they were.'

'So the girls are still listed as missing.'

'In some dusty database.' Gwyn Arthur leaned back in his rickety chair. 'Tell me… are you – or, indeed, Francis Bliss – seeing a connection here with PC Winterson's disappearance?'

'Just me at the moment. Not particularly on anyone's behalf.'

'Christian duty?'

'Unwanted holiday. Bit of a loose end. Just doesn't feel right walking away.'

He nodded.

'Christian duty.'

Merrily smiled. He'd been very patient, so she told him how, because of what she did and the kind of people she occasionally had to mix with, Bliss had asked her to take a look through Rector's library. How she'd wound up looking into matters that he wouldn't, especially with Brent at the wheel, be permitted to waste time on.

'Become your case then, has it? I'm not being patronizing here—'

'Don't really like sticking my nose into police business.'

'People in this area do tend to. A vast area, it is, with not so many people. Or noses. Few longer than mine.'

The bar's swing door had opened. Several people had come in, including a man and a woman silhouetted against the globe lights. The woman had blond hair and the man came with a walking stick.

46

Naked talk

PARKED NEAR THE entrance of the Oxford Road car park, Bliss called Annie. He guessed she'd be at home, at the flat in Malvern, but he rang the mobile.

'Francis.'

He pictured her in her pale-green bathrobe on the sofa, soft towelling around those sharp bones, freshly washed hair in a turban. The unexpected domestic side of Annie, what a turn-on that had been, along with the shop-talk: talk dirty to me, talk to me about criminal investigation.

'What's been on the telly?' Bliss said.

'You don't know?'

'Just tell me.'

'Never watch daytime TV, as you know, but it was second lead on the radio news. Just the basics. Hunt for a missing police-woman on the Welsh Border. Soundbite from Brent, appealing for anyone, et cetera, et cetera.'

'No background? Nothing about a feller helping with inquiries?'

'Is there one?' He could almost hear her sitting up. 'Does that mean it's known that she's dead?'

'I'm sure Brent's hoping she is. Be a career-sealer in Hereford, pulling a cop-killer. Or a first-class ticket out of Hereford.'

Telling her about the seller of weird books who'd left his truck on the car park overnight, got drunk and claimed to have slept in his shop. Who, on being grilled in the street by the latently thuggish Stagg, had not sounded convincing.

'Doesn't seem all that likely to me,' Bliss said. 'You start disturbing the surface, creeps like this will always come crawling out, blinking in the daylight.'

'Takes the pressure off you, anyway.'

'I'm not with you.'

'Oh *hell*—' Annie sighed irritably. 'I was hoping to tell you this in person. Brent phoned me early this morning.'

'He fancy you or something?'

'Actually,' Annie said, 'he fancies you, and not in a good way. He thinks you may know more about Winterson's disappearance than you're admitting.'

'Well, he would. I'm a wild card, me.'

'No listen,' Annie said. 'In its ridiculous way, this is worse than you realize. Sheer wishful thinking on his part, but he has a way with psycho-jargon. Which I'll translate for you. Just don't over-react, all right?'

'Hang on, I wanna better signal for this.' Bliss got out of the Honda and went to sit on the low wall at the top of the car park. 'Go.'

'He thinks you're damaged. Unstable. Unreliable. Before you were hurt you were merely erratic and wilful. You thought you were clever and invulnerable, a city-wise cop amongst the yokels.'

Annie speaking in the old ice-maiden voice to hold his attention.

She had it.

'But then your wife left you for another man. And then, for the first time in your police career, you were badly hurt, physically. Brain damage.'

'He said this to you?'

'He suggested that this, so closely following the discovery of your wife's affair, may have raised you to a different and quite dangerous level of instability. He cites your determination to come back to work before you were fully fit – he suspects some deception there, by the way, some calling in of favours. You had something to prove and not only in the job. You inflate an old man's accidental drowning into a possible murder case and you drag an impressionable young PC into your fantasy. A girl who's already slightly in awe of you.'

The left side of Bliss's head began to pulse all the way down to his shoulder, the top of his arm.

And what about a policeman, Francis? Would she... cop off with a detective, do you think?

He tried to laugh.

'He's such a twat, Annie.'

'I realize he's a twat. But do nothing about this, Francis, you understand? Do nothing. Because if this comes back on me, we've lost everything.'

'Go on.'

'Brent thinks you were leading Tamsin along, constructing an investigation – just you and her – with a view to... getting into her knickers.'

'He actually said that?'

Not Annie's kind of phrase.

'He was thinking, what if it all backfired. She rejects you. Maybe she threatens to report you—'

'And I *killed her*?'

Bliss found himself striding down the street towards the tourist centre like he was about to take off, leave the world.

'He's just flying a kite, Francis. He asked me, as a *trusted colleague* and someone who'd had dealings with you, if I thought it was too outlandish to consider. Bearing in mind that Winterson seems committed to her job in a way that's almost unusual these days... and does not appear to have a regular boyfriend.'

'You telling me I'm on his suspect list for killing... killing a girl who we don't know isn't alive and well? Because if that—'

Bliss felt himself lose it. Could almost feeling it squirming out of his head, dancing down the street in front of him, turning round to make faces at him, gleeful fingers in the corners of its mouth.

'I'm gonna have him for this. I swear to God, I'm gonna take it all the way—'

'Francis, for Christ's sake, he said it to *me*!'

'And you think you're the only one he's said it to?'

'Yes, I do. So far. He feels sure of his ground with me. You and me, long record of no love lost.'

'When this is over... I'm gonna dismantle that bastard. Nobody stops me.'

'Do nothing. Do you understand? Anything you do... *anything*... will rebound. On both of us... on every level. Just go along with everything he tells you to do. And stay out of Hay when you're not on duty.'

Bliss was leaning against the bus shelter, numb down the left side, from his temple to below his knee.

'I'm not on duty now. He sent me home. I don't wanna go home. I hate home.'

'You can come here if you like,' Annie said.

'So you can keep an eye on me?'

'Both eyes. And... maybe the rest of me.'

Mother of God, when did Annie Howe start talking like Mae frigging West?

Only when she was genuinely afraid he might do something that played into Brent's hands.

Not an entirely unfounded fear, he'd concede that.

'I'll come over, then.'

'We can talk about it.'

'Talk,' he said. 'Yeh.'

Not a euphemism. Talk made them compatible. Talking dirty, talking crime. Hard talk, naked talk.

He drove down Oxford Road, for England, but the left side of his head was dragged down with misgivings and the feeling that he wasn't going to make it to Malvern, that something was too close.

47

Blinded to the rest

BETTY FIDDLED WITH the phone until the picture appeared then she pushed it to the middle of the table, folded her arms and became very still.

Merrily remembered this about her, an ability to withdraw into herself as if she was watching the scene on some inner monitor. They'd met twice since the Radnor Valley witch-hunt, but not in the past year. Her face was firmer than before. Not that much older, but certainly stronger. Her blond hair was back off her face, held by an old-fashioned Alice band, her eyes startlingly clear and focused even in the dim light.

'*Where* was it, darling?'

'Gwenda Protheroe,' Gwyn Arthur whispered. 'Proprietor.'

Long wings of thick dark hair. Leaning over the bar, displaying an impressive cleavage.

'Set into the back of the fireplace, upstairs,' Betty said. 'Probably hidden for years.'

'We're just looking for a little help here,' Robin said, 'if it's only to eliminate the possibility of Mr Oliver being Adolf Hitler's long lost grandson.'

The photo in the phone was a close-up, just discernible in the dimness, from where Merrily and Gwyn Arthur were sitting, way back in the shadows. She glanced at Gwyn Arthur, half alarmed; it was like he'd plugged her into some circuit that edited reality, cut to the chase.

'It is though, isn't it? Sort of a swastika.' Gwenda snatched up the phone, hair swinging, then called out, 'Anybody know about any Nazi stuff in Hay, back in the war? Come *on*...'

Holding up the phone displaying the soot-rimed swastika.

'Wossisname,' the man with the wine stain said. 'Hitler's Number Two. Rudolph Wossisname... I got no memory these days.'

'Rudolph Wossisname,' Gwenda said. 'Parachuted down to try and wind up the war, something like that. Wasn't he incarcerated somewhere round here for a while, or was that just a story?'

'Rudolf *Hess*. Abergavenny, that was. Taken there for interrogation. It's only half an hour away. How would that work, then, Gwennie, with the carving on the chimney?'

'Er... no idea.'

Somebody laughed. Merrily recognized Wine-stain now: Gareth Nunne, a name that looked good over a bookshop. A dealer who somehow acquired cheap remaindered copies of books before they even went into paperback.

Betty said, 'What are you guys not telling me?'

Robin said, '*Bets*...'

'*Die, Englisher pig!*' Betty said.

All eyes on her, including Robin's, bagged now. His hair was still long, but less sleek than it had been. He looked like a man from whom something was slipping away. You hoped it wasn't Betty.

'Anybody remember Tom Armitage?' Betty said. 'Antiques?'

Gwenda shook her head. Gareth Nunne grunted.

'Cocky bugger.'

'Only I was talking to him on the phone, because I was interested in people who'd had the shop before, and he was telling me about how they used to find bits of war comics around the place. There was a guy there once who sold them, including rare German comics. Nazi stuff, I assume he meant. He said the guy OD'd on drugs.'

Gwyn Arthur was nodding.

'But you guys,' Betty said, 'when I show you this, you just go rambling on about Rudolph bloody Hess.'

Gareth Nunne looked at her, mock-startled. Gwenda laughed.

'You tell them, girlie.'

A woman said wearily, 'Jab.'

Gwenda said, 'What?'

'Jerrold Adrian Brace. Gorgeous, pouting Jerry Brace. Used to sign his initials, JAB. He's the guy sold the war books and comics.'

'*Connie…*' Gareth Nunne putting on a warning tone. 'You remember what we…?'

'Oh Gawd, Gary, what's the point? It was a long time ago.'

Merrily saw she was quite elderly and sloppy, about six necklaces, and smoking what looked like a slim panatella. Betty turned her wooden chair.

'Sorry, is it Mrs Wilby? Look, we're not having a great day, and I know there's something so much worse going on all around us, right, but it would be helpful to deal with this. That shop's important to us, and it doesn't seem to have a good history. Just helps to know these things.'

'So, like, anything you can tell us,' Robin said, 'be helpful if you didn't hold back.'

'Yeah, go on, Con,' Gwenda said. 'Somebody tell them. Tell *me*. We're all grown-ups here.'

'Nobody remembers now, anyway,' Gareth Nunne said. 'He wasn't yere that long. And when he *was* yere he wasn't yere half the time.'

'Gareth likes you,' Connie said to Betty. 'Gareth thinks we have far too many ugly old booksellers and you would help redress the balance. Gareth's sexist, ageist and everything else ending in ist. And I've been charmed by your insanely dashing, disabled husband, and we knew from the papers what had happened to you, so we wanted you to be happy here. And, as we said, it's a very long time ago.'

'Don't stop there,' Betty said.

'Well, he died, you see,' Gareth Nunne said. 'In the end, that was what most people remembered about Jerry Brace. The way he died.'

'He OD'd,' Betty said. 'That *is* right, is it?'

'Yes, but not quite so many people did in those days, my dear. Not in places like Hay. Not *heroin*, anyway. Bit of a nine-day wonder. Not that there weren't many of *those*, mind – oh, the glamour. The lovely Marianne Faithfull here for a while. April Ashley, Britain's first ever sex-change sailor. Not that poor bloody Jerry was famous.'

'Except for the way he died,' Connie said.

'Flaming Nora!' Gwenda threw a bag of crisps in the air. 'Get to the *point*. I don't know any of this, and I'm furious.'

'Well, of course you don't, dear,' Connie Wilby said. 'It was over thirty years ago. He was an ex public-school boy. Wealthy, titled father with strong fascist leanings. Sir Charles. His Mosleyite mate was Lord Brocket, who lived at Kinnersley Castle, end of the war. And he'd infected his son with his political views. Jerry had this awful obsession with what you might call the dark side of the last war.'

Gareth Nunne grunted.

'Ostensibly. In the shop you'd have books on Churchill and the Battle of Britain and piles of war comics. But upstairs, up past the sign that said "Staff Only"... was the other stuff.'

'We used to think it was just pornography,' Connie Wilby said. 'Sort of stuff you'd sell on the Internet these days. You knew people were going to that shop who never went anywhere else. Men usually, sometimes in pairs, in those short denim jackets. It was only when he died that we found out that it was wall-to-wall heavy-duty Hitler and the SS and satanism.'

'Some of those books,' Gareth Nunne said, 'were actually plain-cover stuff. Interminable tracts full of hatred. Privately published by the neo-Nazi fraternity in the UK. He also – this was the early days of video – would put together old films of the rise of Hitler and those Berlin Olympics, the Aryan fitness dream. And footage from Himmler's magic castle at Wewelsburg. He had a video copier, churning out all this stuff.'

'You'd hear him talking about Hitler when he was pissed,' Connie said, 'like the Fuhrer was some bloody dark angel, and he—'

'Was that his phrase?' Betty's head had snapped up. 'Or yours?'

'Oh, his, I 'spect. He was a bit of a... they'd say he was a Goth now.'

'There was a stage,' Gareth Nunne said, 'where we'd have all these bloody skinheads in town, all filing into his shop. I hadn't got a shop then, see, I was working for the King, and I don't reckon *he* was too happy, but it wasn't like he owned the place.'

Gareth Nunne scowled, remembering, his facial skin flaw shining like beetroot. Gareth Nunne and Connie Wilby... Merrily had been in both their shops once or twice, over the years. She remembered Connie specializing in local history and old maps.

'With hindsight,' Connie said, 'I think Jerry only opened that shop to feed his obsession. His opening hours were ludicrously irregular. Sometimes he'd close for a week and bugger orf somewhere – back to his parents' house – or with some woman, we thought. He was very fond of women. But, as I say, he was terribly handsome. Blond hair.' She looked up at the bar, wistfully. '*Terribly* handsome. Which rather blinded you to the rest.'

Merrily saw Gwenda raising an eyebrow.

'And so *fit*,' Connie said. 'As if he worked out at the gym, which was hardly fashionably in those days. I don't think there *were* any gyms in this part of the world. Not outside schools anyway.'

'You're playing this for all it's worth, aren't you, darling?' Gwenda said. 'And you do keep dwelling on his physical attributes. That mean you... knew him well?'

'Not well,' Connie said gruffly. 'But – yes – I knew him. Once. Couldn't take my drink in those days, that was the trouble.'

'Bugger me.' Gareth turned his chair round to peer at her. 'I didn't know about that, Connie.'

'Thought I was going to be his older woman at first, but he never even looked at me again. Or he looked at me properly and thought, "Oh Christ, what have I done?"'

'You were still in your thirties,' Gareth said. 'Just about. If I'd known you was up for—'

'Oh please! They were heady days, even the King bringing girls back to his castle. Nearest Hay ever came to a summer of love. And *I* didn't know he was a bloody Nazi, did I? It was just war books, then, far as we knew.'

Gwenda said. 'Was this… you and the Aryan beauty… in the shop in Back Fold?'

'Was, yes. I think Jerry was the last person to actually live there. He'd had the walls painted black, and there were posters and things. Joss sticks. Not bad for a man-pad. I remember he just had a bloody big mattress on the floor in the living area. And he'd light a fire in the small grate upstairs. Small burn marks all over the floorboards.'

Connie burst into throaty laughter.

Robin said, 'What happened to all the books and tapes and stuff?'

'Don't know, dear. Somebody must've come to clean the place out, get rid of the stock. I doubt any of us would've wanted to take it on, even as a free gift. We didn't know about his heroin habit. Wasn't so ubiquitous, then, not like now, all those needle bins in the public lavs.'

'A superfit heroin addict?' Gwenda said.

'Perhaps he was just wasted. I wouldn't know, would I? I was a convent girl. Perhaps when he shut the shop and went away he was in some sort of rehab – they have rehab in those days? Can't recall. Anyway, that's why nobody noticed. When he… went.'

She looked at Gareth, who looked down into his beer.

'He'd been dead for well over a week, see, when they found him. What was it, Connie, overdose or a bad batch of something?'

Connie shook her head. Betty didn't react. Merrily wondered if she'd been expecting something worse.

'All too common nowadays,' Connie said, 'but back then, in Hay...'

'Where did they find him?' Betty asked.

'If it was me about to live there,' Gwenda said softly, 'I wouldn't want to know. Don't put yourself through it, darling, he's gone. And you're young. Sterner stuff, what?'

Connie laughed.

48

Messiah

MERRILY HAD DRAWN it, from memory, on the back of a post office receipt – no room on a cigarette packet any more because of the horror photos which could surely only encourage more hard kids to smoke. She wanted to follow Robin and Betty out of the bar, but Gwyn Arthur had shaken his head: not yet.

He'd waited for a couple of minutes after they'd left before standing up.

'Didn't think you were still here, Gwyn,' Gwenda said. 'A little tryst, is it?'

'This is my friend, Mrs Watkins, Gwenda. Person of the cloth.'

Merrily felt the gaze of the close-bearded man standing close to Gwenda, polishing a glass.

'You must have hidden qualities, Gwyn,' he said.

'So well hidden my wife can barely remember them. I'll see you, boy.'

'That's her son?' Merrily said outside.

Gwyn Arthur laughed.

'A customer who once said that was almost glassed. He's... her boyfriend of some long standing. Gwenda has charms which are not so well hidden. As you may have noticed. Some men who've never read a book in their lives patronize that bar just to watch her move.'

Merrily followed him across to a bench near the spired clock tower which she saw, for an instant, as a huge hypodermic syringe. Two cops were talking in its shadow. She took out the post office receipt.

'Quite an unusual swastika. Less angular.'

He shook his head, didn't seem to recognize it.

'I was here when they found Mr Brace. About a year before I went home to West Wales in search of fame and fortune. Welsh-speaker, see, instant fast-track out there. But my wife had never learned, so we came back in the end.'

A cameraman from Sky TV was shooting the two cops against the clock while a reporter studied notes on a clipboard. There was a chilly feeling now that if you turned away you'd miss some development.

'I tend to smell it, in my memory, every time I go past that shop, which is almost every day. The smell from when we broke in, and there was Jerrold Brace, mostly naked, decaying in the bath.'

'Do you know why the Thorogoods have opened a bookshop when they're closing down in all the high streets? Hard enough for a seasoned professional.'

'If things weren't as bad as they are, I don't suppose they'd find a shop here at a rent they could afford. I'm guessing they never quite recovered from what happened to them. And they were welcomed here. The booksellers are glad to have another bookshop to strengthen the foundations. If they hadn't taken that shop, it might've been a nail bar. Another one gone.'

'And that's why nobody wanted to tell them about the death in their bath?'

'I expect it's a different bath now. Wasn't that gruesome, apart from the condition of the body – quite a warm autumn. Brace had apparently been off heroin for a while and then got hold of some particularly pure stuff and... gone. There was the syringe on the bathroom floor and the remains of the unadulterated smack.'

'And he had links with the Convoy? And the missing girls?'

'As Mrs Wilby said in there, he was a good-looking boy and he liked the ladies... No, that's wrong. Almost certainly wrong. It wasn't ladies he liked. He'd grown up with *them*. He liked... if he was a woman or a gay man we'd use the words *rough trade*. He appeared to like the sort of women you might find attached to the convoy. And when Gareth Nunne says he wasn't at the shop for long periods, you might find that one of the long periods was during the magic mushroom season.'

'He'd join the Convoy on the Bluff?'

'He was certainly there when we were questioning them about the missing females. I recall asking him if the older one, Cherry Banks, had ever been seen in Hay. If he'd said he didn't know what Cherry Banks looked like, my suspicions would have been aroused. But no, he admitted to having had sex with her. He said he came up to the Bluff to chill out, or however they put it back then. Chill out and get laid.'

'What about the other girl, Mephista? Was she rough trade? At sixteen?'

'She was... intelligent. But different. Her parents were old hippies. Her dad told me they'd tried to bring her up with their values – live frugally, be at one with nature. I remember thinking, she's too young for all that. She'll rebel. The way her parents rebelled against capitalism, consumerism, shiny suits.'

'What did Brace have to say about her?'

'Thought he knew which one she was. Well, yes, I'm quite sure he did. They were both to be found at Rector's farm – Mephista dragged there by her parents, Brace helping out.'

'With what?'

'I don't know. But, of all the people from the Convoy, he seems to have been the closest to Rector.'

Grainy clouds had slid across the sun, enough to bring out a breeze. Merrily zipped up her coat.

'My information is Rector had a substantial neo-Nazi following from his first book – dealing with the occultism of Nazi Germany. He was distancing himself from it by then... but some of them clearly found that hard to accept. If they even believed it. It was as if they thought he had some secret source that they could tap into. Did Rector know what Brace was?'

'And who is *your* secret source, Mrs Watkins?'

'Erm… I think that had better remain secret for the time being. Reliable, though.'

She wondered if his interest stemmed purely from his own involvement in a case that was still on the books. Did he feel the answer was here, in Hay?

'Did *you* talk to Peter Rector, Gwyn?'

'The Messiah? Not one-to-one, having gone there as bag-carrier to my DI.'

'The Messiah? Who called him that – the Convoy?'

'And others. He'd stride the bare hills looking like a prophet. Hair suspiciously black for a man well into his fifties. But when you spoke to him he was unexpectedly quiet. Almost – what's the word? – diffident?'

'You think working with the Convoy filled some need in him? Like to help the homeless? Or was it more cynical? People who wouldn't tell. Or, if they did, wouldn't be believed.'

'He certainly used to hang around with that chap, the television playwright. Jeremy Sanders…? *Sandford.*'

'*Cathy Come Home*?'

'You remember that?'

'Yeah, seminal TV play about homelessness. We watched it at theological college in connection with something. Man with a strong social conscience. He was there?'

'Lived nor far away, in Herefordshire. Still interested in the homeless. And gypsies of all kinds – a member of the Gypsy Council. And he'd written a book about magic mushrooms. Someone said it was Sandford who encouraged Rector to involve the Convoy in his activities. And there was that other chap, Bruce Chatwin, the writer, he was staying with Rector when we talked to him. Used to stay with him while writing.'

'Both dead now.'

'There we are. Regular little arts festival up there.'

'So why would Brace have a hidden swastika in his shop? Inside the chimney which was obviously still in use in his time and then was blocked up. By him?'

'Don't know *what* to make of it. Set in stone, or brick, like a family crest. His father, Sir Charles, died quite recently.'

'I don't think I've heard of him.'

'Well connected in the City. Second home in Herefordshire, to which he eventually retired. Victorian Gothic monstrosity out near Bromyard which he enjoyed making even more medieval. As Mrs Wilby said, he was a friend of the Nazi-sympathizer Lord Brocket. Also, incidentally, of the fugitive Lord Lucan.'

'He was right-wing?'

'Oh hell, aye. Brace was one of the people mentioned as possibly sheltering Lucan when he was being sought for the murder of his children's nanny. A lot of it going on, then, under the surface. Talk of a right-wing coup, being planned when it was suggested that the prime minister, Wilson, was being controlled by the Soviet Union. Very dark days, and the Welsh Border... little hotbed of prominent fascists. But... being a neo-Nazi was not an offence, except to the sensibilities of some of us.'

'Are they still around? Frannie Bliss is a bit dismissive about their continued potential as a threat. My source... less so.'

'It's an interesting question.' Gwyn Arthur had his pipe going. 'Throughout the eighties and nineties, we were occasionally alerted to the existence of extreme right-wing cells in Mid Wales, Shropshire, Herefordshire. Often indistinguishable from the survivalists in their remote farms, with more weaponry than was legal. You'll still find them on the Internet.'

'You think Brace was actually a member of one?'

'Not sure. Could be he was simply serving a gap in the market. Dealing in the kind of books he knew some of these people would pay enormous prices for. Using his father's contacts.'

'You think there was more, though, don't you?'

He took his pipe from between his teeth.

'Merrily, you dismiss these people as complete crackpots, see, and then something happens. But is there anything here to risk public humiliation by passing on to my former colleagues? I tend to think not. Still... it's been very interesting talking to you. Let's stay in touch.'

She noticed he'd called her Merrily, as if accepting her, at last, as some kind of colleague, a legitimate confidante. And yet...

She watched him walk away, thinking that, for events of more than thirty years ago, they all seemed very clearly defined in the mind of Gwyn Arthur Jones.

One side of the car park backed on to the grounds of Hay Primary School, a TV reporter was standing by the gate, recording a piece-to-camera as children came out, met by parents and minders.

Merrily unlocked the Freelander and got in, slammed the door, feeling tired and frustrated, that elusive moment of illumination at Hay Church far behind her now. Nothing quite added up, just became more complicated, more tangled. She rang Bliss's mobile and filled up his answering service with an edited version of what she'd learn from Gwenda's Bar and her discussion with Gwyn Arthur Jones, who she didn't name.

On the way home, the mobile chimed, and she stopped on the edge of the village of Dorstone, where Tamsin lived, to pick up a text.

Gwyn Arthur:

> I got it wrong. It was not Messiah
> they called Rector. It was Magus.
> The Magus of Hay.
> For what that's worth.

Magus. An archaic term, applied to sundry sorcerers and the Three Wise Men of the New Testament.

Magus of *Hay*?

She texted back at once.

Who actually called him that?
Can you remember?

When she drove into Ledwardine twenty minutes later, her head was still so clogged with it that she turned into the vicarage drive, almost running into the back of Martin Longbeach's Mini Cooper. *Bugger.* Slammed on, backed out and reversed all the way into Church Street.

Parking on the square, she gathered up her bag and her fleece and stumbled down to Lol's cottage, where Ethel was waiting behind the door, slaloming around her ankles, as the mobile chimed.

The text from Gwyn Arthur Jones said,

I think it was the
novelist
Beryl Bainbridge.

She called him back, but there was no answer.

49

Superstition

UPSTAIRS, KAPOOR BENT to examine the derelict fireplace.

Robin said, 'You see it?'

Kapoor straightened up. 'It was an Indian sun symbol, you know that? My gran was always pissed off at Hitler nicking it off us.'

'You notice this one is going backwards? That a negative thing?'

'Dunno, mate. Never heard of a satanic swastika. Coulda phoned my gran, she'd know. If she wasn't dead. Tell you what, put the plate back, forget it.'

'And the fact that a guy obsessed with Nazi black magic was living here? And that it sounds like nobody ever made a success of a business here ever since?'

'That,' Kapoor said, 'is just superstition.'

'Well, yeah. Of course it is. Holy shit, Kapoor, I'm a *pagan*. I'm a superstitious *person*. Superstition is *good*. Superstition is opening yourself to hidden messages. Recognizing what the world's telling you and reacting accordingly. Taking precautionary measures.'

'No, mate.' Kapoor's eyes narrowing. 'That's Obsessive Compulsive Disorder.'

'You know what? Your gran would not like how you turned out.'

Robin looked at Betty who'd followed them up and was standing near the top of the stairs, face clouded with uncertainty in a place once a magnet for razored racists and disaffected street scum. A room that once had shelves packed with *tracts full of hatred*, according to Gareth Nunne – a guy entitled to a degree of contempt by virtue of being about as far removed as you could imagine from the Aryan ideal of superfit manhood.

After a while, Betty said, 'I probably told you about my brief encounter with neo-Nazism.'

Robin blinked.

'Bets, for some reason I have no recollection of that.'

'It was before we met. I went out with one, once. Kind of.'

'And you told me about this?' Robin was blinking. 'I don't think you did.'

'*Once*, OK? All right, maybe it's not the kind of thing you boast about.'

'Take a seat,' Robin said.

'I was about seventeen.' Betty dropped into a cane chair. 'I was with a mate, and we got talking to these two guys in a second-hand record shop in Llandod – Llandrindod Wells,' she said for Kapoor's benefit, 'where we moved when I was a kid. They asked us if we wanted to go to a festival up on the border, towards Shropshire. They seemed quite normal in the shop, but when they picked us up they were in a black van and wearing what I thought at first was just standard goth kit. I was a bit suspicious, but, you know, there were two of us, and I didn't see the swastikas till we got out at the festival. Which, of course, was right in the middle of nowhere and not exactly Glastonbury.'

Robin said, 'You never told me *any* of this.'

'Maybe you weren't listening. Anyway, it wasn't one of my favourite nights, and I've not thought about it much since. We kept away from them, wondering how to play it. They got stoned and came looking for us, and we'd realized by then that we were supposed to camp out with them for the night. So we just took off for the nearest farm and asked if we could use their phone. Spent just about every last penny we'd got on a taxi. But not before we'd listened to all this shit, in the van and then round the fire on the site.'

'Like what?'

'How their generation – our generation – was going to see the birth of a new aeon of Aryan supremacy of which Hitler was only the prequel. How the spirit of Hitler was still out there to initiate the... I don't know, the warrior replacing the wimp-culture. Make war, not love. How the weak should be culled. And the work-shy scroungers.'

'Was everybody there that way inclined?'

'Probably no more than a dozen. It was an acoustic festival run by local beardies, and I think they were a bit pissed off by these guys who were kind of jeering at the music. But nobody wanted to cause any trouble.'

'I'd've caused some trouble,' Robin said. 'Back then.'

'I ran into a few later, on the pagan scene. Always hanging around the fringes of Wicca and Druidry. Lowest kind of goth – heavy metal, death metal, grandiose, sexist. It's mainly a man-thing.'

Robin thought of his paintings for Lord Madoc, the inter-galactic Celt. A lot of violence there. Not that he'd written the stuff.

'You never told me,' he said sadly. 'Not all this.'

'Robin, I was never very interested. I've always followed the Celtic tradition. I knew they were into some of the same things as us – earth energies, green politics. Just in a different way. They reject the matriarchal element in Celtic paganism, the Mother Goddess. And they say we got the back-to-the-land thing wrong. You can't just get by with apple orchards and growing your own veg, you need to kill. Kill the wildlife, cull the population. Get rid of the weak.'

'That's religion?'

'Oh, and democracy can never work. And the name of the God-like Hitler was blackened by us inventing the Holocaust. And all non-whites are a result of our ancestors having sex with monkeys, but you knew that.'

Robin's hand closed on the ram's head knob on his stick, aware of something rising within Betty that didn't occur too often. She'd been the one to suggest they show the picture of the swastika around town, which translated as Gwenda's. Betty had gone in meaning business, Gwenda backing her up, two strong women, both outsiders.

'OK,' he said. 'Whadda we do?'

'If he's left anything here, we need to get rid of it. Starting, I suppose, with the purely practical stuff.'

'The easy bits, huh?' Robin knelt down, ran his fingers over the contours of the crooked cross in the chimney. 'You wouldn't have a stone chisel, Kapoor? I got one back at the bungalow, but we should do this now. Now it's exposed to the air.'

'Well, yeah,' Kapoor said. 'Suppose I can find summink. But if you bring the whole wall down, it ain't my fault.'

'Accepted.'

'Fair enough. Don't go away.'

When he'd gone, Robin was aware of the cold, metallic weight of the air in the room. Maybe imagination, but the ambient calm around Betty wasn't. He knew that calm, like a vulcanologist knew volcanos.

'You're quiet.'

'For too long.'

She went over to the window, looking down into Back Fold, the town slowing down for the evening like some old crustacean settling into its shell.

'They should've told us.'

'Maybe it was just we didn't ask.'

'Crap.'

'Bets, we're—'

'You're right. Nobody's had much luck here, have they? From a back-street antiques dump with a phone number in the window to a failed literary bookshop. And Jeeter's right, people cover up things they don't like. It's like this guy Tom Armitage – "Oh, life's too short for what you can't explain." Wrong!' Betty banged the flat of a fist on the window sill, turned round, glaring at him. 'You explain it, then you *fix it*. Meanwhile... yes, get rid of the obvious. Knock the bloody wall down, if you have to.'

He nodded. Stood up, and the pain went up and down his back like a file. He felt his face go grey. He didn't care.

Bliss was halfway to Ross-on-Wye, the back road to Annie's flat in Malvern to avoid Hereford peak-hour traffic, when the mobile went.

By the time he'd found somewhere to pull in, with the warning lights on, the phone had already stopped, as if it had been a wrong number or a change of mind by the caller. Didn't recognize the number, not one he'd stored, but he called it back anyway.

'Oh. Bliss.'

'Who's this?'

'It's... Claudia Cornwell in Talgarth.'

It registered at once with Bliss that she sounded edgy and not in a barrister way. He kept quiet. He could see what looked like the full length of the Black Mountains from the English side. Against the late sun, they did look unusually black.

'Bliss, I'm not sure how to handle this. I've just seen something on Wales Today. The Welsh news? Well, for a start, I saw you.'

'In Hay, yeh. Apologies for not wearing me suit. Long night.'

'It was just a parting shot in a long report on the missing policewoman. About a false alarm that had the police rushing down to the river.'

'The King of Hay.'

'Yes.'

'Something you want to tell me, Claudia?'

'There is, but I have another call waiting that might have a bearing on it. You going to be around tonight? I mean you, not the police, generally.'

'I could be.'

'You know what I'm saying. There are some things that have to remain confidential. As you must know yourself.'

'And some things where privacy has to take second place.'

'I just need a little more time to think, Francis, and perhaps an assurance that if I tell you something I'm not going to be making what amounts to a formal statement to West Mercia Police.'

'You know I can't make promises with something this big on the go.'

'I'll call you back,' she said.

Bliss called Annie to say he might be late.

'She's a barrister,' Annie said. 'Be bloody careful, Francis. You've had very little sleep, which didn't used to matter.'

'Yeh. Thanks.'

A mile or so further on, he found a gate left open to a field newly mowed for hay. Pulled in, tilted his seat back and slept.

When Kapoor hit the end of the chisel with the hammer, the chisel vanished up to its hilt.

'Blimey. What's happening here?'

'A space?' Robin said. 'There's a space behind the swastika?'

Kapoor dropped the chisel, cupping his hands to catch a little rubble. Concrete, Robin thought, not stone. Spider-cracks were appearing at the top of the swastika.

'Gonna drop out in a bit, anyway,' Kapoor said, 'if I don't help it along.'

'Do it,' Robin said.

Kapoor lifted the hammer and drove in the chisel one more time, Robin cupping his own hands underneath, letting the swastika fall into them in a puff of dust. Robin carried it away, a round of concrete a couple of inches thick, Kapoor scraping out the edge of the hole it had left.

'Torch?'

Betty had the mini-Maglite ready, handed it to him and he shone it around in the hole then came away, turning the head to switch it off, putting it down in the grate, wiping dust from his mouth.

'Just a hole.'

'Lemme see.'

Robin picked up the torch, bent carefully to peer in there, saw a shallow tunnel, like a handful of bricks had been removed. At the back of them, stone.

'Don't get it. It's like another wall.'

'Well, yeah, it is,' Kapoor said. 'It's the castle wall, innit?'

'Yeah.' Robin came out, his hip grinding. 'Gotta be.'

Betty said, 'The castle wall? Can I just...?' She picked up the chisel. 'Jeeter, if you can shine the beam to the back... Thanks.'

She reached an arm into the space. Robin heard the blade scraping at the stones, and then Betty withdrew it and lay down on her stomach and put her face up to the gap in the back of the chimney. Emerging with her face and hair like she was wearing clown's make-up.

Robin smiled; didn't think he ever loved her more than when she was all messed up and didn't care.

'Basically, this room,' Betty said, 'has a little entry to the castle. Right into the wall.'

'Yeah?'

'Does that not ring your bell, Robin?' You were so excited to be living so close to the castle. And you're not even a Nazi.'

'Thanks.'

'You don't get it, do you? This Brace... he had money, it sounds like. He was *from* money. He could've got a better shop than this. Why would he want this one? Maybe the same reason you wanted it, except you just like it because it's old and the nearest thing in Hay to a romantic ruin. But for him... a military stronghold? Dedicated to violence?'

'I don't—'

'It's how they think.'

'Right.'

He was recalling last night, though it seemed like another life. The way he'd seen the castle through the small, square window in the bathroom and felt no welcome there. Thinking how, even when the castle was in ruins, a tradition of blood-flow had continued under the walls.

This would mean nothing to most people. It was in the past. Over.

'It doesn't end there,' Betty said. 'The space. I don't think it ends with the wall. I'm guessing some old stones at the end have been taken out and replaced.'

'How d'you know that?'

'It's not mortared. It's just rubble.'

Robin looked at Kapoor.

'I can't reach that far,' Kapoor said. 'Can't get inside there with a hammer and chisel. You got a crowbar? You know? Like a big tyre iron?'

Robin shook his head.

'Got a spade in the truck I keep for if we get stuck in the snow.'

It had been snowing until well into April, and he'd felt if he'd taken the spade out it would snow again.

'Better than noffing, mate.'

'I'll go fetch it,' Robin said. 'Long as the cops don't see me and think I'm using it to bury someone.'

Wasn't a joke, and nobody laughed.

50

Spartan

'She was at Rector's place when we went to talk to him about the girls,' Gwyn Arthur said on the phone.

Beryl Bainbridge.'

'*Dame* Beryl Bainbridge, I think,' Merrily said. 'Distinguished novelist.' She looked at her cigarette. 'Distinguished smoker.'

'Rector liked writers, as you know,' Gwyn Arthur said.

Merrily lit the cigarette. She'd been finishing her omelette in Lol's kitchen when he'd called back.

'This woman answered the door when we arrived,' he said. 'Quite… petite, long dark hair. Made us a cup of tea. "I'm Beryl," she said. Very pleasant, she was, very nice to us. She said, "I suppose you want to talk to the Magus of Hay."'

'You didn't, by any chance, ask her to explain why she called him that?'

'It was said in a tongue-in-cheek fashion, and I was just a policeman, not a potential acolyte. Why is it important?'

'Puts him in a different light, somehow. It's all stayed with you, hasn't it? Didn't take much memory-jogging.'

He was silent. Time to push him?

'I'm wondering… if there was something that, with hindsight, Gwyn, you feel you could have done that you didn't.'

'Isn't there always? I wish I'd known then what I know now. I wish I'd been a more senior officer at the time. I wish I'd had someone like you with whom to exchange ideas.'

'I'm not—'

'By which I mean someone who can explain aspects of human behaviour by seeing them from a different perspective. Who talks to people who wouldn't talk to me. Or not in the same way.'

She could hear his breath, slow, almost meditative.

'Oh dear. I think I need,' he said, 'to take you into my confidence. Before something happens.'

She stared out of the window into the sandy light on Church Street. This had been a long time coming.

'If it hasn't already,' he said.

He'd opened the shop, selling second-hand crime novels, with the help of an old friend, a long-established bookseller in Hay. Didn't really know why. He liked books, but had no particular aptitude for selling them

'However, the *Brecon and Radnor Express* thought it was worth a story. *Top Detective* – as they were generous enough to describe me – *Turns To Crime*. I get my picture taken between Inspector Wallander and Inspector Rebus on the book covers. After it appeared in the B & R, the story was picked up by a couple of the national papers. Not big, but it was there.'

Weeks later, he said, he'd had a phone call from an elderly man in North Wales, to whom he hadn't spoken since the 1980s, when the man's daughter had gone missing from an encampment on Hay Bluff.

'Mephista's dad?'

'Sounding much the same. Still desperate to know if his daughter was alive or dead. Even more desperate, perhaps, because his wife, he said, was very seriously ill and perhaps there might not be so much time left for her to achieve peace of mind. It made me feel guilty over the quality-time we might have spent soon after the girl disappeared if we hadn't been inclined to suspect it was all a scam to keep the Convoy on the Bluff for a few more weeks. I wondered if we *had* treated them like third-class citizens.'

'Attitudes were different, back then.'

'But... I was retired now. I said – without promising anything – that I'd go back and review the case. They wanted to pay me, but I thought it was the least I could do. And it also gave me a reason to... feel worthwhile again. Every couple of weeks, I've been giving him a ring and going over a few things. Even tracked down a couple of former members of the Convoy – one of whom liked the area so much he came back, to live, with his family. Has a plumbing business now. One thing I *was* able to harden up was the evidence of Mephista's relationship with Brace, which I now know to have been a close one.'

'How close?'

'Extremely close. She had what used to be called a crush on him. Which developed. He'd bring her back to Hay in his vehicle.'

'She couldn't have been here when he died if he lay undiscovered for so long.'

'Couldn't she? What if she didn't want to go back to her parents? Or be called to give evidence at the inquest?'

'But if Brace was dead... where *could* she go? She was just a kid.'

'Interesting, isn't it?'

'With the older girl, Cherry Banks?'

'Cherry's role in this... is uncertain. No mention of her again.'

Merrily watched the clouds breaking up over the vicarage chimneys. Going to be a clear night.

'You learn anything from Mephista's father that you didn't learn at the time?'

'Not a great deal. The truth is that it was not possible to pick up Mephista's trail without access to the Brace family.'

'Sir Charles? The old Mosleyite? How does that work?'

Sir Charles is indeed central to this. I, ah, went to his funeral.'

'Where?'

'Hereford Cathedral. As any detective will tell you, funerals can be... revelatory. Who's shedding tears, who isn't. Who's shedding tears to an implausible extent. I finally struck pay-dirt, as they say, that evening, in discussion with a nephew of Sir Charles who, I think it's safe to say, did not share his politics and was not expecting to receive anything in the will. He only came out of curiosity, to see who turned up.'

Merrily kept quiet. Gwyn Arthur evidently wasn't taking her fully into his confidence. What had given him reason to think the Braces would know what had happened to Mephista?

He told her Sir Charles's nephew had decided to skip the finale at the crematorium, to spend a couple of hours with him in the bar of the Castle House Hotel. Obviously some resentment here. Gwyn Arthur had learned how Sir Charles's estate had been depleted by the arrival of a grandson.

'Seems that not long after the death of their son, Sir Charles and Lady Brace were made aware of a young woman who insisted she was carrying Jerry's child.'

'Ah… And did he believe her?'

'Might have been more resistant had she not been accompanied by someone he knew and trusted – and one can only assume this was in a political context. Perhaps someone who was a regular customer of Jerrold Brace and had got to know Mephista. Anyway – the upshot – he took her in.'

'Adopted the child?'

'This is where it gets interesting. My new friend, the nephew, believes both mother and child spent some time in London, at a hotel owned by friends of Sir Charles, who provided employment for the mother until what may have been her first marriage. The boy gets sent away to a series of famously tough boarding schools. Spending his holidays at one of the farms or communes we were discussing earlier. Where there's a regime of fitness, self-sufficiency.'

'But wasn't Mephista resistant to all that?'

'Hippy self-sufficiency is not the same, is it? This was not benign. It did not involve peace and love. And, anyway, it appears she didn't go with him. Mephista seems to have spent most of her time in London, *whoring around*, in the words of Sir Charles's disgusted nephew. He *may* have exaggerated. But as far as Sir Charles was concerned, it seems, her role, essentially, was over.'

'So Brace's grandson is taken from his mother at an early age... brought up as...'

'As a warrior, I suppose.'

'Sounds almost Spartan. In the original sense.'

'Oh, it was. I was directed to specific websites where I read of young people being turned out into the hills for whole days and nights to live on what they could find, what they could kill or steal. Discovering their inner resources.'

'What the hell kind of man *was* Sir Charles?'

'I'd say a man who was ashamed at his son failing to live up to the Aryan ideal. Deserting his fitness programme, descending into drug use, sexual adventures with unsuitable women of uncertain origins.'

'No other children?'

'Daughter in America. Another son who distanced himself from his father's politics enough to become a radical journalist in Scotland.'

'So Jerry must've been a real loss.'

'One wonders, where did Sir Charles lay the blame for what happened?'

A pause. The clouds had dispersed. Swallows dived for insects, tiny, efficient acts of carnage.

Merrily said, 'Rector, do you think? For betraying the cause?'

'And who supplied Jerry Brace with the raw heroin?'

'What, you think...?'

'Happens in Hay at a time when more or less all the bookshops – all forty-plus of them – were flourishing. When the town was acquiring an international reputation. When the first festival was being planned. So you have a town trembling on the brink of affluence... and, close to its centre, a bookshop trading in the vilest form of political pornography.'

'You think Brace's death was…? That he was seen as damaging to the town's image?'

'Not something ever likely to be proved, one way or the other. Heroin, in the right situation, can be the most effective of murder weapons. But, yes, Sir Charles seems to have blamed what he thought of as the degenerate hippy element in Hay for the death of his… true heir? Rather contemptuous of Independent Hay.'

'But he must've been aware of it happening, Gwyn. If he saw Jerry as his true heir he must've stayed in touch with him. Why didn't he take steps to get him out of there?'

'I don't know. I don't know why Jerrold Brace came to Hay in the first place. I'd guess he was no more a natural bookseller than I am.'

'So are you any closer to finding Mephista?'

'I…' You could almost hear him wondering if he'd said too much. 'The truth of it is, there may be a dilemma here. Would it be better, in many ways, for her father and her ailing mother to remain in ignorance of what became of their daughter?'

'That doesn't sound good.'

'It probably isn't.'

Ethel watched, golden-eyed, from her fleecy bed by the side of the unlit stove as the evening brightened. Merrily carried the empty mug back to the kitchen, which overlooked the remains of the orchard that once encircled the village. Maybe Lol would call tonight. She wished he'd just come home. Being alone was not about freedom.

She Googled Beryl Bainbridge, groaning softly at the result: nearly three quarters of a million mentions. She put in *Beryl Bainbridge, Peter Rector*: nothing to suggest a connection. *Beryl Bainbridge, Hay-on-Wye*: yes, she'd appeared a few times at the Hay Festival, she'd enjoyed it, she liked the place, its eccentricity. Her London home apparently looked like a Victorian museum of childhood, with ornate religious overtones and her funeral had been incense-soaked Anglo-Catholic.

Merrily didn't remember falling asleep on the sofa, only the dream of a darkened church that stank of hash, lit by a single, hovering candle casting no light as she walked towards it along an aisle that went on forever.

A time-lapse, and then the candle was directly in front of her, blinding white, held aloft by a man far taller than her, whose face was a shoal of flitting shadows.

'*What will you do now?*' he said.

When the phone chimed she awoke with a throb, the way you did when the nightmare bucked and you were thrown to the ground, lying there and praying, like a child prayed: Please God, save me from the bad things in the dark.

'Are you doing anything important tonight,' Gwyn Arthur Jones asked, 'or are you available for work?'

'Work?'

'Do you... keep a black bag or something, at the ready?'

'You're serious?'

'Not everyone,' Gwyn Arthur said, 'is an old agnostic like myself.'

She stood next to the open window, hands flat on the sill. No breeze now, the evening becoming the warmest part of the day.

In the distance, the low growl of a tractor in a field south of the village, some farmer starting his haymaking early, remembering last year's drowned summer. The possibility of climate change, and the farmers changing with it, ready to work through the night if necessary.

A now-familiar grey car appeared on the cobbled square where, it being Friday night, about a dozen others were parked, for the Black Swan.

No surprise. It was Sylvia Merchant's car and probably Sylvia who got out. Certainly tall enough, but the woman wore a long, light-green raincoat and, even though this was the warmest dry night in over a month, its hood was up, a hand holding it together over her face. Another woman emerged from the passenger side. She was more seasonally clad in a white linen jacket, and her black hair was uncovered.

They walked across the square and into the vicarage drive, and then the leaner, more serious Martin Longbeach was padding into Merrily's mind.

I hope I've made it clear that it's nothing for you to worry about. You're on holiday and you can relax.

Sylvia wanting Martin to meet her medium. In the white linen jacket, for innocence. Not at all an unhealthy practice, spiritualism. Something the Church might as well accept, in these liberal times. Merrily was thinking, this should be me in there.

The whole thing becoming clearer now. Sylvia Merchant had wanted to put her on the back foot. To feel threatened and make concessions to prevent the humiliation of accusations about the misuse of deliverance, accusations of spiritual bullying.

A Christian woman, worshipper at the Cathedral, who wanted its blessing for communication with the dead.

Pick and mix. Where would it end? Merrily felt a rush of anger. Should go in there, sort this out, not leave it to Martin. He'd be her witness and she'd be his.

And how long would *that* take?

Oh *God.*

Merrily pushed stiffened fingers through her hair, picked up her phone and her car keys and carried her airline bag out to the Freelander.

51

Received wisdom

HALFWAY DOWN BACK FOLD, she jumped, as Gwyn Arthur Jones detached himself from a doorway, like an urban fox.

'Never thought,' he said, 'that I'd be a party to anything like this. But, there we are, I suppose life should never become predictable.'

The evening was unclouded, the castle like a cut-out. Back Fold bumped crookedly down its left flank into the town centre. And you could almost hear an old but well-serviced motor running inside Gwyn Arthur Jones, a man who would always know more than he'd reveal.

'This all comes about, of course, because I happened to mention your name to Mrs Thorogood.'

Holding open a shop door for Merrily, and then she was stepping into a woodland glade on a moonlit night. Tree shadows on the walls, which faded up in shades of blue between the bookcases, to a celestial ceiling.

And like a solemn tableau, amongst the trees: Mr Kapoor in his Mumbai Indians T-shirt, Betty Thorogood in her Alice band and Robin Thorogood leaning not on a stick but a spade.

Betty stepped forward at once, hugging Merrily. Spontaneous but stiff with apprehension, and the hug was not so much a greeting as a transfer of tension, emotional osmosis.

'Betty... you all right?'

'Not totally. Thanks. Thanks so much for coming.'

Betty looking down at the airline bag. Everybody looking at

the airline bag, which contained a Bible, a prayer book, a flask of water and salt.

The swastika brick lay on a console-type table. Gwyn Arthur picked it up, a forefinger following the relief pattern.

'It's left-facing, see. The technical term for which, I've learned tonight, is *sauwastika*. But see how its arms are rounded rather than angular, so it's also two letter esses, crossed.'

Robin looked over Gwyn Arthur's shoulder.

'SS? Himmler?'

'No, no, the circle in the middle is a letter O. Which also represents the sun, in negative.' Gwyn Arthur opened the laptop, already booted, found a bookmarked site and the symbol came up at once. 'The Order of the Sun in Shadow.'

'And that is what?' Robin said.

Merrily bent to the screen.

'It *was* an ultra right-wing sect based not far from here.'

'We're not sure if it still exists,' Gwyn Arthur said. 'It had a newsletter called Dark Orb, which then became a website. The last edition I can find dates back seven or eight years. The symbol has also been changed several times. The one on your brick doesn't seem to have been used for over twenty.'

Gwyn Arthur brought up another bookmarked site dominated by a larger circle, a more angular swastika and the line, *DEFINING A NEW BRITAIN*.

'Could be the Liberal Democrats,' he said, 'until you read about the, ah, cosmic reservoir of untapped dark power left behind after the war. Which, it says here, may be drawn upon to facilitate, at an appropriate time, the opening of an era of what they touchingly describe as *a necessary cruelty*.'

'And I bet they all got a full set of Iron Maiden albums,' Robin said. 'You ever arrest any of these assholes?'

'Ha. The sad and slightly risible truth is that, while we knew some names and my colleagues occasionally had them under observation, none has ever been convicted of so much as a parking offence.'

'But this Jerry Brace was a member, right?'

'If he went to the trouble of installing its symbol in his wall… ' Gwyn Arthur turned to Merrily. 'It now seems that symbol may be masking something else. In the wall. Or, rather, the wall *beyond* the wall. Which is the castle wall.'

'Quite a way in,' Robin said. 'I guess an archaeologist would want to take a small trowel to it and about two weeks sifting the dirt, but…'

He lifted the spade.

'… the hell with that.'

A square of reddening sky lit the upstairs room, where a rug had been rolled back and a pile of rubble made a pyramid on the boarded floor. Merrily peered into a hole in the back of the fireplace that became a shaft.

'How do you know it's not just part of the wall that's been repaired at some time?'

'No mortar,' Kapoor said. 'And we've found two modern bricks on end, like pillars to take the weight, make a space. I'm trying not to dislodge them.'

Robin propped his stick against the wall.

'Can I do something? Getting kinda antsy here.'

'Nah, mate. You been pushing it enough.'

'In fact,' Gwyn Arthur said, 'if I can ask a favour, Robin… there *is* something you could do. Would there be any way we might find out if the Order of the Sun in Shadow *does* still exist? I suspect you have contacts on the… occult fringe.'

'Conceivable the Pagan Federation would have them on a list, even if it was only a blacklist. There's also a guy of my acquaintance, up in Manchester, who knows everybody ever swished a wand. You want me to call him?'

'If you can do it without explaining why.'

'Gwyn, with all respect, I wouldn't *know* why. A swastika in the chimney, a hole in the wall, a guy who died from bad smack... interesting and a tad disturbing... for us. But I'm sensing you're on a different path here.'

You could understand his perplexity, his need for a handle on this.

'Three missing persons,' Gwyn Arthur said. 'I have to do what I can. Humour me, Robin. Now I'm no longer in the modern, bureaucratized police, I am allowed to follow my feelings with impunity.'

Betty had beckoned Merrily down to one of those kitchens which needed a mini-fridge and a micro-oven. It had no window and must, for many years, have served no wider purpose than making tea during working hours.

'Are you... really planning to live here, Betty?'

'Until we're making enough money to rent somewhere better and turn all this into shop, I suppose we are.'

'Things are that bad?'

'*Have* been.' Betty plugged in the kettle. 'For most of a year, Robin could hardly walk at all. Couldn't sit to paint, couldn't stand to paint. Very depressed. Then he – *we* – had the idea of moving to Hay and starting a bookshop. Thinking we could flog our magnificent collection of pagan, magic and earth-mysteries books to kickstart it.'

'Good idea. Maybe not the best time to do it, mind.'

'No. But we've happened upon this place, right under the castle and Robin's all lit up. The castle, wow! Suddenly, the old Robin's back. Love of ruins – castles, abbeys, cromlechs, everything they don't have in America. Even their negative aspects he sees as inspirational. Just moods. Merrily, all I want is to make it work for him. What would *you* have done?'

'Gone along with it, I suppose. We do, don't we?' She looked around the cell-like kitchen. 'How long have you felt something was wrong here?'

'*You* felt it?'

'Betty, I don't profess to feel anything. I just do received wisdom.'

'I don't believe that. And when what I'm getting is plain evil I don't want to mess around. I mean, I don't want you to feel compromised or—'

'*Plain evil?*'

'Got it the first time I came in. Wasn't the smell of a putrefying body, nothing so obvious. Not even that damp sensation of human misery, which is the most common thing you pick up in a run-down house. It was active, bad energy. Aggressive. Sort of thing dowsers pick up sometimes. So half of me's saying, get out, don't touch this dump. But how can I say that to Robin?'

'Did you say anything to him?'

'Hinted there was a slight problem. Would've been stupid to say nothing. But I said, whatever it is we can handle it. We can fix it. And sure, there are some things I *can* fix. Or convince myself I've fixed, which is pretty much the same thing. In the world I was a part of.'

'OK… what's actually happened?'

'Not much. First time I walk in here, I don't like the feel of it, particularly upstairs. Well, big deal. And Robin spending last night here and it's not a very good night – lights coming on, which could be loose wiring or something. And then we find out that a junkie snuffed it on the premises – well, so what? Hardly Amityville, is it? Nobody's ever seen Brace walking past in the night with a spectral syringe in his arm. And yet…'

'I'm not dissing this, Betty.'

'We can dismiss everything as pure imagination, can't we? And then something happens, and it's too late. And I *say* I can fix it… but I haven't done this stuff in quite a while, and if you don't work at it day and night you lose it. You need to meditate for hours every day. Visualize, focus, induce trance states, levitate. But a heavy inner life doesn't leave you much of an outer life. And if you have problems like, say, a disabled husband… hopeless. So when Gwyn mentioned you were around…'

'You want me to try and cleanse the place, best I can?'

The kettle hissed in derision.

'You're carrying two thousand years of tradition,' Betty said. 'Older than what passes for paganism, which actually got cobbled together in the nineteen fifties. Which I'm not denigrating. Not saying it doesn't work, or that it hasn't given me a lot of electric moments over the years, but... I'll do whatever you want. Go down to Father Richard's church on bended knees and confess my... heathen sins.'

'Actually... I should really go down and clear it with him, too. As it's not my patch.'

'I think he's on holiday. It's that time of year, isn't it? '

'In which case I suppose I can get away with squaring it with the Swansea and Brecon Deliverance minister.'

Huw.

'And assuming it's OK...' Betty poured boiling water into the pot. 'What would you be able to do?'

'Depends very much on what we're looking at. If this is just Mr Brace still around, we'd be looking to help him on his way. If, as we suspect, Mr Brace was involved with an occult-based sect which is borderline satanic, it may not be only Mr Brace and that's a whole different—'

'And what if it's well *over* the borderline? What if it's bigger than the shop?'

'You mean involving the castle. As there's nobody living in the castle and it's not my patch, I think I leave it alone. Just make sure that hole's blocked up before we try anything here.'

'Richard Booth never quite got the measure of the castle, either,' Betty said. 'He had a disastrous fire. Now he's finally had to sell it.'

'Let's try and avoid the implications of that... at this stage. I can go so far – minor exorcism, exorcism of place – without an official nod. Beyond that, I'd really need to talk to the Bishop.'

'Which one?'

Betty looked disconsolate. Merrily thought about it.

Of course. Protocol.

'You're right. I'd have to talk to *my* bishop, who's probably still in London, and he'd have to talk to the Bishop of Swansea and Brecon and... *bugger*. Let's just—'

The mobile chimed in her bag.

'—play it by ear.'

The light wasn't strong enough in here to make out the number. A tiny room filling up with steam. She stabbed the keyboard.

'Merrily,' she said.

Bliss said, 'I think I need you to come out again, if you would.'

'Where?'

'Did I tell you about Claudia Cornwell, the barrister?'

'The woman in the red car.'

'She's coming out to meet me. At Rector's place at Cusop. We've arranged to be there in about half an hour, when it's dark. Any chance you can come over?'

'What, as a chaperone?'

'Yeh, to chaperone me. I need somebody who understands what the hell she's on about.'

'In connection with what?"

'In connection with what they found in the river this afternoon.'

'You mean the—?'

'Maybe not a joke.'

'And you're saying she knows about *me*? Or are you?'

'Yeh. She's not unhappy. She's already checked you out online.'

Merrily could hear footsteps on the stairs, raised voices.

'The important thing is you're not a cop,' Bliss said. 'Not an official witness. Important for me, too. I'm stepping outside the box. Several boxes, now I think about it.'

'When did you last sleep?'

'Why do people keep asking me that? Until half an hour ago, actually. In the car. Gorra grab it when you can. Merrily, I'm gonna be a bit out of me depth, that's the thing.'

x

'How long will it take? I'm in the middle of… something else.'

She could hear Robin calling urgently for Betty.

'Couldn't say,' Bliss said. 'It's only an interpreter's job, and if it's nothing to worry about, less than hour. Yes?'

'OK, I'll do what I—'

He'd gone. Betty was backing off.

'Whatever it is, just go ahead. Seriously, just put me in the queue. As long as I know you're there and you're prepared to help…'

'I'll only be at Cusop. But let me do a quick… something before I go.'

Fuse wire, Huw called it. Never leave without applying it.

The kitchen door opened.

Robin, Kapoor and the spade.

On its blade a wooden box, the size of an old-fashioned cigar box, encrusted with rubble dust.

'Maybe it isn't ours,' Robin said. 'We're just the tenants here.'

'I don't think that should hold you back, necessarily.' Gwyn Arthur Jones examining the box, a cop again. 'Do you?'

Merrily watched from the doorway. Could hardly leave here until they'd opened it. If they were going to.

It went quiet. Kapoor looked from face to face.

Gwyn Arthur Jones nodded.

Kapoor fitted the blade of the chisel under the lip of the lid and the box sprang apart, Merrily instinctively taking a step back. Well, who knew what abomination Jerrold Adrian Brace had buried deep in the castle wall?

Robin looked inside.

'Oh.'

'Come on, then, mate,' Kapoor said. 'Ancient stash of smack?'

Robin turned the wooden box upside down over the console table and another slim box fell out, cardboard this time. The word Maxell on it, in big lettering.

Kapoor looked up at the ceiling.

'He buried a videotape?' Robin said. 'That a let-down for you, Gwyn?'

'I think not.' Gwyn Arthur Jones bent over it. 'Brace sold videos. Gareth Nunne mentioned it. Hitler's rallies. He copied them.'

'He buried Hitler in the castle wall?'

'I don't think this is Hitler, do you?'

'Then what is it?'

'I suspect something more contemporary.'

'And it won't wait till tomorrow?' Kapoor said.

'I would not wait half an hour if it could be avoided.'

'Yeah, me neither,' Robin said. 'We need an old-fashioned VCR.'

Kapoor took a look.

'*Extremely* old-fashioned.'

'Gotta be a few still around.'

Kapoor shook his head.

'Wouldn't bet on it, mate.' He turned the tape box around with a forefinger. 'This is Betamax. Big in the nineteen eighties, then VHS swallowed the market. By the mid-nineties they'd vanished completely. I can still sell VHS test-match tapes, or transfer them to DVD, but I won't touch these. We'll be bloody lucky to find anybody who's still got a Betamax player tonight.'

Silence.

'Shit,' Robin said.

Merrily slipped upstairs with the airline bag. When she did the prayer, standing beside the heap of rubble in the lowering, flesh-coloured light, it felt like talking into a pillow pressed over your face.

Or maybe she was just impressionable.

Whatever, she brought out the flask of water.

PART FIVE

Chaos magicians... only get
together to work on specific
projects.

Prof. Ronald Hutton, in
The Book of English Magic,
by Philip Carr-Gomm and Richard
Heygate (2009)

52

The last redemptive project

THE WIND WAS rising. A smoky cloud-mass shaped like a rabbit made a forward bound in slow motion and then came apart over Hay Castle, a mile away on the horizon.

Rector's gate was open and Merrily drove through. She was early, but there was already another car here. A small car, and her heart jumped like the rabbit in the sky.

But, no. Tamsin's car was green, a Clio. What was she thinking? Nerves.

She got down from the Freelander, and saw a woman standing at the top of a paddock next to the house. The other car was a Mini Cooper, black and grey, no sign of a red Audi.

The woman turned, black against a deep red sun frizzling the day's embers. Merrily unzipped the black hoodie to expose her second-smallest pectoral cross. She scowled, slipped it over her head and into a pocket of her jeans. Opened the wooden five-barred gate and they met somewhere in the middle of the paddock.

'Mrs Watkins.' A hand came out. Blue-varnished nails. 'Claudia.'

'You came early then.'

'Worried I might have bothered Bliss for nothing, I suppose.'

'Oh?'

'Actually just worried.'

Claudia was nearly a head taller, a big-boned woman in a sheepskin gilet, pink jeans pushed into soft leather boots. The kind of woman you saw picking up her kids in a Toyota Land Cruiser on the nanny's day off. Merrily followed her back to the gate, and they stood with their backs to it watching the sun set over Hay.

'I read what I could find about you on the Net,' Claudia said. 'And then I rang Athena White.'

'And you still came?'

'She particularly asked me not to tell you what she'd said about you. But, let's say I think you might be quite surprised if I did.'

A rabbit – no, a hare – lolloped out of the farthest hedge, actually towards them, and stopped, becoming a silhouette that might have been a small standing stone, in the centre of the field. Claudia watched it, smiling faintly.

'I'm not going to say anything as obvious as that's Peter, come to see what we're doing.'

The hare didn't move.

Merrily said, 'You think something's happened here?'

'I think there might have been a burglary.'

'In the house?'

'Not exactly. I've had a bit of a dilemma, bit of conscience-searching. I've obviously not been very careful. '

'Letting yourself be seen.'

I'm hoping Bliss will be discreet.'

'He can be. When he has to.'

'In return for which I told him I'm prepared to be *less* than discreet and talk about what was happening here. He wants me to talk about it to you, as someone who might be able to process it. And maybe so he can legitimately deny all knowledge of it if things get difficult for him.'

'Blimey. Have you really only known him a couple of days?'

'I've known other detectives. Ask me what you think he needs to know.'

'You were close,' Merrily said, 'to Peter Rector?'

'Thought I was. When he turned ninety, I offered him an apartment in my far-too-big house, with the use of a large reception room and an outbuilding for his temple. Seemed such a perfect solution to his increasing fear of infirmity that I was quite offended, at first, when he refused. I didn't realize, then, why he couldn't leave here. There were things I didn't know about him for a long time. Things I probably still don't know. More like a revered great-uncle, shall we say, than a grandfather.'

Merrily watched the sun fall behind Hay, which, viewed across empty fields, at this time, in this light, looked like some impossibly romantic medieval settlement.

'And is this about his… last redemptive project?'

'If you know about that,' Claudia said, 'you didn't get it from Athena.'

'You're right.'

'Merrily – can I call you that?' Claudia bit her lower lip. 'I think we're walking around one another, probably unnecessarily. But feel free to take out that cross again and wave it in my face.'

'All right, I don't know what the project is.'

'Thank you. Athena's in a difficult situation. She's charged with making sure it doesn't collapse. That's what Peter wants. How discreet are you, Merrily? Are you bound to report to your Bishop?'

'I'm on holiday.' Merrily looked over her shoulder towards the castle mound and the church of St Mary, Cusop. 'And I'm guessing we have a few minutes before Bliss gets here.'

'Or a little more if he wants to give us time to connect, which I suspect he does. From my point of view, while I don't go out of my way to conceal my private interest, I'd rather nothing appeared in the papers. If only because I don't want any tedious jokes from young solicitors about magicking an acquittal.'

'I can see you wouldn't.'

'I'm an initiate,' Claudia said, 'in an order of ceremonial magicians. A neophyte with aspirations.'

'What kind of initiate?'

'You mean white or black?'

'I doubt it's ever that simple. Why do you do it?'

'I'm guessing you don't want the offensive answer about Christianity, as practised in this country, no longer satisfying people's spiritual needs.'

'Doesn't offend me, Claudia. If we provided much of a buzz any more, congregations wouldn't be going down the toilet. What's the non-offensive answer?'

'It's also an intelligent, challenging, demanding… escape. Into myself. Been meditating since my teens, and this is what comes next if you don't want to get into some incomprehensible eastern discipline. It's been wonderful for turning the mind into a blank screen, increasing one's powers of focus and concentration and… other useful skills. Now, I know for a fact, for example, when someone's lying to me in court.'

Claudia slotted her heels into the bottom bar of the gate and hauled herself up to sit on the top.

'But they're just side-benefits, really. Using peripheral skills to try and become superhuman in a world of ordinary humans, or to score points or make money is… bad karma, if you want to put it like that. Am I gaining your confidence at all, Merrily?'

'My daughter's drawn to paganism. It hasn't turned her into a werewolf.'

Claudia nodded.

'All right.' She looked across the fields. 'The project, then.'

'Can I guess?'

'Do.'

'Is it Hay itself? If he was the Magus of Hay, was the project the Kingdom?'

It had come to her whole, standing so close to the border between England and Wales. Here before her was the Kingdom, right on the frontier. No obvious housing estates or factories visible from here, only the original medieval town. You could almost see the walls.

'If I've got this right,' Merrily said, 'declaring independence was a spontaneous act. Richard Booth didn't think about it, plan anything… he just said it and it happened. Metaphorically speaking.'

'Far more than metaphorically.'

'And when everybody thought it was a joke… to Peter Rector it wasn't. It was something that was almost visionary.'

'Almost?'

'Maybe Booth thought it was a joke too, with his tin crown and his plastic orb.'

'Which, unintentionally, are magical artefacts,' Claudia said. 'Far more powerful than if someone very rich had fabricated the real thing – real gold, real jewels. Here they are, made entirely from recycled stuff. Glass jewels nicked from a dog collar. Everything cobbled together. Worthless.'

'Second-hand. Very Hay?'

'*Yesss!*' Claudia jumping down to the grass, surprisingly nimble for someone her size. 'Breaking all the rules. Saying to the government and the council and tourist and development boards…'

'You don't exist,' Merrily said.

'Exactly. Booth and his supporters were saying, "On *our* level of consciousness, *you don't exist*. If we don't see you, then you aren't there. *We've made you disappear.*" Magic.'

'Is it?'

'Natural magic. A number of factors coming together at the right time. Serendipity. Serendipity is very close to magic. Except it doesn't last. Mostly it explodes. The bubble pops. Unless…'

Claudia walked out into the darkening paddock, the grass sloping towards woodland below the town on the horizon, sparkling now with lights.

Merrily didn't move.

'The last redemptive project was to make sure it continued?'

'The continued powering and protection of a brilliant chaotic mind,' Claudia said.

'So Rector had appointed himself court magician.'

'I never actually thought of it like that.' Claudia looked momentarily disapproving. 'But I suppose you're right.'

She went to stand where the hare had sat.

'An exercise like this stands more of a chance of success if it's set in train at the beginning of something. If it's not a rescue package. Blank canvas. You spot your opportunity and then you move quickly. When you look at Hay now, it's hard to imagine how it was before the first second-hand bookshop opened, most of its shops closed down, its railway ripped up.'

Claudia extended her arms.

'Imagine *this* is Hay. This field. Imagine the gate is the castle. Behind it – as in physical reality – the Black Mountains. Below it, the River Wye. Most of the medieval town walls have gone – but still there, the stones taken to build houses and shops, so therefore still in the town. It's *all still here*. On our mental model, we might choose to put the walls back in their original place, enclosing the heart. The street pattern at the core of the town, if you hadn't noticed, actually forms the shape of a heart.'

'I didn't know that.'

'Look at a street plan sometime: High Street, Castle Street, Lion Street, Bear Street and the rest… all blood vessels shaping and wound around a heart. Peter's self-appointed task was to make it beat. To a strong, persistent rhythm that couldn't easily be stopped. To give it momentum.'

'How does that work? What do you mean by the *mental model*?'

'Something that exists on a higher plan. Constructed in the imagination. Imagine it as virtual reality on a screen into which you can drag images, make things happen. All magic works through will power and the harnessing of energy. Spirits, if you like. Which can be seen either as external forces or processes from deep in the human psyche. In this case, we also have natural energies directed into the town – the power of water rushing down the Dulas Brook, with all its waterfalls, flowing into the River Wye, the best, most revered river in England and Wales. But more powerfully, emerging on the other side of town, you might have something else.'

'We talking about the church?'

'You know it? And the surroundings?'

'I was there this afternoon.'

'It'll be very clear in your mind, then. Go there now. Go on… you're safe. It's one of yours.'

'Not entirely.'

'Humour me.'

She found she didn't have to try too hard. As she stood by the hedge at the side of the paddock, she was, at the same time, below St Mary's Church, following the stream past the waterfall, across the bridge. Then she was in the alley between the almshouses, emerging opposite the entrance to Forest Road, the end of the Gospel Pass, highway of saints, up to another St Mary church, high in the Black Mountains, where the statue of the Virgin raised her crumbling hands to bring down the…

'… sheer power of medieval Christianity, Merrily. In a time when the Church was illuminated by miracles and magic. The blessing and guardianship of the Holy Mother.'

Claudia's voice coming across the twilit field, with a slight echo. Seeming to pick up your unspoken thoughts. The tricks these people played. Merrily said nothing. Found she was holding the pectoral cross in her pocket, sliding her fingers through its chain. Well aware of how the modern Church had let all that dissipate.

'So here's Peter, at the confluence,' Claudia said. 'Where streams feeding the Dulas brook rush past another significant Mary church.'

'Cusop Church. *That* one.'

Out of the corner of her right eye, she could see it: solid, short tower, enclosed, like the others, by yew trees, one said to be nearly two thousand years old.

'Where was he?' Merrily asked softly. 'Where exactly was Peter Rector?'

'In the engine room,' Claudia said. 'And the engine was comprised of people. Living and dead.'

53

Right-hand path

IT WAS LIKE something was preventing them getting close to the truth, erecting barriers.

Kapoor had an old VHS recorder for transferring vintage cricket tapes to DVD, but his only hope of finding a Betamax recorder was getting hold of the guy who repaired his kit.

An anorak, who never threw anything away, who worked out of a shop in Brecon, long closed for the night. And whose name was Jones. And who was unknown to Gwyn Arthur.

Kapoor had started ringing people in the phone book called Jones. It could take a while.

Meanwhile, the videotape sat on the console table that used to be an altar. Upstairs, the hole in the wall made Thorogood Pagan Books part of the Castle.

Robin had a little black book full of pagan contacts. Just didn't carry it around with him, so he'd had to borrow Gwyn Arthur Jones's laptop to track down George Webster, last heard of in Manchester and linked to a Wiccan group operating in the Pennines.

George was, presumably, still editor of Witches' Rune, formerly a quarterly magazine, now only a website which, like most goddamn websites, didn't go out of its way to reveal home numbers. However, the single number given was one for advertisements and subscriptions which, unless Witches' Rune had acquired actual staff, was worth a shot.

Answering machine.

Shit.

'This is Robin Thorogood,' Robin said, 'George, if that's you, for the Goddess's sake, call me the hell back, willya? This is urgent.'

He hit *end call*, turned to Jones.

'George thinks urgent is against the flow and therefore not a pagan concept, so we can only hope he comes back tonight.'

Jones pulled up one of the cane chairs he and Betty had brought from upstairs.

'If you do get a number for someone linked to the Order, I'd be grateful if you'd speak to them yourself. I can brief you on what to ask but I doubt I'd be able to master the jargon or manage not to sound like an old policeman.'

'And you think I talk Nazi?' Robin's phone rang; he lit up the screen. 'Jeez, there *is* a goddess. Hold on…' He listened, grinned. 'Yeah… will do, George.' Lowered the phone. 'I'm calling him back directly. Times are hard at Witches' Rune. Like everyplace, but at least George can lay a curse on the bank.'

He called back.

'George, I guess you're about to start a significant ritual so I won't mess around.'

George's voice was cold.

'What makes you think that?'

Because your whole freaking life's a ritual, George.

'Forget it. George, listen up, I need help to trace a guy who ran a… well, a Left-Hand Path group operating on the Welsh border. This bookshop we're running, someone wants me to try and get hold of some of their original literature. Normally, I'd politely decline, but we only just started up and I don't want to get a reputation for being unhelpful.'

'What's it called?'

'Order of— Hold on, I got the note here. The Sun in Shadow?'

The phone went silent.

'George…?'

'The *Nazis*?'

'That a fact? This guy just said Left-Hand Path. If he'd said like, Extreme *Right*—'

'The Order of the Sun in Shadow once contacted me to place a display ad seeking members. All a bit ambivalent, but it didn't look too harmful at the time, so we ran it and they didn't pay, despite repeated invoices. I'd imagine having a customer who collects fascist occult literature wouldn't be terribly good for your image.'

'Yeah, well, I've promised now. You kept a contact address, phone number for this guy?'

Across the room, Robin heard a yelp of triumph, saw Kapoor throwing his mobile in the air and catching it.

'—always keep contact details of people who owe me money,' George said. 'I'm just looking through the file. How's Betty?'

'She's good,' Robin said. 'She's always good.'

'Yep, here he is. Moved from his original address in Radnorshire, to Solihull. Quite a reputable address – well, suburban-sounding anyway. You want that or just the number?'

'Both, if that's OK.'

Robin wrote it all down in Jones's notebook.

'Just keep my name out of it, Robin. These are unlikely to be terribly nice people.'

'Yeah, the word Nazi was kind of a hint in that direction.'

'I'm serious, Robin.'

'I'm truly grateful to you, George,' Robin said. 'Heil Hitler.'

54

Poppet

'Each of them stationed in a chosen spot,' Claudia said, 'at a prearranged time.'

'Physically?'

'Initially, yes. Someone might, for example, stand at the confluence of the brook and the Wye, down on that little beach near the sewage works where the King was found.'

Here, on the edge of night, Hay-on-Wye reduced to a serrated silhouette against a band of fading red, it all sounded entirely logical, disturbingly persuasive. But Merrily, uncomfortable with it, found she'd put the cross back around her neck.

'If you can have a group of people with the same focus,' Claudia said, 'working with perfect synchronicity in a sympathetic atmosphere, the results can be amazing. Think of the transcendent power of Gregorian chant in a cathedral.'

'So you'd have a group of trained initiates, all focused on the creation of a successful economy founded on books?'

'Nothing so simplistic. You don't concentrate on making booksellers rich. You refine it to something which is, at once, more amorphous and more exact. Think of it in its purest form – illumination, a whole ethos founded upon *the word*. Doesn't matter whether it's the Bible, the Koran, the Bhagavad Gita or Dan Brown. Knowledge begins with the word.'

'Knowledge, enlightenment... books?'

The moon had come out, not far from full. Claudia's broad face shone.

'Because books were central to the aspiration, Peter liked to involve writers. They'd come individually to Hay and Peter, or one of his group, would introduce each of them to a particular spot, perhaps linked to their personality, and show them how to store the images – the sights, the sounds, the atmosphere of the place – in their imaginations. So that, even if they were hundreds of miles away, they'd be able to visualize and to project themselves into a location.'

'That couldn't've happened overnight.'

'No. Some people, it would take a year, two years, of daily practice. And not everyone stayed the course. Using writers was not invariably a good idea. Bruce Chatwin dropped out quite quickly – more interested, I suspect, in what he could get out of it for a novel or a travel book. For something like this to work, it has to be separated from all personal desire. One must maintain a level of complete detachment from what one wants to achieve. That's why most of the people involved were, as they say hereabouts, from Off.'

'Is that why the Convoy were involved?'

'Sorry? Oh, you mean the travellers? Before my time, I'm afraid. Yes, a very convenient human resource in the nineteen eighties. Introduced to Peter by... who was that chap?'

'Jeremy Sandford?'

'Possibly.'

'Supporter of the homeless. Expert on travellers and magic mushrooms.'

'Then it would have been. The mushrooms were never used in the actual working but seem to have been useful for pre-conditioning. Opening people's minds to the limitless possibilities. The wider your horizons, strange as it may seem, the easier it is to sharpen your focus.'

'I'll work that out sometime. What about Beryl Bainbridge?'

'You're very well informed.'

'Psychic powers, Claudia.'

Claudia didn't smile.

'Beryl was... a natural. I met her once. Entrusted with the old marketplaces – the Buttermarket, which even looks like a temple, and the square below the castle. She was famous for liking a certain clutter – house like a Victorian museum, full of statues and icons and stuffed animals. Think of Beryl in the town on a market day, absorbing the atmosphere. Hay market representing commerce – *local* commerce. An unusual talent for projecting herself into a place and time and then condensing it into the essentials. Surrounded herself with chaos, yet her books were models of concise precision – like sigil-magic, where everything is reduced to a symbol.'

'I kind of remember reading once that she was an atheist.'

'May well have been. But when she died, in 2010, her funeral was at the church of St Silas the Martyr in Kentish Town – a service so High Church that some of the mourners didn't realize it wasn't very traditional Roman Catholic. No one has quite managed to explain that.'

Merrily stared at the moon. Miracles and magic.

'Take me through this, would you, Claudia? On a particular night...'

'Might be the night of the full moon or the equinox. But you have a group of people, all over the country, alerted these days by email, who go into some private place in their home at the appointed time... and are sent a specific phrase or a clearly defined concept or an image, and... begin.

'There's a temple. You'll see. A proper temple. With a magic circle and cardinal points, all the necessary stuff. And sympathetic props. The most significant of which was a poppet. You know what that is?'

'That's a witchcraft thing, isn't it? A doll.'

'You take what you need for the purpose, from any tradition. It's become known as chaos magic. Customized ritual, virtually nothing forbidden. Peter liked the idea, whilst believing it was terribly dangerous for a novice magician, on the basis that you can't break the rules with the necessary confidence if you're not fully conversant with the rules you want to break.'

Merrily was thinking of what Athena had had to say about chaos magic.

'So you can take the Christian tradition and marry it to something... else.'

From the heretical merging of religion and magic comes a general breach of taboos. The energy of the perverse.

She was thinking of the figurines in the alcoves in Rector's library: Isis and the Virgin.

'I didn't think you'd find that terribly acceptable. I'm just telling you how it was. The concept's credited to the artist and magician, Austin Osman Spare, whose images you might have seen—'

'In the library, here?'

'The library has drawings by Spare and Eric Gill, who was at Capel-y-ffin.'

'An obsessive Catholic with a taste for breaking taboos,' Merrily said. 'I believe incest was a favourite.'

'I can only assure you...' Claudia was now little more than a shadow '... that however much you might reject his methodology, Peter Rector's intentions towards Hay were entirely positive.'

'Odd, though, how the kind of occultism favoured by neo-Nazi groups like the Order of the Sun in Shadow seems to have absorbed some of the principles of chaos magic.'

Merrily was shaken. There was a tightrope here between good and evil, and the rope was woven from strands of a disturbingly convincing madness.

'He'd left all that behind,' Claudia said coldly. 'As you keep being told.'

'Doesn't mean it isn't still being followed by people inspired by Rector. Do you know anything about Jerrold Adrian Brace?'

'No. Who is he?'

'Forget it. What was your role in the last redemptive project?'

'I was never directly involved. As I've indicated, he still considered me a student. He'd tightened up a lot on the people he used. The days of the Convoy were long over. It was all very clandestine – the chosen few. I've been mainly the help. The one who helped his solicitor handle his affairs, managed his money, went to his bank, made sure David Hambling and Peter Rector lived safely and happily apart. But he trusted me with knowledge of what was happening. All vibrantly exciting. At first.'

Headlights in the lane.

'Go on,' Merrily said.

'Quite dizzying, seeing Hay mushrooming from a forlorn farming town to somewhere known all over the world. I was here when Clinton came to speak in a huge marquee on the green behind the castle. Thousands of people... a limo with smoked glass windows... the world's media. Businesses booming all over town, you could almost hear property prices blasting through the roof.'

'And Rector actually thought he was responsible, in essence, for all of that?'

'And who's to say he wasn't? Who can ever say that?'

'That's a very dangerous time, isn't it?' Merrily said. 'That explosion of fame and wealth. When all kinds of people come in with their own agendas. When cherished ideals can tumble in the scramble for bigger and bigger profits. People can go temporarily mental. Look at the banking industry.'

'That's when the creative, energetic role becomes a guardian role. More serious.'

Headlights turning in.

'So I'm taking it that what you call the poppet was the effigy of the King of Hay.'

'Life-size. Seated on a throne in the circle. So that he was always part of what was happening. Sometimes the focus was purely on the King, if he hadn't been well or had financial problems.'

'Didn't manage to stop him having to sell the castle.'

Claudia didn't reply.

'So how did he end up in the Wye?'

'Merrily, I don't know. When I saw the effigy on the TV, I was aghast. Which is why we're here. Why I'm telling you all this.'

'Where would they have to go to get the effigy, the poppet?'

'That's the burglary aspect. The King lives in the temple. In a magical vacuum.'

'Where's that?'

'You'll see.'

The car braked, a red glow, headlights rapidly extinguished.

'Why would someone take him out and throw him in the river?'

'Or, more likely, in the Dulas Brook, swollen by the rain. The poppet flushed down the brook and washed into the Wye. I don't know.'

Merrily saw Bliss getting out into the deep dusk, quietly closing the car door. He had some thin packages under each arm, the moon glinting on cellophane. Bliss was walking steadily, better in the dark.

'Evening, girls. Do we have consensus on this? I don't want to hang around.'

'Let's assume we do,' Merrily said.

Suddenly very insecure, in this place where imaginary worlds were built and broken.

Bliss gave each of them one of the plastic packages, keeping one back.

'Durex suits,' he said. 'Can't be too careful.'

'What?'

'Don't ask. I hope this is nothing. I hope Claudia's brought us here on a pure whim. What's a doll in a river, after all?'

Claudia said nothing, but her breathing was audibly rapid as she led them beyond the house towards the outbuildings and the engine room.

55

Out of blood

'Name's Seymour Loftus,' Robin said to Jones. 'How'd'ya like that?'

Pretty dark now. Beer-bottle lights on shelves of books, face-out, displaying photos of brooms, pentagrams, the Tree of Life and Stonehenge at dawn. Jones had told him about two missing girls, who would be middle-aged women now.

'You're saying you think they're dead?'

'I'm making no assumptions.'

'Like... detritus?'

'People living outside society disappear all the time. They may be dead, they may be living under different identities.'

'Right.'

Robin was starting to connect with the mindset, and it was both ridiculous and frightening, and it made him mad that there were people like this haunting the beloved British countryside.

Betty was making more tea. Kapoor was on the road to Brecon to pick up a reconditioned Betacam VCR. Robin picked up the mobile, prepared to go to work, like the stupid cops who'd gone to work on him on the edge of the scenic parking lot.

'Where did you get my name?'

'Seymour... that *is* you?'

'Who did you say you were?'

Loftus had one of those downbeat Midlands accents.

'My name's Robin Thorogood. I'm a PF member and also a bookseller. Thorogood Pagan Books, of Hay-on-Wye?'

'Not heard of them.'

'Well, you wouldn't have. We only just started up. We were in the Radnor Valley, we had a bust-up with an evangelical priest.'

'I remember that. It was in the papers. That was you, was it?'

'And now we took over a bookstore that once belonged to one of your members.'

'*My* members?'

'Order of the Sun in Shadow?'

'Nothing to do with me.'

'Seymour… get real.'

What you learned about these guys, through all the years of moots and gatherings, was that no matter how they sounded in a ritual, how sinister they looked in a temple, some of the time they were just people, with insecurities, money worries, marriage problems and fears of the past catching up with them.

'That was years ago,' Seymour said. 'I don't do that any more. I don't even talk about it any more. We started something we couldn't control. It's over.'

'His name was Jerrold Brace.'

'He wasn't a member.'

Oh, too fast, Seymour, just a little too fast.

'And how does it concern you?'

'We have… found signs of his habitation. Cut in stone.'

'What did you say your name was?'

'Robin.'

Not only failed to conceal his number, he'd given the guy his name and address. But it would be crazy to treat him like you believed all the bullshit.

Seymour said very quietly, 'Robin. I was pretty young when I was doing that, had extreme views about the way the country was going, and I wrote some stuff I wouldn't like to be associated with now. I've got kids. I'm on the council.'

'British National Party?'

'No! Green Party, if you must know.'

'And like, do the Green Party know about your roots?'

'Some of them do. And they know I'm not the same person. Half the Labour Party started out as rabid Trots. We all go through these phases.'

'You sure Jerry Brace wasn't a member?'

'I'm still not getting your angle on this.'

'Seymour, I may have to talk to the cops.'

'Why do I care who the hell you talk to?'

'You'd care plenty when they showed up on your suburban front porch with a warrant for your ass.'

'Are you trying to blackmail me? Because I make a point of recording all my calls.'

'Don't do blackmail, Seymour, though I will admit to the occasional death-threat.'

Robin saw Jones smile, looking up from scribbling in a note-book. Remember the main aim is to unsettle this man, Jones had said.

'This is a small town, Seymour, and people have long memories, and your guy, Jerry Brace—'

'He's dead! He's been dead years and years. He was a damaged man. And he was *not* my guy.'

'So you did know him?'

'I knew him by reputation. I can't talk about this, it's futile.'

'And I'm guessing you also know about two girls he used to hang out with who went missing?'

'You're making no sense. I think I'm going to have to end this call. Come back to me when you know what you're talking about.'

Robin stood up.

'Seymour…' He was in pain '… it's not too far for me to drive up there, and if I have to I will. And, boy, am I *loud* on a doorstep.'

Pause.

'He was full of shit,' Seymour said. 'He said he wanted to join the Order. I didn't particularly like the sound of him, and we knew he was doing hard drugs. We said come back when you're clean. Clean and cold. When you can deal with your emotions. When you can prove to us you're ready to move up. *Move up*. That was how we talked, back then.'

'You ever talk to Brace in person?'

'He rang one night. You could tell he was on something. He offered me…'

'Keep going.'

'He was offering the town. He said the town had been magically separated from the rest of Britain and was somewhere we could… establish ourselves. Through him.'

'How?'

'Let me finish. He talked about a remarkable vibe being wasted by useless hippies and if the new aeon was going to start anywhere it was there, and it would start around him because it was his destiny, and we could help each other achieve our mutual aims.'

Jones had pushed the notebook in front of Robin.

ASK HIM IF STILL ANY OSIS-LINKED FARMS OR COMMUNES. SAY IF CO-OPERATES MIGHT LEAVE HIM ALONE.

'… how he'd chosen his place of habitation with great care,' Seymour was saying. 'All the border strife, all the killing it must have seen. How it had grown out of blood and fire. He said he…'

Jones pulled the notebook back.

'What did?' Robin said. 'What grew out of blood and fire? Hay?'

'Its castle.'

'What?'

Jones pushed the notebook back in front of him.

ASK HIM ABOUT THE BOY. WHO WAS LOOKING AFTER THE BOY?

'Brace is long dead,' Seymour said. 'None of this matters.'

'Then you might as well talk about it.'

'He said it was his home. His ancestral home.'

'What was?'

'Work it out.'

'Who was looking after the boy, Seymour?'

Robin mouthing to Jones, *Who's the boy?*

'I've had enough of you. I don't want to hear from you again.'

'Seymour, just unload it.'

Dead phone.

56

Vision and need

MERRILY'S ONE-PIECE protective suit was too hot and far too big. She kept stumbling over its floppy folds.

Claudia Cornwell had stopped at the barn doors, was looking back towards the bungalow.

'In case either of you doesn't know, this was the site of a large farmhouse called Bryn-y-castell – Castle Hill. Reference to the castle mound. The house was left derelict then pulled down, I suppose about fifty or sixty years ago. Some of the stone went into the bungalow and also these outbuildings. But an important part of the old house remains. Important for us, anyway.'

The doors weren't even locked. Bliss had a torch, which showed there was nothing here to steal. It had a layer of bales of straw, obviously old, more of them in the loft. But none of the expected smells of new hay and old manure.

'You can see this place got no more than a cursory going-over from the search team,' Bliss said. 'But then, why should it? How many barns have cellars?'

A few bales had been thrown out of the loft to expose the corners. But nobody had bothered with the floor.

'The barn was simply built over the entrance to the main cellars of the demolished house,' Claudia said. 'Root cellar for apples, wine cellar.'

Bliss said, 'How many times you been here, Claudia?'

'Here… many times. Down there… once. Yesterday. So my DNA's going to be everywhere, isn't it?'

Merrily said, 'So the cellars conceal…'

'The temple, yes. The temple was constructed over about a year. After what happened on the Bluff, Peter wasn't going to take chances any more. Only he and his innermost circle ever came here. A sealed chamber. There was only a handful of them and most of them were over seventy. It's a measure of how important he thought this was.' Her voice faded, as though talk was only delaying the inevitable. 'Could I…?'

Merrily took a step back. Claudia had pulled a bale to one side, pointed at three or four others.

'The trapdoor's under those. There's a blue plastic sheet we need to take up. Peter showed me how to get in if there was an emergency. I was the nearest, at Talgarth. He knew I wouldn't just go down there.'

'But you did yesterday?' Merrily said.

'He was dead. The future was uncertain. As I say, most of his… people… are old. I was the youngest and still outside the core. I came back and wandered around. Shed a few tears, wondered how it could possibly go on without him, even if Athena White could gather a few more suitably qualified people together. I wondered, like you're probably wondering now, if we hadn't all just succumbed to his… his vision… and his need.'

There was the trapdoor, plain oak, sunk into the flags, an iron ring sunk into the oak. Bliss slipped his white-gloved hand under the ring.

'There are electric lights,' Claudia said. 'On the wall on your right when you get to the bottom of the steps. Small narrow ante-room and a plain white door. Here's the key.'

A plain Yale key. She gave it to Bliss. He stood looking down, the big numbers on his baseball sweater just visible through the plastic. He'd tied a white mask over his mouth and nose.

He said, 'You want to go first, Claudia?'

'I think it should be you.'

'Yeh.'

Bliss pulled on the ring. The trapdoor came up easily, with a low, hydraulic whine, Bliss's torch downlighting a rough pine stairway, with a rail. He went down about three steps, looked back, pulled down the mask.

'Just tell me briefly,' Bliss said. 'What will I see? What's the layout?'

'A ceiling of midnight blue.' Claudia's voice was firm, as if she was reciting poetry. 'A black and white floor, like a chessboard. Circles, one inside the other. A triangle. An altar. The coat of arms of Hay above it. On the altar, a chalice of water from the confluence of the Dulas Brook and the River Wye. And a chair. A stiff-backed chair with arms, like a throne. Inside the circle where it would be protected.'

'And that's where the dummy would've been.'

'Where the King sat. His crown askew. Baggy trousers tied at the waist with red and yellow binder twine. All the energy channelled through him, and he never knew. Never even thought of it. God...'

Merrily said, 'Why did you go down there? When you were here on your own?'

'Because... because I'd walked all around and couldn't sense Peter anywhere, I just... He'd gone, you see, and suddenly I couldn't stand that. The man who'd had more impact on my life than anyone at Oxford, any head-of-chambers. I wanted to be with him, one more time. To get some guidance.'

'And was he there?'

Claudia was sitting on a bail of straw, as if she'd felt suddenly weak.

'Don't know. Don't know.'

Bliss looked irritated.

He went down.

Presently, the lights came on in the cellar. Sounds of Bliss unlocking a door, but there was a long period of hush before Merrily heard his moan.

57

English corruption

BETTY SAID, 'FUNNY how you don't see things. Really obvious things.'

Robin held tight to his mug of tea. He'd been resistant to tea for so long; now, sometimes, he couldn't get enough, and it couldn't be too hot, couldn't be too strong.

'You knew, didn't you?' Betty said.

Looking at Gwyn Arthur Jones, an old golem in a drooping suit. A discontinued line in cops.

'Actually, Betty, I didn't. When you have a name like Jones, these conceits seem so far removed from your own kind of reality as to appear quite nonsensical.'

'You think it was a conceit?'

'Perhaps a genealogist would say otherwise, I don't know. Anyone can prove anything. If I had the money and the patience I could demonstrate my own line of descent from the Princes of Dyfed. No, no—' He lifted a hand. 'I'm not serious.'

'But *something* lit your lamp,' Robin said.

'Yes. Something did. Been on the back-burner for so long that I lacked the courage to approach it. What business was it of mine, an old copper with a long nose and too much time on his hands?'

It was actually Betty who'd seen it first, after Robin had come off the phone with Seymour Loftus.

'Brace,' she said. '*Is* Brace an English corruption of De Braose?'

* * *

'Nobody knows that,' Robin said now. 'Coulda come from anyplace. And it isn't always even spelt the same. There's a block of new apartments down the street called De Breos Court, with an e.'

'Always struck me as odd,' Jones said, 'that they should name luxury flats after one of our great historic villains. The man who massacres the Welsh aristocracy over Christmas dinner, then slaughters one of their sons, aged seven. Odd, too, that this forbidding grey apartment complex is – in size – the biggest development in Hay since... the castle, I suppose.'

'But those apartments weren't here when Jerry Brace arrived in Hay?'

'Like's Garage, it was, in those days. You'd never have a hope of filling all those flats back then.'

'So, OK, Brace arrives, conceives the idea he's a descendant of de Braose, the Ogre. Or is that something his old man had told him way back? Is that, in fact, why Jerry fetches up in Hay?'

'Either is possible, boy. It's entirely in keeping with the way these people like to think. And also explains his obsession with the castle. He convinces himself he's the true heir. In essence, it belongs to him, not the interloper, Booth, who takes a fine military fortress and fills it – pah! – with books.'

'Actually,' Betty said. 'If you're looking for the last time this country was subject to a fascist dictatorship you could very well be looking at de Braose's time. Even Hitler never managed what the Normans achieved. OK, not an Aryan invasion, if they came from France, but—'

'No?' Jones lifted a forefinger. 'I may be wrong...' He opened the laptop '... but I believe the Normans were a race apart from the French.'

'Just don't make it any more weird,' Robin said.

'Earlier on, Mrs Watkins was asking me why Brace had chosen to set up his business here, and I was forced to say I didn't know. What I do recall from my reading is that William de Braose was, at first, well regarded by King John and allowed to behave like a king himself in the borderland. They eventually fell out – probably over de Braose's failure to disclose income to which John thought he was entitled. Anyway, he went on the run. Was finally killed and his wife and child starved to death. But, right up to the end, William was insisting he'd return one day to his beloved borders, and he— Ah, here we are. The Normans were descended from Nordic invaders who settled in France. Vikings, in fact. Or Germanic. So there's a case for saying the Normans were Aryans… yes.'

'Tradition,' Betty said. 'Heritage. Destiny. *Hell.*'

'Bets, it's just an elaborate fantasy they built around themselves.'

'It's a… septic obsession,' Betty said.

Robin pulled open the door and walked out to see if there was any sign of Kapoor. It was night now, so no bastard wardens with a licence to kill; Kapoor would park right outside. Robin did not turn, as he usually did, to look up at the castle with an element of possession based on a desire to paint it. He was hearing Betty: *I just think that we might have some work to do. To make it ours. Rather than… someone else's.*

He took a few paces then came back, shut the door hard. The castle walls would be blackening.

'There you go.' Betty turned the laptop away from herself. 'British neo-Nazi pagan factions tend to associate themselves with Anglo-Saxon and Nordic traditions.'

Jones produced his pipe.

'All right if I…?'

'Sure,' Robin said. 'Just don't bring out a pork pie.'

'You didn't finish telling us, Robin. What, in the final analysis, was your opinion of our friend Loftus?'

'He was lying. It all came too easy. He's a local politician now. Green Party. Then again, he could be lying about that, too. I almost told him about the videotape.'

'Perhaps you should have done,' Jones said. 'Time, I think, to start nudging the applecart. Perhaps beyond time.'

58

A dark symmetry

SOMETIMES, WHEN THE worst had happened, you were angry with yourself. You'd thought about it repeatedly, in vivid detail, convinced that self-torture could alter reality. Not only stop it happening but stop it *having* happened.

Worthless superstition.

But *please God...*

When they reached the bottom of the steps, Bliss was coming out, shutting the white door, putting his back against it, snatching off his face mask.

'No point. Nothing to be done.'

Moving his arms, trying to sweep them back up the stairs, like crowd control.

'No.' Claudia Cornwell carried on down to the bottom of the steps until she was face to face with Bliss. 'We need to see this.'

'Claudia—'

'This isn't about the law, Francis, or regulations, this is about what I might be able to tell you that you wouldn't get from anyone else. I need to see. Or else why am I here? Why's Merrily here?'

Bliss tapped gloved fingers against a thigh, his left side, the side that went numb. He looked up at Merrily.

'You all right with this?'

She just nodded, not all right with any of it. She wanted out of here. Wanted to go running back up the steps, tripping over her Durex suit until she could tear it off and keep running into the darkness. She wanted a cigarette.

'All right then.' Bliss stepped aside. 'Remember, you don't touch anything, even with the kit on. Don't lean against any walls. And especially you don't throw up. The first hint of nausea, you get out and into that field. Or, better still, your own car.'

He opened the door.

'Take some deep breaths now. You won't want to in a minute.'

A crypt, with adornments. Uplighting, shaded.

Tiled floor, earth-coloured walls, a low ceiling, a false ceiling.

A ceiling of midnight blue. A black and white floor, like a chessboard. Circles, one inside the other.

Cardinal points.

Michael, Gabriel, Raphael, Uriel, the archangels through which magicians paid tribute to their Hebrew ancestors.

All there.

On the altar, a chalice.

Also fat candles with white wicks, brown-flecked.

And a chair. A stiff-backed chair with arms, like a throne. Inside the circle where it would be protected.

Yes.

Where the King sat.

If only.

'She never left Cusop,' Bliss said.

Stepping away so they could see her. If they wanted to. If they could bear it.

They were spared Tamsin's face. Her head had fallen forward on to her chest, hair screening the wound which had produced all the blood, like waxwork blood now, dry and ridged, and the stink of it all, in this vacuum, was the worst you'd ever know. A sweetness under it, as if incense had been burned in here, the stench of death and evil.

You've gorra big future, PC Winterson.

'I need some information, Claudia,' Bliss said through his mask. 'From when you first arrived in Cusop yesterday.'

Jesus, Merrily thought. *Yesterday.* The hood was tight around her face, a white-gloved hand pressing the mask into her nose and mouth, but the smell got everywhere.

'We've been through this, Francis,' Claudia said.

Her eyes, unexpectedly, hot with panic. A barrister and a magician. A mother. With daughters?

'No,' Bliss said. 'When we went through it, Tamsin was missing. So let's start with the assumption that it wasn't you who killed her.'

Claudia gasped. Bliss pulled down his mask, took a savage breath, did not choke.

'Let's assume somebody saw you come into the barn and uncover the entrance to the cellar. Could've been Tamsin herself, who saw you leaving and then went down. Maybe someone else followed her and then...'

'Her throat's cut?' Claudia said. 'Somebody cut her throat?'

'Claudia, when you were there, in full daylight, did you see anybody else in the vicinity? In Cusop? Anywhere?'

'Nobody. Although people evidently saw me.'

'Kelly James. And – assuming pregnant Kelly has nothing to hide – someone else. There are several possibilities, and the one that seems most likely is that someone saw you go in and, when you'd left, came down here to take a look. What's he find, Claudia. The King's in his chair?'

Bliss was talking faster, battling his condition with an unnatural, forced, clipped authority.

'The King's always in his chair,' Claudia said.

'For Christ's sake, Frannie, *stop it*!' All the breath pumped out of Merrily and thank God it was only breath. 'This is not an interview room, this is... this is...'

But he didn't stop. He couldn't stop.

'The King's robe was red, but not with blood. The King had already gone, right? Whoever it was didn't want the effigy messed up?'

'I don't see why he wouldn't.' Claudia's voice high and hoarse.

'If his intention was to desecrate the temple. Blood, piss… anything. You know what they're like.'

'No, I don't, necessarily. Who?'

'People who'd do this.'

'*Who?*'

'I don't *know!*'

'Frannie, can we get the… get out of here? Please?'

'You didn't have to come in, Merrily. It was your decision. All right, let's say he – or even *they* – came in for a look around.'

'So the intruder just takes the King – *planning* to throw him in the river? Is that what he's come here for?'

'Or in the brook,' Claudia said. 'More likely the brook.'

'Why? Under your… rules. Quick, Claudia. Don't stand there refining it, you're not presenting a defence.'

'All right!' Claudia's hands up in front of her face. '*One* – it was the brook where Peter died. *Two* – lots of rain lately, the water would be high and rushing. Wouldn't take long for it to get washed down to the Wye.'

'Why?'

'A kind of ritual drowning of… all our efforts? The project? *I* don't know, I'm just talking off the top of my head, Francis, and I may be talking balls.'

'Doesn't matter. So Tamsin, having been alerted by Kelly James, turns up, looking for you. Sees the barn door's open and the hatch. Comes down and confronts the intruder, the way she… the way she would. What's *he* thinking, then? He hasn't done anything? He hasn't even broken in. He's just a trespasser. He's just curious. He's like, "*Sorry*, officer, but… well… you gorra admit it's a bit weird in here, isn't it?" That's what he'd say.'

'If he was an ordinary trespasser.'

Claudia stood looking at Tamsin, making herself look, Merrily thought, in case any of this was her fault. Looking at the big cakes of dried blood encrusting the poor kid's T-shirt.

'How does that,' Bliss said, 'lead to *this*?'

Hardening his questions now, Merrily thought. Going for Claudia – almost certainly unconsciously, but it was there – the way so many defence barristers must have gone for *him* in the witness box. But the corpse, in all its pitiful horror, was never in court, where the only smell would be wood polish.

'Do you know all the people in Rector's coven or whatever you prefer to call it?'

'I think so.'

'How well?'

'Christ, Francis!' Claudia snatched away her white mask. 'These are not bloody satanists! They're people – mainly *elderly* people – of a gentle and spiritual disposition. *Learned* people. They don't do… sacrifices. Not of anything *living*.'

'Then who would? What about someone she knew? Say the trespasser is someone she'd talked to. In her spare-time inquiries into Rector's death. Suppose she came face-to-face with someone she'd already had cause to be a bit suspicious of?'

'Wouldn't the killer be covered in blood?'

'That would depend if… if he knew what he was doing?' Bliss went to stand behind the chair. 'I'm inclined to think she'd been disabled first. Maybe barely conscious when she was arranged in this chair like the effigy. If she was already disabled, he could've done it from behind, one slash, jump back, stand in the doorway, watch her…' His breath catching in his throat '… bleeding out.'

Merrily heard Claudia's indrawn breath, or maybe it was her own.

'And then,' Bliss said, 'having hidden his or her own motor in any one of a few dozen places within walking distance, the killer – at some stage – drives Tamsin's Clio back to Hay, with her phone in there, leaves it on the car park and goes back across the fields to Cusop for his vehicle. How long a walk – twenty minutes?'

'Or,' Merrily said, 'if he was on foot in the first place…'

'Someone local,' Claudia said.

Bliss shrugged.

'Can we get out of here now, Francis?'

'Not quite yet.'

'I need to go home tonight.'

'Just be glad you can.'

Bliss was still standing behind Tamsin's body. He had his torch out, directing the beam down to where her hair had fallen forward.

'I won't ask you to examine this, but her head's been mutilated.' Bliss turned to Merrily. 'Remember the photograph you came across in Rector's library?'

'Like I'd forget?'

'Hard to be sure, but two cuts…' He was looking down into the circle of light. 'Two deep cuts on Tamsin's head… crossing over.'

'Dear God.'

'Claudia… thoughts. What are your thoughts?'

'I'm thinking I just want to see my childre— All right, I'll— There's a dark… what I can only describe as a dark symmetry… to the removal of a power-object and its replacement by a dead body.'

'So we're looking at somebody who knows this stuff?'

'I think that's the most likely explanation.'

'And what might he do next?' Bliss said.

Merrily saw the woman's shaven head in a grainy photocopy, the message beneath.

What will you do now?

Outside they stripped off their Durex suits, gave them back to Bliss who stowed them in the boot of his Honda.

He'd inspected the temple in case they'd left anything behind, switched out the lights, sealing the crime scene like some chamber at the bottom of a pyramid in the desert. The hatch had been replaced, the bales of straw moved back.

'We drive out of here at a normal night speed. One of you leave about half a minute after the other. Drive into Hay and we'll meet on the car park, down by the recycling bins. Go.'

Claudia nodded, went to her car. Merrily turned bitterly towards Bliss.

'Why did you do that? Why did you keep us in there? What the hell was the point? As if it wasn't bad *enough*.'

'Needed answers. Before the shock-factor set in.'

His voice muffled because he was bent over, hands on his knees, shaking. As he came up, his face was lit briefly by the lights of Claudia's car and his eyes were hot and pooled.

'Just leave me alone, eh, Merrily.'

She nodded.

As she drove between the broken gateposts, hands cold on the wheel, there was one narrow, pale strip over Hay, like the light under a closed door.

59

Poltergeists

THEY WALKED AWAY from the cars, stood near the bottom of the Oxford Road car park, amongst the moonlit bins: *glass, plastic, cardboard, garden waste.* No more than twenty cars on here and four were police.

'What a friggin' awful mess,' Bliss said. 'For everybody.'

Car-hiss on Oxford Road. Otherwise silence. Merrily felt the sweat forming like cold dew on her forehead.

'You have to tell them, don't you? Now.'

Bliss stared at the foothills of the Black Mountains, embossed on the pale night sky.

'Claudia and me, we'd rather someone else made the discovery. I've been trying to think about how that's achievable. If it is.'

'Think about Tamsin's family. Sitting there, drinking too much tea, waiting for the phone to ring. Reassuring each other over and over. Telling them now isn't going to shorten the suffering, but it'll at least end the crippling anxiety.'

Bliss turned to Claudia.

'You go home, eh?'

'No.' Claudia backed away. 'You're not going to be able to keep me out of this. I told you and I told Merrily that I'd rather my private interests didn't become public knowledge, but… after seeing what we all saw… that doesn't matter. Think about it.'

'What I'm thinking about is you spending several long days beating your head against a wall trying to initiate acting-DCI

Iain Brent, PhD into stuff he thinks wouldn't motivate even the most irrational killer. *You* know how this goes.'

'Yes, I do. And I'm a barrister. I can handle it.'

Merrily's phone chimed. She moved out into the car park.

'Merrily.'

'*Gwyn Jones, Merrily. Where are you?*'

'Back in Hay.'

'*Are you all right?*'

'Yes, I'm all right.'

'*Francis Bliss… is he with you, now?*'

'Not far away.'

'*All right, listen to me, Merrily. Can you ask him to meet me? Just him, nobody else. Next shop along from the Thorogoods. Mr Kapoor's cricket shop.*'

'Gwyn, I'm not sure he's going to want to right now.'

'*Merrily, look, this is going to be too big for me now. Do you understand what I'm saying? It's taken a turn for the serious.*'

A soft drumming, and she turned to see Claudia Cornwell quietly hammering the soft undersides of her fists against the bottle bank's rusting flank.

'… the enormity of it,' Claudia was saying. 'None of our careers are worth this.'

'*Tell him it's important, Merrily. Tell him it's more important than anything in my long career in the police.*'

'Gwyn, what I suggest is you come here. We're at the bottom of the car park, near the bins. Can you do that?'

'*Three minutes.*'

'All right,' Claudia said to Bliss. 'I will go home. I'll go home and drink black coffee and wait for the knock on the door. It's not going away. We don't get rid of a night like this.'

They watched her walking to her car. Merrily saw that the left side of Bliss's face was sagging. He needed sleep, but how much sleep was he going to get when he went to Brent and told him what they'd found? This was awful. Everything tonight was awful.

'Frannie, that was Gwyn Jones. He wants to talk to you.'

'Stall him.'

'I can't. He's on his way down. He says to tell you it's more important than anything in his time as a cop.'

Bliss sighed.

'Gwyn Arthur Jones. One of your bloody poltergeists that doesn't know it's dead. I'll be just like him when they kick me out.'

He leaned back beside a wide metal mouth choking on cardboard.

'All right, tell me quick. What did Claudia say before I arrived. What did she tell you?'

God.

Merrily lit a cigarette.

'Some people called Rector the Magus of Hay.'

'Meaning?'

'Priest in the pre-Christian sense. Someone who works magic. And we're not talking end-of-the-pier. Claudia's a barrister, you don't get to be a barrister overnight. She aspires to work magic and she knows that's going to take her a lot longer. It's psychology, only deeper. It's religion for people who aren't into faith. It demands massive self-discipline.'

'Yeh, we've been here before. Does it work?'

'Works for them. For people who take it seriously, this stuff's bigger than life and bigger than death. You know what I'm saying?'

'And I can just hear meself repeating it to Claudia's mates in the CPS. Now tell me what it means in terms of crime and motive.'

'I can tell you what it means in human terms. Some of it. For Rector, it was about conscience and atonement. He'd written a book explaining how a belief in magic had inspired the most evil regime in history, and he did it so persuasively he was seen as one of the major voices of New Right mysticism. When they found out he wasn't, some people felt betrayed.'

'Enough to kill him?'

'Enough to want to spoil his party, certainly. Rector was

looking for a way to repair his karma. Persuade somebody to leave heaven's gate off the latch. He wanted to devote his last years and all his learning to something essentially… positive.'

'As symbolized by an old clothes shop dummy in a crown? And then replaced by a young copper who gets a swastika carved into her head?'

'Just accept it. All that matters is that enough people believed— Oh.'

'Good evening, Gwyn,' Bliss said.

He was agitated. She could tell that by his breathing. In that, for the first time, she was aware that he *was* breathing. He nodded at Bliss, before turning to her, his voice unexpectedly sharp.

'He knows about this?'

'No,' Merrily said. 'Other things came up.' She paused. Sod it. 'Like… the discovery of a young copper in a cellar. With her throat cut.' Heard Bliss pulling in a furious breath. 'Frannie, for God's sake, it's bloody pointless holding anything back at this stage.'

'You are saying…' Gwyn Arthur Jones swung round to Bliss '… that Tamsin Winterson—?'

'You say nothing about this, Gwyn,' Bliss hissed. 'That clear?'

'And I'll say, Francis, is that you need to come with me. You need to see something.'

'Look, we've got—'

Gwyn Arthur was already walking away, long strides towards the top of the car park where car-beams intersected like shining blades under the castle wall. When they caught him up, he started talking about Jerry Brace and his obsession with the castle. Also a former fascist called Seymour Loftus who was perhaps all that remained of the Order of the Sun in Shadow.

And how none of that mattered after you saw the tape that Gwyn Arthur had already watched on the player borrowed in Brecon. Which he said would put everything into a hellish perspective.

60

Name of my father

THE TV SCREEN vibrated to black.

Chairs and stools were set up in front of the monitor which shared a desk under a cricket bat hanging from a beam, a shadow against the low lights, like some antique punishment device.

Merrily said, 'Where's Betty?'

'Back at the bookstore. Waiting for you.' Robin sounded disconnected, hair sweated to his forehead. 'She... didn't wanna see it again. I'm just here to remind you 'bout what you planned. Tell you she's waiting. When you're through here.' He nodded at a coffee machine. 'Help yourself.'

'Perhaps I'll have one later, thanks.'

Her throat was like a sandpit, but this didn't feel like a social occasion. She'd actually forgotten what she'd agreed with Betty, and there weren't many distractions that made you forget about a proposed exorcism.

She heard the shop door closing, the rattle of a blind coming down.

'This is Francis Bliss, boys,' Gwyn Arthur said, flat-voiced. 'Here to help us.'

Merrily sank down in front of the screen, between Gwyn Arthur and Bliss, who didn't seem up to helping an old lady across the road. Her head ached.

Gwyn Arthur nodded to Kapoor and the screen acquired a shaky image, dark and oily like the inside of an old car engine.

393

Kapoor stepped away, as if he didn't want it to be any clearer. Gwyn Arthur peered at Merrily.

'You all right with this?'

'Tonight I'm all right with anything.' What the hell was coming? 'Sorry, that's not what I meant.'

Gwyn Arthur caught Kapoor's eye, lifted a forefinger. Kapoor set the tape rolling. Robin reached for his stick.

'I'm outa here. Don't wanna leave Betty alone. OK?'

But she knew that wasn't it, as Kapoor followed Robin to the door, held it open for him, and shut it behind him, letting out a staccato steam-train breath as he came back to the TV. On the screen, something glimmering in a shifting darkness.

'Pre-digital,' Kapoor said. 'Very basic camera, I'd guess.'

A face was fading out of the darkness.

'It's night,' Kapoor said. 'The lights in the room are poor. Altogether… a bleedin' mercy, really.'

A woman's face. Grey and indistinct, but you could make out closed eyes. Bliss leaned into the screen.

'Dead?'

Dear God, how much of this could anyone take in one night? But the camera had pulled back to throw the woman into shadow and reveal a second person. If that was a person.

Bliss said, 'What's he gorrover his head, Gwyn?'

'Looks like the corner of a black bin liner. See the point at the top, with a kind of ridge and the way it's pull back tight?'

The eyeholes were no more than knife-slits, crudely scissored around the edges to widen them.

'Wearing the rest of the bin liner, it looks like,' Bliss said. 'Underneath, covering his upper body. More wrapped round his arms. Look at the hands. Looks like friggin' Homer Simpson. Homer Simpson's hands.'

'Rubber gloves. He's dressed for…'

'I can see what he's dressed for,' Bliss said tightly. 'The woman… she's gorra be well out of it. Nobody gonna sit still for this.'

'We had a stack of pictures of Mephista,' Gwyn Arthur said. 'But this is not her. This, I think, has to be Cherry Banks. You can detect slight movements. I think she's sedated. Whatever they used before Rohypnol. I used to know.'

'Someone's laughing,' Merrily said.

A short burst – stifled, muffled. She thought of Jane. Jane laughed like that when she knew she shouldn't be laughing at something. A squeak of instinctive, suppressed mirth.

'Look at the camera shake,' Kapoor said. 'All over the place. Way the camera's suddenly shooting the ceiling.'

Merrily jerked back.

'What's that in his hand?'

Glint above a yellow fist.

'You really don't have to watch this,' Gwyn Arthur said, 'but I'd be glad if you'd listen. Try and make out what he's saying.'

'Bloody hell, Gwyn—'

'Listen. Please.'

She shut her eyes on it, plucking words out of white noise, And then opened them too soon.

'Sound fluctuates,' Kapoor said, his back to the screen. 'Amateurs. Cheap kit.'

'Oh, Jesus,' Merrily said.

Kapoor froze the tape.

'Reverse it, please,' Gwyn Arthur said.

Bliss said, 'What'd he say? *Sacrifice*? He say sacrifice?'

'No – further back, boy. I want us to hear that laughter again.'

Merrily watched the crinkly, shiny blackness unfurling from the woman, rippling in the half-light, the blood – *dear God* – sucked back into the throat.

'All right.' Gwyn Arthur raising a hand. 'Stop. Now run it again.'

She kept her eyes closed, this time, all the way through concentrating on prising the words from the hiss and the laughter.

Bliss recoiled.

'What happened there?'

'Blood-spatter, it is, on the lens. There, see, someone's trying to wipe it away.'

Merrily's gut knotted.

'I ain't watching this again, all right?' Kapoor said. 'Don't wanna be remembering this forever.'

Out of the video, more laughter. Eruption of glee.

'Definitely a woman's laugh,' Bliss said. 'Where's the woman?'

'Behind the camera? Is the woman recording it?'

'What's this? Oh, Mother of God. This is thirty years ago?'

Merrily opened her eyes to the point of the knife, wiped clean of blood, quivering above the top of the lolling head. To the descent of the point. To the welling blood between the hair and the flesh and the bone.'

'Merrily, is this the woman in the photo? Gorra be.'

Wavy lines, a buzz. Merrily let the breath come out, began to lever herself out of the chair. Saw Gwyn Arthur's sorrowful smile.

'Not over, I'm afraid. Break in filming. No actual editing here, just stop-start. But we should take a small break, too.' He signalled to Kapoor to pause the machine. 'You caught those words, either of you?'

'I think,' Merrily said, 'that he was saying, *I sacrifice you...*'

'Yes.'

'*... in the name of my father.*'

'I doubt even Sir Charles would thank the boy for that.'

'I'd guess means his... forefather.'

'The rest,' Gwyn Arthur said, 'takes place in the bathroom. Fortunately, not a long sequence.'

Immediately,

Thack, thack, thack.

The audio was perhaps worse than the visuals. From behind closed eyes you were imagining it in full light. Merrily opened her eyes to the camera zooming in and pulling back, like a crow ripping at roadkill. White enamel, red enamel. Liquids jetting up at the lens, and the glee this evoked splintering through the static and this time nothing could wipe it away.

'It's inhuman,' Merrily said.

Stupidly inadequate.

The last shot before the end of the tape was in perfect focus, the black plastic killer standing up, arms out, triumphant. Chest like a butcher's display tray, a blade in a red hand, only spots of yellow. In the other hand, something like a small red squid.

'Oh God,' Bliss said.

'All right.' Gwyn Arthur Jones was out of his chair. 'Shut it off. How many copies so far, Mr Kapoor?'

'One DVD.'

'You have a VHS recorder of your own, don't you?'

'For transferring match tapes to DVD. It's at home. You want me to fetch it?'

'Would you do that? This is important. We could use at least one copy on VHS. I want to do something.'

Kapoor shrugged.

'I'll go now. Could use some air.'

When he'd gone, Bliss leaned back against the closed door.

'Let me ask this again. You're saying that all this happened over thirty years ago and this bloke is long dead. Is it possible he isn't?'

61

Look what you made me do

BLISS WAS ON his feet, hanging his jacket over a vacant chair, his left eye weeping down his cheek.

'I *can't* go to Brent with this. This is about... what was that word you used about Rector?'

'Frannie—'

'Atonement. I need this bastard.'

'At the cost of sacrificing your career?'

'What's a career?'

Look, Frannie, without sounding like a bereavement counsellor, whatever the poor kid did—'

'Whatever she did, Merrily, she did so she could put something useful on me desk. So I'd remember her name. Me. The battered friggin' hero.'

'There's a flaw in that.' She'd been ready for this, knowing it would come at some point. 'Suppose you'd said, "Don't count on any help from me, Tamsin. Stick to chasing drink-drivers and shoplifters." You know what she'd have said to herself, Tamsin being Tamsin? She'd have said, *I'll show this bastard who should be chasing shoplifters...*'

'Nice argument, Merrily. Almost convincing.'

Gwyn Arthur said, 'This *is*... the same as Tamsin? Thirty years on?

'Except he didn't finish the swastika.'

Bliss telling Gwyn Arthur about the photograph inside the

book in Rector's library. Probably Polaroid. Instant picture. Muddied up in a photocopier to obscure the identity even more.

'Why would he do that? Why would he send it to Rector?'

'Because he's trying to shift the blame?' Merrily said. 'Maybe not so much *what will you do next*? as... *Look what you made me do.*'

'That could be right.' Bliss sat down again. 'Like a peevish kid. And then he dismembers her body in his bath. I'd guess the reason they stopped recording is it went on for two or three hours. You realize what's involved there? How many bin sacks you'd fill? It's not just arms and legs, is it? It's sordid and messy and disgusting, not like...'

'Not like a magical ceremony,' Merrily said.

Jerrold Brace's tribute to his forefather, his liberating performance of something hideously at odds with civilized behaviour, his self-initiation. The electric charge, the magical high dissipating into the hot, greasy grind of pulling a human being apart and packing away the bits, prime cuts and offal.

'There's something else.' Gwyn Arthur went over to the tape player, switched it back on. 'Think I can work this thing. Would both of you mind listening to this bit again?'

He sat close to the screen, rewinding.

'You're listening for the woman's voice in the background. Tell me what you think she's saying.'

Merrily closed her eyes. The thin voices in the cans suggested a climber clinging to a cliff-face in high wind.

'There,' Gwyn Arthur said. 'What are the words?'

Clear enough this time. She took off the cans.

'She's saying... *say it*. Quite urgently. '*Say it, say it, say it.*'

'That's what I thought. Thank you.'

'What's that signify?' Bliss said. 'What's that about?'

In the real world, a phone rang, sending him over to his jacket.

'Assuming this is a copy,' Gwyn Arthur said to Merrily, 'what happened to the original tape, do you think? Would it have been mailed, perhaps, to Mr Loftus at the Order?'

Bliss stood with his phone at his cheek. He stiffened.

'No,' he said. 'I haven't. Where was this?'

Merrily watching him, alarmed. Watching his already disfigured face become an emotional car crash.

'A dilemma for Mr Loftus if that arrived in the post,' Gwyn Arthur said. 'The young master, at the time, of right-wing rhetoric. You can imagine him writing his inflammatory books, self-published under false names, inspired by the early work of Peter Rector. Brace's shop a valued outlet in the days before the Internet, but suddenly here's Brace himself presenting this horror. Saying also to Loftus, *Look what* you *made me do.*'

Silence. Bliss still on the phone, listening, expressionless now. It didn't look like good news.

'Thanks,' he said. 'Thanks, Karen.'

'Perhaps we need to talk to Mr Loftus again,' Gwyn Arthur said. 'Perhaps *I* need to talk to him this time. Or you, Francis?'

'Let's keep Loftus on ice for a bit.' Bliss's voice was dull and beaten as he shut the phone. 'Looks like all hell's about to break loose out there. They've found Tamsin.'

Gwyn Arthur shut off the player.

'*How* did they find her?'

'Anonymous phone call to the Incident Room. Brent's on his way in. Looks like all the key people have had individual phone calls.'

'That was yours?' Merrily said.

'No. Looks like I'm not gerrin one. That was Karen. Me mate.'

'Maybe they didn't tell you,' she said forlornly, 'because they could see how knackered you were when you left.'

'Possible. Not likely.'

Merrily stood up. Bliss's face was like an envelope torn down one side.

'Sounds like we were seen, doesn't it, Merrily? It's unlikely anyone just happened to stumble on that cellar so soon after we left. Sounds like we're stuffed. Me, anyway.'

'Or,' Gwyn Arthur said, 'your friend Miss Cornwell made the call.'

'Trust me, she wouldn't.'

'Or the killer did. Listen, I think... I think if anyone needs to atone it's probably me. Though until I saw the tape I had no real reason to think killing was involved. But it...' He had his pipe between his hands, screwing and unscrewing the stem '... it's pretty obvious to me who we're looking at.'

62

Symbol of intent

Merrily stood in the alley, looking at rooftops, as if there might be visible signs of distress rising through the curling streets, like oil up the wick of a lamp, until a desperate light would flare from a window of the empty castle.

Nothing to see, of course, nothing to hear. Nobody would know yet, except for senior police and the cops in the patrol car who'd followed up an anonymous call and gone down the steps with their flashlights and come out personally sickened and professionally thrilled, to make way for the Durex suits.

Robin came down from the shop next door, saying he and Betty had cleaned the place up. Put the stones back in the chimney, brushed up the dust. It was ready.

'I'll come soon,' Merrily said. 'Very soon.'

Thinking, why? What's the point? What am I for? A walking anachronism. Who cares?

'Sure.' Robin raised a hand. 'Thanks.'

He was looking lost, like somebody had taken an axe to his idyll. Did he really think she might achieve anything other than to make Betty feel a little more calm?

'Hold on.' Gwyn Arthur Jones was at the door. 'Don't go yet, Robin. I think I asked you about the laughter?'

Robin came wearily back into the cricket shop.

'Jesus, Gwyn, what am I supposed to say? It's a goddamn nightmare. Yeah, we both heard it. Yeah, we thought it was like a laugh we'd heard someplace else. I guess a laugh doesn't alter that much over time. You can change the pitch of your voice, go live in some other place and absorb a new accent, but...'

'Laughter's the result of an inner process too deep for control,' Gwyn Arthur said. 'Hard to fake. And who laughs at violent death, in such a gleeful, uninhibited way?'

'Children,' Merrily said. 'Children who've only seen it in horror films. Who've never thought much about the reality of it. It was a young person's laugh.'

Gwyn Arthur came from a different, maybe more reflective era of policing which perhaps had lasted longer in country towns. His aromatic tobacco calmed the air like the incense in St Mary's church.

'The father's name,' he said, 'is Tim Wareham. Retired now, and no more an old hippy than any of us who were around in 1967. I really don't think, but for his wife's poor health, that he would have contacted me at all. I think, even then, he realized that whatever fate had befallen his daughter would be something they might be better off going to their graves without knowing about.'

'You have to wonder,' Merrily said, 'why they called her Mephista. I mean, not everybody would see it as tempting fate, but...'

'They didn't. Her name was Melissa. Which, as a young child, she'd pronounce as *Meffissa*. And Tim, when she was naughty, would change it to Mephista. Which, being the free spirits they thought they were, they found funny and affectionate. And it stuck. Melissa Wareham, her name. And she was often naughty. They stopped keeping pets because of the way she would *have fun* with them. As she'd put it.'

'He told you this?'

'Makes me smile how, when some teenager is missing or dead, the parents appear on TV to tell the nation how you could not wish for a better son or daughter. A beautiful, thoughtful child. And the candles are lit and the shrines are built. Doesn't help. It's what they *don't* tell the nation that might have helped. I said to Mr Wareham that if I was to find her I'd need to know it *all* – the good and the bad. But mainly the bad. And mostly it was.'

'Sorry, Gwyn, you said they were from London?'

'Brighton. Where the girl was joining questionable gangs before she was twelve. Had a tattoo, when it was still an aggressive sign in a female.'

Robin said, 'Where?'

'Left armpit, Robin. Swastika, as it happens. Common enough in those days, though still very much a bad-taste symbol – a snigger against the parents and the grandparents. A wounding form of teenage protest. But then the Warehams were remembering their own protests. They remembered a peaceful rebellion – smoking cannabis, dropping a little acid. And picking magic mushrooms, once, in an area they recalled as a heaven on earth. You see where this is going?'

'To the Convoy,' Merrily said. 'To becoming holiday hippies in the hope that Mephista would absorb the old ideals?'

'But it's not always heaven, see. Tim Wareham remembers an early autumn of rain and fog. No proper heating in their old ambulance. Tim and his wife were excited by the discovery of Peter Rector in a farm nearby, offering enlightenment, for free. But the girl was at her worse. Frequently drunk on cheap cider. In a perpetual rage.'

'This was when she found Jerry Brace? Or did he find her?'

'Brace had dropped out of university. Avoided the military career his father had in mind for him. He was given, as a last chance, a sum of money to build himself a business. Ending up in Hay – like you, boy.' A nod at Robin. 'With a vanload of war books, many purloined from his family's huge library, I'd guess. Including the only one that obsessed him, that he'd never sell. Which, of course, was Rector's book on Nazi occultism – mystical racism and the Aryan Holy Grail.'

Merrily took out her cigarettes then put them away again.

They lacked the appeal of a pipe, and she didn't want to stand in the doorway.

'Was Rector's father into the mysticism?'

'Not so much, I don't think. But the discovery of Nazi occultism was, I imagine, what finally made the rather indolent Jerrold Brace into his father's son. Sending him in search of Peter Rector, the man they'd both come to believe was... a secret master – is that the term?'

'Something like that.'

'He once told his cousin, Roger – my Brace family contact – of his belief that he was receiving telepathic messages from Rector. Did I tell you that?'

'No.'

'Ah, there's so much of this, Merrily. It was said Sir Charles himself once hired a medium to put him in touch with Hitler. Jerry Brace was picking up all kinds of nonsense from the skin-heads and extremists who haunted his shop, bringing their own self-published books and pamphlets for him to sell.'

'I'm guessing,' Merrily said, 'that a lot of this was fantasy magic, only vaguely based on the wartime Nazi mysticism. Which, from what I've heard and seen on TV, was more grandiose and pompous and masonic. Dressing-up games. Were the wartime Nazis as openly satanic? I don't think so.'

'No. But if Jerrold Brace came here to follow Peter Rector and was disappointed, he may have turned to people like Seymour Loftus. Seymour in his more fanatical days, preaching illumi-nation through violence in the approach to his new aeon.'

'And Mephista?'

'Apparently the kind of sixteen-year-old who, today, in Robin's homeland, might be found in a primary school with an assault rifle. Intimate with a man taking too many drugs and fantasizing about being descended from a robber baron. Volatile cocktail, wasn't it?'

* * *

Frannie Bliss was at the open door. You could feel his tension rising with the deepening growl of traffic on Oxford Road at a time when it might normally be dying back. Had he been seen at Cusop? Was Brent looking for him?

Gwyn Arthur Jones was retelling the history of his breakthrough at the funeral of Sir Charles Brace, most of the detective work already done for him by the nephew, Roger Brace, alienated from the rest of the family and attending the old man's funeral for pretty much the same reasons as Gwyn.

Bliss shut the door and came back to hear about the pregnant girl Sir Charles had taken in and yet was careful to keep at arm's length. Finding her and the child a home at a family-owned London hotel, where she was expected to earn her keep.

In the end, Gwyn said, she'd become a junior manager, with a talent for charming guests while ruthlessly culling superfluous staff. She might have been running the hotel by now, if she hadn't begun an affair with the bar manager. Breaking up his marriage and then leaving with him to take over management of a Soho pub. Then marrying him.

'Thus,' Gwyn said, 'becoming Mrs Turrell. The boy also taking the name, under which he was later sent to a prep school at Sir Charles's expense.'

He waited. The name was vaguely familiar to Merrily, but Robin was the first to react. He looked shaken.

'So, uh… what was the kid's name?'

'George.' Gwyn Arthur opened his venerable tobacco pouch, excavating with a finger. 'George Brace Turrell. You can imagine the Turrell part being casually discarded if he met his grandfather's expectations.'

'Shit,' Robin said. 'How bad's this gonna get, Gwyn?'

'Depends how much you want to stay for, boy. Shall I continue?'

His mother hadn't seen much of him after that, for several years. He'd attended private school and spent his holidays at a farm owned by associates of his grandfather, where he underwent fitness training and learned all the right skills. Learned, essentially, how not to be his father.

The stepfather, Mr Turrell, had died in a shooting incident a year after the marriage. Collateral damage in a gang war. Gwyn had made contact with two old colleagues who'd left Wales to join the Met, now also retired and happy to talk, like old cops always did to other cops. One of them had sent Gwyn a scan of an old newspaper story, which included a photo of the young widow.

Gwyn found it on his laptop. She was leaving the inquest, wearing dark glasses, a slight figure in a black coat, black beret aslant on her long blond hair, white in the monochrome picture.

'Doesn't look like her,' Robin said. 'But then...'

Bliss bent to the screen.

'Let's just deal with this. How come nobody recognized her when she came back?'

'Who'd recognize her anyway?' Gwyn said. 'After thirty years? Nobody in the town really knew Mephista. Even the man who was in the Convoy and settled here had no particular memories of her, except for the name. And a skinny blonde, now decades older, dark-haired, heavier?'

'And why *did* she come back?'

'I can speculate, but it's no more than that. I'm not a policeman any more. Can't take statements.'

'Because in my experience,' Bliss said, 'all that about people returning to the scene of the crime is an exaggeration. Just as often, they put as much distance as they can. Especially if they're only an accessory. You're *sure* this is her?'

'Oh, I'm sure of *that*, if little else. Even contriving, on a warm day, to see the remains of the tattoo. No longer a convincing swastika but not entirely removed.'

Nobody had noticed Jeeter Kapoor coming back with the VHS machine.

'Didn't like to say anyfing, but when you close your eyes… that laugh… it is, innit?'

Merrily was keeping out of it. She didn't know these people, hadn't seen them until today. Neither, she assumed, had Bliss.

Had she heard the laugh? Maybe.

You tell them, girlie.

A likeable woman. Sexy and fun. The laugh had come easily. It would be one of the regular sounds that fizzed over the bar-chat, just as it had over the tape-hiss.

'Listen,' Robin said. 'Can we like spell this out? Two questions. *One* – is Gwenda really Gore Turrell's mother? And *two*—'

'Yes,' Gwyn Arthur said. 'Thank you, boy. I think we all know what the second question is.'

No business of his. Not a policeman any more. And even if he were, it was hardly uncommon in the hills. Well, Merrily knew that. Brothers and sisters, mothers and sons, fathers and daughters – consider the famous Eric Gill at Capel-y-ffin. No one harmed, and if there was no under-age business involved, blind eyes might be turned.

'Gwenda and Gore,' Gwyn said, 'they were accepted by the people frequenting the bar. Or at least she was – he was perhaps a bit aloof, but always obliging. A glamorous older woman and a fairly unassuming young man – not a partnership likely to incite much comment. And I had no reason, see, until now, to believe that incest might be far from the worst of their crimes.'

'Somebody must've pointed you at them, Gwyn,' Bliss said. 'Not as if they look much alike, is it?'

'Ah, you settle somewhere in retirement, it's hard to turn off the old instincts. You get to know more people and their back-grounds. Especially the incomers. The white settlers, as we used to call them. Usually happy to talk, lay out their credentials for being here. Gwenda and Gore, now – very friendly, but revealing little. Gore's a mystery. Spends a lot of time on recreational running – but not in an ostentatious way. Often turning out before dawn, arriving back from the hills before the bar opens. Competes in marathons he never seems to win, though always well placed. Nothing to draw attention to himself.'

Merrily glanced at Bliss. Had that been sufficient reason for Gwyn Arthur Jones to investigate these people, delve into their history? Had to be more to this.

'They have an extensive apartment,' Gwyn said, 'behind and above the bar to which few people have ever been invited. But the visiting builders and plumbers of my acquaintance report a quantity of sophisticated fitness equipment. And no books at all. *No books.* An economy founded on books, and their biggest customers are booksellers, but no books… what's that saying?'

'Suggests they aren't particularly… in sympathy with the Hay ethos,' Merrily said. 'What else did you find out?'

'There was a second marriage. And a profitable divorce. A Mr Carter, owner of a restaurant in Cardiff. And then Mr Protheroe, who I know nothing about, yet. Except that he's no longer in the picture.'

On the hottest night of the year so far, Merrily felt physically cold. She saw Bliss's discomfort, saw Robin's pain translated into the paleness of his skin. Jeeter Kapoor just sitting there, blinking, chewing his lower lip, clearly wondering if he should say something.

'All right,' Bliss said, 'the worst of their crimes. What *are* the worst of their crimes?'

His face was mottled with light and dark, slanting shadows around his eyes, like a panda's. He shouldn't be here, shouldn't be working. She didn't know enough about his condition: was he in danger of collapse, a stroke? Was there any of the burden she could take?

'How did they come together, Gwyn?' she said. 'After all these years. Had they been continually in touch?'

'I have no idea.'

'And are they as toxic together,' Bliss said, 'as Brace and Mephista? What, after all, have we got? Encouraged by

Mephista, Brace kills Cherry Banks and disposes of her God knows where. Do we have any evidence of Jerry's son doing it again? And why?'

'Hey, just say that—' Robin was on his feet. 'You said Cherry? Cherry was the dead woman?'

'We think,' Bliss said.

'Holy shit, listen, I don't know if this helps, but when I was here last night, letting myself into the bookstore, there's this old lady – the weird whistling old lady, Mrs Villiers, and she's babbling at me, the way she does, and amongst it all she says – lemme get this right – *Cherry don't... Cherry don't do it no more.*'

'Where was this?'

'Outside the door.'

'That's all she said?'

'No, there was other stuff. She said – this makes some kinda sense now – she said... it was like she'd warned this Cherry not to come.'

'To the bookshop?'

'I guess. And she said she'd put her up at her place. One night. Something like that.'

Gwyn Arthur said, 'You're absolutely sure about this? You were drunk, were you not?'

'Not so drunk I'd get that wrong.'

'This indicates Mrs Villiers knew there was something wrong. Back when she was compos mentis. If Cherry was a prostitute... woman of the night...?'

'If she knew something,' Bliss said, 'how come she didn't come forward at the time?'

'If you'd known Mrs Villiers then and now,' Gwyn said, 'you would probably not ask that question. But we do need to talk to her. *Try* and talk to her.'

'Dead right, Gwyn. Meanwhile, anything any of you *hasn't* told me, you need to bring it out. Gore – why Gore? How did George become Gore?'

'Sigil,' Robin said.

Merrily looked at him.

'Turning words and phrases into magical symbols?'

Bliss closed his eyes wearily.

'No, see,' Robin said, 'if you're making a sigil, you start by like condensing a word to its essence. If a letter's repeated, you take one out. George has two Gs and two Es. You remove the extras, you're left with Gore. Might be just a coincidence.'

'Interesting.' Merrily looked at Bliss. 'Claudia would explain it a lot better than me, but it gives... George... a certain focus.'

'A sigil's a symbol of intent,' Robin said. 'You write down something you wanna happen and then reduce the letters, then make what's left into a symbol you can focus on.'

'Suggesting that Gore was a symbol of someone's intent,' Merrily said. 'Blood and gore.'

'Then you put it at the centre of a ritual... and you make something happen.'

'Like a killing?' Bliss said. Then he shook his head. 'It's not good enough, is it?'

63

The case for atheism

GETTING ON FOR midnight when Robin moved stiffly into Gwenda's Bar. How welcoming it looked, like a softly lit hollow tree. More like a real home than either of his half-homes, all mellow light, a little smoke and comfortable, companionable people.

He ordered a pint of shandy. He was sweating.

'Parched,' he said.

Gwenda placed a cool hand on his moist cheek.

'You can do better than a shandy, Robin, surely.'

'Uh?' Robin put his hands up, shaking his head in mock horror. 'After last night?'

Gwenda laughed. He looked into her eyes and saw how pale they were for a woman with such dark hair. Not eyes you could easily connect with. All the small things you noticed when your cherished world view had fragmented like a smashed mirror.

Gareth Nunne regarded Robin with faint distaste, sucking the froth from his half of Guinness.

'You been running, boy?'

'Shovelling, Gary. Shovelling and scraping till we're knee-deep in rubble.'

'Alterations, refurbishing, I don't do any of that. Anything don't look right I just cover it up with books.'

'Get any of you guys a drink?' Robin said.

'Go on, then,' Gareth Nunne drained his glass. 'Just a half.'

'You feeling generous tonight, Robin?' Gwenda said. 'Or just too tired to know what you're saying?'

She was up on her high stool, low-cut, long-sleeved black top, black leggings. You could eat her.

Robin deliberately didn't answer, accepting his shandy from one of the two women behind the bar. Extra staff on tonight. Good business with all the cops around, chilling out after a heavy day. Only one here now, though.

'We do the right thing coming here, Gary?' Robin fumbled out a ten pound note to pay for his and Gareth Nunne's drinks. 'I dunno. But it was all your fault.'

'Not still bothered about Jerry Brace?' Nunne accepted his beer. 'Cheers, boy.'

'Guy's cast a pall,' Robin admitted.

'Junkie and a loony. Forget about him. You'll come through. You're young, you bastard.'

Robin carried his tankard to the end of the pitted farmhouse table under the bar. In some pain now as he sat down, his stick between his knees, opposite Connie Wilby, edge of the inglenook. He brushed at his jeans.

'Guess this is unlikely, but would anybody here still have an old VCR?'

'What's that?' Connie said.

'Videotape player?'

'Never had one, dear, not even when they were in vogue. I'm what they used to call... damn, can't even remember the terminology.'

Gareth Nunne looked thoughtful.

'A reader?'

'Yes!' Connie raised a finger. 'Of course. That's the word. Thank you, Gary.'

Robin smiled, brought the videotape out of his jacket.

'That better not be a bloody Kindle,' some guy said.

'See?' Robin said. 'How soon everyone forgets.'

Gore Turrell was leaning elegantly over the bar on folded arms. He didn't look happy. Or was that a mood you just projected on him? He nodded at the tape, making a soundless question.

413

'I'm guessing The Best of Adolf Hitler,' Robin said. 'But who knows?'

Robin felt like a wrench was tightening his balls. He looked around at the shiny faces under the teardrop globes. He knew Gwyn Arthur Jones was in here somewhere and also the screwed-up cop in the baseball sweater, Bliss.

Bliss didn't talk like any cop Robin had known. Telling him to stir the shit, flush it all out into the street.

Be loud. They make allowances. You're coping with disability. It's a bastard, isn't it, being disabled? Makes you angry all the time. Makes you wanna deck people, just because you know you can't. You know they're gonna see the first punch coming before you've even made a fist.

But take your time, boy, Jones had said. *Don't make it look like you have a story to tell. Let it get teased out of you.*

They had to be halfway out of their minds to trust a dysfunctional foreigner whose dream was exploding in his face.

It's insane, Bliss had said, *but it keeps screaming at me. We have two murders of young women, thirty years apart, in similar ritualistic circumstances. And one we know was committed by Gore's father with the help of his mother. And we know that Tamsin was asking questions in their bar.*

And then he'd looked at Gwyn Arthur Jones.

We've not gorra shred of evidence. And me and Brent... you don't know the worst of it. And you're retired, and I'm off duty.

And that was when Jones had said,

Let's go and have a drink. Robin looks like he could use one.

'What you looking for, Robin?' Gwenda said.

Gwenda who'd watched a woman getting murdered and hacked up into joints. Fucked her son. And still you could eat her.

'Just making sure Mr Oliver isn't here,' Robin said.

'Oliver came in here *once*,' Gwenda said with a luscious pout.

'Unfortunately nobody knew how to make whichever sophisticated London cocktail he prefers.'

See, that was crap. Unless Jones had all this wrong, couldn't be anything Gwenda didn't know about sophisticated London cocktails.

'And what, exactly, do you not want Mr Oliver to know?' Gore said.

Thank you, Gore.

You kill a cop? A young girl? Did you do that?

'Uh… we had to wreck his chimney,' Robin said. 'The swastika stone… Betty hated it. We decided we were gonna rip it out and put it in the trash. Then we found a hole behind it. A cavity?'

He took a pull on his shandy, not reacting to all the eyes on him.

Gareth Nunne said, 'And?'

'Huh?'

'What was in it? The hole. In the bloody *wall*?'

'Oh. A box. A wooden box.'

'Coffin?'

'A *small* wooden box, Gary. Just big enough for…' he waved the cassette in the air '… a medieval videotape. Only, like most people, we don't have a VCR any more.'

Robin sat up, shook himself, took a drink then called across to Connie Wilby, who was hunched forward, letting the empty inglenook take her smoke.

'This make any sense to you, Connie? What kind of movie might Jerry Brace've wanted to hide in his wall?'

'No idea, lovie. Jerry didn't do pillow-talk. Rocks orf, and I was history.'

'VHS?' Gareth Nunne said. 'Kapoor has one, doesn't he? Copies old test match tapes.'

'Yeah, I, uh… I called him at home. No answer.'

By the time Robin had left the cricket shop, Kapoor had made two copies, one to DVD one to VHS.

'Bugger,' Gareth Nunne said. 'Suppose that means I'll have to fetch mine.'

Some people cheered. Robin lowered his gaze to Gore, who remained expressionless. The TV on the wall to the left of the bar was tuned to a news channel so customers could follow the search for the missing cop.

'Oh, goody,' Gwenda said. 'That should be a fun way to end the night.'

She didn't look at Gore. She just laughed.

Laughed the laugh.

Robin went cold to his spine.

Jeeter Kapoor, still running copies, said he'd leave his shop door open for Merrily, but she told him no.

'Lock it. Don't open it for anybody other than one of us.'

'You fink somebody's gonna try and get this stuff?'

'Wouldn't take any chances. I'd even hide a copy somewhere. *Not* in the wall.'

Jeeter laughed uncomfortably, and Merrily came out into unexpected heat, a moon heading for full, a sky manic with stars. She paused outside Thorogood Pagan Books, suddenly light-headed with dismay. The amorphous nature of this job sometimes made her feel flimsy, slightly ridiculous and, after all she'd seen and heard tonight, irrelevant. Faith seemed naive. As for belief... it wasn't so much what you believed in as the nature of belief itself. What belief could make you do. Belief that killing could liberate the soul. The belief of the suicide bomber who mass-killed in expectation of a parade of willing virgins on the other side.

The case for atheism.

She peered through the window of Thorogood's, where a low-wattage brownish light glimmered grimly. No sign of Betty. She tapped on the glass. No response. She tried the door.

Unlocked. She went in. No sense of forest glade any more, no starry night on the ceiling. You could barely see the ceiling in the smudgy brown light.

'Betty?'

Nobody in the shop. She went between the bookshelves and opened the door to the tiny kitchen, scrabbling for lights but she couldn't find a switch and there was no window.

'Betty!'

She went in, putting out her hands, spinning round just to satisfy herself there was nobody in here, her foot kicking something that turned out to be the airline bag, the Deliverance kit. Wasn't good to have left that in here. She picked it up and backed out, slamming the kitchen door, pausing at the foot of the stairs. She could see a feeble light up there. Were all the lights in this place feeble or was the power being drained?

Power being drained. That happened. Huw Owen said it actually happened, so it must be—

'*Betty!*'

Some moments of silence, and then that hand-on-the-spine sensation of being watched from behind and she spun round and nearly screamed at the sight of a figure at the top of the stairs, white and wafery and vague as a ghost. Plain white dress, blond hair straggly, the Alice band gone.

'Come up,' Betty said.

Merrily hesitated. Betty walked back into the upstairs room, in a desultory way, head bowed.

Merrily went up. Followed her into the room where a trail of dust led to the hole in the back of the chimney as if it had been breathed out.

Robin had said they'd cleaned it all up.

'Have you touched that again, Betty?'

'I got it wrong,' Betty said.

'What have you done?'

'Called them out,' Betty said. 'Both of them.'

Somehow he managed not to look at either Gwenda or Gore unless one of them spoke. Knowing that Gareth Nunne would be back soon with his VHS machine, he was struggling for conversation, aware that people were watching him. People he knew, people he didn't, place was near full tonight. He turned to the woman whose cigar smoke was curling into the inglenook.

'Connie… Brace… I hate to keep coming back to him.'

'Robin, one can only take so much humiliation.'

'Only, he ever talk about some ancestral link with the guy whose big wife built the castle? De Braose?'

'Not to me.' Connie Wilby flaked some ash into the ingle. 'Someone once mentioned it. My own feeling, having read fairly widely on the subject, is that de Braose wasn't quite as black as painted. Killed those Welsh chaps in revenge for his uncle. Nothing to be proud of, but in those days…'

Robin heard the door getting scuffed open.

'… *and* he atoned for it by building and repairing several churches,' Connie said. 'Certainly, the medieval historian Giraldus Cambrensis wrote highly of him.'

'Always two sides to everybody. 'Cept maybe Hitler. Someone told me there are these creeps think he was some kind of avatar and he's still out there? They, like, worship Hitler?'

'Millions of people worshipped him,' Gwenda said. 'Not so long ago.'

'Yeah, but, Gwenda, that was like mass-psychosis. See, maybe there's something I'm missing here, but Hitler, he was into this fantasy about big, blond guys with six-packs, right? And he's like this puny little bastard with flat, dark hair and a stupid moustache who stands on his podium to look big and screams at people, and they're all like, "Hey, Adolf, you're the man!"'

Robin took a big drink, rolled the cold glass tankard around on his forehead.

'That's mass psychosis, guys.'

Clunked his tankard on the farmhouse table. Blinked a little, like he was fishing something from his memory.

'They say he has a son?'

'Who?' Gwenda said.

'Brace. Brace and a girl quaintly called Mephista, they had a son. And Brace's old man, the rich fascist, he adopted the kid? Had him raised as a Nazi, goosestepping from age five. They say he came back here. Possibly to claim what his old man saw as their heritage. The de Braose legacy?'

Gwenda said, 'Where on earth did you get that from?'

'Ah, forget it.' Robin wiped the air. 'Probably crap. Urban myth. My natural romanticism tends to wane when it comes to fascism. I would honestly rather Jerrold Brace had neither lived nor died in the place where we're trying to revive our fortunes. And if we have to exorcize his sorry, smack-addled ass, that's what we'll do.'

He realized he'd snarled at Gwenda, and he saw she'd realized it, too. He saw her expression change, darkening, and he was like, *Oh, shit, shit, shit…* as Gareth Nunne came in, his arms full of VCR. He laid it on the bar and Robin brought out the tape box and placed it on top, and Gareth Nunne stood collecting his breath, the wine stain hardly distinguishable from the rest of his face.

'They've found her,' he said. 'Tamsin.'

The bar noise dwindled into a hush. Like on Armistice Day.

Then the silence was broken all at once, like a signal had been given, everybody moving, chairs getting pushed back. A crush began forming around the bar and the TV on the wall, tuned to the 24-hour news channel, but it was screening something involving sand and tanks. They didn't know yet at the TV station. Only Hay knew.

Robin saw the yellow globes swinging on their wires, heard Nunne repeatedly saying *murdered* and *I don't know, I don't know, I don't know.*

He stumbled and felt his hip screaming, as he was pushed into the corner by several people heading up the book-lined passage for the door as there was a flash and then the lights went out.

64

Physical things

BETTY HAD HER Alice band back in. Her face shone, scrubbed, cold water darkening the neck of her dress.

Merrily lowered the bag to the dust. The bag with the salt and water and the Bible. Her head was full of liturgy she was unlikely to be using. She felt tension pouring out of her, like sweat after flu.

'You said you'd felt evil here, and you were right. We saw it. We saw it happening.'

In this drab building devoted to violent death. From animal slaughter to the savage ritual killing of a part-time prostitute.

Thirty years ago. There weren't prostitutes any more, they were sex workers. The parameters of civilized society were being expanded daily so that no one should feel marginalized any more. No right, no wrong. No black, no white. No good, no evil. And incest was simply a preference.

'You said you called them out,' Merrily said. 'What's that mean, Betty?'

'It was after we saw the video,' Betty said, 'I realized that whatever was here left physical things. A swastika in the chimney, a secret hole in the wall.'

'Mmm.'

'Robin had a bad night here, but he was drunk and he slept in the bath which, if wasn't the same bath, was certainly in the same place where Cherry Banks's body was butchered. He had bad dreams. Who wouldn't? Now I know what happened, I'm inclined to think we're getting something from the victim rather than the aggressor.'

'To which there's an answer, which doesn't involve exorcism,' Merrily said.

'What did you do here when you came up earlier?'

'Just a preliminary. A sprinkling of holy water. I'd felt, I dunno, something smothering. I'm not psychic. Just felt blocked.'

'I felt angry. You probably saw that. While you were down at Jeeter's I came up here and I'm standing in the middle of the room, where you are now, staring at the blocked-up hole in the fireplace, thinking, *How do you want to play this, Jerry? Come on out, you sordid little creep.* The sort of thing Robin says. Then I realized I was shouting it.'

'Nothing?'

'So I did de Braose next. I'm going, *Look at me, de Braose, you grasping, power-hungry, proto-Nazi scumbag. Look at me. I'm a blonde from the north, my ancestors were probably Vikings. Some of them, anyway.* I'm conjuring an image of him in his chain mail and his surcoat – only I put a swastika on it as his emblem.'

'What do you mean, you *put* it on…?'

'Used to do this sort of thing a lot at one time. Before I grew up. Scared the crap out of myself. Not this time. He faded almost immediately. If there'd been anything of him here with any kind of balls it would've clung on. The image would either have re-formed or intensified.'

'Betty, call me an old hen, but that seems like playing chicken on the motorway.'

'Yeah, well, I've done a few things I regret. Bit of candle magic to sell the house. You charge a green candle – with your door key inside – and put it in the window of the house you're trying to sell, and by the time it's burned down… Well, we had an offer that surprised even the estate agent. Some people who'd been to view but hadn't seemed that enthusiastic. Coincidence, or had I imposed my will on them? I don't know, and it didn't make me happy. Would there be a cruel twist because what I'd done was wrong? But my poor, crippled husband felt it was his destiny to live here, and him from Brooklyn.'

Merrily took out her cigarettes.

'This OK?'

'Sure.'

Betty dragged out two of the cane chairs and they sat down, their backs to the fireplace. The micro-flame from the Zippo seemed very bright. Nothing blew it out. Betty was right. Nothing much here. Only spent terror.

'So what I was thinking,' Merrily said, 'was a Requiem Eucharist for Cherry Banks. A funeral mass. You and Robin and anyone who might have known her or this place. I think that might do a lot for the atmosphere. If that doesn't offend your—'

'Oh, Christ, no, that would be good.'

Funny how pagans, even atheists, leaned on Christian expletives in times of stress.

'The evil, of course, is still around,' Merrily said. 'But probably not here.'

'Bringing the tape out of the wall… I'm thinking that might reduce the weight.'

'Actually, I'm wondering now if Jerry Brace put that tape in the wall not for any ritual reason. Suppose he wanted it to be fairly accessible. To prove something, if necessary.'

'Like what?'

'Not sure. But maybe he was thinking that, when he was a long way from here, he could get word to somebody where it could be found. Dunno. Junkie logic. He never had the chance, anyway.'

Betty cradled her hands on her lap.

'Don't go thinking I'm any less scared. People are frightened of ghosts, who seldom harm anybody – just things you saw as a kid but didn't have to bother with, adults you didn't have to be polite to, children you couldn't play with. But… we live in a human world, with human evil, and human evil is… nearly always much worse.'

'Did you hear Tamsin Winterson's been found? Murdered.'

'Oh Christ. Where?'

'Cusop.'

Betty sighed.

'They gave Robin a hard time. We only found the tape because they took the place apart. It's like we were brought here to be some kind of bloody catalyst. What's happened to her?'

'Confidentially – pretty much what happened to Cherry Banks, that's the thing. Gwyn Jones is making connections.'

'Small town. Unusual if things this horrible aren't linked. This is awful, Merrily. You feel you're watching something... forming... out of the past. And we've been made part of it. This guy photographed me in front of the castle. Said it was for a tourist brochure. I didn't believe him somehow. It was like... I don't know. Like being fitted into something.'

'Robin said you heard the laugh.'

'I'm no judge.' Betty stared at the black window. 'I don't know the woman.'

'What's that?'

A whistling outside. Might have been a hymn tune, though not one that Merrily knew. Betty found a tired smile.

'Mrs Villiers. Someone else who seems trapped. In a private world. With ghosts. Maybe it's catching. Just before the guy with the camera, our landlord's wife was telling me she'd seen Dame Beryl Bainbridge, the novelist. On the day she died. In London, I suppose.'

Merrily looked up, startled.

'Where was this?'

'On the square, I think. The marketplace. Near where I was photographed. Does that mean something?'

'I don't know.'

Merrily was at the window. Just when you thought that rationality, however grim and twisted, was offering explanations...

'I can't see her. The old woman who whistles.'

'You always hear her first. And afterwards. It's as if the whistle takes on a life of its own.'

'What does she look like?'

'Not very big. Little round curious eyes, slightly feral. Quite thin, though you're not aware of that because she always wears one of those long stockman's coats. And a hat.'

'I think I need to talk to her.'

'You won't get much sense out of her.'

'I'd like to try.' Might help Bliss. 'Betty, if you don't want to stay here, Mr Kapoor's still in his shop.'

'Nah. I'll stay with Jerry. And his ancestor.'

'Lock the door then,' Merrily said.

Robin didn't look up as he skirted the marketplace into Castle Street. A lot of people on these streets now, drifting out of the pubs: the Blue Boar, the Wheatsheaf, Kilvert's. Sticking together, some women weeping. He'd looked everywhere for Jones and Bliss; no sign. When the lights came back on, most of the customers had left Gwenda's Bar. Including Gwenda and Gore.

The videotape had gone. Might've been knocked off the VHS player. Might've been taken in the blackout. One of the women behind the bar said this kind of outage had happened a few times; Gore had kept saying the bar needed rewiring but nothing had ever been done.

Robin didn't think this was down to bad wiring.

He felt alienated. Locked out of the public grief, but he hadn't known this kid. Wished he had.

He went through the familiar opening between darkened shops, alone in Back Fold.

Well, not quite. Might've expected this.

There he was, outside the cafe, long closed.

'Gore,' Robin said.

'Wanted a word, Robin.'

He wore a short leather jacket, over tight jeans. And gloves. The moonlight had turned his close-cut beard into a mask.

'Caused quite a stir in there, Robin.'

'I get overtired.'

'What's this all about?'

'You don't know?'

'Let's assume I don't. Who's pulling your strings?'

Why was he wearing gloves on a warm night? Despite his private school accent, he was… well, a dull kind of guy, especially compared with the flamboyant Gwenda. His mother.

Too much information.

Robin said, 'You watched the tape yet?'

He didn't reply. He probably wouldn't've had time to screen it, even if he'd snatched the tape as soon as the lights went out.

'You knew about it?' Robin said. 'You knew there was a tape in the wall?'

'No.'

'You knew it even existed?'

'No.'

'Not a big old family secret?' Robin was starting to lose it with this guy, helpful, obliging, diffident Gore. 'I was thinking with your old man being the star. Playing the killer.'

'I don't understand.'

'And Gwenda directing the movie?'

'So you've seen the tape, have you, Robin?'

'Yeah, I've seen the tape.'

'What does it show?'

'It's not Toy Story 3.'

'And does it have anything to do with me?'

'Aw, Gore—'

'Answer my question, Robin, and then I might go.'

'I don't think so.'

Robin stood in the middle of the alley. They were no more than eight or ten paces from a street with people on it. Cops cruising past. Behind Gore, Kapoor, in his shop, with his VCRs.

Gore moved. Robin lifted his stick, a reflex, and it was just as Bliss had said.

It's a bastard, isn't it, being disabled?

Didn't even see it coming, like a wrecking ball into a crumbling building. Pain like a hot blade, a gloved hand wrenching his head back, leather fingers between his teeth choking his scream as he went down, and his head was crunched, once, twice into the tarmac.

He could see the doorway of the Cricket Shop, a dim light behind it and he clawed at the road, crawling away like a boot-flattened insect, the moon shining like a searchlight in his eyes. He looked up to see the castle leaning back, and he could hear its rumbling, stony laughter like it was travelling along the overhead power cables on the central pole around which the whole alley was spinning in his head.

Gore's black-booted foot coming back.

65

The darknesses

THE WHISTLING WASN'T constant; you kept losing it, down among the arterial streets Claudia Cornwell had spoken of. Down past the medieval market place where Beryl Bainbridge had walked, *entrusted with the old marketplaces.*

You could hear the whistling through the Buttermarket's pillars, no particular tune to it any more, but high and piping, like you imagined faery music, underlaid by the old heartbeat, night-drumming, and the gasp and rumble of sporadic traffic up on the main road.

She'd never been very good at talking to old people until she'd become a vicar and found that, with half the average congregation well over seventy, it was a skill well worth developing. The past was always a good way in. Old people were experts on the past, and this town at night was all past, preserved in warm stone, patches of light, hollows of darknesses... and was that a long coat and a hat, hurrying past the post office and into a side street sloping down?

The old lady who knew that Cherry didn't do it any more. Whose middle-aged self seemed likely to have known and even cared about the young woman who came down from the Convoy to turn tricks in Hay.

Every old community had a living *genius loci*, spirit of place, the ambulant mind of the town. In Ledwardine, it had been Lucy Devenish, the folklorist, Jane's mentor – still there, you felt, sometimes, in the cottage where Lol lived— God, what if he'd called? She'd kept switching her phone off to save the battery, and she hadn't spoken to him since the night of the M-word. It was like he was part of a different sphere of existence.

Down past the poetry bookshop, past the modern-ish library, through moonlit streets and streets the moon couldn't reach, and then there was traffic noise and she was out on the bottom road, and behind her was the pointy, gothic tower where the clockface was shining like a coin, like a second moon.

Past the turning to the bridge over the Wye to Radnorshire, down to where the buildings and the lights thinned out in the approach to England, and here was the whistling again, like a trail of bailer twine, unrolling past the hump of ground where the town walls had been.

Maybe this was all pointless, but it was doing something, and Merrily felt her head clearing into an overview. Felt the gathering of ghosts in the town of books. A melding of minds, the atmosphere in certain spots made denser by presences. Unseen.

Well, seldom seen.

Most of the medieval town walls have gone… but still there, the stones taken to build houses and shops, so therefore still in the town. It's all still here.

Did it work, this transference of mental energy? Did it hold up against the powers of government and big business and the sneers of science?

Vehicles continued to go past, one a dark blue police van. Where were Bliss and Gwyn Arthur Jones? Had they managed to stir it in Gwenda's Bar, provoke a reaction? Last of the mavericks, off the walls, but what else worked in Hay?

Wouldn't take much tonight.

Oh God, there she was… a glimmer of movement up ahead, a figure encased in grey from the top of her head to the ground.

She called out.

'Mrs Villiers…?'

But she wasn't there. She'd turned off somewhere.

The buildings had become more widely spaced. A wispy

428

breeze came in from the river. A sense of the river was on the air. The river you couldn't see. Always a river you couldn't see.

Merrily began to run.

The night was setting around him like concrete. And, Jesus, the fear when he managed to roll over on the tarmac, expecting another kick or a pumping leathered fist, black knuckle coming for his forehead like a killing blow in an abattoir.

A door opened and a carpet of light was unrolled across the alley, a complexity of moving shadows bundled out. Nobody speaking, just an indrawn breath, a gasp, the crack of wood on stone or tarmac.

Robin cringed.

Against the white light falling through the doorway of the Cricket Shop, he saw Jeeter Kapoor wielding the cricket bat that had hung over his cash register, a chain still hanging from it. In a slick of light, Robin saw his faithful stick, with the ram's head, lying on the tarmac, and he went crawling after it as the bat came down, ineptly, on leather and Gore's leather hands reached up and grabbed it.

Then there were more hands, Kapoor spinning round.

'Hey! Get off me!'

As Gore Turrell was back on his feet, and Robin saw Betty running down towards him, and he screamed over his shoulder, through the blood from his lips and nose.

'Stay there! Call the cops!'

Reaching his stick, propping it up in front of him, and he began to climb it with his hands, a wild agony bounding up his back. When he made it to his feet, he was sobbing with pain, but he still hefted the stick, went back into the fight.

Until the stick was snatched away. The cricket bat taken from Kapoor. Robin turned, and the man behind him was like seven feet tall, wearing a suit and a tie. A second man, less formally dressed, looking like shit, accepted the stick from the tall guy and offered it to Robin.

'This is my colleague, DC Vaynor,' Bliss said, low-voiced. 'You've done very well, pal, but let's not get overexcited.'

Robin made out the Mr Punch profile of Gwyn Arthur Jones silhouetted against the Cricket Shop doorway, as Bliss and the tall guy moved in on Gore.

The tall guy had handcuffs ready.

'George Turrell,' Bliss said brightly, 'I'm arresting you for assault. You don't have to say a friggin' thing, but it may harm your defence if you don't mention, when questioned, something you later rely on in court. Anything you do say...'

Robin leaned back into his own fist, knuckles in his aching spine.

'Goddamn cops,' he said to Kapoor, blood trickling from his nose. 'Same the world over.'

She ran past a couple walking slowly down and crossed the road and into the narrow lane, not much more than a track by the side of the vet's clinic. Mrs Villiers could only have come down here.

A little moonwashed car park at the end of the track, under an industrial building, a small, windowless concrete castle, rough lawned areas in front of it. You could read the sign: SEWAGE WORKS.

A short slope down to a brown pebble beach, creamed by the moon as it slid into the water.

The Wye. Wider than you expected, an arcade of black trees on the far bank. To your right, another dip, another narrow beach alongside a stream feeding into the river.

The mouth of the Dulas Brook, had to be. Where they found the effigy of the King. All the way from the mountains and it met the Wye beside a sewage works.

If you didn't know that, it would look charming, quite exotic in the moonlight. Two cars were parked here for the night, and there were lights in a house just up the bank.

And was that actually Mrs Villiers?

Sitting in her long coat, leaning against the strong wooden fence of a private dwelling, high up on the bank of the Dulas Brook. Half shadowed, not whistling, just watching the moonlight on the water?

Merrily walked towards her, then stopped.

There was someone else, just below the concrete edge of the car park, also looking across the river, and then turning. You could hardly avoid talking to her.

'Are you OK?' Merrily said.

She wore a tunic, elegant and expensive, over black leggings. Both hands clasped around a long champagne flute between her knees. Her make-up was smudged and her eyes were pale under the moon.

'Could be better, darling,' she said.

66

A social basis

'No, George,' Bliss said. 'You haven't been charged with anything yet. But if we have to detain you against your will we'll probably start with Assault Causing Actual Bodily Harm.'

Elsewhere in the Community Centre, someone was photographing Thorogood's bumps and abrasions. He was still refusing to go to A and E in Hereford.

A metal Anglepoise lamp had been brought into the room they were using for interviews. Bliss had it turned away from himself but wasn't so crass as to point it into Gore Turrell's face.

'Of course that'd just be a holding charge,' he said. 'The interesting stuff... we'll get to that.' He looked across at Vaynor. 'Darth, as there's no lock on the door, perhaps you could carry your chair over and sit with your back to it. We don't want any bugger disturbing us. Especially any bugger with a PhD.'

'Still at Cusop, boss,' Vaynor said.

Also some kind of Oxford graduate but without the college motto tattooed on his forehead.

'Yeh, well, let's hope nobody invites him back. Tell him half of Rector's land's in Dyfed-Powys's domain, that should do it. Now then.' Bliss beamed across the desk. 'Before we switch on the tape, anything you'd like to tell us, George?'

Turrell was compact and muscular, fit-looking, but not exactly Mr Personality. In other circumstances you might even think he was a Regiment man.

'I was attacked in the street, ultimately by two men and I defended myself.'

'And very ably, George, if I may say so. I'm told you're a bit of a fitness freak. Lots of hill running.'

'That's a crime?'

'Go running on your own?'

'Usually.'

'Ever meet other runners?'

'Occasionally.'

Bliss leaned back, tapping an arm of his chair.

'Women?'

'Some.'

'Where were you off to tonight when you were… attacked?'

'Going to pick up my motorcycle.'

'Yeh, that's one explanation for the gloves. Moonlight ride?'

'Always exhilarating.'

'Would you have come back?'

'Tonight? Or ever?'

'You choose.'

Bliss left some silence. Turrell's talk was cool, but you could tell he was out on a very narrow edge. This *should* be taken slowly, circling round the issue, wearing him down. But no knowing how much time there'd be before the community centre started to fill up, and not entirely with friends.

'How's Gwenda, Gore?' Bliss said. 'Doesn't seem to be around.'

Long silence. Car headlights dazzling in the window. A pulsing in Bliss's brow. Please don't let this be Iain Brent.

'All right, George, let's talk about Tamsin Winterson.'

'I was sorry to hear about that.'

Gore's face rigid, his eyes hard.

Interesting.

'You ever meet her out running? Tamsin?'

'Yes.'

No hesitation.

What? Bliss held himself relaxed. With difficulty.

'Yes, you met her?'

'Yes, I met her.'

Bloody hell. Long mountains up there. Deep valleys. You didn't *have* to meet anybody.

And Turrell didn't have to say that.

'Broken heart, darling. End of a beautiful affair.' Gwenda swirled the liquid in the glass. 'Should've seen it coming, but we don't, do we?'

'I'm sorry.'

'He's a cool one. Told me two nights ago. In bed. Well, of course, we agreed to say nothing, behave as if nothing was wrong. We're grown-up people. One of us rather more grown-up than the other. As you may have noticed. People do. He never seemed to, bless him.'

'Where's he now?'

'No idea, darling. We closed, we kissed, he left.'

'You don't know where he's gone?'

'Could be going abroad, anywhere. He has enough money. Didn't ask. Or the name of his new love. Why should I? Grown-up people. Clean break. Life goes on.'

'That's a… difficult situation. With the business and every-thing, too. You been together long?'

'Long enough.' Gwenda turned away from the water to look at her. 'Seen you before, haven't I? Now *where* have I seen you before – no, don't tell me, I know everything.'

'Then I suppose you know about Tamsin Winterson.'

'Who?'

'The missing policewoman,' Merrily said. 'She's been found. Dead.'

'Oh. Yes, I heard that. Shame. Wait! I know who you are. You came in with Gwyn Jones earlier. Tucking yourselves into a corner where you wouldn't be overheard. Pointless, darling. I hear everything.'

Gwenda sipped from her champagne flute. It wasn't wine, smelled like whisky.

'Old Gwyn. The King of Hay's Chief of Police. Unpaid snooper. *He* wouldn't be missed. Pest. He say you were a priest or something?'

'He may have.'

'You're too pretty to be a priest. And probably not even a lesbian.'

'Well, you know—'

'Don't contradict me. Not the night for it. So tired of people stopping me all the time. Oh, Gwenda, have you heard? What a terrible thing! How will the town ever be the same again? What sanctimonious drivel. As if it affects *any* of them. Why I came down here.'

She turned away and walked down on to the beach of sharp brown stones. Lush too-black hair swept back as she walked. Merrily watched her and thought of Mephista watching Jerrold Adrian Brace carving a swastika into the exposed skull of Cherry Banks, very nearly dead, but not dead or there wouldn't be blood. Had she taken that picture, too? Viewing it through a camera lens – did that separate you from the act, turning it into just a lurid movie?

No, it didn't. Try and imagine Jane doing that.

It made you a monster.

'We used to walk here often, very late at night,' Gwenda said. 'Sex on the bank. Good in the rain.'

She stood at the water's edge, black boots, black leggings, tossing her head back, bleach-white teeth reflecting the lesser white of the moon.

It was like all the nerves in Bliss's head were dying. He wanted to lay it down on the desk and sleep. Just five minutes' sleep would do it.

Well, no, it wouldn't.

'Should look after yourself better, Inspector,' Gore Turrell said mildly.

Bliss held on to his temper. Quelled his dismay. Tried to rise above the numbness.

'How well did you get to know Tamsin?'

'Pretty well.'

'You went running together?'

'Yes, we did.'

'Where? Where did you go?'

'Several places. Along the Cat's Back and down to Craswall. Over the Bluff and up to Capel. Down to Llanthony once.'

'When did this start?'

'About a year ago.'

'You're not lying to me, are you, George?'

'Why would I lie?'

'Because little Tamsin's dead and there's nobody left to disprove it?'

Just as no one could disprove it if he'd said he'd never met Tamsin Winterson in his life. Which would have been the sensible line to take.

'You ever meet off the hills?'

'Yes.'

'On a social basis?'

'Yes.' Turrell took a long breath, looking into the corner beyond Bliss, where a pair of wellingtons stood. 'And, later, more than that.'

Mother of God. Bliss saw Vaynor blink.

'Did Gwenda know about this?'

No answer. Bliss rewound Gwyn Arthur in his head.

… recreational running… not in an ostentatious way… turning out before dawn… marathons he never seems to win… Nothing to draw attention.

Tamsin: no boyfriend her family knew about. Dedicated to her job. Staying fit for the Job. Little Tamsin.

'George, are you telling me you were Tamsin's boyfriend?'

Gore shrugged.

'Why didn't you come forward this morning when we were

appealing for anyone who knew her or had seen her in recent days to contact us?'

No reply.

'George… Gore… I want you to think very carefully before you answer this question. Have you ever been to Peter Rector's house, Bryn-y-Castell, at Cusop?'

'No.'

'You're sure about that?'

'Of course I'm sure.'

Mother of God, so many questions, so little time. Going well and yet going badly. What had Gwyn Jones got wrong?

'Did Tamsin know who your father was?'

'Hardly likely.'

'Why?'

'As even I don't know who my father was. Only who I was *told* my father was.'

'People don't seem to know much about your personal history. Where were you before you came to Hay? Do you want to say something about that?'

'Only that I fail to see what it has to do with a short fracas in an alleyway.'

A tapping on the door. Bliss ignored it.

'But you know who your mother is, don't you?'

Silence.

'Gore, you've been very cooperative. But I've been noticing that this is a particular subject you seem reluctant to discuss. Are you refusing to answer questions relating to your mother?'

'Yes,' Gore said. 'I'm afraid I am.'

'Tamsin's death, Gore. Let's talk about that. Did you kill Tamsin?'

'No.'

'When did you find out she was dead?'

'No comment. Isn't that what they say?'

'Did you make a phone call earlier tonight to tell the police where to find her body?'

'No comment.'

'Do you know who killed Tamsin?'

'No comment.'

'Are you angry that she's dead?'

'Yes.'

'Gore, out of interest did Tamsin know about your political views?'

'I don't particularly have any political views. My... apparent grandfather had political views.'

'What about your friend Seymour Loftus?'

'He's not exactly a friend.'

Bugger. He wasn't even denying he knew Loftus.

'He's a member of the Green Party,' Gore said. 'He stands up for the preservation of the British countryside. Against over-crowding, wholesale building and subsequent sharp increases in the crime rate. You mean you don't?'

God, it was a fine line, wasn't it?

'And he follows old religious practices linked to the land,' Gore added. 'Similar to the ones adopted by Robin Thorogood and exalted by his shop. You have a problem with that, too?'

'DI Bliss.' Iain Brent's voice from the other side of the door. 'I'd like a word. Now.'

The door shook. Darth Vaynor held it shut with his chair, but he looked very uncomfortable.

'What are you doing here?'

Brent had him in a corner. Actually had him in a corner.

'Talking to a suspect, Iain. It's one of me functions.'

Brent went through all that about him being the SIO, how everything had to go through him. *Everything.* Bliss asking him, amiably enough, if this extended to a simple assault where he and Vaynor had just happened to be on the spot

'And I had no reason to think you were even here,' Bliss said. 'Seeing you seem to have alerted everyone to the discovery of Tamsin's body except me.'

Taking a chance here. If someone had seen him at Cusop.

But then, if that had been the case, when he'd walked in an hour or so ago, in search of someone reliable, Vaynor would've casually asked him to stay in the building, instead of following him out.

'I didn't have you called because,' Brent said, 'I need fit men. And you're a sick man, Francis. On more than one level, I suspect. Who's this suspect supposed to have assaulted?'

'A bookseller. Robin Thorogood.'

'You're adding insult to injury, Bliss.'

'You gorra suspect yet? For Tamsin?'

'Get this man bailed and go home. I'll talk to you later.'

'Might help you,' Bliss said reluctantly, 'if you talked to me now.'

Brent just turned away. Rich Ford had come in, was activating computers and his small staff, soon to be expanded.

'Conference in half an hour,' Brent told Rich.

'You know what, Iain,' Bliss said conversationally, so Rich could hear and Darth Vaynor and a couple of Dyfed-Powys fellers. 'You're a really shite detective. Did I ever tell you that?'

Brent didn't turn round but you could see some action in his shoulders.

Shoot out. Sunday morning now. By the end of the week, one of them wouldn't be working here any more.

'Oh, and a twat,' Bliss said. 'But that goes without saying.'

67

Crystal tulip

A VEHICLE TURNED into the track leading to the river, and then there were shouts.

Police. Had to be. And they were coming down.

And she hadn't even started praying yet.

Gwenda was saying, 'What've you got under there, darling?'

With the moon-white, self-assured, patronizing smile that said *I know everything, I hear everything, I've done everything.*

Then a door slammed and the voices stopped, and a vehicle accelerated away, and, at the same time, Merrily heard the whine of the vehicle reversing out of the track.

Two different vehicles and the one coming down here had obviously taken a wrong turning, and all the voices had been from the top road

No police. How deceptive sounds could be, especially in darkness, when vision was restricted.

Merrily said, 'What do you *think* I've got here?'

Sweating again. Always a giveaway, and you couldn't hold it back.

They were standing facing one another, just above the river's beach. Merrily began edging up the grass to where Mrs Villiers sat in shadow, up on the bank of the Dulas Brook.

Gwenda pointed at Merrily's chest.

'Unzip.'

'What?'

'When I say I know everything, I mean I *like* to know everything. And I don't know what that is.'

'Oh…'

Warm night. Merrily pulled down the zip of the black hoodie and took it off, hanging it over her right arm. Exposing to the moonlight her white T-shirt and the cross. Compliance.

Gwenda bent and fingered the cross.

'You really *are* a priest?' She stood back, hands on ample hips. 'What the *fuck* is a priest doing here following bloody Gwyn around? You do know he's completely addled?'

'Is he?'

'Something this town does to people, I'm afraid.'

'Erm… how's it do that to people?'

'When you get a large number of mad people in one place…' Gwenda doing it in baby-talk '… it inevitably affects the rest.'

She laughed. They were right about the laugh. It really hadn't changed very much. It was a laugh that squeezed itself out of captivity and then bounded away, taking you with it, making you want to rather like her.

'And you're too inquisitive,' she said. 'What *are* you doing here?'

Always difficult to put on an act when you were facing a direct confrontation. Even from someone you knew was covering up something abhorrent, something hideous.

So don't put on an act.

'OK,' Merrily said. 'There's a shop. In Back Fold. The Thorogoods' shop?'

'Where they found that swastika, yes.'

'Betty Thorogood, I've known her for some time.'

'You're wearing a cross. She's a pagan.'

'I don't have too much of a problem with that.'

Gwenda did a sneery little hiss.

'The touchy-feely Christian Church. Only Islam has any balls these days. What's bothering Betty?'

'Bad atmosphere.'

'A *bad atmosphere*. Oh. We believe in all that, do we? Bad vibes? Evil spirits? Call out demons, do we?' Gwenda took a sip from the champagne flute and walked up the bank. Sat down just below the concrete car park, patted the grass beside her. '*Tell* me.'

'Never actually exorcized a demon.' Merrily sat down, leaving a space between them not quite wide enough to suggest fear. 'Not much call for it. Well… plenty of call, but you usually find it's not justified.'

'So what did you do for the lovely Betty?'

'Nothing yet. We thought it was all about Jerry Brace, but it evidently wasn't.'

'This is the neo-Nazi Connie shagged? Once. She claims.'

'You don't think she did?'

'Not if he was as good-looking as she insisted he was. Anyway, it's all balls, isn't it?'

'You don't believe in these things?'

'Belief's pointless. Faith's babyish. I grew up among believers. Parents were cranks. Mustn't do this, mustn't do that, this is right, love is all you need, this is wrong, bad karma. Thought they were free, but they were just in a different prison. Couldn't stand them once I learned to think for myself. Once you realize that nothing's wrong and nothing's right unless it *works*, your life's transformed. *That's* when you become free.'

'You learned that… from an early age, then?'

'I'll try anything once and if I like it I'll try it twice.'

The smile said, *I've gone through life breaking taboos like dead twigs.*

Merrily holding herself steady, hands on the grass either side, ready to move. Seeing Cherry Banks, mutilated in the smudgy photocopy, and the degradation of the charmingly artless Tamsin Winterson to a limp-haired, blood-caked heap.

And hearing an echo of the car in the track and the car on the top road and the voices that could have come from either.

Gwenda looked at her, a finger alongside her nose, as if puzzled.

'Why haven't you exorcized Jerry Brace?'

'Well... you don't exorcize dead people. Unless you have reason to think there's more to it. I mean, his beliefs were very dark, but Jerry himself... he wasn't up to much, was he? Not by himself. Seems to have idolized Peter Rector, but Rector had changed. Maybe he couldn't adjust to that.'

'Fancy,' Gwenda said. 'One would almost think you'd known the man.'

Merrily followed the moonlight into the pale eyes, trying to find Mephista there. She saw Mephista sitting in an old ambulance on cold, rainy Hay Bluff, watching her dad making notes for his stillborn book on New Age travellers. Making her own plans for the grooming of Jerry Brace, putting him into a situation which, if he went through with it, would put his whole future into her hands. And he *had* gone through with it, he'd killed and mutilated and dissected, Mephista standing behind the camera, urging him on.

say it, say it, say it...

I sacrifice you in the name of my father.

Replaying this alongside the sounds of the car on the top road, the car in the track and the voices. And the voices on the tape. You thought you knew where the voices on the tape came from.

say it, say it...

Came from behind the camera.

I sacrifice you

Came from the figure in black plastic.

Didn't it?

'Did you see the video, Mrs Protheroe?'

'Which video?'

'The one Robin brought into the bar.'

'We didn't have time.'

'So you don't know what's on it.'

'Do you?'

'Well, yes. A few of us saw it earlier tonight.'

'I thought Robin hadn't got a player.'

'They wanted everyone to see it,' Merrily said. 'To see if anyone could throw any light on what was happening on there. We all knew what it looked like. It looked like a murder. A kind of ritual murder. Of a young woman. In that shop.'

'You're serious? Has it been shown to the police?'

'Probably. By now.'

Gwenda looked up and all round. It was very quiet now. Merrily kept her eyes on her.

'Why did you follow me, darling?'

'I didn't.'

'You just happened to arrive here? And on your own. How odd. But then you're a priest. You've got your god with you.'

Gwenda laughed.

Laughed the laugh.

Merrily sprang up, but Gwenda was already on her feet. A well-built mature woman with long legs, muscular legs. She might not go hill running with Gore, but there was all that fitness equipment that Gwyn had been told about, in the apartment. The apartment with no books.

Gwenda gripped the champagne flute. Did something so efficiently she'd obviously done it before. Raised the hand and brought the flute down on the edge of the concrete, very swiftly, at an angle.

'Tell me,' Gwenda said.

'Tell you what?'

'What you think I did.'

The gleaming at the end of Gwenda's right hand was not a knife. The champagne flute was half smashed, Gwenda's fist tight around the stem up against a jagged open tulip of good crystal.

Merrily stumbled over a lump in the grass, nearly went down. Gwenda came another step closer. Lifted the arm with its crystal prongs.

'All right.' Merrily scrambling up, backing off. '*That...* that's what I think you did.'

'Say it!'

'Yeah, right, exactly... Say it... *yes*. That's what you said. *Say it*, you were hissing, *say it*... And because he was bloody terrified of you by then, he said it. He said, *I sacrifice you in the name of my father*. And that was... that was all you needed. All you needed was his voice, saying the words. *His* voice, *your* blade, and that was all he had to do. That and hold the camera while you stood there. Killing Cherry Banks. The detritus. That's what I think, Gwenda. That's how I think it went.'

Limping away, gasping. Her left foot had found a hollow in the grass and, stepping out of it, she'd twisted an ankle.

Oh God, don't let her see you limp. Divert her... anything...

'Was Cherry your first? Easy... easy to get her down from the Bluff?'

'Told her there was a wealthy guy in Hay who was into trashy girls. Dirty girls. You didn't have to tell her twice.'

'Jerry say she could use his place?'

Gwenda seemed to relax.

'We took her to Jerry's place, and the wealthy chap obviously didn't turn up, so Jerry fucked her himself, then we had a threesome, and gave her some sleepy pills. Just another homeless scrubber tagging along with the Convoy. She told us this would've been her last time anyway as she'd seen the *Holy Mother*... in the air at Capel-y-ffin. Well, that fucking did it, far as I was concerned.'

'She said she'd seen the Lady of Llanthony? When did she tell you that? Before she was drugged? Before she was part of a threesome?'

'Don't remember, darling. Except that it was like a sign. Prostitute discovers faith. How lovely.'

'And what did it feel like afterwards? After you'd done it. An explosion of consciousness? Halfway to the astral plane, was it, Gwenda?'

Gwenda took a step up the bank, the crystal flute swinging at her side.

'Or was it just about initiation? Your initiation... Jerry's initiation... whose was it? Never going to be able to prove it wasn't him, so that… gave you a hold on him. The ultimate hold. You and Jerry going all the way together. How… how *touching*.'

'Thank you,' Gwenda said, 'that makes it a lot easier.'

Swinging her arm like a pendulum, a keening whisper in the air and Merrily's left arm was ripped from wrist to elbow.

Oh.

The temperature dropped.

'How can you—?'

She was trembling now, in severe shock.

'How can you *do* this? How can you go on doing it?' How can—'

Pop.

Was it extreme fear that did this? The inner camera pulling back, the blur of images, the vivid sense of yourself under a milky moon, not quite full, an arm banded with bright blood.

Your fresh blood. Cherry's black blood. Tamsin's dried, waxwork blood.

'Tamsin? Was that you, too? *Was* it?'

… and the blood matted on Tamsin's chest and the blood that flowed back into Cherry's throat in the rewinding video. Outside of all this, you saw the actual hatred burning inside you like a blue light, like a gas jet turned up full.

You saw Mephista lunging with the glass at your face and losing her footing in a patch of mud and starting to slide down the bank, unbalanced.

And you might not be able to walk, but you could throw yourself down the bank, giddy with rage, breath pumping, until you had a hand under her jaw and the other groping for the eyes.

Seeing it happening, as if from somewhere else, higher up.

As if through the round eyes of Mrs Villiers, sitting directly above where you were pushing Mephista's head under the water, where the Dulas Brook emptied itself into the Wye.

The old woman's eyes reduced to smudges of shadows, her jaw fallen.

Her whistling in your head.

68

Martyr

FIRST FLUFFS OF white in the sky, blue and orange beacons on the ground, radio crackle. The futile scurryings of baffled cops. Bliss's Honda parked at the edge of the market square, under the castle.

Merrily in the passenger seat, still unable to keep a limb still, a white bandage on one arm, to the elbow.

'Tried to kill herself,' Bliss said. 'Ostensibly. She threw herself into the river, and she let herself float out on her back, and there she is like the Lady of friggin Shallot, screaming at them not to try and reach her. I'd got there by then. You know what I did, Merrily? Stood there and had a bit of a laugh.'

'As you do.'

'As you do when you know she's just furious at being upstaged by a little vicar.' He turned on her. 'Merrily, *why?* Why did you run it so close to the wire? Why didn't you just run the other bloody way? In that situation, on me own, even I'd've run the other way.'

'What, like you did with a cellar full of the cockfighting fraternity?'

'Why?' Bliss said again.

'I don't know. I don't know why I did it.'

Well, she did. And that was the blackest joke of all.

'We're gonna tell Gore later,' Bliss said. 'Tell him what happened down by the river. To see whether he laughs as well. So to speak. It's interesting that he'll talk, in his faintly refined way, about everything. Everything but his family. Everything but his upbringing. Everything but his mother.'

'It's a very peculiar relationship.'

'Did she do it all? From the beginning?'

'I think you'll find she did. A psychotic teenager exposed to – whether it was happening or not – black magic and a celebration of violence by educated, persuasive people who claim that doing bad things is not only excusable, it's important for the future of the planet...'

'Did you see the devil in her, the yellow satanic eyes? I'm not being fatuous.'

'No. I wanted to, but it's like she's got past that stage. She's a mature woman now, it's become habitual. Smashed all the barriers. Sold her soul a long time ago. What's left looks like... nothing. Something dead. What scares me most was that it's like there was some kind of transference. Something happening inside me. For just a second or so, on the riverbank, I just wanted to... Frannie, I'm a bloody vicar...'

'Yeh, well, you didn't.'

'What if they hadn't come when they did?'

'No illusions, kid, she'd've had you. You'd be a friggin' C of E martyr. Saint Merrily.'

She watched the pink entering the clouds, like a little blood soaking through the bandage on her arm.

'Who told them, anyway?'

'Somebody in one of the houses, complaining about the disturbance. They thought you were both pissed.'

She started to laugh.

'Why was she there anyway? Why did she really go there?'

'That little beach? There's talk of a boat being seen on the river, in the vicinity. What if somebody was waiting to pick her up? Both of them, or just her. Get them quietly away down the Wye? How traditional is that?'

'What kind of boat? Whose?'

'Interesting, isn't it? All the rich and influential, deeply right-wing people with land near the Wye. Downriver and into oblivion. But I fantasize… We're never gonna know, are we?'

They were silent for a few seconds. From inside the ambulance, she'd heard them bringing Gwenda out of the river, Gwenda – typically – threatening to bring charges. Merrily getting out of the ambulance very rapidly in case Gwenda was coming in.

'When I first met her down there,' she said at last, 'she was rambling on about Gore leaving her for another woman. I thought it was all just bullshit, off the top of her head. But it does begin to look like something happened between them. Something conclusive.'

'She's possessive, to put it mildly. Her son and her lover – can you imagine that? Finding the son and lover is two-timing her?'

'Are you going to be able to prove that Gwenda – for whatever motive – killed Tamsin?'

'Lorra work to do there. Had she been watching Tamsin? Had something alerted her when Tamsin went to the bar to ask questions?'

'Some visible chemistry between Tamsin and Gore? Where's Gore now?'

'Out there somewhere. Charged with assault and bailed. It'd make it a lot easier for everybody if he buggered off. I wonder if he will.'

'You're not watching him?'

'Dyfed-Powys's baby now, and Brent will've explained about my condition. If Gore sticks around, we'll need to work on him. He may've killed nobody and might well walk. A man raised by Nazis.'

'Where's Tamsin on this? Did she know about that? Or was he just some uncomplicated, quiet fell runner?'

'It's conceivable that Gore was finally starting to react against his own upbringing. Although, to be honest, I wouldn't trust him at all. Thorogood told me a silly little tale about Gore helping him to put up his shop sign and nearly taking Kapoor's head off with a big slab of oak. Like something was bred into him – if you gerra chance to kill or main an ethnic… Yeah, right.' Bliss shook his head. 'I don't know where this starts, Merrily, but I've a good idea, with the state of the West Mercia Police budget, where it's likely to end.'

'Yes.' Merrily watched the dawn. It didn't seem like a dawn. 'Mrs Villiers… do they know what happened to her?'

'You gonna tell me about that?'

But she couldn't.

'Well,' Bliss said. 'Only time and Billy Grace will tell. Gorra be off, Merrily. Thought we should touch base for a few minutes, but I've gorra big day ahead. Trying to pull something together. Avoid gerrin Brent's knife in me back.'

'You need rest, Frannie. You know you do.'

Bliss grinned.

'Funny thing,' he said. 'I feel better than I've felt in a long time.'

69

Spirit rising

Windows wound down for the birdsong, cow parsley waist-high on the verge of an empty road, she steered stiffly into the driveway at The Glades at not long after six-thirty. Because of the horse-chestnut trees on either side, a dull lantern was still ambering the Victorian dressed-stone of the porch when Mrs Cardelow let her in.

'She'll refuse to come down, Mrs Watkins. Far too early.'

'Mrs Cardelow, I saw her curtain twitch as I drove up.' She hadn't, but it was worth a try. 'Could you tell her I have just one question. Which is, who killed—?'

'Cardelow – *out!*'

Miss White was standing at the top of the stairs in a long, tubular quilted dressing gown that made her look like a carnivorous caterpillar.

'Clearly, I was wrong,' Mrs Cardelow said. 'Would you like tea or coffee with your copy of the Official Secrets Act?'

'My room,' Miss White said.

As usual, no books were on show but the floor-to-ceiling cupboards spoke for themselves. An occult library in every sense.

Merrily was allowed to sit on the bottom of the bed, twisting to face Miss White who was lodged in what looked like a reconditioned barber's chair, the Zimmer within reach.

'I had several phone calls either side of midnight, Watkins.

Was able to make a useful response to virtually none of them. For which I blame you.'

'I've never seen you without make-up before,' Merrily said. 'I'm shocked. Close up, you look almost innocent.'

'What happened to your arm?'

'Glassed. By a woman who then used it on herself to avoid answering questions about some deaths, one of them a young policewoman.'

'You seem unusually bitter,' Miss White said.

'I've been trying to work out whether that's a sin. Also...' Merrily leaned forward '... how much lower the casualty count would be... *if you'd told me the truth.*'

Miss White sniffed.

'I did tell you the truth. Just not all of it. Couldn't, anyway. Be in breach of the terms of the bequest. These deaths – are we still talking about neo-Nazis?'

Merrily sighed, starting to feel very tired.

'You know what, Athena? I couldn't tell you. I don't know where the fantasy starts or where it ends. There's a man called Seymour Loftus – don't even know whether that's his real name.'

'It is. And he's a practising magician of some long standing.'

'You know him?'

'I don't *know* him. Know very few people now.'

'What about Sir Charles Brace?'

Miss White made a sound like dirty water in a blocked drain.

'Oh dear, oh lord, yes. We all knew him.'

'*We?*'

'The people I don't talk about. Brace was a foolish blimp of a man. Always planning some military coup with a bunch of gammy-legged old colonels. Lived in a dreadful fake castle with an alleged pair of Himmler's specs in a showcase. Became more or less insane in his later years.'

'What about his children?'

'Disowned most of them for lack of backbone. Despaired of

finding a suitably cranky heir and was forced to skip a whole generation after one of them made away with himself.'

'Jerrold Brace?'

'The names escape me.'

'What about his grandchildren? One called George. Known as Gore. The son – and partner – of the woman who did this?' Merrily lifted the bandaged arm. 'Brought up – allegedly – at Sir Charles's expense, in some kind of right-wing survivalist commune in Mid Wales. Your colleagues investigate any of those?'

'They may have existed. And Loftus may have served as an instructor, if you like, at one or more. Loftus is an unimpressive man, but he knows his stuff. They were taking existing magical systems and modifying them to serve their political and philosophical ambitions. Which are mostly doomed in the short term, but they seldom think short term. They think in terms of aeons. Imagining they'll still be around, in some etheric sense, to watch the cosmic revolution. Could never be arsed with people like that.'

'They still out there?'

'Oh, they're still there, but in what form? I don't know. These training camps – it's a possibility, but if you were to raid one all you'd find would be a smallholding with a rather eccentric library. To go back to old Brace and his grandson – I *can* tell you something. Usual rules.'

'Of course.'

'This might be urban mythology. Only the lawyers know the truth but, given the transparent lunacy of it and Charles Brace's obsession with breeding suitably Aryan descendants... there *was* talk of a Secret Trust. Do you know what that is?'

'No. Don't make me ask Uncle Ted.'

'Let's say that Brace leaves a sum of money – say a few million – to a particular person, who is then trusted to turn most of the money over to the grandson when the grandson meets certain conditions. In this case, it might be – I'm speaking hypothetically here – the production of a properly Aryan child. Boy serves up a sprog who looks like bloody Boris Johnson and he's quids-in. Once the child's been verified as his, of course, and the mother's credentials have been approved.'

'Who's the trustee?'

'*I* don't know, it's a bloody secret, isn't it? But you can imagine the appalling George perpetually on the lookout for a suitable carrier for his sperm. What's the matter?'

'Nothing, I—'

So when a lovely young woman arrives in the very shop, at the foot of the castle where Gore's parents had performed their seminal sacrifice...

Look at me, de Braose. I'm a blonde from the north, my ancestors were probably Vikings.

A young woman who'd thought she was under observation, whose image had been captured in front of the castle.

This was, of course, insane. So much here that would never be understood, and some of it had only ever existed in people's skewed minds.

'And the mother's alive?' Miss White said.

'They pulled her out of the Wye. She's in hospital, under guard. Refusing to say anything. Told *me* a few things, one to one, but... her word against mine.'

'Don't be naive, Watkins. You're a minister of the Church. She left you with a serious wound.'

'You know too much, Athena.'

'Or she might do away with herself while on remand. You can but hope.'

Merrily said nothing. Only one issue remained.

'Who killed Peter Rector?' Miss White's face was serious and, without the Alice Cooper eye make-up, appeared guileless. 'Did you ask Claudia Cornwell, whom I gather you encountered?'

'May have. In a roundabout way.'

'She tell you nobody killed him? That they simply... attended his demise, if you like.'

'You going to explain that, Athena?'

'Oh, *Athena*, is it?'

'Whatever you want.'

'I *want* somebody to relieve me of the responsibility of finding someone to accept his legacy. All right... I *surmise* – and will go no further than that – that Peter Rector was worried on a number of fronts. One, that he might be losing his faculties. Not so much his mind as his capacity for... using it... and other functions... for a particular purpose.'

'The last redemptive project.'

'If you like. He could always detect shadows. A few of which we've just discussed. He thought – I *surmise* – that it was time to go. For... some of him to go. In a purposeful way.'

Maybe she didn't need to know this.

'You've doubtless read of the elderly male witch who volunteered for a sacrificial death by hypothermia on a beach on the south coast during the war. Part of a ritual to prevent a German invasion. The psychic Home Guard. You *have* read about that, I suppose?'

'Mmm.'

'Peter loved that story.'

'I don't think I like where this is going.'

'Where do you see it going?'

'He wants to make himself part of the... the project?'

'He can only do this for a time. When the physical body dies, the astral body may remain extant for some time. Longer, if sustained by... shall we say the energies of others. And, when necessary, it may be able to function... through... living persons. Requires someone... receptive. You should be able to work this out for yourself, so I'll say no more. But it might be seen to be assisted by a ceremonial departure.'

'I see,' Merrily said. At last, she felt a kind of smile coming. 'Tell me when I go wrong.'

She sat, straight-backed, on the bottom corner of the bed, placing her hands in her lap and closing her eyes.

'OK. I can visualize the temple under the barn made active. I can visualize people stationed at significant intervals along the Dulas Brook, from close to the source, up in the mountains… perhaps close to the stone circle on the Bluff or even the place where the Virgin was made manifest. People in deep meditation, all the way to the access points, in Hay… down by the sewage works… or even below St Mary's Church… both linked by the wonderful River Wye, anyway. Which is hidden from the everyday business of the town… like the chancel from the nave.'

'Not bad,' Miss White said softly.

'And, at the appointed time, when he feels himself psychically supported, I can visualize Mr Rector throwing his hat, symbolically, in the pool and… following it. His spirit rising to follow the brook's energy down to the sacred Wye. And as it rises…' *Dear God…* 'as it rises, a strange light is cast over Cusop around the castle hill and Bryn-y-Castell farm so that the land itself becomes translucent. God, Athena, I think I'm going to cry…'

'Don't be disrespectful,' Miss White said. 'Now get out.'

70

An occasion

'DOESN'T END, MERRILY,' Gwyn Arthur Jones said.

She took his call in the picnic place – one of Herefordshire's rare roadside gestures to the tourist – on the edge of Hardwicke.

'Message on my machine to call Tim Wareham as soon as I got in, regardless of time. I call him back, intending to let it ring three times and then hang up, so as not to disturb his wife. But he picks up at once. Having heard on the radio that Tamsin had been found murdered.'

'I'm trying to think how that would affect him. I mean personally.'

'Well… it's interesting. He never met Tamsin, but when he saw her parents on television, he was reminded of a holiday they spent on the Winterson farm. Years before Tamsin was born, this was, when her father had not long taken over the farm and was diversifying into tourism. Opened two fields as a campsite. The Warehams hired a pitch for a week.'

'With Mephista?'

'Mephista found the farm *boring*. Would walk around leaving gates open. Mr Winterson explained to her the problems caused by allowing animals into a potato field. Mephista left even more gates open, with predictable results, causing Mr Winterson to lose his temper with her. Not a girl, as you know, who appreciated admonishment. That night, a barn catches fire. Well, no proof. Fulsome denials. The Warehams invited to leave. Could you blame the farmer?'

'Erm… no. What did you tell Mr Wareham? About Mephista.'

'Told him a certain amount and left it to him to join the dots. I think he'll choose to shiver alone rather than tell his poor wife.'

Merrily watched the sun explode through the dead flies on the windscreen.

'You realize there are now *three* possible motives for a psychopath like Gwenda to kill Tamsin in Rector's holy of holies. If you get inside her head, it has a horrific logic.'

'Much of which,' Gwyn Arthur said, 'would be shredded by a defence counsel with half the skills of, say, Ms Claudia Cornwell.'

'There's ironic.'

'But perhaps Gore had taken as much of this as he could stand.'

'Bliss told you about Gore and Tamsin?'

'The murder of Tamsin would surely bring about a fundamental change in a relationship very much dominated by Gwenda, in her dual role.'

'He wanted to end it and get out? Do we really know why they came back to Hay?'

Explaining that, Gwyn said, might thrust them back into the world of the mystical and the symbolic. The King withdrawing from public life. The castle changing hands. Bookshops closing. The possibility of change and decay. A sense – to Merrily – of Rector's magic breaking down. Gwenda nourishing an old hatred for both Rector and Hay itself.

Dualism, Merrily thought. The prospect of being there in the fading of the light, darkness rising.

'I think,' Gwyn Arthur said, 'that after the murder of Tamsin Winterson, if Gore had made it to his motorbike last night, he might never have been seen here again. Amidst all the talk of blood legacy, blood sacrifice and ushering in a new aeon of violence… it's small breath of possible humanity, isn't it?'

'How's Robin?'

'Bruised. Angry. I feel a terrible guilt about that boy. We used him. We have a debt to repay. We – the booksellers – are having a collection for them. Of books. Not many of us won't have the odd pagan-oriented item on our shelves.'

'You might have a problem getting Robin to accept charity.'

'A problem to which we are now applying ourselves.'

'I had a similar idea.'

Involving Athena White and a small but meaningful portion of Peter Rector's library. They couldn't all be relevant to the future of the last redemptive project.

'Gwyn... one thing...'

'Yes.' He sighed. 'Go on.'

'Gwenda describes you, more than a bit disparagingly, as "the King's Chief of Police".'

'Now how would she know a thing like that?'

'She knows everything, Gwyn.'

'Well, it's a joke, obviously.'

'Is it? Like the Kingdom of Hay itself?'

'Look... Even as a working policeman, I was always a tacit admirer of Richard Booth, for whom life was not always easy. Over the years, there have been many attempts by people in local and national government to discredit him. Some – usually by rival businessmen with far more money – quite public. Others shady and scurrilous. I have, at various times, been in a position to provide what you might call counter-intelligence. I tend to prefer the term Internal Security, to police. Please don't broadcast this.'

'Of course not. Thank you. That explains a lot. Including why you offered to look after the wet effigy. I expect he'll be returned to the right hands.'

'Already done, Merrily. Not that I would admit to giving any credence to, ah... However, the matter of Mrs Villiers...'

'Gwyn... I don't know what to tell you.'

'Natural causes, they say. A heart attack is likely. There'll be a post-mortem. She'd... been there quite a while, it seems. Dead. DS Dowell, who was the first to examine her, tells me there were obvious signs of rigor mortis around her mouth and jaw. Even in warm weather, which apparently accelerates the process, it's at least three hours before that happens.'

'Yes, that… in view of one thing and another, that's odd.'

'And died there. Where the Dulas Brook enters the Wye.'

'I'm going to try not to think about it for a while,' Merrily said.

But couldn't stop thinking about something Athena White had said, relating to the immediate afterlife of Peter Rector.

She parked on the square at Ledwardine at just after eight a.m. Sunday. Locked the Freelander, shouldered her bags, started down Church Street to Lol's cottage. Then stopped and turned, dragged out the church keys and went back across the square to the lychgate.

The main door was already unlocked.

Colours.

On the step outside, a scrap of something light blue, a fleck of something yellow. She slid through the lifting shadows, into the nave. The flush of red apples in the stained window and Martin Longbeach, emerging, pink-faced, from the chancel with a covered dustpan.

'Oh,' he said. 'Merrily. Are you up early or…'

'Home late. You know what it's like, clubbing, you lose all track of time.'

'Yes,' he said, as though he believed her.

'Everything OK?'

'Oh. Yes. Everything's… fine. Absolutely fine.'

'Am I right in thinking Ms Merchant was here last night?'

'Last night? Oh… yes. Can't imagine you'll hear from her again. Much better now. She left very happy. Very happy.'

'With a friend?'

'With a friend, yes. Indeed.'

She sought his eyes.

'What's in the dustpan, Martin?'

'Ah, Merrily… we all do what we think best, you know?'

'An occasion?'

'A small occasion, yes. Under cover of night.'

'The friend was her medium.'

'Her name's Gillian Williams.'

'Able to channel Alys.'

'So she says. But who knows?'

'So Alys was there, too. As it were.'

'As it… were. Yes.'

'What's in the dustpan, Martin?'

'Oh…' He didn't lift the lid. 'Dust… you know… bits of paper.'

'Coloured paper.'

Martin shrugged.

'It's confetti, isn't it?' Merrily said.

Closing her eyes.

She didn't want to talk any more. She wanted to go to bed and smother her screams in Lol's pillow.

Notes & Credits

For reasons of credibility, the eccentricity of Hay has been underplayed.

The histories of Hay read by Robin Thorogood and others include Kate Clarke's *The Book of Hay* (Logaston Press) and the large-format *Planet Hay* by Huw Parsons (Peevish Bee Books). Richard Booth's *My Kingdom of Books* is published by Y Lolfa.

I've known the King of Hay for many years, since doing stories for BBC Wales on his various enterprises. *Candlenight* was probably the first totally new book he ever had in the window at The Limited. What a coup, huh? The second was probably, *My Kingdom of Books* which I helped launch, memorably, at the Hay Festival.

I also followed the late Supt. Ralph Rees, head of Dyfed-Powys Police in Brecon, who became a (much-missed) friend, on his adventures with the Convoy on Hay Bluff.

Capel-y-ffin is a fascinating place. Above the hamlet, you can still see the monastery of Fr. Ignatius, the remains of his church and the statue of Our Lady of Llanthony, a mystifyingly neglected apparition.

The waterfall in Cusop Dingle can be seen by the roadside, also the site of Cusop Castle. Good parking at the ancient church.

Hay Castle is in transition – again.

The Hay Festival lasts for about ten days around the end of May, under the direction of the ever-resourceful Peter Florence, and has spin-off festivals all over the world. St Mary's Church in Hay, where Fr. Richard Williams holds his fascinating Anglo-Catholic services (you're welcome to take your dog to mass) is indeed surrounded by an intriguing collection of natural water features, and a pathway does lead from the church to the mouth of the Gospel Pass.

The history – not all of it apocryphal – of satanic neo-Nazi groups on the Welsh Border is chronicled in considerable detail in *Black Sun*, Nicholas Goodrick-Clarke's authoritative exploration of Nazi occultism. If you thought all this was made up, you would be very wrong, though the extent of its support remains debatable. The Nazi-sympathizer Lord Brocket, who seems to have attended Hitler's fiftieth birthday party, lived at Kinnersley Castle, a few miles from Hay, around the end of World War II. On the day this novel was finished, the front page lead headline of the Midlands' Sunday newspaper, the *Mercury*, was EXTREMISTS IN BID TO REVIVE FASCIST PARTY. The faction, whose 'spiritual leader' was the late Sir Oswald Mosley, was described as a 'sinister organization with many members claiming to be pagans or followers of satanic or Wiccan cults.'

Tracy Thursfield was hugely helpful with research into the esoteric and lots of discussion, as was Gary Nottingham. David Conway's autobiographical *Magic Without Mirrors* is extremely convincing and very funny, and Gareth Knight's *I Called it Magic* is another revelatory and rather heartwarming account of how a magician gets by these days. The magic of Gareth Knight, the most obvious heir to the great Dion Fortune, is also a key element in T. M. Luhrmann's authoritative analysis of contemporary ritual magic in Britain, *Persuasions of the Witch's Craft*. Peter J. Carroll's *Liber Null* remains (I think) the definitive guide to practising chaos magic. Read it and give up. Thanks, as ever, to Sir Richard Heygate, co-author with Philip Carr-Gomm of *The Book of English Magic*, already a classic work destined to live forever. And to Prof. Bernard Knight, who never fails to answer my desperate, eleventh-hour forensic-pathology questions.

You can find the unexpurgated facts about Eric Gill in Fiona MacCarthy's biography, *Eric Gill* and the artwork-oriented *Eric Gill and David Jones at the Capel-y-ffin* by Jonathan Miles. The big Fr. Ignatius fanbook is *The Life of Father Ignatius, the Monk of*

Llanthony by Beatrice De Bertouch and the embittered antidote is *Nunnery Life in the Church of England* by Sister Mary Agnes.

Also…

Hilary Morris for tales of old Hay. Betty and Robin's much-valued neighbours, Haydn Pugh and George Greenway, of Back Fold.

The Prince of Hay and scourge of the Kindle, Derek Addyman.

Rob Soldat, author of *A Walk Around Hay* and fount of curious knowledge. Victor Hutchins, of Cusop Dingle. Anne Brichto, Hay bookseller. Ronald Verheyen, who had to come all the way from Antwerp to point out what I was missing on my own doorstep. i.e. Cusop.

Bev Craven, designer to the gentry, Mark Jones, farrier to the stars. Alan McGee, founder of Creation Records and a possible contender for the vacant role of Magus of Hay. Cathi and Thom Penman. Barbara Erskine, author of *Lady of Hay* which deals in depth with the de Braose family, a big novel now widely recognized also as an important reference work on the medieval Welsh border. Jessie and the late Ken Ratcliffe (a legend) who saw the light at Cusop. Duncan Baldwin for super-fast legal advice.

Nick Talbot, who is the band Gravenhurst, whose lines 'To understand the killer, I must become the killer' infiltrated the end of the book.

Mairead Reidy, ace researcher. Anne Holt and Tom Young. Caitlin Sagan. Iain Finlayson. Dai Pritchard, master of all trades. Terry Smith, marketing executive, and the legendary composer Allan Watson, whose work can be heard on the two (so far) Lol Robinson albums, *Songs from Lucy's Cottage* and *A Message from the Morning*. See the website, www.philrickman.co.uk.

My ever-helpful agents, Andrew Hewson and Ed Wilson. My unbelievably accommodating editor, Sara O'Keeffe. And Anna Hogarty for the painful final haul…

And – don't know where to start – I owe Carol so much on this one. Weeks and weeks of late nights and early mornings.

Reading different versions of the same chapters over and over until we get to the essence. Any flaws that remain unidentified are definitely not hers.

Read on to discover more about

The Magus of Hay

Q&A with Phil Rickman

1. This is the twelfth novel in the Merrily Watkins series. Did you imagine it would go on for so long?

I didn't think there was even going to be a second one after *The Wine of Angels*. I'd got quite fond of Merrily and Jane, but I just couldn't imagine a village vicar getting involved in murder twice. And no way was I going to write a cozy 'clerical mystery' series – I do have *some* principles.

And then…it came like a revelation. What if, after her difficulties settling into a possibly haunted vicarage, she was to be appointed diocesan exorcist? I knew they existed, having interviewed a couple over the years. So I rang Hereford Diocese and they directed me to the local exorcist, or deliverance minister as they are now known, and he was unequivocal about the unpleasant people you were likely to encounter in his job. I asked him what it would be like for a woman. He said it would be rather dangerous, for several reasons. And so a series was born.

The actual series begins with *Midwinter of the Spirit*. Think of *The Wine of Angels* as a prequel. It was, after all, meant as a stand-alone. And – this series is not a soap – you can read the novels in any order.

2. When you describe these novels as 'mystery', what exactly do you mean?

Crime novels – particularly in the US – are routinely described as 'mysteries'. Usually this just means a puzzle for a detective to solve.

All of the Merrily novels involve crime, handled as realistically as I can. But Merrily is not a detective in the normal sense (if you ever see that awful term 'clerical sleuth' it won't have come from me). We're looking here at mystery in the widest application of the word, in that there's usually an element of the paranormal, or at least the peripheral. Some of it might have a psychological explanation. And while some of it may, scarily sometimes, be less easy to interpret, it's not horror and it's not fantasy – both of these genres tend to invent explanations for anomalous events while, in the Merrilys, I tend to accept the mystery. Just like real life.

3. Virtually all of the locations are also in real places along the Welsh Border. How does this work – and have there been any complaints from Hay-on-Wye about the eeriness and evil in this book?

Does Oxford complain about Inspector Morse? Does Edinburgh moan about Rebus? The fact is, Hay is a very eccentric town, and nothing in this novel travels far from the truth or people's actual experiences: the anomalous lights at Cusop, the element of neo-Nazism in the hills, the alleged apparitions of the Lady of Llanthony, the magic mushroom convoy…it's all there, or used to be. And, of course, the King of Hay. I was actually accused by someone in America of making it all up. In this area you need to make up very little…

And that's how I think (hope) that the series stays fresh after a dozen novels. Each one relates to a specific location. I follow an idea to a particular town or village or patch of countryside, and other ideas just walk out of it…out of history, folklore, the landscape. Even occasionally out of the newspapers – the kind of crimes that actually occur in this area are usually extraordinary. If you really want to check all of this out, I've done an illustrated book called *Merrily's Border*, with photographer John Mason, about the background and locations.

4. There's been comment about the absence of some regular characters from _The Magus of Hay_. Does that bother you?

Hmm…very little of Lol or Jane, and just a walk-on part for Gomer Parry. Well, so what? It's not a soap, and in real life people don't go everywhere with an entourage. In _The Magus of Hay_, I wanted to take Merrily out of her comfort zone to face a challenge on her own. It's taken a few readers out of their comfort zones as well, but most people seem to have enjoyed the excursion. It's interesting…everybody seems to have a different favourite character, and I practically get death threats if Ethel the cat doesn't appear. But – I'm sorry – when it gets predictable, it'll be time to stop.

5. Do you have any actual plans to stop?

Well, no. I find it really strange when writers like J.K. Rowling (even under her adult crime-writing alias) say there will be _seven books_ in a series. It's like saying, _This is not a real world, you know – I make it all up, I'm the boss, and if I decide there's going to be seven, that's it._

I was once talking to Jo Brand at the Hay Festival and, possibly to wind her up, suggested one of my reasons for writing about a woman was so that I didn't have to make any decisions. ('You're dead, Phil,' Jo murmured, in that way she does.) But it's true, in a way. Merrily is not me in a skirt and, very occasionally, a dog collar. And I don't know how she's going to react to situations, where she's going next or what's going to happen to her belief system. Finding out is interesting.

6. Where next, then? Do you have any idea at all?

The next one, _Night After Night_, is not a Merrily (the absence of the word 'of' in the title is a clue). But I've had a vague idea, or theme, for another Merrily on the back burner for quite a while, not quite daring to do it. Actually, it's two ideas that seem to fit together. They switch from the city of Hereford to an area very close to the Border that I've never touched before. It could be that the time has come…

Coming soon…

NIGHT AFTER NIGHT

Contains scenes some viewers may find disturbing…

Leo Defford doesn't believe in ghosts. But, as the head of an independent production company, he does believe in high-impact TV.

Defford hires journalist Grayle Underhill to research the history of Knap Hall, a one-time Tudor farmhouse that became the ultimate luxury guest house…until tragedy put it back on the market. Its recent history isn't conducive to a quick sale, but Defford isn't interested in keeping Knap Hall for longer than it takes to make a reality TV show that will run *night after night*…

A house isolated by its rural situation and its dark reputation. Seven people, nationally known, but strangers to one another, locked inside. But this time, Big Brother may not be in control.

Praise for Phil Rickman:

'Few writers blend the ancient and supernatural with the modern and criminal better than Rickman' *Guardian*

'First-rate crime with demons that go bump in the night'
Daily Mail

'Compassionate, original and sharply contemporary' *Spectator*

Publishing in hardback and e-book in October 2014…